"**A**re you ok?" Alma asked.

Mitch grimaced. "Yeah. I'm fine."

She gave a long look, honestly assessing, and Mitch forced himself to meet her look with a smile.

"I promise," he said. "I can handle it."

She hesitated a moment longer, then nodded. "Ok."

The Terrier was heavy with the extra fuel, soggy on its wheels, waddling awkwardly into the turn that lined them up on the runway. Mitch eyed the length of it uneasily as he waited for the flag. It should be more than adequate, but the air was still and the weight of the supplemental tank sat uncomfortably toward the tail. Alma was frowning, too, making the same calculations, and Mitch gave her a shrug. It would be enough or it wouldn't. He thought it would be. Just.

The flagman waved them on, and Mitch pushed the throttles forward, bringing up the power as quickly as he dared. The Terrier rumbled forward, the big engines howling; the tail lifted, and dropped again, and Mitch looked at the airspeed indicator. Close, but not there, not enough. He cursed the lack of headwind. If he couldn't get more out of her, if he couldn't get the tail to lift—They were almost at the point of no return, fly or die, crashing ignominiously off the end of the runway.

"Come on," he said, under his breath. The speed was creeping up, the tail starting to lift. "Come on."

STEEL BLUES

Book Two of the Order of the Air

by Melissa Scott & Jo Graham

This novel, the second in the Order of the Air, following the novel *Lost Things*, ties in with the Crossroad Press original series O.C.L.T.—featuring the novels *The Parting* by David Niall Wilson & *Incursion* by Aaron Rosenberg, as well as the novellas *Brought to Light* & *The Temple of Camazotz*. *Steel Blues* occurs in the past, but O.C.L.T. members were there…

For our families of choice

Chapter One
Colorado Springs, December, 1931

Lewis Segura looked out the kitchen window in the gathering dark. No new snow was falling, but five inches of powder littered the yard with only the path between back door and driveway dug out neatly. There was nothing really to see except the garage and the slope that backed it rising steeply, covered in aspen trees long since shorn of their leaves. In the fall they made a glorious display, but in winter the bare branches wrote dark shapes against the snow.

From the front windows he could look toward town, down the two lane graveled road that rose from flatter land in the valley toward the old farmhouse. Looking east the view was breathtaking, possibly one of the reasons Gil had picked this house for his bride. Of course Gil had been dead nearly six years, and Alma was Lewis' bride now—his wife—strange as it felt to say those words.

From the living room came the first strains of music, a jazz band beginning their set and getting louder as Jerry Ballard tuned the radio. It had a good beat to it, real pure New Orleans jazz, and Lewis wondered what station Jerry was picking up. Jerry had been doing some work today, unlike the rest of them. He'd spent most of the morning with his books and papers spread out all over the living room, working on a peer review of an article about the defeat of an Assyrian king by a pharaoh of Egypt whose name Lewis couldn't remember, though Jerry had told him twice. Better still, Jerry was getting paid for it, though the fee was modest.

They could use it. Two years had passed since the stock market crash had plunged the nation into the worst economic crisis anyone could have imagined, and it just kept getting worse. Unemployment had now reached twenty-five percent, one out of every four men, and President Hoover seemed to be doing nothing to stop it. In fact, it felt like he was making it worse. A few months ago he'd decided to pull all the contracts for carrying mail from the small carriers and consolidate them among the four biggest air companies—nice for their stockholders, but death for small businesses like Gilchrist Aviation. They'd lost their mail contract, a good half of their business.

With the Depression, passengers weren't paying good money to travel by air. Maybe Hollywood millionaires could still afford it, but precious few people in Colorado could. And January was not a spectacular month for crop dusting.

Come April or May they'd probably have to head for California and do some itinerant work, spraying crops wherever the jobs were available. Worst of all, they'd probably have to split up, as nobody needed three pilots. Either that, or they'd have to start selling off planes, beginning with Alma's beloved Jenny.

As it was, they were lucky to get one job a week, and the long months until April or May stretched out cold and bleak. There had to be coal for the furnace and fuel for the planes, food for four people. None of those things could be compromised on.

Lewis turned his attention back to the pot bubbling away on top of the stove. It wasn't much, just some cheap ground beef and kidney beans, a can of tomatoes and a couple of onions, dressed up with some spices out of the cabinet. Just chili con carne, but on a cold Friday night in December it hit the spot. The cornbread was already out of the oven and cooling on the butcher's board.

"They're back," Jerry called from the living room. He could see down the road as Lewis couldn't, and it was a moment before Lewis heard the sound of the engine, Alma's Ford Runabout truck chugging up the grade in the snow. She and Mitch had taken the truck down to the airfield. It was much too cold and wet for Mitch's Torpedo. His sporty convertible was under a tarpaulin in the garage.

"I hear them," Lewis called back, turning to get bowls out of the china cabinet. Bowls, spoons.... He poured the hot water through the top of the coffee pot and set it on the back eye of the stove, listening to it drip through cheerfully. The Dixieland Jazz dipped and swayed on the radio.

Jerry appeared in the doorway leaning heavily on his cane. His thick brown hair was touched with gray at the temples, and with his gold rimmed glasses and moleskin sport coat he looked every inch the distinguished professor he should have been. "That smells good."

"Thanks," Lewis said.

The back door jangled as Alma and Mitch stomped in, Mitch stamping his boots on the mat outside rather than just tracking snow the way Alma did. Her knit hat had a bobble on it that bounced as she shook the snow off. "Oh that smells good." She took the hat off her bobbed blond hair.

"Just like your mama made?" Mitch asked cheerfully, stripping his gloves off. He looked like the high school football star he had been, just gone to seed a bit—thirty-nine and a touch more rugged, though his Southern accent was still thick enough to spread on bread.

Lewis frowned. "I think I picked this up wildcatting in Texas." He didn't remember his mother making anything of the kind. This was Tex Mex, not Californian, not the roasted meats and ristas of peppers he remembered from his childhood.

Alma had gone over and taken the lid off the pot. "Oh yes," she said with a blissful smile as she smelled the steam. "I'm half frozen."

"Any charters?" Lewis asked.

"Dr. Hambly says he might need to go to San Francisco at the end of the month," Mitch said. "But he's not sure yet."

"That's a nice job if it happens," Lewis said optimistically.

"If it happens." Alma divested herself of her coat and draped it over the back of her ladder back chair before dropping into it. "And I don't see anything else."

Uncharacteristically, it was Jerry who stopped the slide into gloom. "Come on, Al," he said. "It's Friday night. No more work." He brandished one of the bowls at Lewis. "Have some dinner and let's enjoy the music."

Mitch glanced toward the living room door. "That's real New Orleans jazz. Who've you got there?"

Jerry shrugged, still holding the bowl for Lewis to fill it. "Band out of Chicago, Louis Armstrong and the Stompers, I think the announcer said."

"Real nice," Mitch said appreciatively. "Nothing like New Orleans jazz."

Jerry tilted his head. "And when were you ever in New Orleans, Mitch?"

Mitch shrugged, not looking at Jerry as he got the coffee cups and poured carefully, putting them each on the table, then going to the icebox to snag Alma's sweetened condensed milk. "I don't know."

"Thank you," she said.

Mitch smiled. "We know you can't do without it."

Lewis neatly flipped the cornbread out of the cast iron frying pan upside down on a plate and put it on the table before he sank into his chair.

He barely got his eyes closed before Mitch said, "For what we are about to receive, may we be truly grateful."

"Amen," Alma said quietly.

Jerry looked vaguely miffed. "That was perfunctory."

"Oh come on, Jer," Mitch said, cutting into the cornbread. "If you'd said grace it would have been nine psalms long and taken half an hour."

Alma laughed, and after a second Jerry cracked a smile. "I suppose it's the thought that counts."

"So what's up with the magneto on the Terrier?" Lewis asked, referring to the mechanical problem that Alma and Mitch had gone down to the field to fix. The Terrier was their largest plane, a trimotor that was Mitch's beloved, and recounting its woes took most of dinner. Full dark had come and there was the faint ticking of freezing rain falling against the window.

Mitch lifted his head and looked out, though there was nothing to see. "Rotten night."

"We're nice and warm," Lewis said, and Alma smiled back at him, nudging him under the table with her knee.

"That we are," Jerry said. "Though the way this country is going...."

"Jerry...." Alma said.

Lewis frowned. "If we don't get some business soon," he began. He wasn't an owner of Gilchrist Aviation—Alma and Mitch owned it jointly—and he was acutely aware that if he hadn't married the boss, if he were still a hired pilot, he'd be out looking for work. They didn't have work for one pilot full time, much less three. Not anymore.

"I'll sell my car," Mitch offered. Silence greeted that, and he shrugged, spooning in another mouthful of chili and chewing carefully. "That ought to get us a little ways."

Alma shook her head. "Mitch, that's your car, not the company's."

"And it's your roof over our heads." He glanced around the warm kitchen. "Gil bought a house and I had a couple of really nice cars."

"You pay rent," Alma argued. "You pay more than your fair share now."

Jerry put his hand over hers. "We're all family, Alma. Let us each do what we can." He glanced at Lewis over the top of his glasses. "We stick together."

Lewis had come late to this, to this fellowship that they called the Aedificatorii Templi, the Builders of the Temple, a magical lodge dedicated to the august goal of perfecting the world. He'd never dreamed something like this really existed. Or, if it did outside the world of penny dreadfuls and Black Mask Magazine, he'd imagined it peopled by serious men in dark suits, leaders of industry and science, meeting in secret in basement chapels hidden away at country estates. Not by ordinary people, aviators and college professors, who lived in an ordinary house in an ordinary town. Colorado Springs was a pretty ordinary place.

Of course some of the things they'd done were pretty extraordinary. Two years ago he'd been aboard a transatlantic airship, trying to save passengers and crew from a man possessed by a demon. Two years ago he'd killed a man in the woods above Lake Nemi, taking on the age-old task of being the priest of the goddess Diana, her chosen one.

Unfortunately, that job didn't come with a salary.

The jazz on the radio had given way to a message from the show's sponsor, Ford Automobiles. One day he might buy a Ford. Well, when things got better. Surely they would eventually, even if there was no light in sight at the end of the tunnel.

"We do stick together," Alma said, squeezing Jerry's hand and releasing it. "And don't think I don't know how you've been hustling for work."

Jerry shrugged. "Every little bit."

"Shhhh," Mitch said. "I want to hear this."

"...most exciting aeronautical event of our time! The Great Passenger Derby ushers in a new era of excitement in the air! A no holds barred contest of skill and speed featuring the greatest pilots of our time in a thrilling race from Pacific to Atlantic! Taking off from Grand Central field in Los Angeles on March first, the finest teams will compete to reach the ultimate goal—sunny Miami, Florida! With a purse of $25,000, the stakes have never been higher! The sky is the limit! So stay tuned to this station for complete coverage of the Great Passenger Derby!"

"We could win that," Mitch said.

"If we had a $500 entrance fee to blow," Alma said. "For that matter, if we had $500, we wouldn't need to enter the race."

"Are you kidding?" Lewis asked. "It's a $25,000 prize! That's a small fortune. We'd be set for a couple of years, all of us."

Alma frowned. "It's bound to be really competitive, but the Terrier could handle it."

"The Terrier could win it," Mitch said. He scooped some more butter onto his cornbread. "We could win it. The three of us? Come on, Al. Who's better? There are a lot of people as good, but I'd stake any money that there's nobody better."

Lewis nodded. "We're a good team." Three pilots would give them a lot of leeway, and Al was as good a mechanic as anybody was likely to ever see, better than him.

Al looked at Mitch, her blue eyes grave. "We don't have $500," she said levelly.

"Henry does."

Everyone looked around at Jerry who shrugged expressively. "Henry Kershaw has the money, and he designed the Terrier. Don't you think he'd like to see a plane he designed and built win a high profile race? It would mean thousands and thousands of dollars in orders for him. Besides," Jerry picked up his coffee cup. "Don't you think Henry owes us one for saving his business, not to mention his life?"

Henry had been one of the people possessed by the demon two years ago, and without their interference would certainly have been dead. But....

"Don't you think you've milked that for all it's worth already?" Mitch asked. "The first class steamer tickets home?"

"It never hurts to ask," Alma said. She looked at Lewis. "Henry can say no."

"He can," Lewis said. There was the same bright thing in her eyes that he always loved, the thrill of a challenge in the air that spurred him on. A coast to coast air race, no holds barred.... Something prickled at the base of his spine, the faint touch of sight he was beginning to use, beginning to rely on. "But he won't."

Lewis dreamed, and while he knew in some part of himself that he lay safe beside Alma, some other part of himself seemed to walk distant streets.

The sounds of jazz filled the night air, not from the radio but pouring out of windows, out of clubs and bars and restaurants and homes alike, pure New Orleans jazz. The Devil's Music.

He paused in the light of a cast iron streetlamp, his face lost in the shadow of his hat. The devil's music indeed, bright and intoxicating, no pale imitator of the music of savage rites, but music intended to wean the soul from God. Even here, in the shadow of the Cathedral of St. Louis, the devil's music penetrated every shadow.

As he had demanded. He had written the newspaper and told them: anywhere he heard the devil's music he would not kill.

It was a heady thing to have a city of half a million people obeying him. Everywhere in the city of New Orleans people were listening to jazz tonight, even people who hated it, because the Axe Man said that he would not kill if they embraced his father's music. Like the Ripper half a century earlier, his idol and his model, he was his father's son. And any who embraced the devil would survive....

Quietly he turned away . He would not kill tonight. Eight times he had struck before, and eight souls sent wailing to that hell from which he had come. Many, many more had embraced darkness out of fear, while others let the devil in right this moment, let him come winding through their senses in the intoxicating strains of jazz. The music would possess them and they would never be free.

The twentieth century had dawned in hard, bright light, and it would end in primeval darkness, twisting down into oblivion like an airplane in a stall. He was the devil's retribution on this world, and even music gave the devil his due.

Lewis woke, his heart pounding in his chest, the dream fading even as he opened his eyes in the darkness of the bedroom. Beside him, Alma slept on. The radiator rattled softly, steam rising in the pipes from the furnace below. Outside, there was the faint ticking of ice against the window. There was no music.

He got up, padding to the window and pulling the drapes aside. Nothing moved in the yard, the trees limned darkly with water not quite frozen. The lights were still on in Mitch's apartment over the garage. It must not be that late. Mitch was a night owl and he stayed up past any of the rest of them, listening to the radio in his place where it wouldn't keep anyone awake. Was it Mitch's radio that had woken him, that had wormed its way into his dreams? It would have to have been awfully loud with all the windows closed. And there wasn't a sound now.

Lewis shook his head. A bad dream, one of the ones that didn't make sense. Not about something happening now, he thought. Something that happened a long time ago, not something coming. It felt different. A memory, not a precognition. Only not his memory. He frowned. The more he tried to remember, the more the details of the dream escaped him. Streets and rain and jazz, and something bad that happened… It was gone, washed clear. The dream faded even as he reached for it. A bad dream, Lewis said. But one that required no action. Whatever it was, it was over and done.

He crawled back under the mound of blankets, snuggling up to Alma. And surely they had trouble enough without borrowing more.

It had been nearly a month, and no answer to her letter to Henry Kershaw in his Los Angeles office. Maybe he wasn't there, he had half a dozen shops at airfields across the country, but it was time to stop thinking about the Great Passenger Derby and start worrying about more likely work. Alma bent over the ledger in the narrow room she used as her office when it was too cold to work at the hangar. Which it definitely was now, with the price of coal what it was, and the jobs so few and very far between. Better not to try to heat the office at the hangar, and do the books here, after she and Mitch had made their daily check on the planes. The cold wasn't all that good for them, but at least they could fire up the engines now and then, make sure the oil was ok and all the fuel lines and control wires in good shape. Admittedly, that cost money—fuel money, coal money, her own time and Mitch's—but they couldn't afford to get a job and discover that the machinery wasn't ready.

She looked at the ledger again, at the balance dwindling in the far right column. No work for two weeks, not since a piddling little job that barely paid for the fuel they'd burned; she'd pared the cost to something Harriman could afford, on the theory that he'd recognize what a better deal it was and hire them again, but the weather had been rough, and she wasn't sure he'd risk being sick again even if it did save him four hours each way.

Maybe she could save a little more on the groceries. She'd already stopped buying clothes, was still wearing the winter coat she'd bought four years ago, though the fur collar was looking a bit moth-eaten, and she was almost ashamed to let Lewis see her lingerie. Of course, if it wasn't for the odd skills Lewis had picked up here and there, they'd all be walking around in socks that were out at toe and heel: it had seemed odd, at first, to see him settle down by the radio with yarn and needle and a darning egg, but she couldn't argue with the results.

If only they hadn't lost their mail contract. That still rankled, all the more so because they hadn't done anything wrong. She and Mitch and Lewis had played by the rules, applied for their contract and won it fairly, delivered the mail every day to the main feeder line in Denver. They'd even made enough money to hire a fourth pilot, and she'd counted on that money to get them through the hard times. When the Air Mail Act passed the previous year, she hadn't been worried. Yes, the way the payments were made changed, and it was no longer a flat subsidy for flying mail, but they had the Terrier and it looked as though it would be easy enough to switch to a combined mail and passenger service, just the way the government seemed to want. Ok, they didn't run a daily passenger service of at least 250 miles, but they came close and were prepared to step up and make it happen, and they'd held a mail contract for more than two years anyway. But then the postmaster general had pulled the rug out from under everyone, taken all the contracts away from the smaller carriers and handed them over in a chunk to three giant airlines, two of which he'd more or less created by forcing smaller companies to merge if they wanted to get the new contracts. There was no room at that table for a little company like Gilchrist Aviation, with two planes and three pilots. And with that contract, they'd lost their only steady income, except for Jerry's salary for teaching at the high school. You couldn't run a company on that—you could barely feed and house four people on that, never mind have anything left over.

She rubbed her eyes, trying to make the numbers take better shape. Mitch had offered to sell his car, but he wasn't likely to get a decent price for it. Nobody was in the market for sports cars these days. At least she owned the house outright, Gil's last gift to her—maybe she could mortgage it, if they got desperate for cash, although how she'd make the payments was another question entirely. Sell a plane—sell the Jenny, sadly, her baby, but, again, no one was in the market for aircraft right now. No, if she was going to sell the Jenny, better try to hold off until summer, when somebody might need a crop duster badly enough to pay close to what it was worth....

Somehow they had to scare up more work, that was all there was to it, but for the life of her, she couldn't see how. They were known, they were reliable, everybody's first choice, but nobody else had any money to spare, either. She reached for her pocket knife, unfolded it to whittle her pencil to a sharper point. The Great Passenger Derby still nagged at her—$25,000 to the winner—but she shook her head. Unless and until Henry answered her latter, there was no point even thinking about that money. It cost $5.00 just to send off for the entry forms, the one that disclosed the actual race route; it was $500 to enter the race, and, while Jerry might talk about Henry owing them, she wasn't convinced he had the money to spare, either.

Lewis thinks he does. Lewis thinks he will.

Her hands faltered on the pencil. Lewis saw things, sometimes, possible futures and inevitable outcomes, mostly in dreams but now more and more under conscious control. And if they had money, they could afford to send him to someone to learn to use his talent—there were still lodges out there that could be trusted, who could teach a natural clairvoyant to make best use of his skills. But that was out of the question, too. They simply couldn't afford to be without his income.

There was a knock at the door, and she looked up. "Yes?"

The knob turned, and Lewis stuck his head through the open door. "May we come in?"

He was smiling like a kid at Christmas, and Alma's heart lifted in spite of knowing better. "Sure. Is there a job?"

"I got something for you," Lewis said, and tossed a thick white envelope onto the ledger. Jerry and Mitch were behind him, crowding into the little room.

Alma looked down at it, a typewritten envelope addressed to A. Gilchrist, Gilchrist Aviation, the return address TexAv Fuels in San Angelo, Texas.... She reached for the letter opener, already knowing what it would be: the entry forms and the route information for the Great Passenger Derby.

"Lewis, you shouldn't—that was five dollars!" A week's groceries, if they were careful.

"I won it off Jerry in a poker game," Lewis said, straight-faced, but Mitch spoiled it by snickering. Lewis was a terrible poker player, but Jerry was the only one of them whose money wasn't tied up in the business....

"Chicago paid me a little extra for that last article," Jerry said, gently. "I figured it was worth a shot."

Alma shook her head, unfolding the pages as though they might bite. The top sheet was typewritten, a form letter thanking "Mr. Gilchrist" for his interest in the race, and then the rest were mimeographed entry forms and half a dozen pages listing the legs of the race and the various requirements and extra contests.

"They're only allowing stock planes. And you have to carry a passenger," she said, skimming through the rules. "Someone who's not a pilot."

"Jerry," Mitch said, promptly, and Jerry shook his head.

"I'm out, Mitch. School's in session, remember?"

"Damn." Mitch looked genuinely stricken, and Alma shook her head.

"Nothing's decided. It's still $500 just to enter."

She turned over the pages as she spoke, eyes flickering across the blurred print. A full transcontinental race in six legs, Los Angeles to Coconut Grove—a suburb of Miami, the route notes helpfully pointed out, with a private airfield. Six legs, one mandatory layover, with inspection—well, technically they were expected to stay overnight in each leg's destination city, which made sense. Night flying was always a bitch.

The route took them across the southern states, probably in an attempt to stay in good weather during the early part of the year. Los Angeles to Flagstaff, Flagstaff to San Angelo, San Angelo to Little Rock, then to New Orleans for the mandatory stop, with full inspection. Then New Orleans to Pensacola, where they'd be expected to land, refuel, and stage a mail drop—well, they'd done that half a hundred times in the mountains, that shouldn't be that hard. And then one final leg, from Pensacola across the Florida panhandle and down the coast to Miami.

There was something.... She flipped back to the beginning, frowning thoughtfully. Any passenger plane could enter, but the specifics meant that the advantage would go to the big trimotors like their own Terrier. The other contestants would be flying mostly Fords and Fokkers, and if they were, if Gilchrist had the only Terrier in the race, or at least the only Terrier backed by the manufacturer....

"Oh," she said. "We need to wire Henry."

"What?" Mitch blinked.

"I thought you didn't think that was a good idea," Lewis said.

"We can win this," Alma said. In spite of herself, she was smiling. "It might have been made for us."

"We could fly to Los Angeles tomorrow," Mitch said. "It's not like we've got anything on the books."

"Day after tomorrow," Alma said, and tried not to think about the fuel costs. "We need to let Henry know we're coming."

Chapter Two

The dead man was standing in the rain outside the restaurant at the corner of Chartres Street. He was a big, heavy man in a Panama hat, and he was watching everyone who went into the restaurant closely. Stasi looked away, concentrating on the treacherous cobblestones and her high heeled black shoes with ankle straps, but he saw the movement of her eyes and knew she'd seen him. "Excuse me, ma'am. I was wondering if you might do me an itty-bitty favor?"

Stasi stopped under the green awning and rolled her eyes. "Only in New Orleans!" she said. "None of this 'ooga booga boo' or 'I have returned from beyond the grave!' Oh no! In New Orleans it's 'excuse me, would you do me a favor?'"

The dead man looked hurt. "I was trying to be a gentleman, seeing as how you looked like a lady."

Stasi sighed, patting at her damp hair, long and black and curled neatly in a bun at the back of her neck, the front done with pins in finger waves. "What do you want?"

"My brother Milward, he's the chef. Would it impose too much on you to go give him a message? Please, ma'am. I've been standing out here the better part of a week trying to get somebody to do it."

She looked at him levelly. "Do I look like a sucker to you?"

"You look like a kind-hearted lady." His blue eyes were painfully honest. "We Dead can tell things like that."

"Fine." Stasi rearranged her pocketbook, hoping that made loitering under the awning look natural. "What do you want?"

"Tell Milward that I put the strongbox down the dry well at granny's place. He'll know what I mean cause we used to play there together."

"You put the strongbox down the dry well at granny's." Stasi sighed again. "Fine. I'll tell him if I get a chance."

"I can't tell you how much I appreciate this, ma'am," the dead man began, but she brushed him off, opening the swinging door and stepping into the restaurant.

It was crowded on a rainy night, gleaming brass railings separating sets of white draped tables, every table filled, while waiters in black tie fairly flew about, trays of steaming crawfish etouffeé and Creole rice in hand.

The maitre d' met her before the door closed entirely. "Do you have a reservation, ma'am?"

"I'm meeting a gentleman." She looked around him, scanning the dining room. "Mr. Lanier."

"Ah yes." The maitre d' almost bowed. "He's expecting you. Right this way."

It was a table in the front bow window, romantic and thus a little isolated from the clatter of the dining room. Lanier stood up as she approached. He was tall and rugged, good looking in a way, with prematurely gray hair somewhat at odds with a face that couldn't have been quite forty. "I'm so pleased you could join me," he said, his accent thick enough to stand a spoon in. He stood while the maitre d' held out her chair and saw her into it, but waited until he left before he spoke again. "Miss Smirnoff, is it? I thought that was a brand of vodka."

"It's Rostov," Stasi said, unfolding her napkin.

He sat down, smiling. "War and Peace."

"Ivanova."

He spread his hands, a generous grin on his face. "I don't much care, Miss. Call yourself whatever you like. I've heard good recommendations of your work and I'm pleased you'll undertake this little commission for me."

"If the price is right," Stasi said. "And the particulars are as you say."

Lanier nodded slowly. "Five hundred dollars. Half now, half on delivery. And I would advise you to take care with the piece." He paused. "It has a history," he said delicately.

Stasi's plucked eyebrow rose. "A history?"

"You know how objects acquire history," he said pleasantly, reaching for the basket of angel biscuits in the middle of the table. "But I shouldn't have to tell someone with your talents to be cautious."

"I'm always cautious," Stasi agreed. "But you'll have to be more specific."

He looked thoughtful, as though he were saying less than he knew—typical for a buyer, but unpleasant. "The object in question has been purchased by a very wealthy man who has an interest in the occult. I won't say expertise. I won't credit him with that. But he does take precautions with his possessions."

"You said there was a safe," Stasi said. "You didn't say anything about occult protections. What kind of protections?"

"I would assume that his home is warded. Beyond that, he probably has specific deterrents on the location of the safe." Lanier picked up his butter knife. "Things to make it unobtrusive, or at least unattractive to passersby. Possibly there are specific measures to confound ordinary burglars."

"Well," Stasi said with a brilliant smile. "I'm not an ordinary burglar."

"Indeed not, Miss," he said. "Which is why I came to you. You have a reputation for handling objects with unusual protections on them."

"Or unusual objects," she said.

"That too." Lanier said cheerfully. "So I'm sure you're the perfect connection for this. I have every faith in your success. And I imagine you'll find the object…interesting."

"What tradition is he working in?" She spread her fingers. "It does matter operationally, you know. I'll need the proper countersigns."

"It's an offshoot of the Golden Dawn," Lanier said.

"Humm." Stasi took a sip from her water glass, considering. "Formal Hermetics. A Lodge tradition. Stuffy and stogey and completely predictable." She shrugged. "That shouldn't be too much of a challenge for me. Two fifty now and two fifty on delivery." She held out her hand briskly. "That would be two fifty now."

His smile broadened. Lanier reached into his pocket and took out an envelope, which he gave her. "It's a pleasure, Miss Ivanova. Will you stay and join me for dinner?"

Stasi took the envelope and opened the flap, fanning through the stack of tens and twenties. "I don't have the time. I have a train to catch."

"Of course you do. Good luck."

"I always have good luck." Stasi stood up. "I'll be in touch."

She threaded her way between tables and waiters out to the front. The rain was falling in solid sheets, gray and chilly. But there was a taxi just across the street. The dead man was still pacing. She turned to the hovering maitre d'. "Do you have something to write on?"

"Beg pardon?"

She hooked an order pad off the shelf behind his reservation stand and tore off the top sheet. "Can you please give this to the chef? It's terribly important."

"Of course."

Stasi wrote across it swiftly. *Milward—your brother put the strongbox down the dry well at your granny's place where you used to play together.* She folded the note and handed it to the maitre d' with a smile and a quarter for his trouble. "Thank you."

"I'll give it straight to him," the maitre d' promised.

"You'd better," Stasi said, and gave him a sideways smile. "It's a good thing to stay on the right side of the beyond." And with that she walked out into the rain.

It took two days to make the arrangements, and then the third day to fly into Grand Central. It felt weird not having Jerry in the back seats, especially after their last trip to Los Angeles, but Mitch managed to ignore the absence. He took the last leg, bringing the Terrier neatly onto the runway in the early dark, and taxied the plane to the hangar they'd reserved while Alma ducked into the terminal to change out of her flying clothes. They weren't staying at the Roosevelt this time—Henry wasn't paying and they couldn't afford it on their own dime—but Alma had managed to find them a cheap place not too far from the field. The diner across the street was still open; they wolfed a late meal, and retreated to their rooms.

It was warm in the little room, at least by Colorado standards, and the noise from the street came clearly through the thin walls, making it hard to sleep. Mitch rolled over, trying to punch his pillow into a better shape, wondering why they'd even bothered. This whole trip was a waste of time and money. Henry wasn't going to risk $500 on them, not right now. Whatever he owed them for saving his life was long ago paid. Lewis was good, but his talent was untrained. He might not be able to tell Sight from wishful thinking…

Mitch folded the pillow again, frowning at his own pessimism. He shouldn't blame Lewis for his own bad mood, particularly when Lewis had never shown any sign of making that sort of mistake. If anything, he was more likely not to mention his hunches, which had its own drawbacks. . . . He cut off that line of thought with the ease of long practice. There were plenty of things that didn't bear looking at, and this was one of them. They were meeting Henry in the morning; time enough then to be disappointed.

"I don't know why I put up with you people," Henry Kershaw said, sitting down on the edge of his desk and looking at the three of them.

"Because we're the best and you know it," Alma said briskly. At forty-one she was still a handsome woman, tall and curvy, with blonde hair cut in a tidy short bob. She wore a conservative tweed suit, but her long legs drew the eye anyway.

In Mitch's boyhood, the sight of legs like those would have started a riot. Two years younger than Alma, he'd been born in 1892. Victoria had been on the throne of England and Benjamin Harrison had been President of the United States, which had only had 44 states instead of the current 48. The massacre at Wounded Knee had been less than two years old and the Ghost Dance was still alive and well. Mitch didn't think he'd ever seen a woman's legs other than his little sister's until he was in the army, and trying to catch and diaper Evelyn didn't exactly count. Not that it mattered much now, but he could still look. And not that Alma had ever been anything but a good friend to him. Usually he was able to keep his mind off such things; it must be being in Los Angeles that was making his thoughts drift.

"And we can win the Great Passenger Derby for you," Alma went on. "Because we fly a Terrier Trimotor. It's the best in its class, hands down—a beautiful design, beautifully built."

Mitch nodded. The Terrier was the sweetest passenger plane around, way better, faster and more versatile than the Ford Trimotor which dominated the class, better made than the Fokker that was Ford's other big competitor. If Henry wanted a genuine ace to endorse his plane, Mitch was perfectly happy to express his honest opinion.

"I know it's a good plane," Henry said. "And I know I sold Gil the top of the line. But I don't see how that guarantees that you'll win. Even if you were to—exercise other available options—I can't see that you can promise me that."

Henry had been part of the same lodge back during the war, though he'd moved on since then to a lodge that practiced a more experimental form of the art. "That would be cheating," Mitch said, solemnly, and surprised a grin from Henry.

Alma smiled too, though more gently. "I can't guarantee a win, of course. But I can show you why we have a better than average chance of taking the big prize."

She took the sheets of paper out of her purse, and Henry shifted himself to let her spread them out on the blotter.

"Mostly the race alternates short and long legs," Alma said, "except that there are two short legs to get us from Little Rock to New Orleans to Pensacola. The long leg from San Angelo to Little Rock—that's the third leg, here—that's just about 600 miles. The Fords, and you know most of the planes are going to be Fords, can't make that jump without refueling."

"Unless they have long-range tanks installed," Henry said.

"Which I wouldn't," Alma answered. "Not when their cruising speed is already on the slow side. I wouldn't want the extra weight even with them empty."

Henry nodded slowly. "Go on."

Mitch held his breath. When Alma had spelled it out for them back in Colorado, he hadn't quite believed it either, but she'd gone over the math patiently until he finally got it.

"The Terrier is designed to be an all-purpose aircraft," Alma said. "Swap out two seats, add a daybed in the cabin. Need more cargo space? You can move the rear bulkhead forward. Need more range? Put in a supplemental fuel tank."

"Ah." It was barely a breath, but it sounded as though Henry was there ahead of her.

Alma went on anyway. "If you'll send our supplemental tank on ahead to San Angelo—where I know you have hangar space—then it will be waiting for us when we land. We install it that night, and we'll be able to make Little Rock without refueling."

"You're not just going to be flying against Fords," Henry said. "The Fokkers have the range. I don't know about some of the others...."

"The Terrier's faster than a Fokker," Alma said. "Not to mention more reliable."

"That kind of change isn't against the rules?" Henry picked up the sheaf of papers, began sorting through them.

"Not that I can see," Alma said. "The planes have to be stock, but the supplemental tank is stock, and we're treating it as a stock item. We're installing and removing it just the way we would for any ordinary set of jobs."

"Which is a very nice selling point for me," Henry said. "I do see that." He paused, still looking at the papers in his hands. "What are you going to do if there's another Terrier in the race?"

"Fly faster," Mitch offered. Lewis smothered a snort of laughter.

"We are very good," Alma said, demurely.

"Not to mention smart," Henry muttered. "What exactly do you want from me, Alma?"

"I need you to put up the entry fee," Alma said. "And pay for any fuel that's not supplied by the race. We'll pay you back out of our winnings."

"Assuming you have some," Henry said. "There aren't any guarantees in air racing, as I'm sure you'd be the first to tell me."

"There is, of course, a manufacturer's prize," Alma said. "If you wanted to enter that part of the competition as well."

Henry sighed. "At another $300? Hell, why not? All right, Alma, it's a deal. But I'm going to work this for every bit of publicity I can get. Are you game?"

Alma nodded in turn. "We're game."

Mitch nodded, too, and hoped it was true.

Jerry Ballard levered himself out of Mrs. Holton's Model T. It was an awkward process, first getting the wooden leg to the ground, and then the cane, swinging his body around to get his hands on the door's frame to lift and balance. It was worse in the snow, and he made himself take his time even though he wanted to be out and gone, to walk off the anger filling him. He made sure he was steady, and turned carefully to lean back into the car.

"Thank you, again." He couldn't drive any more, of course, not with the missing leg, had had to cadge rides to school from his fellow teachers, and Catherine Holton lived only a little further up the road.

"Oh, my pleasure, Dr. Ballard." Her smile was as false as his, and he only hoped his worry didn't show as clearly as hers. She had two children, and her husband had already been out of work six months.

"Will you be all right?" he asked abruptly, and her eyes fell.

"We'll have to be, won't we?" She reached for the gearshift, and Jerry took a step back, closing the car door gently. She put the Ford into gear with equal care, and Jerry turned to make the long walk up the drive. At its end, the farmhouse waited—Gil's house, Gil's and Alma's; Alma's and Lewis's now, and Mitch's. And his, too, except he didn't want it. Not like this, anyway: his dream had been summers in the Near East, a dozen different dig sites mapped out in imagination, and winters here in the mountains, coming back to friends and lovers only long enough to write his papers and ready himself to leave again. Gil had never wanted that much travel—he was a pilot, not an archeologist; he needed a home base, a home field, and there had been a few months when it all seemed as though it would come together. But the war had ended that. He shook himself and fished in his pocket for his key, his breath steaming in the thickening dusk, fogging his glasses.

He let himself into the hall, balanced carefully as he unwound his muffler and freed himself from his topcoat and gloves. He took his time putting them all away—there was no good way to tell his news, and it was even worse, coming on top of Henry's decision to back them—and Alma's voice came from the living room.

"Jerry?"

He braced himself. "It's me."

"Everything all right?"

"Yes." And it wasn't a lie, not in the most essential things. He limped toward her, his cane and his leg tapping on the wooden floor.

She was waiting in the living room, wearing one of Gil's old cardigans against the chill. She still had a book in her hand, her finger holding the place, but she was frowning, undeceived. "What is it?"

Jerry sighed. "They're closing the high school early, and laying off the teachers—laying off everyone, from the janitor to the principal. They'll hire some people back in the spring when they open—if they open. But—not me. They don't need a Latin teacher right now."

"Oh, Jerry." Alma stopped. "What do you mean, if they open? They can't just close down the high school—can they?"

"There's no money to pay the teachers," Jerry said. "No money to heat the building, either, so the school board's closing down until spring."

"Which puts us into planting season," Alma said. "So they probably won't start up again until the fall."

Jerry nodded.

"Oh, Jer," she said again.

"I've got other options," he said, though the words felt hollow. "Reviews, the occasional article, translations—there's still work out there for a specialist." Except that there were half a hundred specialists in exactly the same things competing for those jobs, and most of them were in Chicago or Cambridge, not Colorado Springs. "It's people like Catherine Holton and Martha Betts that I feel sorry for."

Alma nodded. They all knew who'd been out of work for a year, who was pawning the family radio, whose watch no longer had a chain or fob.

"And it's not as though I particularly love teaching high school," Jerry said. He couldn't seem to stop talking, as though he might convince himself. "I won't be sorry to see the backs of a few of those boys."

Alma turned to the sideboard, where the decanter stood half full. It wasn't good whiskey, exactly, but it was better than the local homebrew Mitch usually scrounged for them. She poured them each two fingers of neat spirit. Jerry lowered himself into the chair by the radio and took the proffered glass. His stump was aching, and he took a long swallow.

"Say," Alma said, and sat up straighter in the chair opposite. "This means—Jerry, there's no reason now that you can't be our designated passenger."

Jerry blinked. He'd resigned himself to not being part of the air race, done his best to pretend he didn't hate being left behind, and now—Alma was right, there was nothing to keep him here. "Every other team is going to be bringing some one hundred pound starlet," he said, scrupulously. "Not only are they a good deal more photogenic, but I weigh nearly twice that. Every ounce could make a difference, Al."

"Leave that to me and Mitch. You've got other advantages."

"Let's hope we don't need them," Jerry said, and felt his heart lift in spite of everything.

Chapter Three

On February 25th they took off to fly to California, spending the night in Las Vegas along the way, because this time they weren't flying into Grand Central but a bit beyond, to the private field at Henry's hacienda outside the city. There were no lights there, no flagman unless Henry detailed someone to meet them or, even less likely, deigned to wave them down himself, and there was no point risking a landing at dusk, not when even a small miscalculation would bring them in after full dark. At best that would force them to divert to Grand Central, and no one wanted to make them look bad just when Henry was ramping up the publicity for the race.

All of these were things that Jerry understood, even though he wasn't a pilot and never would be one. He'd begun as a scholar, a classicist, survived the Great War as an artillery officer, and even before they'd had to amputate his foot and most of the lower leg, he'd meant it when he told Gil he had no desire to learn to fly. He'd always been happy to leave that to Gil, and then to Gil and Alma, and now to Alma and Mitch and Lewis. That was what they were good at; his skills lay elsewhere.

In research, for one. He refolded the last of the newspapers he'd bought in Las Vegas, a New York Daily Mirror only a day old, studying Winchell's column. Winchell was already talking up the race, and most of his jibes seemed to be reserved for the amateurs from Fair Harvard—"Charles Parker Salstonstall, George Peter Newhouse, Miss May Saltsonstall, and Rob-Roy McIsaac... guess which one didn't go to Harvard, boys and girls... and it's not the lady!"—but they were bound to draw his eye eventually, if only because Alma was leading the team.

The pitch of the engine changed, the plane tilting in a wide turn, and Jerry glanced out the window to see a tile-roofed house passing below the wing. It looked enormous, three wings and what looked like a stable forming a square around a verdant inner courtyard, and Jerry shook his head again at the amount of money involved. Henry had lost a bundle on his failed airship, and it was hard to believe he was selling many airplanes these days, but he still seemed to be doing all right. Which was a good thing, if it meant he could sponsor them in the race.

The Terrier tipped again, swinging around over the house a second time, and Lewis leaned across the aisle.

"We'll be landing soon."

"Yeah." Jerry ground out his cigarette and folded the newspapers back together. He could feel it now himself, could see the descent out the window, the dry grass rushing to meet them, the mountains a purple smudge in the distance. And then they were past the grass and onto tarmac, and he felt the lift fail as Mitch brought the plane neatly down onto the runway.

"I can't believe Kershaw's paved the strip," Lewis shouted, over the noise of the engines as the plan shuddered and slowed to a decorous pace.

"I can," Jerry said. Henry didn't do things by halves. If he was going to have a private airstrip at his house in the country, it was going to be a good one. He'd have hangar facilities and a workshop—yes, there they were, a long low building off to one side, vanishing as Mitch turned toward it. That left him with a view of the house, also built long and low, with stucco walls and red tile roofs, small windows shuttered against the sun. It wasn't as old as it looked, he guessed, looking at the way it fit the land around it, but it was every bit as expensive.

Mitch brought the Terrier to a halt just outside the hangar, and Lewis jumped to open the door and let down the folding stairs. The air that rushed in was dry but not as hot as Jerry had expected, smelling of dust and gasoline. He worked himself to his feet, the artificial leg tricky on the metal floor, and Mitch and Alma emerged from the cockpit, both of them looking tired but pleased.

"Everything went well?" Jerry asked, and Mitch nodded.

"She's in pretty good shape. I'd like to tweak the motors just a little more, but—yeah. It was a good flight."

Alma rubbed his shoulder lightly. "She ran like a dream," she said. "Let's not push too hard."

"Just a tweak," Mitch said, and Alma followed him out of the plane.

Jerry tucked his cane under his arm and levered himself carefully down the stairs, taking most of his weight on his arms. Henry was waiting, along with a man Jerry vaguely remembered as Henry's senior shop manager. Mitch and Alma were already talking to him, Lewis hovering quietly, and after a moment he and Mitch disappeared into the hangar's shadows. Jerry braced himself on his cane, and moved to join them, accepted Henry's jovial handshake and a tap on the shoulder.

"Good flight, I gather."

Jerry nodded. "From a passenger's perspective, entirely uneventful. I read the papers most of the way."

Henry gave him a shrewd look. "You're getting into the spirit, I see."

Lewis and Alma had followed Mitch and the engineer into the hangar, but Jerry hung back, lowering his voice just a little. "I thought I'd better. There's going to be a lot of press interest in this event."

"There is," Henry agreed, his voice neutral.

"And a great deal of it focusing on personalities."

"You've been following Winchell?"

Jerry nodded. "Of course."

Henry gave a crooked smile. "He'll eat Alma up. With a spoon."

"Yeah."

"And I'm going to let him," Henry said. "It's all good publicity for me."

Jerry glanced over his shoulder, to see Alma leaning on Mitch's shoulder, Lewis still at her back. He looked more like a bodyguard than a husband, standing there, and his frown made him look unhappily possessive rather than just tired. "Too much gossip might not be good for you," he suggested, and Henry shrugged.

"If the press wants to turn Alma into a femme fatale—well, good luck to them. I can't see it." He spread his hands hastily. "Don't get me wrong, Alma's an attractive woman, but—"

"I expect you don't see it because it's not true," Jerry said, with a bit more edge than he'd meant. They were skating on thin ice here, and he'd never known just how much Henry knew or suspected, back when they'd all been part of the same lodge. Jerry had been Gil's lover then, Gil being Alma's late husband; he and Alma had shared Gil until Gil's death, a highly unconventional arrangement but one that had worked for them. And if you looked too far back into his past, there was a regrettable affair that had very nearly gotten him kicked out of school and had cost him his scholarship... But he couldn't exactly say that out loud, so he settled for the next best thing. "But my point is, we're going to be taking—precautions—all through the race. Nothing that would count as cheating, nothing that will influence the outcome, just—protective sigils, things like that. And we want to be free to act if we have to, without being trailed by every reporter who wants to catch one of us with his pants down."

Henry nodded slowly. "I see that, yes. All right, I'll do what I can—"

"If you could stick to professional opinions," Jerry began.

"If I did that, they'd assume she was sleeping with all of you," Henry said. "I'll be calm and soothing and talk about how sweet it is that Alma's found new love after being widowed so young." He paused. "Your job will be to keep her from killing me when she reads that."

"I'll do my best," Jerry said, with a grin.

Henry had promised nothing too fancy, at least for their first night, but even so, the dinner was impressive, and Lewis was glad he'd bought a new suit for the race. Alma had a nice dress, not too fancy, but not severe, a rich rose-red that flattered her golden hair, and a matching spray of silk roses in place of a hat. Henry's wife Mabel was far more exotic, graceful in her silk pyjama suit, and Mitch had been quick to light her cigarette and refresh her cocktail before dinner. Henry didn't seem to mind, and if he didn't, it was none of Lewis's business, any more than the starlet Henry had brought on the airship trip with him. Jerry had fallen into conversation with Henry's daughter, Rose, a tall, solemn girl with glasses who managed to make a green silk sheath look oddly dowdy. Alma and the shop manager, Nowak, were talking about the magnetos, and Lewis concentrated on the food in front of him. The roasted pork was delicious, and the corn relish was lightly touched with chiles, a flavor familiar from his childhood: a Spanish cook, he guessed, but that was no surprise, in California.

After dessert, they retreated to Henry's lavish sitting room, where a uniformed maid brought coffee and Henry offered a selection of liqueurs. Mabel excused herself, pleading an early start the next day, and took Rose away with her, and Nowak made his departure a few minutes later. Henry leaned against the mantel, swirling the brandy in his glass, and Alma put her hands on her hips.

"All right, Henry, out with it."

"I received the final list of entries today," he answered, and nodded to his desk. "No surprises."

Alma crossed to the desk, putting her drink aside, and Lewis came to join her, peering over her shoulder at the neatly type-written list. No, there weren't any real surprises: all three of the newly-created passenger and mail lines had entered, Transcontinental and Western Air, United Aircraft and Transport, and American Airways, all flying Fords. He was a little surprised that American had managed to field a team. Less than a year ago, they'd been a collection of more than eighty small airlines, some of them no bigger than Gilchrist. It was impressive that they'd pulled themselves together. He'd heard of Consolidated Aircraft, too, and was surprised that they weren't entering one of their own machines: Floyd Odlum was supposed to be taking an interest in them, after Transcontinental had been forced into the merger with Western. The others, though...

He stepped aside to let Mitch look, and Alma relinquished the paper to him, fixing her gaze on Henry. "Who should we be worried about?"

"All of them," Henry answered, and Alma rolled her eyes.

"Seriously, Henry. What do you know about the smaller teams? This Jezek Corsair, for instance—"

"Connie—Conrad Jezek use to work for me, and I was sorry to lose him," Henry said. "They're being a little cagey about their specs, and I think they had to lean on the organizers a bit to get in at all— you can't really call it a stock plane when they've only built one of them—but it looks to me as though they've traded size for speed. They're going to be carrying a smaller fuel load than you are, and that's going to cost them."

"How about Bestways?" Lewis asked. "Or Comanche?" There was something familiar about the names listed for the latter, though he couldn't quite place them.

"I don't know much more than what it says on their entry papers," Henry said. "Bestways is out of the midwest, Chicago, I think. And Comanche is a bunch of Army Reserve guys from Oklahoma."

That was where he'd heard the name. Lewis said, "If that guy Rayburn is who I think he is—I met him at a Legion meeting a while back. He's a good pilot."

Alma nodded, visibly filing the information. Mitch looked up from the sheet of paper. "And—Crimson Air?"

"The Fair Harvards," Jerry said, and blinked as they all looked at him. "I'm not drunk, that's what Winchell's been calling them. They must've leaned on the organizers, too. I can't see them being a serious aviation company."

"That doesn't mean they can't fly," Lewis said.

Jerry paused, visibly trying to remember what the gossip columnist had said. "The two boys are cousins, just out of Harvard, and they've been flying since the younger one was twelve."

"And they've got a ringer," Mitch said. "Isn't Rob-Roy McIsaac the guy who used to fly liquor out of Canada for all the hot-shots in New York?"

"That's the one," Henry said.

"Hell of a way to go straight," Jerry said.

Mitch put the list aside, and Lewis picked it up again, scanning the entries. Pilots aside, and they wouldn't know how good any of these people were until they were in the air, it was the planes themselves that were going to make the difference. Five Fords, two Fokkers, and the Corsair... The Corsair was an unknown quantity and there was nothing they could do about that, though he trusted Henry when Henry said it would be carrying less fuel. The Terrier was better than the Fords, and as for the Fokkers—well, the Harvards were flying one of them, and he'd back Alma and Mitch over a bunch of college boys any day. And Bestways was small enough that they might not be able to keep the plane in top conditions, and the Fokkers were notoriously prone to problems. And that, he knew, was partly wishful thinking, but on balance he was starting to like their chances.

"There's one other thing we need," Alma said, looking at Henry. "You told me you wanted us to repaint in some sort of flashy scheme."

Henry spread his hands, the remains of his brandy glinting in the warm light from the lamps. "It's all publicity. I've had a couple of my people draw up some designs, nothing gaudy, but a bit brighter than raw metal—"

"I'll paint it purple if you want," Alma said, and Lewis saw Mitch wince. "But you don't touch the rondels—in fact, we need to repaint them ourselves, to reinforce their protection."

"I figured those were sigils," Henry said. "Yes, of course, you can use the shop—I'll tell Frank you're making some secret modifications, that'll keep him happy. Just don't leave everything smelling of aftershave this time."

Lewis felt himself blush—two years earlier, they'd borrowed Henry's machine shop in Chicago to create protective sigils, and the only scent available to consecrate the equipment had been a bottle of Mitch's aftershave—but Jerry laughed aloud.

"Needs must," he said.

Alma grinned. "I expect we can be a bit more subtle this time."

Henry lifted his glass. "A toast, then. Luck and victory."

Lewis raised his glass and drank with the others, hoping for both.

Alma leaned back in her chair, stretching her toes into the sun that crept onto the edge of the shaded patio. It was lovely and warm in California, when there was still snow back home; she had bought a pair of daring pumps, cut low in the toe with three thin straps across the foot, and she eyed the dark green leather with renewed admiration. Henry had insisted on supplementing their wardrobes, buying each of the men a nice new suit and casual slacks and jacket, and her a green crepe jacket-dress with the new higher waist and the pumps to match. He had wanted her to buy jodhpurs as well, for interviews, and she'd reluctantly agreed, but refused the matching middy blouse. She particularly liked the way Lewis looked in his new cream-colored suit, so she was willing to forgive Henry a great deal at the moment—well, for that and the lovely coffee. It would be far too easy to get used to living like this, sleeping in every morning, rising to a breakfast expertly cooked by a polite and attentive staff, taking her last cup of coffee out to the patio before she had to face the business of the day... Not at all like home, where only Lewis could be relied on not to burn the bacon, and where there were always grounds in the coffee no matter how many eggshells she put in the pot.

"Good morning, Mrs. Segura."

Alma looked up to see Mabel Kershaw making her way through the French doors, elegant in wide-legged trousers, her hair held back in a silk scarf. She held a cup of coffee, too, and settled herself in the chair next to Alma, smiling pleasantly.

"You don't mind if I join you?"

"Not at all," Alma said, already marshaling her excuses, and Mabel took a long drink of her coffee.

"Henry said he took all of you on a shopping trip yesterday."

"Yes," Alma said, and extended her foot. It was size nine and a half, but the pump managed to make it look elegant.

Mabel nodded appreciatively. "Oh, that's nice! I do like those— you won't mind if I pick up a pair, will you?"

"Not at all," Alma answered, surprised and rather touched. That was unexpectedly gracious, and hardly necessary, and she found herself warming to the other woman.

"It occurred to me—my beautician's coming today," Mabel said. "And I thought you might like her to cut your hair, too."

Alma paused. "That's very nice of you," she said, carefully.

Mabel set her cup down and leaned forward. "Please don't be offended. I don't mean that I think you need it, or—anything bad." She sounded suddenly younger, less sure of herself. "It's just that there are going to be so many reporters and the newsreels and everything, I thought you might like to get a proper cut before the race starts. It's not like for the men, they can just go to the nearest barber shop."

"I doubt Mr. Kershaw does that," Alma said, and Mabel gave a sudden grin.

"No, he most certainly does not. And his manicurist is more expensive than mine." She sobered abruptly. "It matters how you look out here, Mrs. Segura. Especially with the press involved. The better you look, the better you'll be treated."

That was probably true, Alma thought. She'd seen it in the way reporters covered society gossip, though that was more Jerry's hobby than her own. She'd been willing to paint the Terrier any outlandish color Henry wanted, for the sake of the race; surely a Hollywood hairstyle was a lesser sacrifice? "It'll have to be something I can manage without setting," she said.

Mabel nodded. "Dolores is a genius. She'll be here at three."

Dolores turned out to be a stout elegant woman in a neat blue suit, with delicately tinted nails and unobtrusive makeup. She had brought a pair of younger women to help out, and Alma let them pamper her with orange-blossom shampoo and a foot massage. By the time those were done, she was relaxed and agreeable, happy to let Rita paint her toenails, though she turned down the manicure with only mild regret.

"I can't keep my nails in any kind of shape," she said, glancing up at Dolores. "And whatever you do with my hair, it has to be something I can take care of—that I can make look good—on the road."

Dolores nodded seriously. "Yes, Mrs. Kershaw explained that you will be in the Passenger Derby, Mrs. Segura. I am seeing—something not so very different from what you are wearing now, just a bit updated. More suitable to a world traveler."

Alma grinned at that, but leaned back and let her get to work.

When they were finished, her hair washed and cut and styled, makeup applied with a feather's touch by pertly smiling Olive, she stared at her reflection in the mirror with some surprise. It really wasn't all that different, just a little change in the angles that framed her face, and yet the woman who looked back at her was somehow much more sophisticated, even elegant.

"You must keep the lipstick," Dolores said, very seriously. "It is not an easy color to find, and it becomes you."

"Lipstick and powder will take you everywhere," Mabel agreed.

Alma didn't try very hard to refuse, but as she changed for dinner, she regarded her new self warily in the long mirror. She only hoped Lewis liked it.

She paused at the top of the two steps that led down to the dining room, bracing herself, and Mitch turned with a whistle.

"Yowza."

Jerry peered over the tops of his glasses, looking slightly stunned, and Lewis came to offer his arm, neat in his new pale suit.

"You look gorgeous," he said, low-voiced, and she tucked her hand into his elbow with a quick grin.

"A new look for the race."

"You'll be the best-looking pilot in the bunch, that's for sure," Mitch said, and the bell sounded for dinner.

"I hope she knows what you're getting her into," Mabel Kershaw said softly behind her, to Henry, but Lewis drew them away before Alma could decide whether to respond.

The California sun was warm though it was only March, and Lewis took his jacket off the moment he got in the hangar. The good thing about working on the Terrier in Henry's hangar was that it was top-notch. There was every piece of equipment you might want, and all of it was good and worked right. Also, since Kershaw had built the Terrier, there was no making do with parts intended for a Fokker or a Ford. Everything was factory sharp, just what the boss ordered.

The bad thing was that there were always people hanging around. Henry had a shop manager, one of his senior mechanics. A bunch of his designers worked out of this hangar. And he had a full crew all the time, tending to a couple of other planes either pre or post production. The Gilchrist Terrier that was going to be in the air race was a source of pride to everybody, and being alone with the plane was like trying to court a girl before her quinceañera. Alma had concluded that while a big robed ritual to bless the plane might be preferable, it was not going to happen. The magic was going to have to be in the paint job itself, in the repainting of the sigil on the Terrier's tail, rather than in a working that accompanied it.

Alma and Mitch were already in the hangar, the sleeves of Alma's mannish shirt rolled up to her elbows as she stood by Mitch survey-ing the basic job. Henry's guys had put the first coat on, solid white from nose to tail, and Lewis had to admit it looked good. A lot better than bare metal, anyway, which was what they'd had. The wing tips had also been painted, a bright medium blue that Lewis frowned at. It would change the profile of the plane against the sky, make it harder to identify.

Apparently Mitch had been saying the same thing, because as Lewis walked up Alma replied, "Yeah, but we're not worried about friendly fire! A little confusion might be good for us."

Mitch put his hands on his hips. "It's pretty. I'm just saying that it will make us look like a smaller plane. It's going to make us look like one of the Fords from a distance."

"Does that matter?" Alma asked.

"Consolidated's colors are blue and white too," Mitch said.

"They've got red on the tail," Lewis said, joining them. "You can tell us apart."

Jerry came around the other side of the plane, pushing his glasses back on his nose. "I've got it drawn out and ready," he said, waving a piece of paper at Lewis. "Do you think you can do this?"

Lewis took the paper and studied the design. It was a circle cut into four parts by an equal-armed cross in the center, like a compass or a Templar cross. An outer ring around the outside sported 'Gilchrist Aviation' around the top of the circle and 'Ps 22 16-17' around the bottom, all rendered in the same celestial blue as the wing tips. "I can do it that size," he said. "It's big enough. What, about 36 inches across there on the tail?"

"Sounds good," Alma said.

Lewis eyeballed it. "So the letters are a couple of inches tall. Sure. I can do that with a fine brush."

"It's the Sixth Pentacle of Jupiter," Jerry said in a low voice so it wouldn't carry to shop employees. "It serveth for protection from all earthly dangers, regarding it each day devoutly thou shalt not perish."

"Sounds good to me," Mitch said. "I like not perishing."

"I'll keep that in mind," Lewis said. "I'll need a big compass or calipers or something to trace the circle onto the plane."

"Fortunately I have one of those," Jerry said, his eyes amused. "Vital equipment for the modern magician."

"Ok," Lewis said. "Let's have a look."

The wind blew in through the hangar door, tinted with scents of a spring evening, lifting Lewis' hair off his brow and teasing the edges of the flaps as though the Terrier yearned for the sky. Not a terrier, Lewis thought. One of Diana's greyhounds, born to run. She was ready to stretch her wings over the whole continent.

And she would. Pacific to Atlantic, over mountains and deserts and plains and bayous, over cities rising hopefully toward the sky. Celestial blue, the color of ocean. Lewis carefully traced the circle, going clockwise around with the paintbrush. Pacific to Atlantic, we will be safe. We will be safe under heaven.

The cross was simple, broader brush strokes, clean lines. He'd seen it on airplanes before, not so different from the cross on the Luftstreitkrafte planes he'd fought against in France, only enclosed in the circle and without concave curvature to the arms, a compass that could never waver. A compass. Wherever they wandered, the Terrier would bring them home.

Celestial blue, the color of sky.

"That looks real nice," Mitch said, looking up.

"Thanks," Lewis said.

Jerry didn't speak, just nodded, not wanting to interrupt.

Gilchrist Aviation across the top of the circle, Alma's name when he'd first met her, his family now. Lord protect us, Lewis thought, filling in the letters carefully with the smallest brush, the oldest prayer. Lord, protect my family.

Celestial blue, the color of the Virgin's robe, the color of prayer.

And the verse last. "They pierced my hands and feet. I may tell all my bones." A funny thing to paint on an airplane, he'd thought at first, but it made sense now. No matter what travail, no matter what sorrow, grace never wavered. "Yea, though I walk through the valley of the shadow of death..." Lewis had walked through that valley. He'd been there more than once, but there was always morning on the other side. This was morning. This was bright day, everything he could reasonably ask for out of life—flying and friends and a bride who loved him, who he loved heart and soul. He hadn't thought he could love Al more, but he did, every day that he woke up and saw her open her eyes and look at him.

Celestial blue for Alma's eyes. Celestial blue for love.

Love carry us, and love bring us home safe.

"It's perfect," Alma said as he finished the last letter. "Perfect." Her pride in him made his heart swell with joy.

"You're very talented," Jerry said, and reached up to give him a hand down. Lewis hadn't realized he was so stiff. The sun was almost setting.

"I wish I had more training," Lewis said. He might have meant painting.

"We'll have to work on that," Jerry replied. There were too many people around to say more.

"We need to get changed," Mitch said. "Henry's guests will be here any minute."

"And the press," Jerry said.

Chapter Four

If Henry's previous parties had been sumptuous, this one was over the top. Alma looked around the terrace over the swimming pool with something like dismay. Red Japanese lanterns hung in long ropes, reflecting like fat moons in the still surface of the pool. A full orchestra was playing under a pavilion across from the pool house, white tie and tails on every one. There was a bar at the other end serving up French champagne and everything stronger, while a crowd of women in gorgeous evening gowns and men in black tie mingled around the pool, on the terrace and lawn, and through the wide French doors into the house where a buffet was set up. Here and there the crowd was livened by the occasional strobes of flash powder going off—reporters and their photographers snapping movie stars and aviators, sportsmen and executives.

Alma tugged nervously at the hem of her dress. It was India ink blue, spangled with stars, her best dress rescued from the wreck of the airship Independence two years ago, and it was the nicest dress she'd ever had. Compared to the ones she saw going by, she might as well have been wearing a sack.

"It's ok," Henry Kershaw said under his breath. "You look great." He took her elbow with an expansive and leonine smile. On her other side, Lewis looked as spooked as she did. Maybe more spooked. "I just want to introduce you to some people," he said, steering her through the crowd. "Aviation people. Our crowd."

Alma refrained from saying that somewhere in the last ten years Henry's crowd had diverged a lot from hers. They'd all been in the same lodge once, all stood pretty much as equals when Henry and Gil had both left the Army Signal Corps at the same time, Gil to start a little air passenger service in Colorado and Henry to start one in California. Gilchrist Aviation was still a skin of the teeth operation, while Henry's Republic Air had grown and branched and grown again. Apparently hobnobbing with Hollywood stars was now all in a day's work for Henry.

"You've got to meet this guy," Henry said, steering Alma around a white-jacketed waiter, Lewis following along. He tapped a slight man with glasses on the shoulder. "Floyd! Glad you could make it, buddy!"

The other man turned around, champagne glass in hand, breaking off conversation with the pretty twenty-something brunette beside him. "Had to come take a look at the competition, Henry," he said with a grin, shaking Henry's hand. "My boys are going to lick yours, you know."

"Bah," Henry said good naturedly, pumping his hand. "Not with a Ford Trimotor, they won't! Why don't you put up a team flying your own plane instead of a Ford?"

"Because you can't land a sea plane in the desert?" The other man grinned. "The Catalina's going to be big, Henry. You wait a year or two. The Catalina is going to dominate the market for flying boats."

"But not much use in the desert," Henry agreed. "Floyd, I want you to meet my team captain. This is Alma Gilchrist—Alma Segura, she is now. She owns and operates the Terrier that's going to bring home the cup. Alma, this is Floyd Odlum."

"Pleased to meet you," he said.

"A pleasure to meet you too, Mr. Odlum," Alma said smoothly, hoping her nerves didn't show on her face. She could have swatted Henry for not warning her. Floyd Odlum was the owner of Consolidated Aircraft, one of the biggest manufacturers in the country, and also a part owner of RKO Pictures. In aviation you didn't get much bigger.

Odlum looked her up and down with a smile that was distinctly appreciative. "Much prettier than my team captain! Call me Floyd."

"Floyd, then," Alma said, dragging Lewis to the fore. "This is my husband, Lewis Segura."

"Mr. Segura." More handshakes.

"Lewis won the DSC in France, and he'll be flying part of the race."

"Flying together then?" The brunette beside Odlum spoke up, her smile for Lewis quite genuine, her eyes on Alma's face. "I can't imagine anything better than sharing the skies."

Odlum put his arm around her waist. "This is Mrs. Cochran. Jackie flies too, don't you darling?"

The brunette nodded. "Yes, but I've never entered a race."

"Perhaps you will," Alma said. "We need more women in the air."

"That's what I think too." She lifted her chin, a surprisingly strong jawline on such a pretty face. "Are you going to win?"

"Yes," Alma said simply.

Odlum laughed. "Well, Henry, I'm glad to see your team has confidence."

"And I have confidence in them," Henry said smoothly. "There's no better team out there. Mitchell Sorley is the third member, and he's a genuine ace. Mark my words, they'll bring home the prize."

Odlum offered his hand again. "Well, good luck to you. May the best man win!"

"Or woman," Jackie said, and her eyes met Alma's with a smile.

Henry steered Alma off into the crowd again, Lewis trailing after silently. Alma hoped she didn't look as nervous as Lewis did. "Is she Odlum's wife?" Alma asked.

"His protégé." He managed not to put a sneer in it. "She worked in a hair salon in New York. No idea how Floyd ran into her, but now she's flying his planes and sharing his house." Henry shrugged. "You know I could care less about other people's domestic arrangements."

He'd certainly overlooked hers at various points, though Lewis bristled a little. He'd shared Alma's house and bed for months before they were married, and Henry hadn't said a word about them sharing a cabin on his airship. Of course he'd been possessed by a demon at the time, but he wouldn't have minded even if he hadn't been.

"Smile!"

Henry turned around, half pulling her around with him, a big smile on his face. "Hello boys."

The newspapermen grinned back. "How about a big smile for the paper, Mr. Kershaw? Is this your team?"

"Two of them," Henry said genially as Alma tried to plaster a smile on her face too. "This is Alma Gilchrist Segura and her husband, Lewis Segura, of Gilchrist Aviation. They'll be taking my Terrier to Miami and bringing home the prize."

"Smile!" one of them said, the flash going off blindingly enough that Alma saw spots. "Smile!"

"Where is Mitch anyway?" Lewis muttered.

"Hiding," Alma said under her breath.

Lewis finally escaped the throng of reporters on the pretext of getting Alma a drink. There was a bar set up by the pool and a couple of guys waiting for the bartender's attention, which at least gave Lewis a minute to think and cool off. Trying to be perfect every moment was nerve wracking, but apparently this was how the game was played. He couldn't help but wonder how much better Gil would have been at this than he was. It seemed like everybody had liked Gil, one of those guys who somehow effortlessly moves between different groups of people who can't stand each other and leaves everybody thinking he's a good guy. And after all, it must have taken some diplomatic skill to be married to Alma and carrying on with Jerry at the same time with everybody happy as a clam. Lewis couldn't figure out how anybody in the world could do that. After that, dealing with hordes of reporters would probably be child's play.

Not that Alma ever compared them. She never said Gil would have done better. She never implied that Lewis wasn't up to standards. But still it was pretty clear that this was a world he'd never be at home in, one where he'd never be acceptable. No matter what he did, he'd be Alma's gigolo in the eyes of all Gil's old friends.

There was a prickle at the edge of his consciousness, like a faint sound too low to hear, a prickle he was learning to associate with his sight. The last time he'd been to one of Henry Kershaw's parties all hell had broken loose on a psychic level, so Lewis started around, looking for the source of the trouble. Or was it trouble? More like a manifestation of some kind, work being done quietly and skillfully.

There was another terrace down from where they'd set up the bar, screened from above by big bushes, but when he stepped away from the bar and the music Lewis could hear faint voices, two women talking. Another step and he could see.

They were sitting at a cast iron table, chairs pulled close together. One of them was their hostess, Henry's wife, Mabel. The other was perhaps thirty-five or so, shorter than Alma and very thin, with black hair and long scarlet nails and a black dress. Her eyes were outlined in black like Theda Bara playing a vampire, and her face was powdered pale. She bent over the cards laid out on the table, a cigarette in a long holder in her hand, a little black handbag lying on the table by the cards.

"I really can't tell anymore, Mabel," she said, peering at the cards. "As far as I can tell his ventures are just fine." She turned another over, showing the picture to Mabel. "See?"

It was the cards, Lewis realized. The prickle was the cards and whatever she was doing to manipulate them. They were a focus for sight, just like Alma's pendulum was a focus for her affinity with earth. He'd seen old women tell fortunes with playing cards, but the pictures on these were unbelievably more complex, a full language of rich symbols rather than rudimentary forms. He wanted to see them, to handle them and get a better look.

She looked up, the black haired woman, and her ruby lips parted in a wide smile. "We have company, Mabel."

Mrs. Kershaw turned around, momentary alarm flitting across her face. She relaxed when she recognized Lewis. "Oh! Mr. Segura." She beckoned for him to come down the last two steps. "I was just asking the Countess to read on Henry's wagers on the air race."

"Um?" Lewis said.

"It looks very good," Mabel said reassuringly. "The stars seem favorable."

"I hope Mr. Kershaw bet on us," Lewis said.

"Of course!" Mabel said. "Henry would never bet against his own team. I just couldn't resist asking the dear Countess to give me a teensy weensy peek into the future. She's absolutely the best medium in town, you know. Much better than those overpriced Hollywood ones." Her voice dropped confidentially. "You know she faces a terrible exile for her talents."

Lewis blinked. "Do you?"

"Oh yes." The Countess put her elbows on the little table, gloved hands clasped together with the cigarette holder between. "I was trained by Rasputin himself. And so of course when the Revolution came I had to flee for my life, darling! Of course I would have anyway, because of my rather distant kinships with dear Nicky. The Czar, of course. I called him Cousin Nicky. We were all so familiar at those rustic retreats at the dascha, just family and Rasputin!" She closed her eyes rapturously.

"What do you do?" Lewis asked.

"She reads the cards," Mabel said. "And she speaks with the Dead."

"It causes me great suffering," the Countess said in her throaty voice. "But it helps set those poor souls at rest. What else can I do except put myself through the most excruciating agonies if it will bring them peace?"

Lewis felt a chill run down his spine. It wasn't that he didn't believe it was possible. But surely of all magics that was the one that should be played with the least, the awesome and horrible act of disturbing the rest of those laid in consecrated ground, or of listening to the torments of those who did not rest in peace. He looked at her, frowning. He'd felt the frisson of real power. She was doing something. But speaking with the dead?

No, he thought. She had to be a fake. There were charlatans, that he knew, and Alma had warned him there were those who sought membership in a lodge to legitimize their own schemes. Speaking with the dead was for priests, for those who were most serious about their spiritual vocation, not for would-be dragon ladies who apparently charged for card readings, vamped up in black dresses and too much makeup!

The Countess smiled at him stiffly, as if she'd read every thought on his face. "But I don't believe you need my little talents, do you, Mr. Segura?"

Lewis swallowed. "There isn't anyone dead I need to talk to." And he sincerely hoped there wasn't anyone dead Alma wanted to talk to either. He glanced down at the cards again. They were beautiful. And there was no way he was going to ask to see them, not if he had to ask her.

"How nice for you," she said, casting her brilliant smile on Mabel Kershaw again. "Then shall we go on, darling?"

"I just came out to get Alma a drink," Lewis said. He took a step away. "I'll do that, if that's ok."

"Of course," Mabel said.

Henry cast en eye over the crowd, checking the progress of the party. So far, so good: they'd had photos by the Terrier, which had been pulled out into the middle of the field with the Republic name large on the hangar in the background, Alma had given an excellent interview, and at the moment it looked as though the aviation people, the money people, and his carefully selected friends from the various lodges were mingling amicably. In fact, Odlum might owe him a favor or two, if the look on his face was any indication. Greg Potts still had money to lend, and that was saying something, these days.

He turned toward the bar, pausing to exchange a polite remark with Reverend Fell, who was a sometime member of the Los Angeles lodge and a chaplain to the stars. He didn't much like the man, but his presence meant that certain others might make an appearance, and that was worth it for the extra publicity. The bartender had his drink ready before he asked for it, a Manhattan cocktail poured over extra ice, and Henry took a sip before nodding in approval. The bartender grinned and turned to serve someone else.

In spite of himself, Henry's eyes turned to the Terrier, the white paint almost glowing in the dark beyond the pool. It was a risk, putting up the money, especially now, when no one was flush any more. He was tapping capital, and had been since Independence crashed; if he didn't get the cash flow moving in the right direction soon, he was going to be in trouble.

He scowled into his drink, all too aware of the irony of his thoughts. For him, "trouble" meant selling a house, if he could find a buyer, or closing a shop, or Rose not being able to spend next year at Julliard. There were too many people for whom "trouble" was no work and no money, foreclosure and water soup. But if he had to close a shop, he'd just be adding to the problem. Eight hundred dollars to keep the San Angelo shop open, or Miami: it was worth it. And Gilchrist would come through. They were damn good flyers, all of them, and having Alma in charge was a pleasing novelty that would keep the press interested. Of course, nobody could guarantee there wouldn't be a mechanical failure, or just damn bad luck, but on balance it was worth the risk.

"Quite a party, Mr. Kershaw."

That was one of the reporters, a stocky, sandy-haired man with a better suit than most of his peers and a bright and cynical eye. Carmichael, his name was, Henry remembered, and he was a source for Walter Winchell. And that made him dangerous: Winchell's gossip column was carried in newspapers nationwide, and his Sunday night radio show reached tens of thousands all across the country. And Winchell made very sure it didn't pay to get on his bad side.

"Thanks," he said, cautiously.

"Eat, drink, and be merry?" Carmichael asked.

Henry winced, thinking of the rest of the quotation. "Let's hope not."

"I never thought you'd be superstitious."

Henry forced a smile. "Come on, Carmichael, have you ever met a flyer who wasn't?"

"Lindbergh."

"He doesn't have to be."

"Touché." Carmichael grinned. "Say, about your team—which is it, Gilchrist or Segura?"

Henry considered pretending he didn't know what the reporter meant, but that would only put him at a disadvantage. "I believe it's still Gilchrist professionally," he said. "She married Lewis—Mr. Segura—last year."

"She's a hot ticket," Carmichael said. "So she and Sorley are partners—business partners—and then she married this Segura? While he was working for her. Would you say she wears the pants there, Mr. Kershaw?"

"That's a hell of a question."

"Off the record," Carmichael said.

Right. Henry would believe that about the time he got an invitation to go ice skating in hell. He said, "Alma's first husband died too young—he was gassed in the war, and never really recovered. I'm just pleased she's found someone."

Carmichael's eyebrows quirked up. "And what about this Dr. Ballard? What's an archeologist expecting to dig up in the air? Or is he just another of Mrs. Segura's friends?"

"Off the record?" He still didn't believe it, but at least it bought him time.

"Off the record, Mr. Kershaw." Carmichael's voice was suspiciously solemn.

"Dr. Ballard's done some test work for me before." He winked. "We've got a few tricks up our sleeve."

For a second, he thought he'd gone too far, but then Carmichael nodded slowly. "Thanks, Mr. Kershaw. That's good to know."

"Off the record, mind," Henry called after him, and received a wave in answer. Alma wasn't going to be happy, he thought. Hopefully she'd be too busy flying to notice.

Mitch had found a nice quiet spot indoors beside the buffet table, where he'd loaded a plate and then retreated to a corner to browse. It wasn't that he was so hungry, but nibbling gave him something to do, a reason to look busy. He couldn't very well just stand in a corner like a suit of armor all night. He certainly didn't want to trail along after Alma like Lewis was doing, looking like a vaguely threatening bodyguard behind her. Lewis hadn't been more than two steps away from her all night and was managing to look like every stereotype of the jealous Latin husband who was afraid to let her out of his sight. Of course Mitch knew it was probably that Lewis was scared to death, and hanging onto Alma's sleeve was the way to make sure nobody ever talked to him. Alma, on the other hand, seemed calm and smooth as a breeze. Sure, she did this every day.

Mitch put his empty plate down on a side table and glanced over the titles on Henry's bookshelf. It was fairly quiet in the house, most people out by the pool, crowded around the bar he could see through the open French doors. Maybe he could just pick out something and settle down and read in Henry's study for a while. His fingers walked along the shelves. *Undine* and *Sintram* by Friedrich de la Motte Fouqué....

"You like fairy tales?"

Mitch turned around and looked way down. The woman was a good foot shorter than him, with graying chestnut hair cut in a bob at the back of her neck, perhaps closer to forty-five than forty, with brown eyes and a smile that made you want to talk to her. "Sometimes," Mitch said.

"So do I," she said. "There's something wonderful about those old stories we grew up with, isn't there? The watersprite who traded her immortality to be with the man she loved."

"Sprites are good, but I think I like the valkyries better."

At that her smile broadened. "Oh so do I," she said. "You must be Mitchell Sorley."

"Must I?"

"Well, you're on Henry's team and Lewis Segura is out there, and you're certainly not Mrs. Segura." She glanced toward the doors. "So that makes you Mitchell Sorley, doesn't it?"

"Guilty as charged," Mitch said. "But I've got no idea who you are."

"Beatrice Patton," she said briskly. "I know Henry through his other work." She paused. "Not his aviation interests."

"Ah." He'd known Henry had invited a bunch of Lodge people from all over the network he corresponded with, and most of them were strangers to Mitch. "You're here in LA then?"

She shook her head. "DC at the moment. But my husband is originally from LA and we're here on family business. Henry asked if we'd like to drop by." She shrugged, her eyes drifting to the crowd by the bar. "My husband is mad for aviation. He says it's the wave of the future, so of course we had to come."

"He's probably right."

"He's often right. Except when he's colossally wrong." She smiled again, her too high heels shifting on the mission-tiled floor. "Are you going to win Henry's race for him?"

"We're going to try," Mitch said. He pulled the copy of Undine off the shelf. "But right now I think I'll settle for hiding from the press."

"They are persistent, aren't they?" she said. "I confess I'm a little shy myself."

She seemed about as shy as an organ grinder's monkey, but Mitch shrugged. "Do you Work with Henry?"

"Not with his group, but in the same tradition. You?"

"The same," Mitch said. "We branched a few years back."

"As so many did: Alpha and Omega, Stella Matutina, Whare Ra, Isis and Serapis..."

"Aedeficatorii Templii," Mitch said, identifying his own branch.

"Isis and Serapis." She smiled again. "That makes us almost kin."

"Kissing cousins, as my mother would say. Well, if my mother had ever heard of a Lodge."

"So how do you find the Work?" she asked.

There was a racket as a group of six came through the French doors, two reporters and a group of men around a woman Mitch thought looked vaguely familiar. Her white evening gown and platinum blonde permanent was very Hollywood. She gave the reporters a brilliant, lipstick pout.

"Maybe we should move this conversation down the hall," Mitch said. "Henry's office should be quiet."

"Indeed."

It was at the end of the hall, down the long tiled corridor covered in its bright Turkish runner, the one light on a side table halfway along turned off. Mitch frowned. Henry kept a good many esoteric things in his office, but there was no prickle as they approached the door, no familiar desire to go do something else that should signal a warding to keep random partygoers out. There was no reason for anything stronger, just a simple thing to make sure that anyone wandering around the downstairs didn't find that end of the hall very appealing. And yet there was nothing. No prickle. Nothing.

Beatrice frowned as though she thought it was odd too.

Mitch put his hand to the door handle and opened it. There was no resistance. And that was wrong. There should at least be something, a sense of breaking through a barrier, of being somewhere a guest shouldn't be. And that's what it would feel like to an ordinary person—a sense of guilt, of discomfort at intruding sharp enough to make it unpleasant to enter.

The office was quiet and empty, leather chair behind his desk, the lights off except for the green shaded reading lamp. The curtains were drawn on the window which overlooked the pool terrace. Everything was quiet, everything in place. There was no reason for anyone to be in here tonight or probably tomorrow either, unless Henry planned to get some work done in the afternoon after the race began. He sure wouldn't be here at the crack of dawn. He'd be over at Grand Central watching his team at the starting gun.

Her frown deepened, and he saw Beatrice sway just a moment on her feet, eyes unfocusing.

Mitch came around the desk. "Are you all right?"

"Fine," she said. For a moment her eyes had looked black, the way Lewis' did when he was seeing something that couldn't be seen with outward sight. Then they focused on his face, brown and ordinary. "But there's something wrong."

Mitch nodded. "I know. There are no wards."

"Someone's taken them down." She looked at him. "In the last hour. Someone's been in here and they were up to something they shouldn't have been." She cast her gaze around the walls. "They stood right over there. I can feel the residue. They dispelled the wards rather than breaking them."

He drew a deep breath. Something was well and truly rotten in the state of Denmark. "Ok. Stay right here. I'm going to go get Henry."

Jerry Ballard had escaped. Since he wasn't technically part of Henry's race team, just a passenger, he didn't actually have to make nice to the photographers and race sponsors. He didn't have to answer a million questions or try not to. He could leave that to Alma, who seemed to revel in it, and find something quieter to do. He chatted with some old acquaintances from Henry's lodge that he hadn't seen in years; it was nice to catch up and talk shop in his own field rather than aviation. He ran into Bullfinch by the pool and had a nice gab about the ongoing excavations at Halicarnassus, a useful and interesting topic.

By ten o'clock he'd talked enough. Alma was determined to get down to the airfield at dawn and that meant getting up around four, something he didn't enjoy at the best of times - and this was not the best of times. It was looking like this party was going to drag on interminably into the wee hours.

But at least he didn't have to stay inside. Jerry looked out across the lawn beyond the swimming pool toward the circular drive, the hangar buildings paler shadows beyond that, barely lighter than the hillside. The Terrier was pulled up on the grass just where they'd left it when they'd all posed for photos earlier, right out in the middle of the lawn where anyone approaching it would be in full view of the entire party. Yes, it had gotten dark since then, but with no trees to shade anything the Terrier gleamed in the moonlight, the roundel on its tail shining faintly. Jerry knew it was a trick of paint, not anything more esoteric, but he still found it obscurely comforting.

The ground was firm beneath his cane, and Jerry started off across the grass toward the plane at a good clip. Nobody seemed to notice he'd left, and Jerry popped the side door. He'd just climb in and get comfortable in one of the rear seats. Maybe he'd even take a nap until the others were ready to turn in for the night. Then he'd speak to Henry about having someone watch the plane overnight, just in case. He turned the handle and stopped. A shadow moved. Someone was standing at the nose.

"Who's there?" Jerry called, his hand tightening on the heavy walnut grip of his cane.

A woman stepped out from behind the plane, striking a pose against the distant lights, slender silhouette in a drop waisted dress, a little handbag in one hand and a cigarette holder in the other. "Dr. Ballard," she said in a throaty alto. "I was hoping to catch you alone."

"You were?" Jerry asked. He had no recollection of ever having seen her before.

"I saw you earlier," she said. "When they were taking photographs." She took two steps forward, a thin woman in strappy black shoes that buckled around her ankles, black as her hair and her simple dress. "I hoped that I might have a chance to talk with you alone."

"About what?" Jerry said.

Another step, and she raised the hand with the cigarette holder to his lapel. Her nails were long and scarlet, but she wore no jewelry at all. "Your work is so fascinating. I've followed it breathlessly for years."

"You have?"

"You can't imagine how it feels to finally meet you," she said, dark eyes meeting his on the level, closer to thirty-five than twenty-five, and wearing no cologne for all her sophistication.

Jerry fumbled for his handkerchief to clean his glasses off. "I'm charmed, I'm sure," he said. "And just who are you?"

"Countess Anastasia Rostov," she said. "Oh, the title is just a courtesy now days, I'm afraid! What with that horrible man in the Kremlin and my dear family scattered to the winds!"

"I'm terribly sorry," Jerry said, though the Russian Revolution was decidedly not his fault.

"Oh don't be!" she said, lifting her other hand to his lapel as he stepped back. "Like you, I now lead a gypsy existence, a lonely exile. So lonely."

"Um," Jerry said, stepping back again. Unfortunately, that put him directly against the open door, the steps against the back of his knee.

"But I know that you are the other half of my wandering soul."

"Not really," Jerry said, putting one hand on her arm to push himself around her. "I think we'd better get back to the party, don't you?"

"But isn't this the perfect opportunity for us to get to know each other better?" She gave him a sultry glance beneath black eyelashes.

"Dr. Ballard, I know that you and I will be the best of friends."

"Friends," Jerry said swiftly, maneuvering her away from the plane. "Let's be friends. And let's go back to the party."

Those eyelashes batted again. "Are you afraid that if you're alone with me you'll compromise my reputation?"

"Exactly!" Jerry said. He could feel cold sweat running down the back of his neck. "I'd never want to do that. Let's go back to the party!"

"But the night is young, and this is such a lovely airplane," she said. "I bet it has nice seats inside."

"I'm sure it does." Jerry slammed the door. "But we're not supposed to be out here. Let's go join the others before Mr. Kershaw gets upset."

She shrugged prettily. "If you think so, but...."

"I do," Jerry said quickly.

"But who knows when this opportunity will come again." She took a step closer, lips opening.

"It might be a long time." Jerry took her arm and all but dragged her away from the plane, making his best time across the lawn with her in tow. "But c'est la vie. Que sera, sera."

"Carpe diem. Mazel tov," she said. "Dr. Ballard, I want to know you better."

"And I'm going to find the necessary," Jerry said quickly, dropping her arm at the edge of the terrace. "Bye."

He all but bolted into the pool house and its changing facilities, the ones marked MEN. Hopefully that would put her off for a bit. God help him, these parties of Henry's were getting stranger by the year!

Beatrice was still standing there when Mitch got back with Henry in tow. She'd turned on the floor lamp and also lit a white candle in a brass holder on the table between the two windows, laying the match book down as they opened the door.

Henry checked. "Mrs. Patton?"

"Someone took your wards down," she said, turning around briskly. "Nothing looks disturbed, but I wouldn't know, would I?"

"Does anything look out of place, Henry?" Mitch asked.

"Not that I can see." Henry turned around, his gaze raking over the glass fronted book cases, the desk with its pristine green blotter. "But normally I wouldn't be in here until day after tomorrow. No reason to be here tonight, and tomorrow I'll be at Grand Central first thing in the morning for the beginning of the race. Since I'm already over there and I've got an office off the shop, I probably wouldn't be in here at all. I'd just work over there tomorrow." He reached down and pulled on the desk drawers. "Still locked," he said.

"That doesn't mean anything," Mitch said.

Henry gave him a sharp look. "I know that," he said, fishing his keys out of his pocket and opening the drawer. Mrs. Patton looked politely away as he pulled out a sheaf of currency and counted it. He unlocked the lower drawer and rummaged around in it as well. "Everything's here," he said.

"What's in the drawers on the other side?" Mitch asked.

Henry opened them. "For your inspection, Captain?" Stationary, envelopes, two bottles of fountain pen ink, a box of paperclips...

"Office supplies," Mitch said with disappointment.

"This is my office," Henry said. "I keep office supplies in my desk drawers."

"And very sensible of you too," Beatrice said.

"I like to think of myself as a sensible man."

"Is there any other place you keep valuables?," Mitch asked.

Henry shot him a sharp look, but Beatrice appeared unperturbed. "I'll check," he said, moving aside a picture on the northwest wall to reveal the door of a safe.

It was closed and locked, but Beatrice frowned. "Mr. Kershaw," she began, but Henry was already dialing the combination, his body blocking them from seeing.

The door swung open and Mitch looked. Several envelopes of currency like the ones in his desk drawer and a couple of small velvet boxes from jewelers.

"It's not here," Henry said. He lifted everything out, then put it back, four envelopes, three small boxes.

"What isn't?" Beatrice asked.

"My wife's necklace. Well, not really her necklace yet. I hadn't given it to Mabel. For some damned good reasons." Henry turned around, his brows knitting. "It was in a black velvet jewelry box about so big." His hands sketched a rectangle the size of a cigarette case, small enough to fit easily in a pocket.

Mitch blew out a breath. "Diamonds? What kind of necklace?"

Henry shook his head, still shuffling the other boxes in his hands, opening one to make certain the contents were inside, revealing a stunning ruby necklace in the style of the turn of the century. "It's Berlin Iron."

"But that's not terribly valuable," Beatrice said. "Certainly not compared to those rubies."

"Antique," Henry said. "And no, not so valuable in itself, but it was beautiful."

"I have no idea what Berlin Iron is," Mitch said. "Somebody help me out here."

Henry opened a ring case, checking an elaborate sapphire and pearl ring.

"During the Napoleonic Wars, Queen Louise of Prussia asked women to give their jewelry to the war effort," Beatrice said. "They were supposed to donate their gold and jewels to help defeat Napoleon and instead wear ornaments of iron. Some of the pieces were absolutely beautiful—very delicate flowers and leaves and tracery wrought very fine in iron—heavy as fetters and strong as cannon, but looking like delicate roses or lilies or acanthus leaves." She smiled a sideways smile. "I had one myself, a long time ago. Steel flowers."

"It was gorgeous," Henry said shortly. "The jeweler said it came from an estate sale in New Orleans and that it had been in the family for a century."

"But you hadn't given it to Mabel yet?" Beatrice asked. "You were saving it for a special birthday or anniversary?"

Henry shook his head. "I hired a guy to look into its history. A researcher, not a PI. I wanted to be able to tell Mabel a little more about its provenance."

Mitch nodded. Henry might pretend to just be interested in planes and money, but he knew an awful lot about archaeology and classical history for a layperson, just as Mitch did. It came with the Lodge work. It didn't surprise Mitch that Henry would have wanted to know exactly what the story was behind the necklace. "What did he find?" Mitch asked.

Henry took a deep breath. "The necklace is supposed to be cursed. The legend is that it belonged to a Prussian noblewoman killed by French hussars for her jewels, and that one of them looted the necklace and brought it to New Orleans. However, a few years later his wife was murdered, supposedly by voodoo. After that it went to their daughter when she was grown, but the first night she wore the necklace at a ball she was found dead in the morning, her throat cut. Both of her sisters were died in the next few years under mysterious circumstances. After that nobody wore the necklace for a long time, but about forty years ago one of the descendants did. A few weeks later she was strangled to death and her murder was never solved. The necklace was pretty well known in New Orleans and so was the story of the curse, so some later descendant sold it to a jeweler on the west coast who'd never heard of it." He took a deep breath. "Every woman who wears it dies by violence. So I wasn't about to give it to Mabel. I put it in the safe and kept it locked up. The curse only activates if a woman wears it. As long as nobody does, I figured that was as good a place for it as any."

"Oh boy," Mitch said.

Henry gave him a sharp look. "Well? You're Southern. Do you think the curse is for real?"

"Henry, I'm from eight hundred miles northeast of New Orleans," Mitch said. "My people are Moravian, not French. You might as well ask a Navajo as me, or some Scandinavian from Minneapolis!" Something felt wrong even as he said it, like he'd heard this story before somewhere, only he couldn't remember where. He might have been in New Orleans once. He wasn't sure. It all belonged to that period he didn't remember and didn't try to. Maybe somebody had told him about it. Maybe that was it.

Mitch shook his head. Beatrice was talking and he'd missed the first part of it. "...if you still had the necklace, my husband could have a look at it. He's fairly good with reading artifacts."

"If I still had the necklace it wouldn't matter," Henry said. "The problem is that it's been stolen." He reached for the telephone on his desk. "I'm going to call the police."

"That's probably best," she said.

Henry picked up the receiver. "Mitch, will you go find Miss Patterson and tell her to ask the security guy at the gate not to let anyone out? If somebody stole the necklace they're going to try to leave as soon as they can. Nobody leaves until the police get here. Got it?"

"Got it," Mitch said. The story prickled at him still, but he shook it off, trying to keep the strangeness at bay. He had a job to do about a real thing, a burglar who'd cracked Henry's safe. That was a job for the police. Probably some jewel thief had bagged the necklace earlier during the party and was standing around with it in his pocket waiting to waltz out at the end of the night. The police would catch him and that would be the end of it.

Alma and Lewis were talking to another set of reporters. Or rather, Alma was explaining the technical aspects of the Kershaw Terrier's superiority to the Ford Trimotor while Lewis stood behind her glowering and the reporters' eyes glazed over. Presumably they wanted some kind of better story about an air race than a discussion of the planes.

"How long have you been married, ma'am?" one of them asked.

It was a matter of public record, and no sense dodging a factual question. "A little more than a year," Alma said. "Now, the Trimotor is smaller than the Terrier, but almost the same weight. One of the advantages of the Kershaw Terrier from the point of view of the owner of a passenger service is that you can seat two more passengers comfortably on the Terrier and have the weight of the plane be equivalent. Weight equals fuel consumption, gentlemen."

"How did you and Mr. Segura meet?"

"At an airshow when he was looking for work," Alma said shortly. "And fuel consumption equals range. In other words, the longer a plane can fly without needing to stop and refuel, the more efficiently it can move passengers."

"And you and Mr. Sorley have known each other for a long time?"

"Mr. Sorley is my partner in Gilchrist Aviation," Alma said. "Mitchell and my first husband founded the company."

"Is Mr. Sorley married?" another reporter put in.

"You will have to address your personal questions to him," Alma snapped, and then thought better of it. The last thing Mitch wanted to be asked was why he wasn't married. "But he is not."

The reporter scribbled something in his notebook.

Lewis shifted protectively. "I don't see why you're asking these personal questions," he said. "It's disrespectful."

"No disrespect of a lady intended," the reporter said, touching the brim of his hat. The other one scribbled something else. "Just a little human interest." He broke off, his head lifting. There was the distant sound of a police siren.

Lewis turned too, ears pricking like a hound.

"It's getting closer," one of the reporters said.

Indeed it was. The cypress trees along the side of the pool were suddenly washed in blue light as the police car turned into the circular drive. No, cars. There were two.

Alma frowned.

"I wonder what's going on?" Lewis asked. The reporters had already started shouldering their way through the crowd without a word of goodbye.

A tall fair haired man in evening dress who had been standing with his back to them in the next group turned around. "I don't know, but if there's trouble my wife is probably in the middle of it." A snake ring twined around the middle finger of his right hand next to a heavy class ring, a Lodge of some sort, Alma thought, though not one she was immediately familiar with. It was no real surprise that Henry would have guests from a variety of traditions.

Alma refrained from commenting about who else was likely to be in the middle of it. "Let's go see," she said to Lewis, offering him her arm.

The tall man looked amused. "By all means. Let's see if she's eloped with a movie star or looted the Vatican or is fighting a duel with Errol Flynn."

"Is Errol Flynn here?" Lewis asked, an expression of almost comical dismay on his face.

"Not that I've seen," Alma said.

"I expect he runs with a faster crowd," the other man said.

"Surely your wife doesn't usually fight duels or loot the Vatican," Lewis said as they maneuvered through the crowd.

"There was the incident with the leper colony," he replied cheerfully. "But I don't think she's fought any duels lately."

Four uniformed police officers were crowding into the foyer of the house, one plain clothes detective with them, as Henry elbowed his way through to them. "Thanks for coming so quickly, boys," he said.

"Sure thing, Mr. Kershaw," the detective said, scanning the crowd with very blue eyes, as though he were already looking for a guilty party. He didn't look around at the officers with him. "Don't let anybody leave."

One woman let out a squeak. "There's been a murder! Oh my God, Stanley! There's been a murder!"

"I'm afraid not," Henry said calmly. "But someone has cracked my safe and stolen some very valuable jewelry."

"That's why I always keep mine in the bank," a woman behind Alma said to her companion. "So much more secure."

"A jewel thief?" The reporter started scribbling again. "High society jewel thief strikes Hollywood party...."

Mitch came down the hall from the office accompanied by a woman a little older than Alma in a green dress, tiny next to Mitch's bulk as he stood across the corridor like a guard.

"No one but Mr. Kershaw has touched the safe," she said to the detective. "So you can dust for fingerprints."

The man beside Alma let out a resigned sigh. "And there's my wife now."

"We know how to do it, ma'am," the detective said. "Mr. Kershaw, can you show us the safe?"

"Of course," Henry said, starting to move down the hall. The entire crowd followed.

The detective looked around. "Without the whole party, people. Just Mr. Kershaw."

"And these two," Henry said, gesturing to the woman and Mitch. "They're the ones who found it disturbed."

"You two, then." The detective and one officer accompanied Henry and the others down the hall toward the office.

Alma let out a sigh. "Just like Henry," she said to Lewis. "Trust Henry to get burgled on the eve of the air race!"

The tall man dropped his voice. "It's great publicity, isn't it?"

Alma blinked. "Henry would never...."

"Set himself up? For the jewelry to be found in some innocent place tomorrow?" His mouth twisted in a half smile. "No harm done, just an honest mistake? And a big newspaper headline?"

"Well...." Alma couldn't say that was entirely unlikely.

Lewis shrugged. "It doesn't really matter to us," he said. "Not one way or another."

"Except that Mitch has gotten himself tied up in a police investigation," Alma said. "When we need him fresh for the start tomorrow. Honestly, if he has to go downtown and talk to the police all night!"

The tall man looked at her keenly. "You must be Henry's team."

"We're the Gilchrist Aviation team," Alma said proudly. "We're flying a Kershaw Terrier."

"The three of you?"

"And our passenger, Dr. Jerry Ballard. You know all the planes have to carry a passenger."

"Where is Jerry anyway?" Lewis asked. "I haven't seen him in an hour."

"I have no idea," Alma said, glancing around, though Jerry didn't seem to be part of the crowd milling around in the house.

"There he is." Lewis was rubbernecking, and Alma looked around to see Jerry coming up the back steps from the pool terrace toward the house, leaning on his cane on the slick steps. He raised a hand. "Jerry! Over here!"

Jerry came up and stopped to clean his glasses with his handkerchief. "What's going on?"

"Somebody cracked Henry's safe," Alma said. "And of course Mitch found it, so he and Henry are talking to the police. Where have you been?"

"Hiding from that dreadful woman," Jerry said. "Do you see her?"

"What woman?"

"The Russian Countess," Jerry said. "She's horrible. She cornered me out by the Terrier and practically ripped my clothes off."

Lewis blinked. "She what?"

"Came on like a tiger," Jerry said, his voice dripping with annoyance. "I've been dodging her ever since. What in the hell is wrong with some people? I'd never even met her before."

Alma frowned. "No offense, Jerry, but why in the world would she do that? Women don't generally just go around throwing themselves at strangers like that."

"I don't know. I went out to check on the Terrier, and there she was like a lioness lying in wait to stalk me! She's a nut!"

"Out by the Terrier," Lewis said flatly, and Alma knew he was thinking the same thing she was, only a moment sooner.

"Where is she now?" Alma asked.

Jerry put his glasses back on. "I don't know. I've been hiding in the pool house."

"The Terrier," Lewis said. There were a hundred reasons why someone might sabotage the Terrier. There were 25,000 of them.

"Hey wait!" Jerry called as she and Lewis took off for the Terrier at a run.

Chapter Five

"So let me have this again, Mr. Sorley," the detective said. "You and Mrs. Patton came in here and saw that the safe had been disturbed. What did you see that made you think that?"

Well, not that the wards were down, Mitch thought. "The picture was ajar," he said. Of course now the picture was taken down entirely, lifted out of the way by Henry when he opened the safe.

"So you knew the safe was there?" The detective looked at him keenly.

"I've done some business with Mr. Kershaw in the past," Mitch said. Of course it hadn't involved the safe in this house, but how would the detective know that? Beatrice glanced at him sideways, and he hoped it was to keep their stories straight. No clairvoyance, no wards, no hocus pocus at all—just a nice clean story about nice normal things. "I saw the safe then and I knew he kept cash in it."

"I see." The detective gave Mitch a calculating glance. "Mind telling me what kind of business?"

"Not at all," Mitch said easily. "A couple of years ago Mr. Kershaw received some threatening letters. Not anything signed, not anything he could take to the police, but threatening letters concerning the launch of his airship, the Independence. He hired me and a couple of colleagues to ride along on the ship's maiden voyage and keep an eye out." He shrugged modestly. "Turned out it was a good thing."

The detective put his head to the side. "Why you, Mr. Sorley?"

Mitch put on his best self-effacing look. "Well, I'm a pretty fair aviator. I've known Mr. Kershaw since the war. We served together at the front, and I reckon he thinks I'm reliable. I landed Independence after it was sabotaged, and I expect that has to do with why he's sponsoring me in the air race." Which all followed. Nothing he said wasn't true. It just wasn't the whole truth.

The detective nodded over his notes. "So you're the ace on the team that the paper was talking about."

"You didn't mention you were an ace," Beatrice said.

"I don't like to brag, ma'am," Mitch said with as much Southern charm as he could manage without overdoing it. One of her eyebrows twitched, but she seemed to accept that at face value.

"So you saw the picture ajar," the detective said. "Then what happened?"

"Mr. Sorley said that something was wrong because there was a safe here. He told me to stay here and not to touch anything while he went to get Mr. Kershaw," Beatrice said.

"How long was he gone?"

"Perhaps five minutes," Beatrice said. "I didn't touch the picture."

The policeman who had been dusting for fingerprints looked around. "She's telling the truth about that, boss. No prints on here but Mr. Kershaw's."

The detective shrugged. "So they wore gloves."

"A woman then," Beatrice said. The detective glared at her. "It's a very warm evening. None of the men are wearing gloves."

"Save us from middle aged female amateur detectives," the policeman muttered.

"Anyone can put on a pair of gloves, ma'am," the detective said.

"Listen," Mitch said. "I've told you everything I know. Any chance I could get out of here? It's nearly midnight and I've got a race to fly tomorrow."

The detective nodded. "Ok. But you need a pat down before you leave, same as all the other guests. Whoever grabbed this thing is probably thinking they can walk out with it." He looked at Beatrice. "We've got a policewoman to do a pat down of all the ladies."

"Of course," she said.

By the time they got back to the front hall the crowd had thinned, about half the guests queued up to be searched before they left. Some of them were protesting, but most seemed to find the detective work an exciting feature of the party.

"Well," Mitch said. "It's been a pleasure meeting you."

"And you," Beatrice said. "I hope we'll have a chance to talk more some other time."

"So do I," Mitch said. "But now I'd better find my team and see if we can all get some shut eye."

"Good luck in the race!"

"Thank you," Mitch said, and started hunting for the rest of them. For that matter, where was Henry?

He found them all out on the lawn clustered around the Terrier, and for a moment his heart skipped a beat. Nothing could be wrong with his plane. Nothing.

"...we need to get gassed up and out of here right now," Alma was saying to Henry.

Mitch took the last yards at a dead run. "What's wrong?"

"Nothing, as far as we can tell," Lewis said. He'd climbed up on the fuselage to check out the rudder control surfaces, his black tie gone and his hair mussed out of its slicked back Valentino style.

"As far as we can tell," Alma said. "But Henry, you know as well as I do that we can't see a damn thing out here! It's dark."

"So taxi her back over to the hangar," Henry said. "You can look her over there, the shop's certainly good enough."

"I will," Alma said. "I want to make sure she's airworthy. But then we're flying down to Grand Central." She held up her hand, forestalling Henry's protest. "No offense to you or your people, Henry, but I know they're keeping a close eye on the competitors' hangars."

Henry seemed inclined to protest, but Mitch ignored him. "What happened?"

"Nothing," Jerry said shortly, leaning on his cane. "But there was a strange woman hanging around the plane, and then it was entirely alone while everyone was hunting for Henry's damned necklace in the house. Alma thinks some other team may have tried to sabotage it."

"Might have," Alma said impatiently. "Might. We've done a cursory search and there's nothing amiss, but I can't break the engines down in the dark or get a good look at the fuel lines. If someone wanted to bring down an airplane or get us out of the race, that would be the way to do it."

"I don't see anything wrong right now," Lewis said. "But it's hard to tell in this light."

"We were going to fly out before dawn anyway," Alma said, to Henry. "Grand Central will like us better coming in late rather than early, and we'll know it's secure with the race authorities watching it.

And I can go over it with a fine-toothed comb."

"We'll go over it," Mitch said, a sinking feeling in the pit of his stomach. Nothing could be wrong with the Terrier. Nothing he couldn't fix.

Henry nodded. "Ok," he said. "Maybe the whole necklace thing was a diversion. And if that's true, then I need to take a hard look at my people. That's some big money riding on the race, especially when you figure in the whole publicity angle. I sure don't want my plane having to bow out."

"My plane," Alma and Mitch said at the same time.

Henry grinned, though he looked tired. "Your plane, kids. Just promise me you'll be sure the fuel lines are clear before you take off?"

"Absolutely," Alma said.

"Then I'll call Grand Central and tell them to wait up for you," Henry said.

"Perfect," Lewis said, starting to climb down.

"Not you," Alma said. She reached up and took Lewis' hand as he slid down onto the wing. "Somebody's got to be fresh to fly the first leg tomorrow. You stay here at Henry's like we'd planned, you and Jerry, and get a good night's sleep. Mitch and I will take the Terrier apart. We can nap when you're flying tomorrow."

"I thought Mitch was going to fly the first leg," Lewis said. He looked at Mitch. "It's your baby."

"You can fly it," Mitch said, and it only gave him a little twinge to say so. "I'll take her apart tonight. I can fly the third leg, the one you were supposed to fly."

"Ok." Lewis gathered Jerry into his gaze. "Then we'll hit the sack."

Henry started off toward the house, calling for Miss Patterson, and Alma dusted her hands off on her ink-blue evening gown. She gave Mitch a rueful smile. "Every time I wear this dress, something strange happens."

"Leave it at Henry's," Mitch said. "It's already been in one air crash. No need to jinx us."

It was a long night. It hadn't taken long to be sure the Terrier was at least safe for the short hop to Grand Central, or to follow the tower beacon in to a safe landing, but after that had come the niggling job of making sure there was no more subtle sabotage. By five Mitch was scrubbing his eyes as he made one final check of the rudder controls. Perfect, just like everything else they'd looked at. Alma looked as tired as he did, lip rouge long since worn off, dark circles under her eyes. "I can't find a thing," Mitch said, climbing down and coming over to her.

Alma nodded. "I haven't found anything wrong either." She gave him a wan smile. "Probably I just kept us both up all night for nothing."

"Not for nothing," Mitch said. "If somebody had sabotaged the Terrier.... I don't even know."

"I do," Alma said. "If something went wrong tomorrow, when we're over the desert..."

"Today," Mitch said. "The race starts in three hours."

Alma sat down in the doorway, her legs out before her. "Not much point in trying to go to bed now."

"Henry will be here soon, and there will be a million reporters." Mitch stretched, trying to unkink his back. "But Lewis had a good night's rest. That was a smart move. He can get us through the first stage."

"There are already some fans outside." Alma glanced toward the hangar doors.

A couple of dozen people were milling around in the growing light, hardcore fans who wanted to get the best places, or maybe to get a glimpse of crews and planes preparing. Most of them were men, but Mitch caught sight of an angular brunette in black trousers who was reading the posted information with interest. High cheekbones softened by finger waves, with the kind of smile he liked...

"Mitch?" Alma waved her hand in front of his face. "I asked if you wanted to go get a cup of coffee. Henry's guys can watch the plane and they're not about to let anyone monkey with the engines."

"Sure," Mitch said. He was not quite falling down tired, but some coffee would be a good thing. "Let's do that." He put his arm affectionately around Alma's waist as they went out, just in time for a flash to go off in his face. "Aw crap," he said as the reporter smirked. "Mrs. Gilchrist stumbled."

"If you say so, buddy." The reporter danced back out of their way, camera in hand. The brunette fan gave him an arch look.

"I hate these reporters," Alma muttered.

"We'll lose them in the air," Mitch said. Dawn was coming. It wouldn't be long until takeoff.

Lewis hopped out of Henry's car at a quarter until six, Jerry making his way more sedately behind him. Though the sun wasn't yet over the horizon there was quite a crowd around the entrance to Henry's hangar, twenty or thirty people milling around while Henry's mechanics chatted with them. Inside, the Terrier stood under big work lights. Everything looked ok from where he stood.

Alma was drinking coffee out of a paper cup by the wing, and Mitch was glancing over the weather report spread between them.

"How's the Terrier?" Lewis asked.

"Fine," Alma said. "Mitch and I can't find anything wrong. We've been over her thoroughly, and she looks ok to us."

"Good as new," Mitch said. "Better than new, if we can make her that way." He looked tired but like he was getting his second wind. He'd probably spent as many early mornings on the flight line after a sleepless night as Lewis had, during the war. Of course that was more than ten years ago, and both of them were closer to forty than twenty now.

"Good to hear," Lewis said, walking around the back. Everything looked trim and shipshape. Even the paint gleamed.

Mitch reached down and latched the exterior luggage hatch. "We're ready. And it looks like the weather's going to be just about perfect for the first leg. A hot start and a fast pace."

"I'm game," Lewis said.

"Did they ever find Henry's necklace?"

Lewis shook his head. "The police found the box in the bushes by the pool but no necklace. They searched all the guests but I guess somebody smuggled it out somehow." Lewis dropped his voice. "Unless Henry snitched it himself and hid it somewhere and it will turn up in a day or so."

Mitch looked shocked. "Why would he do that?"

"Publicity." Lewis shrugged. "That's what some guy at the party last night said."

"I don't think so," Mitch said. His voice was also low. "Why would Henry break his own ward? The police wouldn't know the difference.

He could just not ward the thing."

Lewis' reply was forestalled by Henry and Jerry approaching, Jerry looking uncommonly keen and fresh given the hour.

"All ready?" Henry asked cheerfully.

"Ready," Alma said.

"Passengers here, please," the man with the clipboard called. "Official passengers, over here."

Jerry turned slowly, careful in the crowd and on the concrete floor of the hangar. The last thing he wanted was to go sprawling, tripped up by his artificial leg. He felt reasonably rested, despite the late night; he'd shaved carefully and worn his own best suit, the one he'd had made in Chicago four years ago. It was a little old-fashioned, but it wouldn't disgrace the team.

Mitch frowned. He hadn't had time to shave, and there were circles under his eyes. "What—is this the drawing?"

Jerry nodded. This was the first of the publicity stunts: the passengers would draw their teams' starting position an hour before the first plane left. He thought it was unfair, leaving everyone stewing and in doubt about their strategy, but Alma had just shrugged, and he'd left it at that. "Any particular position you want me to try for?"

He was good at influencing probabilities—dice, cards, lotteries—and he could see Alma consider it for a moment before she shook her head. "No. There's ten minutes between each start, and it's all elapsed time anyway, so—let's save that for later."

"Ok," Jerry said, and started for the door.

The organizers had gathered the official passengers at the steps that led up to the platform, and one of the handlers was checking them off on a clipboard.

"Dr. Ballard," he said, making his mark. "Gilchrist Aviation. Please stay right here."

"Of course," Jerry said, and leaned more heavily on his cane. At least he wasn't the only man in the group. Comanche Air's passenger was a craggy-faced man with the weathered skin of a cowboy; he caught Jerry's glance and gave him a wry grin and a flick of the eyebrows that encompassed the gaggle of pretty girls surrounding them. Jerry smiled back, but didn't move any closer.

It was easy to pick out the girls who belonged to the three mail lines, all of them blonde and curvy, with expensive makeup and dresses cut to make a show without actually being immodest, and all of them practiced at catching the camera's eye. Up-and-coming actresses, all of them, Jerry remembered, though the one flying with American was supposed to be engaged to one of their pilots. The girl from Consolidated was a brunette, pert and pretty and equally at home in front of the cameras, a long scarf in Consolidated's colors wound about her neck. She was a contract player at RKO, Jerry remembered from the party, and a would-be flyer herself. The remaining women had done their best, but next to the starlets they looked positively drab. May Saltonstall's suit was well-cut, an expensive gray wool that would look perfectly fine in Boston, but in California made her look twice her age, and her face was pink from sun and nerves. The other two, representing Jezek Air and Bestways Air Transport, had done their best, but their frocks were last year's colors, and the woman from Jezek had opted for an artificial silk that wilted in the morning heat. She was doing her best to pretend it didn't matter, but Jerry could see the strain behind her smile.

"You're from Jezek?" he asked, and she turned, relaxing slightly as she realized he wasn't a reporter.

"Yes. And you're—Gilchrist?"

Jerry nodded. "Mr. Kershaw warned us we'd need to watch out for the Corsair."

She snorted. "Connie—my husband—tried to sell him on the design when he worked for Republic. But—we'll see."

"Hey! Mrs. Jezek! How's the Polish Jalopy holding up?" That was one of the photographers, moving closer with his big camera.

Mrs. Jezek closed her eyes for a moment. "We are Czech, actually."

"How about a smile?"

She managed one, and the girl from Consolidated linked arms with her, offering a bigger smile and a flash of leg.

"Don't let 'em needle you, hon," she said, under her breath. "They're all going to follow Winchell's lead."

Mrs. Jezek managed a more natural smile, leaning closer to the Consolidated girl, auburn hair against rich brown, and the photographer raised his camera.

"Nice one! Hey, Doc, how 'bout you join them?"

Jerry moved in, forcing a smile of his own, and the photographers snapped away.

"Passengers! Passengers on the platform, please!" one of the organizers shouted, and Jerry pulled away, hanging back a little so that he could go last, where there would be room to haul himself up in spite of the artificial leg.

"Gentlemen on the ends, please," a young woman was saying, as she sorted them into the most photogenic pattern. "Miss Collins in the middle, you ladies here—yes, perfect, thank you."

She stepped back, and Jerry looked down to find himself next to May Saltonstall. She gave him a wry smile. "Quite a production—Professor Ballard, is it?"

Of course she'd been to Radcliffe, just as her brothers had been to Harvard. Jerry nodded. "A pleasure to meet you, Miss Saltonstall."

"I think we have a mutual acquaintance—"

A crackle of static from the speaker above them drowned out what she might have said, and Jerry composed himself to listen as the day's master of ceremonies—the manager of Grand Central, a nice bit of publicity—stepped up to begin the proceedings. He ran through the race rules for the benefit of anyone who hadn't been reading the papers—six legs from Los Angeles to Coconut Grove, all planes to be stock passenger planes, each one to carry a non-pilot passenger—while the sun beat down on the open platform, and Jerry felt the sweat begin to worm its way down his back. He kept his face unmoving, schooled to the same bland smile he'd worn under bombardment, and beside him May Saltonstall dabbed nervously at her mascara. Below them, a couple of hundred people crowded onto the tarmac, reporters and photographers filling the first rows, while the newsreel cameras ground away, black boxes poking up out of the edges of the crowd.

"—draw for starting positions," the manager said at last, and another pair of pretty girls in bright red dresses made their way up onto the platform. They carried a long silver tray between them, nine envelopes laid on in a row against the polished metal. "Hold on to your envelopes, please, until everyone has chosen. Ladies first."

They began with Mrs. Jezek, who hesitated only for an instant before grabbing the middle one. The girls in red moved down the line, letting the women pick, so that there were only two envelopes left when they got to Jerry. He considered for an instant, then took the left-hand one, and the girls brought the almost-empty tray back to the man from Comanche Air.

"Ladies—and gentlemen, of course," the manager said. "You may open your envelopes now."

Jerry ripped his open, saw the others doing the same, and unfolded his paper to reveal a large number five printed in heavy black ink. The girl from Consolidated held hers up at chest height, displaying a big 2, and the other women copied her. Jerry did the same, glancing down the line. United was first out, then Consolidated, then the Corsair—a nice break for them, if only for the publicity—then TWA. Gilchrist would follow them, with the Harvards next, and Comanche, Bestways, and American rounding out the field. For all that Alma swore the starting order didn't matter, Jerry couldn't help wishing he'd drawn a higher number. Below them, the camera shutters clattered, the photographers calling *smile* and *look this way*, and Jerry obeyed mechanically, looking over the crowd toward the hangar. It was time to get underway.

Chapter Six

Lewis leaned over Alma's shoulder, looking at the fuel calculations she and Mitch had been struggling over. Despite the late night, he felt pretty good—yeah, he could have used another couple hours' sleep, but he was certainly ready. Mitch and Alma both looked worse, dark circles under Alma's eyes, Mitch showing an unusual hint of stubble. Lewis touched his own chin in reflex, reassuring himself that he still looked presentable. He had a heavy beard, and had to shave twice a day if he wanted to look decent, and the last thing he wanted was to disgrace Gilchrist. Or Henry, he supposed, but it was really Alma who mattered.

He made himself focus on the numbers. "We're not going with full tanks?" he asked, pitching his voice low to keep from being overheard.

Alma shook her head. "Mitch and I worked it out," she said, lowering her voice to match. "Two hundred twenty gallons still gives us a decent margin, especially with a light tail wind predicted the whole way. And we'll be three hundred pounds lighter."

That would make a difference, all right, though Lewis couldn't say he really liked it. Not when the shortest route took them over the Mohave most of the way. But those were the choices: fly north or south of the most direct line, and have towns and highways for landmarks to supplement the compass readings, or trust your dead reckoning and strike out for Flagstaff by the quickest route. The trouble with that plan was that if anything went wrong, mechanical trouble, weather, anything at all, there was nowhere to land but the desert itself. Or the broken badlands in between. "We've got extra water on board?"

Alma stopped, fixing him with a look. "Do you have a bad feeling here?"

Lewis paused, considering the question, trying to find the still center that would let him give a truthful answer. "No," he said at last, and shrugged. "Guess it's just preflight jitters."

"Ok," Alma said, and nodded.

"Problems?" Mitch asked.

Lewis shook his head before Alma could answer. "Just going over the details."

"We're fueled and ready," Mitch said. "Now it's just finding out where we start—"

There was a roar from the crowd gathered outside the hangar, and Lewis looked over his shoulder to see the first of the reporters scurrying toward the planes. "I guess we're about to find out."

At the back of the hangar, a man in one of the red-striped jackets that marked a race referee lifted a megaphone to his mouth. "Teams, you may start your engines!"

"Not until we find out where we start," Mitch muttered.

"Fifth," Alma said.

Lewis craned his neck to see where she was looking, and spotted Jerry limping through the crowd, holding a piece of paper over his head that was emblazoned with a big number five. "No hurry, then," he said. There was a ten minute gap between starts; no need to waste fuel or worry about overheating by idling on the runway.

"Go ahead and start the preflight, though," Alma said.

Lewis climbed into the Terrier, glad to be out of the crowd's eye for the moment. It was warm in the fuselage in spite of the new white exterior, and he shrugged out of his jacket, leaving it neatly folded on a rear-facing seat. By rights this should be Mitch's leg—the Terrier was his baby—and Lewis meant to do right by him. He settled himself into the cockpit, fitting himself behind the familiar controls, and ran down the checklist that was becoming as familiar to him as breathing. Everything was in order, just the start sequence left, and he leaned forward to peer out the narrow side windows. Across the hangar, the Ford in United's colors fired its engines, spitting flame and smoke before it settled to a smooth roar. A moment later, Consolidated started up, and the race marshals began moving the planes out of the hangar.

Mitch brought the ladder over, climbed it to turn the big propeller, making sure everything was clear, left wing, right wing, nose. Lewis heard the familiar clatter of Jerry pulling himself into the passenger compartment, and then Alma joined him in the cockpit, settling herself into the copilot's seat.

"Ok," she said. "Fire her up."

Lewis glanced out the windows again to be sure Mitch was clear, then pumped the primer a couple of times. Throttle closed, fuel at "Full Rich," spark at "Full Advance." Starter on, starter dog engaged. He took a breath, and switched on the ignition and the booster magneto. The center engine caught and fired, and then the pair on the wings; he adjusted the spark and eased the throttle open, watching the oil temperature climb.

He heard the rattle of the stairs being folded in, and then the bang of the cabin door sealing. A moment later, Mitch stuck his head into the cockpit.

"We can taxi when ready," he said. "Follow the flagman."

"Right," Lewis said. The oil was warm now, the engines turning over nicely, and he looked at Alma. "Ready when you are, Al."

"Let's do this," she said, but her expression was grimmer than her words.

Lewis lowered his side window and waved to the flagman, signaling that they were ready. The man waved back, and Lewis eased the throttle back to idle and followed him decorously out of the hangar.

A plane had just taken off, little more than a bright dot disappearing into the eastern sky, and the TWA Ford was taxiing slowly toward the end of the runway. Lewis let the Terrier creep slowly forward, engines at idle, watching the engine temperatures climb and then hold steady, testing flaps and rudder one last time.

"Flag's up," Alma said. "There goes TWA."

Lewis nodded, watching the big trimotor turn into the wind. It trundled forward, clumsy at first, then more graceful as it picked up speed. The pilot let the tail come up, and the Ford rose neatly into the air, banking as it turned south toward the Banning Pass.

"We'll all be going that way to start," Alma said. "After…"

After that, they'd see who the real gamblers were.

Lewis eased the Terrier into position at the end of the runway, revving the throttle and tightening the brakes as the last minutes ticked away. At the end of the runway, the flag went up. He released the brakes and shoved the throttle forward, fuel once again at "Full

Rich" for the takeoff. The Terrier responded eagerly, leaping forward, the tail coming up almost at once, and he couldn't help grinning as the ground fell away below them. At three hundred feet, he banked south and east, Alma calling out the heading for the Banning Pass, and he watched the compass turn, straightening the plane to come smoothly onto the new course. For an instant, he thought he felt something shift in the tail—no, not even a shift, just an odd heaviness, something off, but then it was gone again. He checked the instruments, saw nothing wrong.

"Everything all right?" Alma asked.

"Looks good," Lewis answered. Maybe a suitcase had fallen over? If it happened again, he'd send Mitch back to check.

They had the TWA Ford in sight for most of the flight to the pass, and Alma, peering through binoculars, swore she'd caught sight of the Corsair ahead of them. "They're making good speed," she said, tucking the binoculars away again, "but they'll have to stop for fuel. I wonder if they'll go north or south?"

"I'd go south," Lewis said. "There's a string of railroad towns on the southern edge of the desert there."

"Me, too," Alma said.

As they began the climb to Banning, Lewis frowned at the fuel gauges. It seemed as though they were burning fuel a little faster than he would have expected. Well, once they were over the pass, he could dial back the mixture again, that would help. He was glad they hadn't tried to hop the mountains.

"We weren't supposed to hit a headwind, were we?"

Alma shook her head. "Not much wind at all, and supposed to be at our tail. Why?"

"Fuel consumption's up," Lewis answered. "I'll thin it out once we're past Banning."

Alma reached for her clipboard, frowning as she scribbled notes. "Keep an eye on it. I allowed almost an extra hour's flying time—"

"We're making good time," Lewis said. "I've just been running a little rich, I think."

"Keep an eye on it," Alma said again.

They threaded the Banning Pass in the TWA Ford's wake, a bright dot far in the distance, and leveled out again at a more comfortable cruising altitude. Lewis adjusted the fuel mixture until he was running more than usually lean, listening for any signs of discontent from the engines. They sounded all right, and he squinted at the fuel gauges. "What do you think?"

Alma bit her lip. "We'll save at least forty-five minutes taking the direct line." She glanced at her clipboard again, at the papers covered with figures. "Even if we're burning a little more fuel, we should have the margin."

"We'll do it," Lewis said. He glanced at the compass, settling onto the new heading. The TWA Ford was gone, he realized, and glanced out his side window to see the bigger plane turning north, following the highway. Their loss, he told himself, and focused on flying.

An hour into the desert, and he was beginning to think they'd made a bad mistake. They were still burning fuel at a faster rate than they should be, and as the tanks emptied, he was beginning to feel drag in the tail. Alma bent over her clipboard again, came up frowning.

"We're still good," she said, "but—I don't like not knowing why."

"I can't cut back the mixture any further," Lewis said. "And we're tail-heavy all of a sudden."

"Maybe one of the suitcases slid," Alma said, unfastening herself from her seat. "I'll tell Mitch to take a look."

"Thanks," Lewis said. They were no longer flying into the bright sun of morning, a relief to the eyes, but the Mojave stretched pale and empty beneath his wing, broken only by darker ridges of rock. Ugly country, too barren even for the Indians. He glanced at the fuel gauge again, willing its motion to slow.

The cockpit door opened, and Alma slid back into her place. "Mitch is checking—"

There was a crash and a thumping from the cabin, enough to unbalance the Terrier for a moment. Lewis steadied it, casting one wild glance over his shoulder. Alma was already out of her seat again when Jerry flung the cockpit door open.

"We have a goddamned stowaway," he announced.

"What?" Alma's voice scaled up.

"That soi-disant countess," Jerry said. "She was in the baggage compartment."

"All the way?" Alma grimaced, knowing it was a stupid question.

"Yes." Jerry paused. "Mitch said we deliberately went light on fuel."

Alma closed her eyes. "We did."

Lewis took a deep breath. That was why they were burning more fuel than expected, that was why everything was just that little bit off. They were carrying more weight than they'd thought, and so the numbers didn't add up. Couldn't add up.

"We could dump her," Jerry said.

"No, we can't," Alma said firmly.

"I could."

"No." Alma shook her head. "Get back there, find out what she wants—"

"Oh, my God," Jerry said. "She stole Henry's necklace. What do you want to bet she was hiding it on the plane when I found her? Though why she stowed away—"

"I don't really care," Alma said. "Just make sure she can't do any more harm. I need to figure out if we're going to have enough fuel to make Flagstaff."

Jerry backed out, closing the door behind him. Lewis looked at the fuel gauge again, and then made himself look away. "We'll be cutting it close."

"If we can make it at all," Alma said, and bent over her clipboard again.

"He wouldn't really do it," Mitch said. He looked at the woman sitting on the floor against the bulkhead, her hair falling out of its loose bun, the heat pulling the shape out of her finger waves. She looked utterly unrepentant, though he thought she was probably trying to look pathetic. "We don't really throw people out of planes, ma'am."

"Make me walk the plank?" She lifted her head with a hint of a challenge in her eyes.

"Don't tempt me," Jerry said. He glanced forward at the cockpit where Lewis and Alma talked in low voices, consulting over the controls and the no doubt disturbing instrument readings. "You do realize that you may actually kill us all."

"Surely..."

"Surely I'm being dramatic?" Jerry demanded. "Do you have any idea what will happen if we run out of fuel over the desert? Do you know what happens when a plane runs out of fuel in mid air?"

A tiny wrinkle began between her brows and she looked at Mitch.

"We're not going to crash. Probably," Mitch amended. "If we get to that point, Lewis will set us down."

"Well, then…" she began.

"Only there's no field, you see," Mitch said. "Just Arizona desert. If we have to put down fifty or sixty miles short of Flagstaff, it's going to be an awfully long walk." And one Jerry couldn't make, but that went without saying. A guy with a wooden leg tramping through fifty miles of desert with inadequate supplies and the temperature in the 90s was a recipe for disaster. No, he'd have to take either Lewis or Alma and go for help, leaving the other one with the bogus countess, Jerry and the plane. And he was looking forward to that like a root canal. Not to mention that it would pretty much mean they'd lose the race.

She cast around. "Isn't there anything you could throw overboard?"

"You?" Jerry asked.

Mitch shook his head. "There's the emergency supplies, but those are the things we'll need if we have to land. I'm not about to start chucking the water out the hatch."

Her eyes glittered. "You like to play it safe?"

"I do," Mitch said. "There's no point in taking a bet you'll probably lose."

The countess tossed her disheveled head. "And I thought you were the ace."

"I'm the ace who's still alive," Mitch said, more sharply than he intended.

"You really don't get it," Jerry said. "The weight is calculated very, very carefully for an air race. We have exactly enough fuel to get us where we're going as quickly as possible. If we add a couple of hundred pounds…"

"Hardly that, darling."

"Well, better than a hundred and fifty," Jerry snapped. "If we go down, you're going down too."

"I didn't think I was going to have to stay on the plane," she said, drawing her knees up, her voice ripe with exasperation. "I waited outside the hangar until you and Mrs. Segura left. I thought you'd go have breakfast since you'd been there all night! Silly me!" She threw up her hands. "How was I to know you'd be back in ten minutes? So I had to stay in the luggage compartment. Then you," she looked daggers at Mitch, "fastened the latch! What was I supposed to do then? Bang and yell for you to let me out?"

"In which case you'd have been caught red-handed in LA with the stolen necklace which you did actually steal," Mitch said. "But what if we hadn't found you until we got to Flagstaff?"

"I thought once you did you'd surely get off the plane," she said. "Then I'd crawl out the inside hatch and be on my way."

"With the necklace," Jerry said. "As soon as we get to Flagstaff, we're calling the police."

"Oh, come on now!"

"You stole the necklace from Henry, you're a professional thief, and you tried to make your escape on our plane. Tell me one reason we shouldn't call the police." Jerry glared right back.

"But I'll go to jail!"

"I expect so," Jerry said.

She turned dark, pleading eyes to Mitch. "Surely you can't go along with this! Darling, if only you knew…" She blinked furiously. "I admit that my life has been checkered, but if you had any idea the terrible things that have caused me to end up this way…" Her voice choked and she looked skyward. "I wasn't born like this. And if my husband hadn't been killed in the war…"

"I'm sorry to hear that," Mitch said.

"It was terrible," she said. "We had only been married a few weeks before he left for the front. And then there I was, amid the chaos of the Russian Revolution, amid unspeakable violence…"

"What city were you in?" Mitch asked.

"Minsk," she said. "Minsk. It was horrible. The things that happened…"

"So he was in the Russian army?"

A momentary flicker of something crossed her face. "Yes, of course. Being Russian."

"Ah," Mitch said. "Not Polish or Hungarian."

She gave him a grand smile. "Why would you think that, darling? I told you I was Russian. White Russian."

"A White Russian countess from Minsk," Mitch agreed. "And after the war you went to…"

"Poland," she said quickly. "During the Second Polish Republic."

"Ah," he said. "Poland. Logical place for a Russian countess."

"Absolutely." She gave him a brilliant smile. "Poland was absolutely full of Poles."

"Not Hungarian Jews," Mitch said.

She blinked. "Why would there be?"

"No reason," Mitch said. "So then you did what?"

"I stayed with a tragic relation in Prague," she said. "Tragic. He was dying of gout."

Mitch felt his mouth twitching, and she saw it with a prim look, Jerry looking back and forth between them as though he were watching a tennis match.

"Mitch, what the hell?" he said. "When were you in Eastern Europe?"

"Right after the war," Mitch said, his eyes on the countess instead. "I spent some time in Budapest as a military attaché. Right before the White Terror. Strangely enough, I recognize a Hungarian accent."

"How very nice," she said. "If I meet any Hungarians I'll be sure to tell them."

"So how did you become a jewel thief?" Jerry asked, as though he found this weirdly fascinating.

"Do tell us," Mitch said. "I'm sure it's a fascinating story." He sat down, leaning back in the seat. "This is after Prague?"

"My second husband was a master criminal," she said, crossing her ankles in their pretty strappy shoes. "I met him in London and I had no idea, of course. I thought he was a perfect gentleman. I had no idea that he was using all those house parties as a way to rob people! I thought he just went to Monte Carlo for his health! I had no idea that we were there so that he could burgle a maharajah!"

"Ah," Mitch said. "I take it you distracted the poor guy with your feminine wiles while your husband robbed him blind?"

"Something like that." She rewarded Mitch with another smile. "I left him, of course, but the damage was done! I was hopelessly morally corrupted! It's the old story, I'm afraid. An innocent girl led down the primrose path, not realizing what she has become until it's too late." Her eyelashes fluttered closed. "I still pray that a good man may save me from this life."

"You're a pathological liar," Jerry said flatly. "Or you're nuts."

"And being a good man I should trust that you're really reforming and not turn you over to the police," Mitch said.

"Exactly!" The countess beamed. "I knew you'd catch on."

"Humm," Mitch said. "I suppose that does bear thinking about."

"We are calling the police when we get to Flagstaff," Jerry said. "Mitch."

"But you've got the necklace," she said. "You can give it back to Kershaw when you see him. It's an ugly old thing anyway. And there's no harm done. You just give it back and we're all square."

"Except for the part about you being a felon," Jerry pointed out.

"Darling," she said. "Must you use that word?"

"How about thief?" Mitch said.

"So déclassé."

"Cat burglar? Second story woman?" Mitch grinned. "There's always a dame?"

"Clearly you and I read the same magazines," the countess purred.

"A match made in heaven," Jerry snapped. "She steals a necklace, stows away, and may yet crash the plane, and you're playing some scene out of Black Mask!!"

"With extra plum dumplings," Mitch said, not looking away from her. She did twitch, just a little. "I'll tell you what. If you behave until we get to Flagstaff, and if we have to put down early you're helpful and useful, then maybe we won't call the police."

"Darling, I knew you'd be my champion!" she said. "I'll be such a good little girl. You'll hardly know I'm here."

"Oh God," Jerry groaned.

"But if we crash the plane, you'll probably die," Mitch said, getting to his feet. "So I'm just going to mosey on up to the cockpit now and see how the fuel consumption is playing out." He looked back at the countess. "By the way, do you have a name?"

"It's Anastasia," she said brightly. "Like the lost princess."

"Of course it is," Mitch said. He shook his head and leaned into the cockpit. "How's it looking?"

Alma glanced up from the co-pilot's seat. "You want to trade with me?"

"Yeah," Mitch said. That meant it wasn't good. The Terrier was his plane more than anyone else's, and if push came to shove he'd want to take the controls.

Lewis looked at him sideways. "Everything ok back there?"

"I think I've talked Jerry out of making her walk the plank," Mitch said. "And maybe talked her into behaving until we get to Flagstaff."

"If we get to Flagstaff," Lewis said.

"We can't make it," Alma said, opening the cockpit door again. "The extra weight—if we'd known it was there from the start, maybe… But we can't make it."

"I can run leaner," Lewis said, reaching for the mix control. He dialed it back a little further, and the port engine coughed and sputtered before it caught again. He shoved it back to the previous position. "Ok, maybe not."

"There's a limit," Mitch said. He looked over his shoulder. "What if we cut out one engine?"

"What?" Lewis blinked. The Terrier would fly perfectly well on two of its three engines, except for landings.

"Will that save enough fuel?" Mitch asked.

Alma looked at her clipboard. "Maybe? Let me run the numbers."

The cockpit door closed again, and Lewis looked at Mitch. "What if it doesn't?"

Mitch made a face. "We find someplace flat and set her down. Hopefully not too far from something like civilization." Right now they were over a sheet of sand, like he'd always imagined the Sahara, crossed by the line of a dry riverbed. Ahead the sand turned into crumpled hills, with only the slightest haze of color on the horizon to suggest there might be trees.

"Maybe if we turn north?" Lewis asked. "Aren't there some towns north of here?"

Mitch rummaged around beside his seat. "I'm not really seeing anything. And if we try, we'll have to set down and refuel. No, our best bet is probably still Flagstaff."

"If we can get there," Lewis muttered. "What the hell was she thinking?"

"She didn't know," Mitch said. "And she kind of got trapped. Apparently she stuck Henry's necklace in the tail back at the party, and tried to get it out when Al and I went to grab some coffee. Only we came back too quickly, and I locked the compartment."

Lewis glanced sideways.

"I suppose it was kind of my fault," Mitch said.

* * *

Alma opened the cockpit door again in just a couple of minutes. "Ok," she said, "on two engines, we can just make it. Two engines running as lean as we can."

"They won't run as lean if they're doing the extra work," Mitch said.

"I know," Alma said. "Just—do what you can."

"Right," Lewis said. He'd flown the Terrier on two engines as part of his training, and it handled better than you'd expect, but… You needed three engines to land, and the longer they had the center engine off, the harder it would be to restart.

"You ready?" Mitch asked, and reached for the controls.

"Go ahead," Lewis answered, and tried not to tighten his hand on the wheel.

Mitch closed the throttle, letting the engine burn through the last of the gas in the line, then shut it down completely. Lewis could feel the shift in the handling, an absence of power that made him wince even as he reached to adjust the fuel mix again.

"That's as good as it's going to get," Mitch said. He shook his head. "Damn it, even if this works, we're going to lose time."

"Hope that's all we lose," Alma said, and closed the door again.

Then there was nothing to do but wait, keep the Terrier on course and hope that Alma had done the math correctly. Lewis watched the sand unreel beneath them, and then broken hills spotted with scrub, and finally more sand dotted with trees. The fuel levels were dropping steadily, even at this most economical speed. Lewis looked away, reviewing the ground, searching for landmarks, but he couldn't keep from checking the gauge again and again.

"There," Mitch said, and pointed.

A road cut through the scrub, dirt and apparently unused, but definitely a road. Paper rustled as Mitch consulted the map.

"Ok," he said. "We're in business. That should be the fire road, we can follow that right in to the airport."

Lewis nodded, not trusting himself to speak, and lined the Terrier up on the streak of brown. Twenty minutes passed, then half an hour, and Lewis bit his tongue to keep from asking how far out Mitch thought they were. It didn't matter what he thought, didn't matter what any of them thought. All that mattered was following the road, keeping to their safe slow speed, and waiting for the airport to appear.

Finally there it was, the long stretch of runway, and the tower, and the long streamer of the windsock welcoming them in.

"I'll take her now," Mitch said, and Lewis gladly handed over the controls. This was Mitch's plane, and if anybody could make this work, it was him. Lewis looked at the fuel gauges again, the bars resting on the red warning mark, and shook his head.

"Can you land her on two?"

Mitch shook his head. "I'm landing her on three."

"Is there enough gas?"

"There's going to have to be," Mitch answered. "Get ready to start her up."

As long as we don't have to circle, Lewis thought, as long as the runway's clear and Mitch can just bring her down… He bent his attention to the controls, priming the center engine, setting spark and throttle.

"Now," Mitch said, and Lewis flipped the ignition. The engine choked and died; he hit it again, and this time it caught, ragged at first but steadying.

"Got you," Mitch said, softly, big hands easy on the controls, throttling down, lowering the flaps as the ground rushed closer. "There you go." The starboard engine missed, but caught again, Mitch never wavering from his steady line. And then they were skimming the ground, speed cut to stalling, and Mitch lifted the nose to set them gently down again.

"Oh, you kid," he said, and Lewis released a breath he hadn't known he'd been holding.

For a long moment everyone just sat there, Lewis with his hands still clenched, Mitch with a silly grin.

"Ok," Alma said. Her voice wasn't shaky at all. "Ok. Let's taxi around if we can and see the board."

"Fourth," Jerry said as their tail swung and he could see. "Fourth. We're right behind that damn Fokker from Bestways."

"Fourth out of nine," Lewis said, a dismal tone in his voice, blaming himself for something that couldn't be helped.

"It could be worse," Mitch said. "We could be dead last."

"We could be dead," Jerry pointed out. He gave the Countess a dirty look. "No thanks to you know who. As soon as we stop, Al, get the tower to call the police."

"Please don't!" There was an actual note of panic in her voice, and Alma looked around. The other woman's hands clenched on the seat back. "Please don't. There's no harm done. You've got the necklace and you're safe in Flagstaff. You didn't crash and you aren't in last place." She looked at Mitch imploringly. "You said I could go when you got to Flagstaff if I didn't make any more trouble."

Alma took a deep breath. "Did you actually promise that, Mitch?"

Mitch looked uncomfortable. "Sort of. Yeah."

Alma shook her head. Sometimes Mitch and Lewis were as gullible as a pair of wood sprites.

The Countess met her eyes frankly. "Come on," she said. "A girl's got to make a living." She lifted her chin just a fraction, but what was in her face was real. Fear. And after all, there was no harm done.

"Call the police," Jerry said.

"No, I don't think so," Alma said slowly, her eyes on the Countess. "The publicity would be bad for Henry and it would probably get us tied up with police statements. We might miss our start tomorrow." She watched the color come back to the woman's face. "You can clear out. And as you say, no harm done. We'll give Henry his necklace back when we see him."

"Oh come on!" Jerry said.

"I knew you'd be ok," the Countess said with a brilliant smile. "Didn't I tell you I liked her, Mr. Sorley?"

"Um," Mitch said, sure proof she'd said nothing of the sort but he was too polite to contradict a lady.

Lewis shook his head, following the flagman around to the third hangar. He cut the engines neatly in front of it. They sputtered as they died. "Not enough fuel left to light a match," he said.

Alma got up stiffly and went back to pop the door. "Ok," she said. "You can go. And don't let us see you again."

"I can't believe you're letting her go!" Jerry said.

"Let it be," Lewis said. "You know, people who are down on their luck do some crazy things…"

"Like turn into jewel thieves? We're not talking about panhandling here!"

Mitch got down and unfolded the stairs, and the Countess hopped nimbly down. "Well," she said cheerfully, "It's certainly been fun. Toodle-oo!"

"You might want to give back the necklace first," Mitch said.

"I have the necklace," Alma said.

Mitch shook his head. "Nope. She picked your jacket pocket while she was standing behind your seat in the cockpit. Excuse me, ma'am." He reached around her and shoved one hand deep in the front pocket of her black slacks.

"Darling, I didn't know you cared," she said as he rummaged about very improperly with his big hand.

Mitch smiled as he pulled the necklace out like a magician drawing a rabbit from a hat. "Now you can go."

"That little sneak!" Jerry said.

"Out," Alma said sternly. "Before I change my mind and call the cops."

"Call the cops about what?" The first of the reporters had jogged up, following the taxi way from the stands.

"This lady was just leaving," Mitch said. He gave the reporter an urbane smirk. "You know, they follow you around like crazy. Sorry, Toots. Not interested."

Her mouth opened and closed. "My name's not Toots."

"How are you feeling about the race, Mrs. Segura?" the reporter asked, shifting his attention from the all too familiar byplay. "Is a fourth place finish what you'd hoped for?"

"This was a tough leg, no doubt about that," Alma said. "But it's not the finish. This is just the first leg, and I think we've shaken a few kinks out. I'm confident we're in good shape. This is just the beginning of the race."

"What is your name then?" Mitch asked. "Trouble?"

"You know it, darling," she said. "But you can call me Stasi. With an i."

Alma was trying to keep her mind on her game.

"What kind of trouble, Mrs. Segura?"

"Just a few technical issues that need to be resolved," Alma said smoothly. "Nothing major. A desert course is a challenge for any aircraft. That's why this leg is a good test for all the planes in the race."

"Mitch," Jerry said.

"And easy on the eyes," Mitch said.

"Darling, if you're looking for trouble…"

"Trouble usually finds me."

"Is somebody paying you for this dialogue?" Jerry demanded. Lewis made a noise suspiciously like a snicker.

Alma looked around with her best irritated schoolmarm expression. "Gentlemen, maybe you had better see about the post-flight check list? Lewis? Mitch?"

Mitch looked abashed. "We had better."

"How do you feel about your starting position tomorrow, Mrs. Segura?"

"Well, we don't know for certain," Alma said. "After all, things may change a little in the start order with the on-the-ground competitions, but I'm confident we won't be far off the optimal time. I think we're in good shape for tomorrow's leg to San Angelo, Texas." When she looked around again the Countess was gone.

Chapter Seven

It took another couple of hours for the next four planes to land, with only American Airways trailing the pack. The teams milled in the hangar, warned to wait for the publicity events and a "surprise" inspection that might happen, and Jerry settled himself on the steps of the Terrier. Not only did it ease the ache that came with standing too long, it meant nobody could get into the plane without walking over him. He still felt like kicking himself for having missed what the self-proclaimed "countess" had been up to at Henry's party.

Alma and Mitch checked the big rotary engines—it was never good for them to be fuel-starved too long—and Lewis wandered off toward one of the Comanche team who'd landed twenty minutes behind them, chatting with a group of race officials gathered by the hangar doors. He was back in less than half an hour, trying valiantly to suppress a grin.

"American's had a mechanical," he said, and Alma slid down off the ladder. "They're still in, at least for now, but they won't be here before dark. The race officials have decided to go ahead without them."

"What went wrong?" Mitch asked.

Lewis shrugged. "It's not entirely clear. I heard they broke a fuel line, or maybe had a leak? But they had to set down about halfway along the northern route, and then wait for somebody to mend the part, and then they had to fly out on regular gasoline."

"That puts them out of the race," Alma said. "They've lost—oh, at least four hours already, and they're not in yet, and running on regular gas is going to play hell with the engines."

"One less thing to worry about," Mitch said. He was looking tired, Jerry thought, the beginning of a frown creasing his brow. And no wonder: the last hour and a half of the flight had been no picnic for anyone.

"Attention, competitors!" That was one of the referees, hoisting a megaphone like a dance-band leader. "Attention, competitors! Pilots, please remain with your aircraft for the referees' inspection. Passengers, please proceed to the terminal for the evening round."

Jerry hauled himself up, got his leg and his cane under him with a grimace. He only hoped it was something he could do without making a complete fool of himself.

"Good luck," Lewis called after him.

Jerry waved in answer and limped toward the referee waiting by the hangar door. It took a few minutes to gather everyone—the girls from the studios had obviously taken time to change clothes and freshen their makeup, and Jerry made a note to carry a fresh shirt in the cabin on the next leg so he would look a bit less wilted himself. Comanche's passenger joined them, giving Jerry a wry grin.

"Good flight, Doc?" He held out his hand. "Jed Pelletier."

"Jerry Ballard." Jerry returned the firm handshake, remembering that Comanche's Ford had landed behind them. "Not bad. How was yours?"

"Got the bugs out, I expect," Pelletier said.

They were still one woman short, even accounting for American's absence, and then May Saltonstall came running toward them, her Cuban heels clattering on the concrete.

"I'm so sorry—"

"If you're all quite ready?" the referee asked, and May did her best to become invisible. "This way, please!"

"Do we know what the competition is?" Jerry asked, as they started across the tarmac toward the terminal building.

Pelletier shrugged. "Games for dames," he said, with a grin. One of the starlets gave him a sharp look, and he spread his hands in apology. "Sorry, Miss."

A low stage had been set up on the far side of the terminal, and there was a crowd gathered on the grass beyond the roadway. Jerry had been expecting reporters and the newsreel cameras, but not quite so much of an ordinary audience, and he checked in spite of himself. Pelletier's jaw dropped, but then he plastered a grin on his face, and followed the women up the short set of stairs to the stage.

Jerry grabbed the rails with both hands and hauled himself up after them all.

The stage was dominated by what looked like a giant roulette wheel set on its side, with two pretty young women wearing sashes that proclaimed them "Miss Flagstaff" and "Miss Ponderosa" standing to either side. There was a cluster of radio microphones toward the front of the stage, and the newsreel cameras were already whirring. The crowd began applauding as the organizers herded them into a line, and the starlets responded with smiles and waves. Jerry tipped his hat, and let himself be urged into place at the end of the line next to Mrs. Jezek. They had been the last ones in, and she was looking grim. Even as he thought that, however, she straightened her spine and put on an almost convincing smile.

"Ladies and gentlemen!" That was the master of ceremonies for this event, a stout man in a pale suit, an American flag pinned to his lapel. "Let's welcome the competitors in the Great Passenger Derby to our fair city of Flagstaff!"

The crowd cheered. Jerry shifted his weight to ease the pressure on his stump, tuning out the florid rhetoric. Even in the late afternoon, the sun was hot on his back, and he had to admire the starlets' practiced grace. Next to Mrs. Jezek, May Saltonstall stood with her hands clasped behind her back, looking more like a gawky schoolgirl than a Boston sophisticate.

The crowd seemed fascinated, though. There had to be several hundred people there, including quite a few families, and it looked from the baskets and blankets they were carrying as though they'd made a day of it, picnicking to wait for the planes to land, then staying to see the festivities afterward. And that was good—good publicity, good for Henry and all the other sponsors, and good for Gilchrist Aviation as well.

The MC finished his speech and turned the microphones over to the sponsors' spokesman, "Mr. Hickson from Texas Aviation Fuels." Hickson was taller, leaner, hard-faced under his pale ten-gallon hat, and mercifully to the point.

"Since we've required each airplane to carry a passenger, it seemed only fair to allow those passengers a chance to win something for their teams," he said. "Today, the ladies—and gentlemen— the passengers—have a chance to win a little extra time for their teams. As you see, the big wheel behind us is marked with twenty numbers, each of which represents the subtraction of either five, ten, or even fifteen minutes from a team's elapsed time. With the help of our lovely assistants, Miss Flagstaff and Miss Ponderosa, each passenger will spin the wheel and see what she can do to help her team, beginning with—Miss Ruby Lee, for Transcontinental and Western Airways."

Miss Lee waved prettily, and stepped up to the wheel. One of the other girls said something, and she grabbed a spoke, pulled hard to set the wheel spinning. It whirred loudly, then slowed and settled.

"Five minutes!" Hickson announced. "That's five minutes subtracted from Transcontinental's already race-leading time!"

Jerry studied the wheel as the girl from United took her turn. There were two blocks worth fifteen minutes, four more worth ten, and the rest were worth five. If he wanted to—if he concentrated, he could shift the probabilities, gain the maximum time for Gilchrist. But, no, it was probably better to save that trick for later, when they might really need it. It wouldn't do to look too lucky. Hickson called his name, and he stepped up to the wheel.

"Grab one of the high ones," Miss Flagstaff said, "and pull real hard."

He gave her a smile of thanks, and did as he was told, yanking the heavy machinery into motion. It seemed to take forever to stop, but at last it slowed, drifting past five after five to settle at last on a bright orange ten.

"Ten minutes for Dr. Ballard of Gilchrist Aviation," Hickson announced. "Ten minutes to be subtracted from Gilchrist's time."

Jezek won fifteen minutes, putting them almost even with the Harvards ahead of them, but May shook Mrs. Jezek's hand with what looked like genuine pleasure. And then at last it was over, and Jerry hung back to let the others leave the stage before him.

As he made his way across the tarmac toward the hangar, a handsome brunette in a pretty crepe dress fell into step beside him. She was carrying a notebook, and there was a reporter's tag pinned to her wide white collar; he tipped his hat, but didn't slow his step.

"Peggy Martin, *Cococino Sun*," she said, with a smile that showed very white teeth. "Mind if I ask a few questions, Dr. Ballard?"

"Not if you can do it walking," Jerry said. "I need to get back to my team. I'm sure you understand."

"Absolutely," she said, without great sincerity. "I just had a few questions, anyway. How'd a distinguished professor of archeology end up as the passenger for Gilchrist? No offense, Dr. Ballard, but I'm sure they could have found someone a bit more—mobile."

Jerry forced a smile of his own, tamping down the automatic anger. "And more decorative, too. But I've worked with Gilchrist for many years, and I was delighted to have the opportunity."

"Worked as what?" Peggy asked, and Jerry cut in quickly before she could expand on the question.

"Mrs. Segura's first husband and I were in the War together."

As he'd hoped, that deflected her onto another path. "I understand Mr. Segura and Mr. Sorley are also veterans?"

"Decorated aces," Jerry said, stretching the truth only slightly. Mitch was the ace, Lewis had the DSC. "And Mrs. Segura drove an ambulance on the Italian front."

He became aware that another reporter was listening as well, and the man grinned cheerfully and shoved his hat back further onto his head. "Mrs. Segura's quite a dame," he said. "What happened to husband number one? That was Gilchrist, right?"

"Gil died five years ago," Jerry said. "TB, from being gassed in the Veneto."

Peggy, at least, looked slightly abashed, but the other reporter kept his cocky smile. "And Sorley's worked for her all this time? And Segura?"

"Mr. Sorley was Gil's partner," Jerry said, austerely. They were, mercifully, at the hangar doors, and there were race officials poised to turn away the press. "If you'll excuse me, Miss Martin?"

He ducked inside without waiting for her answer, found himself next to the girl from Consolidated. She gave him a smile, and Jerry said, "You don't happen to know who that guy was, do you?"

She lifted an eyebrow. "You mean you didn't?"

Jerry shook his head.

"His name's Carmichael," she said. "Freelance, but lately he's been one of Winchell's stringers. You better watch him, it sounds like Winchell's decided your boss is some kind of hot ticket."

Alma is going to kill someone. Jerry swallowed the words. "That's all we need."

The girl from Cosolidated shrugged. "It's all publicity, right?"

"That's the idea," Jerry said. He only hoped it was true.

Lewis sat on the edge of the hotel bed in boxers and undershirt, listening to the sound of water running in the private bath. He ought to be dead tired, what with the early start and the demands of the race, but he was too keyed up to sleep. He'd felt like this during the war sometimes. The day was over and by all rights he ought to take advantage of the opportunity to sleep, but his body just didn't believe it. They were safe. There was no war. Here they were in Flagstaff, Arizona, in the Hotel Monte Vista, the nicest place for miles around, two rooms next door to each other, nice and quiet.

Ok, yes, the other teams were also in the hotel. Likely some of them were in the speakeasy downstairs, but that probably wasn't a good idea. The college kids might think this was a game, but for Lewis this was deadly serious. This was their livelihood on the line. He hadn't brought much to this marriage, not like a man ought to. Alma owned the house and the business. She owned the planes and the truck. All he brought was his skill. Lewis knew she prized it. She'd put her trust in him over and over, even when he hadn't learned to trust himself as far as this esoteric stuff went. But he did trust his skills as a pilot, and that was all he'd brought her.

He ought to feel good that he'd pulled it off today. It had been a flight to be proud of, even if it looked easy to the waiting crowd. Aviators knew it was no picnic. Alma knew that. She'd said so. But everything still felt off.

Lewis took out the necklace and spread it out on the white sheets. It was weirdly beautiful, he thought. Wrought iron, but so delicately made that the flowers seemed to be real, as if true petals had been somehow dipped in molten iron without losing their shape, a parody of life like those wax figures that were really the bodies of dead women hidden in wax in one of Mitch's horror magazines. Lewis shuddered. He didn't like horror stories. He only read those lurid things when Mitch left them lying around. He'd seen enough real horror to make them either absurd or disturbing. It was kind of twisted, people reading about the desecration of the dead for their amusement.

Lewis reached out and traced one perfect flower. It was beautiful, though.

A jolt of cold ran through him as though he'd touched ice. No, colder than ice, the skin of an airplane that had been at altitude on a cold day, colder than ice ever got, cold enough to freeze to your skin in a single instant.

Snow. Ice that never melted. Cold fire, drawing you deeper into the snow, deeper into the heart of winter...

Lewis jerked his hand away. The necklace lay on the white sheets, beautiful and inert. It looked unbelievably delicate. It would be gorgeous on Alma, dark tracery against her white skin. Surely it couldn't hurt to just try it on... The thought of her wearing it caused a visceral reaction, desire sharp as pain. She could just wear it for a few minutes, just wear it to bed tonight. Henry would never have to know...

No. It was almost as though someone had spoken behind him, a voice inside his head like his mother's, gentle and forbidding at once. No.

Lewis blinked. It lay on the white sheets, just a necklace, yes, but glittering with an oily sheen, as though malevolence lurked beneath the surface. His stomach turned. No. It was Her hand he'd felt, clearly as if Diana had stood beside him. He was Her priest, and this thing's evil allure couldn't touch him. Not through Her. Not through the bright clarity of the moon. Dark things fled from the moon in the sky and could not bear Her silver touch.

Lewis reached for his handkerchief and bundled the necklace up in it, links heavy in his hand. He tied the corners across and across again. Henry was right, he thought. This was a dangerous thing. It had no business being loose in the world where it could hurt people. As soon as the race was over it was going straight back in a safe where it could stay. And in the meantime he'd make certain that nobody else touched it, nobody without Diana's protection.

Lewis nodded slowly. He was Hers, and his life was Hers to take. That meant nobody else could take it without Her permission, without it being part of a proper challenge. So he was probably the safest person to watch over this. Certainly Alma shouldn't touch it, not even once. He shuddered, imagining the temptation. How tempting it would be to try on something so beautiful, just to put it on for a moment and look in the mirror! Alma pretended she didn't care much for looks, but she'd want to see. Just for a second, just in private. She'd put it on in front of the mirror just out of curiosity.

Not if he could help it. Lewis tucked the bundled handkerchief into the pocket of his flight jacket. He'd wear it against his heart, and hope Diana's protection would do for them both.

"I can't believe Al let her go." Jerry sat down on the other side of the bed and loosened his tie.

"Let it go, Jerry," Mitch said. He hadn't taken his suit coat off yet since the news pictures after dinner. He grimaced at himself in the mirror over the dresser.

"She's a professional thief!"

"We got that, Jerry." Mitch ran his hand over his chin. He didn't need to shave yet. Well, a gentleman is always well groomed.

"Don't you think…"

"No, I don't, really," Mitch said. He felt unaccountably antsy tonight, for all that there was no reason for it. It was true they'd have liked to have grabbed an early lead in the race, but he'd known that was unlikely. Everyone was going to be in top form for the first leg. They'd finished forty-five minutes off the leader, and the spread of the whole field was less than three hours. This race was a week long, seven days transcontinental. Nobody was going to have a significant lead after the first four to five hour leg.

Jerry looked up over the tops of his gold rimmed glasses.

"I can't settle down yet," Mitch said. He glanced at his watch. "It's barely ten o'clock. I'm going to go take a walk around."

"Around where?" Jerry asked.

"Just around the hotel," Mitch said.

Jerry shrugged. "Wondering if they've got a speakeasy in the basement?"

"I know they do," Mitch said. "The bellman told me."

Jerry snorted. "Well, don't wake me up coming in. I need my beauty sleep." He looked toward the right hand wall. "And I expect the newlyweds will be cranky if you wake them up."

"They may like to go to bed at ten," Mitch said. "But I'm going to get some air." Alma and Lewis always went to bed early. Hell, Al had for years before Lewis was anywhere in sight, but for some reason tonight it seemed particularly annoying. Not their fault, Mitch said to himself. People have a right to be happy. If Al and Lewis want to shut the door and spend time together, it's nobody's business. They're married and they get to. No reason to be an ass just because… Because what? Because it's kind of a weird, unsettled night?

Nothing that a shot of whiskey wouldn't solve. "I'll be back in a little bit," Mitch said. He snagged the room key off the top of the dresser. "Night, Jerry."

"Night, Mitch."

He closed the door behind him and locked it so Jerry wouldn't have to get up, went down the hall to the elevator. The cage opened and the attendant looked out. Mitch stepped in. "Down to the bottom if you please."

"The Lounge, sir?"

"If that's where they keep the Kentucky bourbon," Mitch said.

The attendant chuckled. "That it is, sir."

Alma came out of the bathroom in her combinations, her robe loose on her shoulders. She'd needed that bath, the long soak that washed away not just the sweat and dust but the lingering fear. They'd come through, safe and sound, and were in good shape for the long leg to San Angelo in the morning. That was more than she'd expected in those hours over the desert.

She didn't need to be thinking about that again, not when she'd finally managed to stop replaying all her choices, all the chances she'd had to spot the stowaway, and she slid onto the bed next to Lewis, who looked up with a smile. He hadn't bothered dressing after his own bath, was propped up against the headboard in his underwear, the stubble heavy on his chin. His hair had come out of its careful pomade, lay in heavy dark waves threaded here and there with gray, and she leaned against his shoulder. His arm went around her, settling her more comfortably, and she sighed in content. He looked a bit like Ramon Novarro, mostly the dark eyes and the stubbornly curling hair, and she rubbed her cheek against his.

"I really couldn't call the police," she said.

"Jerry really wanted to," Lewis said.

"I know." Alma moved to sit up, but Lewis tightened his hold, and she subsided willingly. "It would have taken too long, though. The last thing we need is to be tangled up with the police."

"Oh, yeah." Lewis shifted again, tucking her into the curve of his shoulder. "She was at the party, you know. I mean, I saw her there."

"Oh?"

"She was telling Mrs. Kershaw's fortune," he said. "That was kind of a surprise. I didn't think Mrs. Kershaw went in for that sort of thing."

"She's not involved in lodge business." Alma shrugged. "But that doesn't mean she doesn't have other interests. I suppose fortune-telling, being a medium, that sort of thing, would be a good way to get into a house like Henry's."

Lewis nodded. "Makes sense."

"A bit more excitement than I was hoping for today all around," she said.

"Me, too." Lewis frowned, and Alma sat up, catching the change in mood.

"What?"

He looked away, his gaze fixing on his flight jacket where it hung over the back of the ladderback chair in front of the desk. "Henry's necklace." He stopped then, shrugging in his turn. "I don't like it."

Alma's content vanished. "What do you mean?"

Lewis shook his head. "I don't—I'm not really sure? It's a strange thing, and I think I was—warned away from it."

"Let's take a look," Alma said.

"I don't think that's a good idea."

"Why not?"

Lewis grimaced. "I believe Henry when he says it's cursed, that's for sure."

"All the more reason to see what we're dealing with," Alma said. "If Diana warned you away, no, we won't do anything except take a quick look."

"All right." Lewis got up with visible reluctance, came back with something bundled in his handkerchief. He undid the knots, opening the fabric to reveal a strand of blackened metal flowers. It didn't look like much, Alma thought, just a jumble of iron, but she trusted Lewis too much to risk touching it.

"I don't feel anything," she said.

"Neither do I," Lewis admitted. "I don't know, maybe I was imagining things?"

"I doubt it," Alma said. She eyed the tangle of metal dubiously.

Maybe they should take it to Jerry, see what he had to say—but it was late, the end of an exhausting day, and they had an early start in the morning. "Well, we can give it back to Henry when we get to San Angelo. Then it's his problem."

"I won't be sorry." Lewis bundled the handkerchief back over it, returned it to his jacket pocket. "Better him than me."

It was a real nice speakeasy. The little tables had white cloths and there were actual waiters, a small stage off to one side for live shows, a placard propped on an easel saying that the Fantastic Fernando Mariachi Players were on at 11. A bar ran the full length of the other side of the room, mirrors behind it reflecting hanging amber lamps. It must cost a pretty penny in bribes to keep the joint open, but Mitch wasn't complaining.

Several of the other teams were in evidence, the Fair Harvards at the far table, a couple of guys from Comanche at another with a guy who might have been one of the Bestways pilots. One of the reservists tipped a wave to Mitch and he responded in kind, but didn't go over to join their table. Instead he slid onto one of the barstools at the far end by the empty bandstand. "Kentucky bourbon," he said. "With a dash of soda if you please."

It wasn't even raw stuff, but oaky and smooth, either left over from before the war or… Yeah, that was it.

"Seventy five cents, sir," the barman said and Mitch put it out without complaining. It was what he'd spend on a whole bottle of regular stuff, but this must be aged twenty years, sure as shooting. He took another sip, savoring the taste. Smooth, rich as amber.

"Can I get a light, stranger?" She slid onto the stool next to him without looking at his face, just meeting his eyes in the mirror behind the bar, still in the same black slacks and black blouse.

"I suppose," Mitch said, fishing out his Ronson automatic and flipping it open.

"You'll have to give me a cigarette first," Stasi said. She crossed her legs nonchalantly.

He grinned. "You don't have any?"

"Did you notice a cigarette case when you patted me down?" She held out her hand. He slid one between her fingers and she bent to light it. Her ruby nail polish was chipped, and she took a deep inhale, puckering her lips on the paper. "Oh, that's good," Stasi said. "I've been simply dying for hours, darling."

"I'm surprised you're not halfway back to LA," Mitch said.

"Well." She reached for his drink but he scooted it back out of the way.

"I don't suppose you came in here thinking that you could get one of the other teams to give you a ride along to San Angelo," Mitch said, holding his drink firmly.

"You're so suspicious."

"Let's just say I think you're resourceful."

She turned her head and gave him a brilliant smile. "That's so sweet of you!"

"Well, it must have taken a certain amount of moxie to escape the Russian Revolution," Mitch said.

"Yes, terribly," she said, arching her neck and waving for the barman. "Yoo-hoo! I'll have what he's having."

"The hell," Mitch said, but he let it ride. There are some stories worth seventy-five cents.

Stasi took another draw. "I'm sure I would have been killed if not for my Uncle Vanya. He smuggled me out of the country in a sled, darling. Simply covered in furs! We were pursued by howling wolves. It was utterly terrifying."

"In Minsk?"

"This was before Minsk, darling. We escaped down the Volga on the cutest little houseboat."

Mitch took a sip of his bourbon. "Playing the balalaika and wearing furry hats."

"Of course not." She downed half hers in a gulp. "The balalaika upsets the reindeer."

Mitch nearly inhaled his bourbon, which would be a pity, as it was way too good to inhale. "Eight of them, no doubt."

Stasi beamed. "How did you guess?"

"Traditional number for a reindeer team. Go on. I'm riveted."

"So there we were, galloping across the snow, just me and my dear Prince Andrei…"

"I thought it was Count Bezukhov in the book," Mitch observed. She gave him a dirty look over the rim of her glass and he shrugged. "I did read *War and Peace* too."

"What is it about you Americans?" Stasi demanded. "Have you all read *War and Peace*?"

Mitch shrugged. "I wouldn't think so. I read it during the war. It was about the only book in the billet, and I think the whole squadron read it twice each."

"Western Front?"

"Veneto," Mitch said, touching his glass to hers. "Over on the other end against the Austrians in Italy and the Balkans."

"Which would explain why you can find Budapest on a map," Stasi said.

"Can I?"

"I imagine you can." She shook her ash into the ashtray. "Are you really an ace?"

"Where'd you hear that?"

"One of the other teams."

"You shouldn't trust everything the other teams say," Mitch said.

She tilted her head back, dark eyes roving over his face for a moment. "I expect that's true though. Is it?"

"Yes." Mitch took another sip of his bourbon. It seemed to be disappearing very quickly. "So I gave you one truth. You give me one. Why are you still here?"

"Did you find a wallet when you were rummaging around in my pockets?" Stasi asked. "I was jumping on the plane for a moment to get the necklace back, darling. I didn't bring luggage."

"Oh." Mitch frowned. "You mean you're flat broke."

"Not a penny. No cash, nothing." Stasi took another draw and then stamped out the end of her cigarette. "Not a dime for a telegram." She looked around the other teams in the speakeasy. "I hoped someone would be…obliging."

"Oh." Mitch felt a slow flush creeping up his neck. "Well. I suppose I could let you have five dollars for the train back to LA. I mean, since it was my fault."

"Your fault?" Her eyebrows rose.

"I locked the hatch."

Her lips parted in a long, wide smile. "I suppose it was your fault at that, darling. I'd be extremely grateful. Especially since I have no place to stay."

"I don't have the necklace," Mitch said. "And I'm sharing a room with Jerry. So don't even get on that bus."

Her eyes widened. "How could you think! Why, I should be so insulted that I'd never speak to you again!"

"Before I give you the money for the train?" Mitch asked.

She smiled again, and Lord that smile was 100 watts. "After, darling. I'm only insulted after."

Mitch shook his head. "Good policy." He opened his wallet and of course there was only a ten, and it would have been awkward to ask the barman for change, never mind that it was most of what he'd figured he'd spend on the whole trip, money being tight as it was. But if they won he could afford it and if they lost they'd be so screwed it didn't matter, so he handed it over with a shrug.

Stasi frowned. "What's the extra for?"

"Breakfast," Mitch said, getting up. He drained the last of his bourbon and put the glass on the counter. "Train doesn't leave until seven. I expect you'll want some."

"Where are you going?"

"To get some sleep," Mitch said. "I've got a race to fly in the morning." She was still frowning after him when he turned the corner to the elevator at the end of the hall.

Chapter Eight

If it had been her choice, Alma thought, they'd have taken off as soon as the sun was well up, flying east into the rising light, into quiet early morning air before the promised wind came up. But the start times were set for the newspapers and the public, the first takeoff at 9:30, so that the reporters could wire their stories ahead, setting up their colleagues in San Angelo with the latest standings and gossip, and the fans had a chance to take their coffee breaks early to see the planes leave. She leaned against the hotel window, feeling the warmth already rising through the glass. A beautiful day for flying...

"Al?" Lewis put his arms around her waist, and she leaned back into his embrace.

"It's going to be a gorgeous day," she said.

He tightened his hold. "Looks it. And, I hate to say it, we should get breakfast."

Alma sighed and nodded. "Right. Are Mitch and Jerry up?"

"I don't know. I said we'd meet downstairs at seven."

Alma glanced around the room—spacious but unnaturally tidy, their bags already packed and ready for the bellhop—and nodded. "Let's go. You'll probably have to wake them, though."

To her surprise, the others were ahead of them, settled at a corner table as far from the other teams as they could manage. Lewis nodded to the guys from Comanche as they passed, and pulled out Alma's chair for her when they reached the table.

Jerry looked up from his paper long enough to nod, and Mitch said, "American got in about nine last night, and they've been working all night to make permanent repairs. Sounds like they're out of it."

"Well, that's good news for us," Alma said. The waitress appeared, and she placed her order, eggs and toast and bacon, accepted her cup of coffee with a grateful smile.

The food was good and plentiful and—best of all, to Alma's way of thinking—on the race organizers' tab. It was all too quickly finished, however, and a referee appeared to herd them onto the waiting bus. The three actresses greeted each other with hugs and giggles, posing even without the cameras watching as the bellhops loaded the bags.

"I've never been to New Orleans," one of the girls said. "It's—mysterious, isn't it?"

"Hot city, cool jazz," one of the Harvard boys said, with a cheerful grin that encompassed all of them without quite being a leer.

The girl from Consolidated shook her head. "I've been there on tour, and what I saw was hot and dirty. People selling magic dust in back alleys. Strange place."

"It's full of voodoo," another one said, drawing out the vowels. She was smaller and rounder than the others, her platinum hair carefully waved, scarlet nails to match her scarlet lips. She smiled at Mitch. "Isn't that right, Mr. Sorley?"

Mitch removed his hat. "Isn't what right, Miss James?"

"That there's voodoo in New Orleans. Black magic."

Something crossed Mitch's face like a shadow. "There's no such thing," he said, shortly, and visibly caught himself. "A lot of good music, though."

Alma linked her arm through his, not liking the change of mood. "Pity we won't have time to hit some of the clubs," she said. "I remember you sent us a telegram from New Orleans once, before you came out west. Gil laughed at all the words you spent on the music."

"Did I?" Mitch's frown deepened. "I don't really remember."

Oh, dear, Alma thought. The last thing she wanted was to make things worse. "But maybe they'll have some good bands at that party we have to go to."

She felt Mitch's arm relax under her hand. "There are plenty to choose from."

They filed aboard the bus, the Harvards leaving the front seats for Jerry and the rest of Gilchrist without making a fuss about it. Alma settled herself next to him, turning to look at Lewis and Mitch behind her. Lewis looked almost placid, and Mitch's taut expression had eased again: a good thing, Alma thought. She was flying the first leg, and had planned to have Mitch as co-pilot before he took over from the refueling stop in Albuquerque. Maybe Lewis should fly shotgun the whole way? She put the thought aside. Mitch was looking like himself again, and he was the one who could get the best out of the plane at the finish. They'd stick with the plan.

There was a small crowd gathered by the terminal, and the starlets waved gracefully to them, drawing cheers. The pilots copied them, sheepishly, and there were more cheers and clapping as the bus drew up at the entrance to the main hangar. A couple of newsreel photographers were set up, grinding away as the teams made their way off the bus. Alma clutched at her hat in the rising breeze, glad she'd worn slacks, and the starlets laughed and made a production of showing their legs while pretending to try not to. Lewis grinned appreciatively, but Mitch looked away, rolling his eyes.

"That wind's going to be a nuisance."

"If it stays," Alma said, and glanced over her shoulder at the windsock on the terminal's tower. It rose and fell, rippling gently, stretching toward the northeast. "It's a tail wind, though."

"That's something," Mitch said.

"I'll get the weather report," Lewis said, with a quick glance at Alma, and hurried away. Jerry had fallen behind as well, folding his paper into a neater package, and Alma gave Mitch a stern look.

"What's going on?" she asked.

"I'm fine," Mitch said, but he didn't meet her eyes.

"Mitch."

He sighed then, and managed a rueful smile. "I'm ok, really. Just nerves. And it was a hard day yesterday."

Alma nodded. It had been, and Mitch had been brilliant, coaxing every bit of performance out of two engines. "Lewis could take the first leg," she offered, "and I could land her."

"No," Mitch said. "No, I'm fine. I promise, Al."

She studied his face, his stance, and nodded again. "All right."

"Let's get started," he said, and sounded entirely himself again.

They ran through the preflight with practiced ease, call and response down the clipboard. Across the hangar, Alma could see American's team still working on their main engine, shook her head without comment. As far behind as they were, it had to be tempting to just drop out, spare the plane—but then, it was a company plane, and the publicity was probably worth the effort.

Across the hangar, an engine coughed to life: TWA, first in, and first out. United followed suit, and then Bestways, and then the race referee was waving at them. Alma hit the priming gun, then waved for Lewis to turn over the propellers, drawing fuel into the lines. Mitch moved the throttle back and forth, and after a moment Lewis gave a thumbs-up from outside.

"Go," Mitch said, and Alma hit the starter on the port engine. It coughed, steadied, and she started the starboard engine and then the center as Mitch adjusted the throttles. They sounded good, a solid, healthy roar, and she grinned, unable to suppress the sheer joy she felt every time she got ready for another flight. It was still hard to believe she'd been this lucky.

"All secure," Lewis reported, leaning in past the open door of the cockpit, and Mitch looked over his shoulder with a wry smile.

"Did you check the baggage compartment?"

"Twice," Lewis answered, and backed away.

The referee waved again, motioning for them to taxi out. Alma advanced the throttle and released the brakes, letting the big plane follow in Bestways' wake. As they made their way along the edge of the runway, TWA took off, rising into the sun. A few minutes later, it was United's turn, and then Bestways made the turn onto the runway. It seemed to take the Fokker forever to lift, and she frowned.

"They look heavy."

"They do," Mitch said. "Wonder if they're trying to carry extra fuel?" Or an extra body. If Miss Ivanova or whatever her name was had taken his money and not caught the train to LA. But she wouldn't try the stowaway trick twice. Surely.

"All the better for us," Alma said. The flagman waved them forward, and she turned the Terrier onto the runway, lining up into the steady breeze.

"All clear," Mitch said, and she released the brakes. The Terrier lurched into motion, the tail popping up, and she pulled back on the wheel, lifting the big plane gently into the air.

She let the Terrier climb steadily to the west, gaining altitude before she turned back, searching for the compass line. She gave the field a wide berth, seeing Comanche lift from the runway as they passed, banking into a tight turn before they were more than a few hundred feet in the air. The Ford straightened, still rising, arrowing into the rising sun. They'd gotten a jump on her with that maneuver, taking a risk she wasn't prepared to take just yet. She scowled, checking airspeed and heading, and Mitch leaned forward in his seat.

"Is that—? Damn."

Alma opened the throttle just a notch, feeling the tail wind beginning to take hold. It was rougher than she'd expected at this altitude, and she eased the wheel back, searching for calmer air higher up. It was better at nine thousand feet, just under the edges of the cloud cover they'd been warned was waiting for them.

"It'll be better at ten thousand," Mitch said.

"How's your dead reckoning?" Alma asked.

Mitch shook his head. "I'd rather have landmarks."

"The tail wind will help us," Alma said, with more confidence than she actually felt. Far ahead, sunlight glinted briefly, a hot pinpoint of light against the thickening haze. Probably Bestways, she knew, and settled herself for the long chase into Albuquerque.

They passed United three hours in, the Ford laboring at a lower altitude, and arrived over Albuquerque with no other planes in sight. She circled the field, lining up for the landing, while Mitch pressed his nose to the side window.

"One plane on the ground. Son of a bitch!"

"What?"

"That's Comanche. How the hell did they get ahead of us?"

"We'll worry about that later," Alma said, and eased the Terrier toward the runway.

They took off from Albuquerque under a cloudless blue sky, eighty-four degrees, wind out of the southwest at 8 mph—ideal flying weather. They'd been on the ground twenty-two minutes, long enough for the refueling truck and a necessary pit stop. United's Ford trimotor had landed eighteen minutes behind them, the pilot pacing around outside with his cigarette while he waited for the truck to finish with them, four extra minutes lost waiting.

Lewis hopped into the shotgun seat beside Mitch, watched him taxi and get up to altitude with a steady hand. As he circled around, turning dead east for the flight to San Angelo, Lewis craned his neck looking out over the right wing. "There's another trimotor coming in," he said. The shape was plain against the distant line of desert, even if he couldn't tell the markings. "Blue on white, maybe? It might be Consolidated's?"

Mitch shook his head, giving the Terrier a little more power.

"They'll be twenty minutes behind United," Lewis said with satisfaction. "They'll have to wait on the truck too."

"I'm not worried about who's behind me," Mitch said. "I'm worried about who's ahead of me. That damn Comanche shouldn't have passed us in the first leg!"

"They're good pilots," Lewis said. "I met that guy, Rayburn, at a Legion meeting one time. I thought he looked familiar. He was a Signal Corps pilot in France. Now he flies for the Reserves in Oklahoma. Real good pilot." Lewis shifted in his seat. "And this is his home turf." Lewis glanced out at the shapes of canyon and desert, a thousand shades of red and ochre. "I bet he knows every thermal."

"They're the team to watch," Mitch agreed. "And TWA. I don't know how they got out in front so far on the first leg."

"A little something extra in the tank," Lewis joked. "Put some moonshine in there with the aviation fuel. Just give it that little something."

"Both Ford trimotors, though," Mitch said. "We'll get them in the next leg. You wait. Tomorrow's going to be our day. We need to get as far forward in the pack as we can on this leg, and tomorrow we'll leave them in the dust. We'll pick up close to an hour not having to refuel. If we can be less than that off the lead..."

"I'm game," Lewis said. The field at Albuquerque was no longer visible. Down there on the ground the United pilot would be gnashing his teeth, wanting to get back in the air. Every minute he spent on the ground was a mile and a half they lengthened the lead. "And once we get past Little Rock, those Oklahoma guys probably won't have flown the route before either." He shaded his eyes against the sun, looking out. "I've never flown it, anyway. Have you?" He couldn't see the Comanche plane ahead, but it was awfully bright. Mitch didn't answer, and Lewis glanced at him. "Have you? Flown that route before?"

"I dunno," Mitch said. There was a crease between his brows but his sunglasses hid his eyes completely.

"You don't know?"

"After I got back from overseas I traveled around for a while," Mitch said. "Don't remember if I was in that area or not."

"You don't remember if you flew in the whole southeast?" Lewis could remember every field he'd ever landed on, clear as Alma remembered every train schedule in the US or Jerry about six dead languages.

"No, I don't remember," Mitch said shortly. "Drop it, ok?"

"Ok," Lewis said. "Sure." Everybody seemed a little cranky and out of sorts this morning. The necklace was a heavy iron weight in Lewis' pocket, and he wondered if that had something to do with it. Could a curse work even if you didn't put it on? At least make you feel bad? Maybe so. It sure gave Lewis the heebie jeebies, and that was a feeling he was learning to trust. But they'd get it back to Henry and then he could lock the thing up where it would be safe. "Hey," Lewis said, "good thing we got rid of that woman, right?"

"Yeah," Mitch said. "A good thing."

Stasi turned away from the Western Union window with a feeling of intense satisfaction . The world was a lot brighter and cheerier with a hundred dollars in her pocket rather than ten, or than $6.74 rather. Wiring for money was a godsend, but it took money to do it. Fortunately, Mitchell Sorley was a soft touch.

Stasi carefully folded the money and put it in her pocket. A change of clothes or two, a small suitcase, and the ticket for the train. Oh, and lunch. There would be time for lunch before the train left at three.

And he bought good drinks with no strings attached.

Most men had strings. Most men were made of strings, like big bouncy balls of twine that just kept on unraveling until they were completely gone.

It was a rather nice metaphor. She should remember that one and use it. The audience for those sorts of sayings were small, but worthwhile. Now, Sorley could be counted on to get it and laugh, every double entendre in it, all the way down to the truth at the bottom. She'd say it archly and he'd laugh, but he'd know exactly what she meant too, take it seriously and take her seriously even when she was being deliberately absurd. Most men either found it ridiculous or charming. The ones who thought she was ridiculous, like Dr. Ballard, tended to conclude that she was a lunatic. The others tended to have strings.

"I am a lunatic, darling," she'd say to Sorley and he'd give her that big slow smile that showed that he believed her and he didn't mind at the same time. And he'd say... what? Well, she didn't really know. Stasi stopped under the awning of the train station and frowned. That was the thing. She didn't know. Men were utterly predictable, 99% of them, whether alive or dead. But she really couldn't guess what he would say. Not that it mattered in the slightest, as she would probably never see him again.

And that was also annoying, as he was really quite a lot of fun, for a captor-cum-benefactor. But wait! Of course she would. Business would require it. The game wasn't over, and he'd probably be livid to know how neatly he'd fallen for another of her schemes. Which of course was what had happened. Livid? Or amused? Or fascinated? One could spend some time contemplating which reaction was most likely and preparing the proper crosstalk for all occasions. One couldn't do it all off the top of one's head.

Stasi pushed the door open and went up to the ticket counter. "One Pullman berth on the Sunset Express," she said.

The girl behind the counter didn't look up from her schedules. "Leaving at three ten this afternoon," she said. "Destination?"

"All the way through to New Orleans," Stasi said. Going direct, she'd beat the air race to New Orleans by at least twelve hours. And then she'd get the necklace back and it would be payday.

Chapter Nine

The Terrier flew on into the waning afternoon, the sun behind them now, the wind steady at their tail. Mitch worked his shoulders, feeling the fatigue settling into neck and back, and glanced again at the instruments. Fuel consumption was good, exactly what it should be, unlike yesterday, and the compass showed them steady on the air line into San Angelo. Lewis had the maps in his lap, folded to show the terrain they were currently passing over. He glanced out his window now and then, but his expression was relaxed, almost placid: still on course, and making good time.

"Looks like we're about seventy miles out," Lewis said, as if he'd read Mitch's mind, and Mitch nodded.

"Thanks." Mitch did the math automatically. A bit more than half an hour, give or take, factoring the tail wind's help and their lightening fuel load. He squinted at the horizon, but there was no sign of Comanche's Ford. He was still angry that Comanche had gotten ahead of them, even if he agreed with Alma that there was no point in taking risks this early in the game. Certainly not before they pulled their rabbit out of the hat in San Angelo.

It was all laid on, or at least it should be. Henry should have shipped the tank ahead of them, should have it waiting in the hangar. Installation was two, three hours' work—and they'd done it before, they knew exactly how to fit the pieces together—and then they'd be ready to make the jump from San Angelo to Little Rock without refueling. Alma figured that would gain them at least forty minutes on everybody else, maybe as much as an hour, and that would put them solidly into the lead. Assuming everything was waiting as promised, but Henry was reliable for things like that. Mostly.

He switched his attention from the horizon to the view out his window, where a dry riverbed meandered through pale and broken land. There would be a road soon, Lewis had said, and then the unmistakable brilliance of alkali flats—and there was the road, just as promised.

In the same moment, Lewis said, "There's the highway."

"Got it." Mitch banked slightly, lining the Terrier up on the thread of beaten dirt. "It takes us straight to the field," Lewis said.

"Good," Mitch answered. They'd passed Bestways about an hour out of Albuquerque, a bright speck against the blue. That had been a bit of a surprise, but a welcome one—maybe Alma had been right about them trying to carry extra fuel. Or maybe they were having engine problems. The Fokkers were notoriously cranky that way. The whys didn't matter, so long as they stayed ahead. "See anything off your side?"

Lewis shook his head. "The fueling stop spread us out pretty good."

Which was as close as Lewis was likely to get to telling him to stop asking, and Mitch swallowed his next sentence. Lewis would keep looking, right up until the minute they landed, and Mitch didn't need to tell him his job.

There were the alkali flats, and then, as promised, the road curved south, revealing the airfield and the triangle of runways. No grass here, not in this dry country, but the dirt was beaten hard and groomed for the race. Mitch circled the field once, checking the windsock and the landing strip itself, and saw the flagman waving him down. He adjusted the flaps and brought the Terrier neatly down onto the rough ground. A second flagman waved him toward one of the two hangars, and Lewis said, "We're third. Behind TWA and Comanche."

"Damn it," Mitch said, and taxied the Terrier into the hangar.

Alma undogged the hatch and lowered the stairs, the warm, machine-smelling air of the hangar swirling in. She took a deep breath, enjoying the familiar scent, and looked around for Henry or his people. TWA was in ahead of them, tucked in its corner; the guys from Comanche were still working on their plane, which meant they hadn't gotten in much before the Terrier. She turned, looking for a leader board, but the big chalkboard beside the office was still blank. She was willing to bet they'd gained some time, though.

"Alma!"

That was Henry, brushing his way past a couple of reporters and a race official.

"Nice flying," he went on. "You're only twelve minutes behind Comanche."

"We shouldn't be behind them at all," Mitch muttered, coming up behind them.

"This is their turf," Lewis said. It had the sound of an on-going argument, and Alma frowned. It wasn't like Mitch to be so down on them. "Past Little Rock, we'll be even."

Alma bit her tongue. There was no point risking a crash this early in the race, she wanted to say, especially not when they were in position to take the lead on the next leg. She looked at Henry. "Thanks. Is everything here?"

"Ready and waiting." Henry grinned, and waved toward the back of the hangar. The supplemental tank and its fittings were stacked on a wheeled pallet, ready for them to go to work, and Alma couldn't help a smile of her own.

"Thanks, Henry."

"I'll fetch it," Lewis said, and started off at a trot.

"Twelve minutes behind Comanche," Mitch said, and shook his head.

"And what behind TWA?" Alma asked.

Henry reached into his pocket, consulted a notebook. "They're thirty-five minutes ahead of Comanche, so—forty-seven minutes."

Alma nodded in satisfaction. "Right where we wanted to be."

She could hear engines outside the hangar, another plane down and in, and craned her neck to see the flagman bringing United through the open doors. Henry checked his watch.

"About twenty-five minutes there."

Lewis had collected the pallet, and he and a couple of guys in Republic coveralls were pushing it toward the Terrier, drawing sharp looks from the two other teams. Comanche's chief pilot straightened up, and a moment later he and his co-pilot had collected one of the referees. A moment later, TWA's pilots joined them, gesturing broadly, and the whole group started toward the Terrier.

"Trouble," Mitch said.

Alma shrugged, bracing herself. She hadn't really expected to get away with this without a protest, but she was sure she'd covered her bases. The pallet trundled closer, and she raised her voice to be heard over the rumble of its metal wheels. "Problems, gentlemen?"

"Possibly, Mrs. Segura," the referee said. "I'm Hiram Nichols, by the way."

Alma extended her hand. "Nice to meet you, Mr. Nichols."

"And you," Nichols mumbled, looking faintly embarrassed. "Mrs. Segura, Mr. Rayburn and Mr. Russo have both pointed out that the rules state that all participating craft must be standard—stock planes as sold by the manufacturer."

"And this is a stock part," Alma said. She could see a couple of the reporters coming closer, attracted by the unusual discussion. "The Kershaw Terrier comes with a supplemental fuel tank as well as optional cabin fittings. We're simply installing a standard part."

"Oh, come on," Rayburn said. "Nobody sells that as part of the package."

"I do," Henry said, looking smug.

"If you'll check the specs that I filed with our entrance forms," Alma said, to Nichols, "you'll find that the tank is listed as part of the standard equipment."

"I'll have to check on that, yes," Nichols said, and waved for another referee. "Bill, run back to the office, fetch our copy of Gilchrist's paperwork."

It took another hour to settle the matter, in which time Consolidated and Bestways landed, but the paperwork she had filed was clear. The supplemental tank was ruled as much a part of the Terrier's stock equipment as the passenger seats in the cabin, and its installation was approved.

"Hang on," TWA's pilot said. "Just hang on one minute, here. Ok, the rules say this is kosher, fine."

"It's pushing it," Rayburn said, and Consolidated's co-pilot, who had joined the group as soon as they'd seen what was going on, nodded in morose agreement.

Alma pasted a polite smile back on her face, spread her hands.

"It's also in the rules that all non-emergency maintenance is supposed to be done by the flight crew," Russo said. "So they can't be getting help from those guys." He pointed to the mechanics still waiting by the pallet.

"Mr. Russo is correct," Nichols said. "Mrs. Segura—"

"Of course," Alma said firmly. She'd expected that, though it had been worth the attempt—and it let the other teams feel as though they'd gotten something back. "We'll take care of it ourselves. That's not really a problem with this design."

There was a clamor from the reporters who had gathered to listen, and she shook her head.

"Sorry, boys, we've got to get to work. Mr. Kershaw can answer any questions about the plane."

"Thanks," Henry said, under his breath, but he was grinning. "Glad to help, gentlemen, if I can."

Alma put them out of her mind, turning her attention to the pallet. They'd practiced this, she and Mitch and Lewis; they could do it in about three hours, and be settled into their hotel for a good night's sleep. "All right," she said. "Lewis, grab a hoist, and let's get started."

Mitch lay on his side in the stripped cabin, a flashlight beside him as he peered down into the opening where the floor had been. The gas lines were permanent, of course, which made the job a lot easier, but the fittings had to be connected perfectly, and the valves had to be tested and re-tested. That was Alma's job—she was the best mechanic of the lot—and at the moment she and Lewis seemed to be arguing about something toward the nose of the plane, their voices muffled by the aluminum of the fuselage. Mitch let himself relax, easing himself up so that he was sitting with his back against the door of what had been the baggage compartment. The spare tank fitted neatly into that space, was bolted down and properly secured, all the access panels checked and triple-checked. And one good thing, he thought, with a sudden grin. There wasn't room for stowaways any more.

Stasi—Anastasia seemed unlikely, though less so than Rostov. His grin widened. He really shouldn't find her so charming. She was an admitted thief and a liar and she'd come close to getting them all killed, though she hadn't exactly meant to do that. But she had style, give her that, even if she did try to crib entirely too much from *War and Peace*. His hand still remembered the feel of her body through the fabric of her slacks.

He really didn't need to be thinking about her. Alma would kill him if she thought he was distracted, and Jerry would like nothing better than a reason to murder poor Stasi. He snickered in spite of himself, knowing he wasn't being fair. She wasn't Jerry's type, not in any conceivable way. Jerry liked things serious or unspoken, not embroidered. And if you were going to steal from the classics, get it right.

It was Stasi's bad luck that he'd read *War and Peace*. Not that he would have believed her in the slightest, not when her accent was Hungarian and not particularly high class at that, but—well, it was his good luck he had read it, because it was fun to let her know he knew and watch her carry on. She had a brain, that one. It was work to keep up with her.

He'd only read *War and Peace* because it was there, the only book in English in the huts at Aviano for the first four months they were stationed there. Jeff had flatly refused to read it at first—"I'm not reading anything with War in the title", he'd said—but by the second month, when the only choices were *War and Peace* and the battered *New Testament* that Coleman had left behind when he was killed, Jeff had broken down.

"Here," Mitch said, helpfully, handing him a bunch of pages. The spine had been broken to start with, and the whole thing was starting to come apart. The covers were tied in place with a twist of string. "You can read just the 'peace' parts."

"I'll do that," Jeff said.

He'd stuck to that for about a week, then started asking Mitch to fill him in on what he'd missed. Mitch obliged, though he made up more and more of it until finally Jeff sat bolt upright on his cot.

"Wait just a goddamn minute."

"What?" Mitch had gotten hold of a three-week old French newspaper, and was laboriously working his way through the shipping news for lack of anything better. He was starting to dream about the libraries back home, frustrating dreams where he wandered the stacks but couldn't find the book he wanted, or, when he did finally find it, couldn't read the smudged and alien printing.

"You said—you told me—" Jeff sputtered to a stop. "Son of a bitch. Was anything you told me true?"

"Denisov's in the cavalry," Mitch said promptly, and Jeff threw his pillow at him.

Mitch fended it off, laughing. "You're going to have to read it, Jeff. That's all there is to it."

"Son of a bitch," Jeff said again, a comprehensive epithet, but he managed to collect the rest of the book, and settled down to it.

Mitch smiled to himself, and picked up the wrench again, reaching into the gap in the floorboards to give the connector a final twist to be sure it was firmly seated. Jeff had been his closest friend in the squadron, closer even than Gil, but he'd been transferred out while Mitch was in the hospital. It was a pity he hadn't managed to go see Jeff after the war, that year that he was traveling. Even with everything he'd managed to forget from that time, he'd have remembered spending time with Jeff. Surely.

"Mitch!" That was Alma, sticking her head into the cabin, her hair held back by an untidy scarf. "Open the valves, will you? We're ready to test it."

"Right," Mitch said, glad of the distraction, and hurried to obey.

Lewis reached into the pocket of his jacket, checking again to be sure that the handkerchief-wrapped bundle was still there. It had fallen out in the elevator on the way down to the lobby, drawing curious looks from the operator and a pretty young woman in an art-silk dress, and he wasn't going to take any more chances. He found the house phone, tucked into a quiet corner of the lobby, and asked the operator for Mr. Kershaw's room.

"The Cactus Suite," the girl said. "One moment, please."

There was a long silence, and finally an unfamiliar voice said, "Mr. Kershaw's office."

"Uh." Lewis paused, regrouping. "May I speak to Mr. Kershaw, please? It's Lewis Segura."

"Oh." The stranger—one of Henry's many assistants, Lewis assumed—seemed just as taken aback. "Oh, I'm sorry, Mr. Segura, Mr. Kershaw's stepped out. I'm afraid I don't know when to expect him back."

Lewis hesitated for a moment. He couldn't really leave the necklace with a stranger, even one of Henry's employees. It would require too many explanations, and, anyway, the curse made it too dangerous. He slipped his hand into his pocket again, shoving the necklace deeper into security. "Would you ask him to call my room when he gets back?"

"Certainly." The smooth voice sharpened. "Is there a problem with the plane?"

"Not at all," Lewis said. "Tell him the tank installation went off just fine, it's all in order. I'd just like to have a word with him tonight if it's possible."

"I'll give him the message," the stranger answered, and hung up.

Lewis replaced his own receiver more slowly, wondering if he needed to do more. Leave Henry a note, maybe? No, if that got out, it would just make trouble—and he didn't really trust any of the hotels' staff, not with the pack of reporters following the race, all ready to offer a five-spot for anything remotely scandalous. They'd have to catch Henry later.

Henry slid onto the stool at the counter of the little diner around the corner from the Cactus Hotel, responded with a nod and a smile when the waitress offered coffee. She brought it and the menu, and he barricaded himself behind it, grateful to have a moment of quiet and relative privacy. Big fans were turning on the wall behind the counter, and the lights were dimmed, which at least gave the illusion of cool. The Cactus Hotel had actual air conditioning in its lower lobby, but right now he needed to get away from anything related to the race.

He craned his neck to check the specials chalked on the blackboard—meatloaf and two sides, baked ham ditto, green chili pie—then turned back to the menu. He didn't really care what he ate, something hot and wholesome and maybe a slice of pie, just enough to take his mind off what the Gilchrist team was up to. They knew what they were doing, he knew that. He'd seen them install the tank and pull it out, practicing in the hangar at his house in the hills until they were all confident the switch would go smoothly. Still, he couldn't stop worrying. He wanted to be back at the field, watching from a distance since the referees had ruled he couldn't help, but Alma was right, his being there would just raise doubts. He could safely leave it to them.

He ordered a hamburger steak and a slice of the cherry pie, then unfolded the paper he'd bought in the hotel lobby, scanning the headlines. It was the afternoon edition, and the coverage of the race was excellent, a big story above the fold, a stop press box giving the first three arrivals, and another box promising full coverage in the next issue. We'll give them something to talk about, all right, he thought, and accepted a refill for his coffee. The waitress brought his plate, and he applied himself to the food, trying not to think about what was happening at the hangar. The wires would already be humming.

"Hey, Mr. Kershaw." Carmichael slid onto the stool next to him, raising one finger to the waitress. "Just coffee, Toots, thanks. Black."

The waitress slapped the heavy china mug down in front of him, filled it with the last of the pot, and stalked away. Carmichael shook his head in mock sorrow.

"There is no pleasing some dames."

There was no good answer to that, and Henry waited, chewing another bite of mashed potatoes that was suddenly, unaccountably tasteless.

"So how's the food?"

"Good," Henry said. It was both polite and true, but he still didn't feel safe saying it.

Carmichael slurped at his coffee, nodded once. "Not bad. I like it better with a little chicory in it myself—just like they make it at Café du Monde. Black coffee with chicory and a plate of beignets. There's nothing like that anywhere else."

Henry made a noncommittal noise, and took another bite of his steak.

"But that's not the point," Carmichael said, after a moment. "Clever girl, your Mrs. Segura. Or Gilchrist. That's a pretty smart trick she pulled there."

"I try to hire people with brains," Henry said.

"I'm a little surprised the referees let her get away with it," Carmichael said. "Seems kind of like cheating to me."

Henry put on his best smile. "Come on, Mr. Carmichael. I not only built that plane and the supplemental tank, I designed it that way. It's a stock part, included in every Terrier we sell. You can't expect me to say it's not kosher."

"Well, no, I wouldn't expect that," Carmichael agreed. "It's just whether the public will see it that way."

Henry's eyes narrowed, but he made himself finish his last bite of hamburger before he spoke. "I don't know, seems to me that the public appreciates a smart move."

"People don't much like trick plays," Carmichael said. "That's why they're illegal."

"Except that this move is legal," Henry said. "The referees said so. As long as they install the tank themselves—and I'd think that would be enough of a handicap for anybody—Gilchrist can use it. And you know as well as I do that it doesn't guarantee anything."

He nodded to the waitress, who took his plate and replaced it with the slice of pie, the cherries and syrup spilling deep red across the chipped plate.

"True. It'd just be a shame if the public took it wrong." Carmichael beckoned to the waitress. "Say, I'll have a slice of that, too." He waited until she slapped it in front of him to say, "Funny thing about Mrs. Gilchrist—I mean, Segura. I was kind of getting the impression it should have been Mrs. Sorley."

So that's the game, Henry thought. Give me more gossip, or Winchell will make your team look bad. Winchell could, too, and with his audience… It was a chance he couldn't afford to take.

"Or Mrs. Ballard," Carmichael said.

"Ballard's a rolling stone," Henry said carefully. "He's not really the marrying kind."

"Mrs. Segura seems fond of him."

"They've known each other a long time," Henry said. "He and her first husband knew each other in the war."

"I thought that was Mr. Sorley," Carmichael said.

"Him, too," Henry said, and hoped he wasn't getting them all into a tangle. "I think if Alma had wanted to marry Sorley, she could have had him any time."

"So instead she marries some Mexican nobody?" Carmichael shook his head. "Who was she trying to spite?"

"Segura's one hell of a pilot," Henry said. That, at least, was absolutely true. The rest… He chose his words with painful care. "I don't think Alma could stand being married to someone who wasn't a pilot, and Segura—well, like I said, he's good. She'd marry a man because of it."

"Huh. Women." Carmichael looked down at his plate, the casual words not quite disguising his sudden eagerness. "There's no telling, is there?"

"Nope," Henry said. He hoped he'd done more good than harm, though if Alma found out—when Alma found out, he corrected dispiritedly—he was going to have some more fast talking to do to keep her from hitting him. It wouldn't be a lady-like slap, either, but a solid roundhouse, and he probably deserved it.

"Well, thanks for the pie," Carmichael said. "I'll be seeing you around."

Henry swore under his breath, recognizing that he'd been stuck with Carmichael's bill as well as his own. Still, he had—he hoped—defused Carmichael's threat, given him enough gossip to distract him and by then Henry could put a word in some other reporters' ears, talk up how smart Gilchrist was, how plucky... He turned over his bill and Carmichael's, reached in his pocket to count out two bits, plus a nickel tip. Time to start calling in some favors of his own.

The passenger competition tonight was a trivia contest, sponsored by a group of local businesses and held in the ballroom of the Cactus Hotel. It was an impressive building, fourteen stories tall, and if the rooms were anything like the public spaces, Jerry wasn't going to complain about the accommodations. The ballroom stretched the full width of the third floor, Romanesque arches supporting a rounded ceiling hung with a trio of massive crystal chandeliers. To the left of the stage, the arches held floor-to-ceiling windows, their velvet drapes drawn against the rising dusk; to the right, French doors gave access to the hotel proper. At the moment, the ballroom was about three-quarters full, the sponsors and their wives and various local dignitaries who'd paid for what looked like a decent dinner sitting at little round tables toward the front, while fans and gawkers and the less enthusiastic of the reporters filled the rows of chairs that stretched toward the back of the room.

The more enthusiastic ones—including Winchell's stringer, who supposedly had hired a private plane to follow the race on his own—were crouched at the base of the stage, pressed up against the curtains that hid the temporary platform's somewhat rickety underpinnings. One of RKO's cameras was grinding away at the side of the stage, but everyone's attention was on the man at the center of the stage. Charlie Bolton was in his element, ten-gallon hat pushed back on his head, a fistful of index cards in his hand, bouncing back and forth in front of the three big radio microphones. The contest was going out live on KGKL and a network of NBC stations, one of the girls had said, and Jerry had tried to forget that as soon as he'd heard it. The idea of making a fool of himself on nation-wide radio had been enough to make him feel faintly queasy.

Luckily, though, the questions hadn't been anything too hard, at least not yet, and while Bolton was quick to tease the girls, he'd stopped short of anything too harsh. He was also taking plenty of time to talk up the local businesses and TexAv Gasoline, the race's main sponsor, and Jerry took a deep breath, willing himself to relax. The first prize was a hundred dollars and fifteen minutes off the team's time, and he thought he had a decent shot at it.

The girls from American and TWA were the first to be eliminated, followed shortly by Consolidated, who managed a sassy exit line that Jerry knew would be repeated in every paper across the country. Miss Gray was doing no harm at all to her career.

The next round of questions were civics-class standards, and eliminated two more, leaving him with Mrs. Jezek, the girl from Bestways, and May Saltonstall. Mrs. Jezek was eliminated on what should have been an easy horse-racing question—*but why would you name a horse Onion?* she asked, and drew a sympathetic laugh—and Miss Bestways failed to spell "halleluiah" correctly.

"And that leaves Dr. Jerry Ballard of Gilchrist Aviation and Miss May Saltonstall of Crimson Air," Bolton announced. "It's the battle of the brains, folks, but first—have you heard about the new Black and White Grocery opening over on Pruesser Street?"

He slid smoothly into the advertisement, swapping index cards with practiced zeal, and Jerry gave Miss Saltonstall a wry smile. She smiled back, grey eyes very determined, and said, "No hard feelings, Dr. Ballard."

"None at all, Miss Saltsonstall," Jerry answered, and felt his attention sharpen.

The next round of questions was straight American history, details of the Revolution and the Civil War, and they swapped answers through the series, neither one missing a question. There was applause when they'd finished, led by Bolton.

"What'd I tell you, folks? The battle of the brains! Dr. Ballard's a professor and Miss Saltonstall just graduated from Radcliffe College—but let me tell you, boys, she doesn't look like a brain!" Bolton shuffled his index cards again. "And it's on to the next round. The subject— oh, dear, Miss Saltonstall. It's baseball."

May leaned in closer to the microphone, her hands clasped behind her back like a little girl's. "Well, that may be a tough subject, Mr. Bolton, but I'll give it the old college try."

Jerry kept his smile bland and polite, but his attention sharpened. He'd heard the tone before, and he wasn't going to be suckered.

"I'm sure you will," Bolton said. "Miss Saltonstall had the last correct question, so it's over to you, Dr. Ballard. Can you tell me which pitcher set a record for most saves in a season, back in 1926?"

"Firpo Marberry," Jerry answered. He'd been a fan as a kid, but Ruth and the long ball had ruined the game as far as he was concerned. He had a feeling he was going to wish he'd paid more attention when Mitch and Lewis had the games on the radio.

"Correct!" Bolton said. "Miss Saltsonstall, can you name either of the two teams who were the first to put numbers on their players' uniforms—purely for the benefit of the fans, we're sure, not the umpires."

"The New York Yankees," she said. "And the Cleveland Indians."

"Correct on both counts, Miss Saltonstall!" Boltson beamed at her. "I might even think you were a fan yourself."

"I am from Boston, Mr. Bolton," May said, primly.

Jerry swallowed a profane comment. She wasn't just from Boston. She was a Boston fan, a Royal Rooter to the core, and he hadn't been giving baseball his serious attention since about 1924… He held his smile steady with an effort, and hoped he wasn't about to lose too badly.

"Dr. Ballard," Bolton said. "What did Ty Cobb do for the last time in his career on June 15th, 1928?"

Jerry took a careful breath. He did remember this one. Cobb might be a bastard, but he played the game the way it was meant to be played. "He stole home, Mr. Bolton."

"Indeed he did," Bolton said. "Miss Saltonstall!"

They went back and forth twice more, Jerry struggling, May quietly confident. He remembered the year the Yankees won their first World Series, dredged up the name of the Brooklyn pitcher who hit a home run in his first major-league at bat. May countered with the name of the pitcher who beaned—and killed—Ray Chapman, and, with a wince, named the Red Sox as the team that lost 107 games in 1926.

"And the last question, for Dr. Ballard," Bolton said. "Name the American League's home run leader in 1925."

Jerry paused. It had to be Ruth, surely. He'd won that title year after year, and he wasn't showing much sign of slowing down. "Babe Ruth?"

"Oh! Sorry, Dr. Ballard. It was not the Babe." Bolton turned to May, still waiting with her hands behind her back. "Miss Saltsontall. If you can answer this question correctly, you win one hundred dollars for yourself and fifteen minutes off the elapsed time. Take a deep breath, that's a lot of new shoes!"

May gave him a rather distant smile. "It wasn't Ruth, but it was a Yankee, Mr. Bolton. Bob Muesel."

"Absolutely correct! Miss Saltsonstall is our winner, folks, with a gritty performance. That's one hundred dollars for you, and fifteen minutes for the team!"

Jerry offered his hand in congratulations, and May shook it, grinning openly now.

"Well played," he said.

"Thanks."

Flashbulbs went off all around them, capturing the moment, and Jerry fought to keep his smile. He'd get fifty dollars out of this, and ten minutes off the team time; Alma would be pleased, and the Harvards were seventh out of nine, so fifteen minutes wouldn't do them too much good. But—he truly hated Babe Ruth.

Chapter Ten

You would be so beautiful, it whispered. So beautiful.

The necklace lay on the bed where it had spilled from Lewis' jacket pocket, iron lace against the matelasse bedspread. It looked just like that, like black lace over white skin. She'd seen a very daring set of combinations once, black lace with no backing, so that every inch supposedly covered was actually rendered all the more shocking, peeking through the fine tracery. Even the bottoms were lace, and she hadn't been able to help wondering if one was supposed to shave beneath it, so that everywhere there was the gleam of marble half veiled.

Alma felt her face heat. The necklace was like that, but you could wear it in public. It was perfectly decent. It would only be your throat that showed like that, only your throat that promised hidden pleasures. Surely it wouldn't hurt to wear it just once. Henry wouldn't mind.

Henry wouldn't... There was something about Henry. Alma blinked. Henry said something about the necklace...

That it was beautiful. That it was lost. He said it made any woman who wore it beautiful.

Alma picked it up, feeling the cool links in her fingers, curved like soft, waiting skin. She could put it on, look at herself in the mirror. It begged to be dragged over skin, begged to lie cold against sensitive places...

She lifted the necklace up, feeling the weight in her hands. She could just put it on for a moment. Henry wouldn't mind.

Henry...

It was hard to remember what Henry had said. Something about not giving it to Mabel. Something about the necklace.

It was like pushing through dark water.

There was a curse. The necklace was cursed and every woman who wore it died by violence.

Her hands shook and Alma dropped the necklace, falling like thunder against the white bedspread.

Her head was clear. "Oh, God," Alma whispered. She'd come so close to putting it on, so close. She got up and crossed the room, not even wanting to touch it, not even through a piece of cloth or something. Its attraction was too fatal. Instead she opened the door and went across the hall, knocking on the door opposite. "Jerry?"

Jerry opened the door a moment later, his jacket off but his glasses still on his nose. "What's wrong?" he asked, frowning at the tone of her voice.

"That is," Alma said, gesturing to the necklace on the bed. "I can't be around it right now. Can you take it?"

Jerry didn't ask questions. He just plunged across the hall, taking out his silk handkerchief and carefully gathering it up in it. Once it was inside the insulating silk where she couldn't see it Alma breathed a sigh of relief. "Better?" Jerry asked. He looked concerned.

Alma nodded. Out of sight, out of mind. "That thing is powerful," she said. "I nearly put it on."

Concern flared in his eyes, and Jerry put his arm around her. "You didn't, though?"

"Not quite," Alma said. "Not quite." She took another breath, glad of the solidity of his arm, of his rock-solid psychic strength. "Jerry, I don't know what I'd do without you."

Jerry's face suddenly went grim. Beyond her through the open door one of the reporters was watching avidly. "Get the hell out!" Jerry said.

"Mrs. Segura and Dr. Ballard," the reporter said. "More than just friends? A tender scene in a hotel room seems to suggest…"

Jerry slammed the door in his face.

"Not again," Alma said, burying her face in her hands. "Am I having an affair with you or with Mitch?"

"Both of us," Jerry said. For some reason he looked amused.

"I have no idea what's funny," Alma snapped.

"I was just thinking that Gil would think this was the funniest thing in the world," Jerry said and squeezed her again.

"That he would," Alma said, resting her hand against his

shoulder. "Oh, that he would!"

He held her for a moment longer, but she could feel his weight shift as he looked around the room. "Where's Lewis?"

"He wanted to talk to Rayburn—the guy from Comanche," Alma said. "I think he said he was taking Mitch with him."

"I thought he was going to give the necklace back to Henry this afternoon."

"He was," Alma said. "But Henry wasn't in his room, and he didn't want to leave it with the secretary."

"No," Jerry said fervently. He fished in his pocket for his watch. "Well, let's get rid of the damned thing now. I'll just call his room, and he can come down and collect it himself." He released her, went to the phone as he spoke, and she heard him ask for the Cactus Suite.

"What?" Jerry's voice and eyebrows rose together. "Oh. Ok. Thank you." He hung the receiver back on the stick, shaking his head. "Henry's left. He checked out this evening."

"To catch the New Orleans train," Alma said. "Of course he'd have to. I should have thought of that."

Jerry reached into his pants pocket, closing his hand over the wrapped necklace. "We'll see him in New Orleans. Do you want me to keep this until then?"

"Yes," Alma said. "Please."

Lewis eased his key into the room lock, hoping he wouldn't wake Alma. He hadn't meant to spend quite so much time talking to Rayburn, but they'd been stationed along the same part of the front, though not at the same time, and that had broken the ice. At least Rayburn wasn't taking the business with the supplemental tank personally—he wasn't happy, but he wasn't holding a grudge. That had seemed to disappoint a couple of the reporters, but Rayburn's co-pilot had told them in no uncertain terms to get lost, and they'd spend another half hour griping about the newspapers and the radio. But that's what paid for the race, they'd agreed, and Lewis came away feeling as though he'd at least kept from making an enemy.

To his surprise, the bedside light was still on. Alma sat up against the headboard, book in her lap, but she looked up alertly as he closed the door behind him, laying the book face down on the sheets. The title glowed yellow against the green background, above the stylized image of a man and a woman in an expensive convertible beneath a full moon: *Kept Woman*. Given the gossip, Lewis thought, it seemed a bit too appropriate. Except that nobody kept Alma.

"I didn't think you'd still be up," he said, and shrugged off his coat.

"I couldn't seem to get to sleep," Alma answered.

There was an odd note in her voice that made him look sharply at her. "Everything all right?" He reached for his flight jacket as he spoke, slipping his hand into the pocket where he'd put Henry's necklace, and found only empty silk.

"It's not there," Alma said. "I asked Jerry to take it." There was definite color in her cheeks, but she met his eyes squarely. "I almost put it on earlier tonight."

"But you didn't," Lewis said.

Alma shook her head. "It—wanted me to."

"It's strong," Lewis said. He hesitated, but he owed her his story, after she'd given him hers. "The curse—Henry was right, I think. There certainly seems to be one. I was looking at it, and all I wanted was to see it around your neck. Luckily, something—She stopped me." He shivered in spite of the room's warm air. "Henry said every woman who wore it died."

"It wants to kill," Alma said. She shook her head. "And it wanted me to put it on. It was—very persuasive."

The color was back in her cheeks, an unsual blush. Lewis sat beside her on the bed, and after a moment, she leaned into him.

"I feel stupid."

"Don't," Lewis said. "If it hadn't been for Her, Her hand—I'd probably have asked you to try it on, and that—" He couldn't bring himself to finish. "I should probably get it back from Jerry."

"I'd rather you didn't." Alma's color deepened, but she forged on. "I don't want to be around that thing right now."

Lewis hesitated. "I was thinking that She, Diana, might be some protection—"

"I'm sure She is," Alma said. "But I still nearly put it on. I don't want to have to worry about it, not with the race to think about."

And that was fair. Jerry would certainly be able to keep it safe. After all, he was trained, he knew what he was doing. Lewis closed his eyes, wondering how a curse like this could be broken, how it had come into being in the first place. For a moment, the room's light dimmed and wavered, like the light of candles streaming in a steady breeze. Men in green uniforms trimmed with red and gold swept through the parlor of a house, while a woman shrieked in the corner, blood staining the front of her thin white dress. Hate rolled from her like heat from a furnace, hate and desperate fury, sweeping over them deadly as chlorine gas, to gather at last in a strand of iron…

He shuddered, and Alma laid a hand on his arm. "Are you all right?"

He nodded. "Yeah. But the sooner we get that thing back to Henry, the happier I'll be."

"Me, too," Alma said. "Me, too."

In the morning the bus brought them back to the airfield in good time, drawing up in front of the terminal where a small crowd was already waiting. There were more adult men than Mitch would have expected for a weekday morning, and he wondered just how many of them had jobs to go to. The local paper hadn't exactly been encouraging—the front page had held three articles on the race and the money it was bringing in, but the fourth big article had been the closing of an ore processing company, the third to go out since the previous January. They mostly seemed happy, though, and there were quite a few kids—who surely ought to be in school—among the adults, so maybe they were just taking a holiday.

All around him, the actresses were drawing themselves up, giving themselves the little bounce that settled them into their on-camera personalities, and Mitch tested a smile. Alma smiled back, but Lewis just looked grave. He wasn't flying today, and that always made him nervous; Jerry looked tired and cranky—he hated losing—but even as Mitch met his eyes, Jerry straightened, his face easing into something that resembled equanimity. They were last off the bus, to spare Jerry's leg, but they got a nice cheer anyway, an announcer with a bullhorn calling their names.

"—Gilchrist Aviation. Pilot and owner Alma Gilchrist Segura, decorated pilot Lewis Segura, Great War ace Mitchell Sorley and passenger Dr. Jerry Ballard."

Alma smiled and waved just like the starlets, and Mitch made himself do the same, grateful to finally duck into the shelter of the hangar. He was beginning to hate the casual way the race promoters called him an ace. It hadn't been so bad right after the War, because then everyone remembered exactly what it meant. An ace was a man with at least five kills, five dead men or more; Mitch had seven, and he remembered every one.

"Right," Alma said, hands on her hips. "Lewis, get us fueled up—make sure they get the supplemental tank full. Jerry, is there anything for passengers this morning?"

"Not that they've told us," Jerry said.

"Good," Alma said. "Ward off the reporters, will you? Mitch and I will start the preflight."

Mitch nodded, and Alma's gaze slid past him, fixing on something behind him. Mitch turned to see the referee coming to join them, and Alma sighed.

"Scratch that. Mitch, would you take the preflight? It looks like Mr. Nichols wants a word."

"Sure," Mitch said, and climbed aboard. He didn't really mind doing the preflight check on his own. He liked having time with the plane, time to think through the flight plan, and he settled himself easily into the pilot's seat. The leather was starting to come unstitched along the inner edge of the seat back, where everyone grabbed and pulled as they climbed in. They'd want to get that fixed, once it was over. He could get Frank the saddler out from town to take care of it, look over the rest of the planes at the same time...

He shook the thought away, and made himself pick up the clip-board. By now, he could do the routine in his sleep, but it was better to have the check. He went down the list, trying to concentrate, but the announcer's words kept coming back. Mitchell Sorley, ace. Well, that's what he was. He had the medal and the citations to prove it, seven kills in the air over Italy. And the Austrians were damn good—the best of them had trained with the German *jadgstaffelen*, and come back to teach their own squads the same methods, and they were flying the best planes they could get their hands on, just the same as everyone else.

They burned like everyone else, too. He'd had a knack for fire, though he never meant to aim for the fuel tanks. Five of the seven went down in flames, and nobody carried parachutes. Two of the pilots jumped, pinwheeling black against the sky to vanish in the trenches; the rest stayed with the burning mess, though he thought most of them were already dead. One had fought it all the way down, trailing smoke and flame, but he'd died before they could pull him from the wreck. Gil had said he couldn't have lived, but that was still the one that bothered Mitch the most. All that effort, slipstreaming, turning, fighting the air to keep the flames at bay, and for nothing. The Italian pilots had called him Il Incendario, the Arsonist, behind his back, and the Americans had called him the Fireman to his face until Gil put a stop to it. Jeff—Jeff had managed to smash the squadron's record of The Firemen's Rag, and Mitch would be in his debt forever for that one.

He had wondered, after he was wounded, when he knew he was going to live and he had all the time in the hospital to think about it, if it was payback. Karma. There were worse things than burning.

"Got the weather?" Alma asked, sliding into the co-pilot's seat, and for an instant Mitch couldn't remember what the sky had been like that morning, could see only the cold blue of Italy. Cold blue, and the bright golden-brown of the enemy planes, each with its own heraldry, skull and crossbones and a knight's plumed helmet and a six-pointed star... "Mitch?"

It was cloudy out. He remembered that with a gasp. The sky here in San Angelo was covered with thin, pale clouds that would follow them east, though the forecast in the newspaper said the rain would peter out before it reached Little Rock. He made a show of looking at the clipboard, and shook his head. "I haven't seen the latest."

"Lewis will get it," she said, and slid back the side window to call to him. Lewis lifted a hand in acknowledgement, and a few minutes later, Jerry brought the sheet up to the cockpit.

"They're just about ready," he said, handing it over, and in the same moment the referees shouted for the leaders to start their engines.

"Are you ok?" Alma asked.

Mitch grimaced. "Yeah. I'm fine."

She gave a long look, honestly assessing, and Mitch forced himself to meet her look with a smile.

"I promise," he said. "I can handle it."

She hesitated a moment longer, then nodded. "Ok."

The Terrier was heavy with the extra fuel, soggy on its wheels, waddling awkwardly into the turn that lined them up on the runway. Mitch eyed the length of it uneasily as he waited for the flag. It should be more than adequate, but the air was still and the weight of the supplemental tank sat uncomfortably toward the tail. Alma was frowning, too, making the same calculations, and Mitch gave her a shrug. It would be enough or it wouldn't. He thought it would be. Just.

The flagman waved them on, and Mitch pushed the throttles forward, bringing up the power as quickly as he dared. The Terrier rumbled forward, the big engines howling; the tail lifted, and dropped again, and Mitch looked at the airspeed indicator. Close, but not there, not enough. He cursed the lack of headwind. If he couldn't get more out of her, if he couldn't get the tail to lift—They were almost at the point of no return, fly or die, crashing ignominiously off the end of the runway.

"Come on," he said, under his breath. The speed was creeping up, the tail starting to lift. "Come on."

"Mitch," Alma said, quietly.

Now or never. Mitch ignored the airspeed, concentrating on the feel of the plane under him, the air on the wings. They were almost there, almost ready, the engines full open—and they were almost at the end of the graded strip. He felt the power building finally, the wings catching lift, the whole body lightening at last, and he eased back on the yoke just as the wheels left the graded dirt. The Terrier wobbled and flew.

He kept the angle shallow, catching his breath, letting the plane steady under them. It was a good thing they were in the desert, not someplace with trees ringing the field, or telephone lines... But they were up and flying, the airspeed rising now, and he tugged the yoke back just a hair, increasing the angle of climb to something a bit more normal. She was still heavy, still awkward, but that would improve as the extra fuel burned off, and they wouldn't be landing again until Little Rock.

"Well," Alma said. Mitch glanced at her, and saw her crooked smile. She tapped his shoulder in answer. "Nice flying."

Comanche's Ford was a silver dot in the distance, a speck of fire when the sun caught the bare metal of the fuselage. They were overtaking it, Mitch thought. Not as fast as he would like, but the fuel was burning off in the supplemental tank, and he could see the airspeed creeping up. TWA was further ahead, out of sight in the haze that thickened the eastern horizon, but TWA was a Ford. They didn't quite have the range they needed to reach Little Rock on a single tank of gas.

"Where do you think they'll stop?" he asked, and Alma looked up from the map and clipboard.

"Dallas. Maybe Texarkana, but if I was TWA—I'd go light on the first leg, try to build a lead, and then be first to refuel."

That made sense. Take off with the lightest fuel load possible to get them to Dallas, flying at full throttle, then be first in line so that they spent only the minimum time on the ground. The TWA team knew Gilchrist could make the jump without stopping, but they'd be slower at the beginning, burdened with the extra fuel and the tank. At worst, they'd end up second, still within striking distance.

"I'd be more worried about the Fokkers," Alma went on, "except I'm pretty sure Bestways doesn't have the range. The Harvard boys might, but even if they try it, I don't think they can make up the time."

"McIsaac might take the chance," Mitch said. The ex-rumrunner would know how to get the most out of his machine, that much was certain.

"And if they don't, they'll at least try to stretch it to Texarkana," Alma said. "At least, that's what I'd do."

"Yeah."

They were coming up on Dallas. Beneath the wing, the road that was their landmark had acquired more houses, more settlement, the long rectangles of cultivated land. Ahead, Comanche's Ford had taken on shape, wings and fuselage distinctly visible. The Terrier was overtaking more rapidly now, and a moment later the Ford tipped sideways, banking into the turn that would take it down to the field at Dallas. One down.

And maybe two, if Alma was right and TWA had tried running fast and light. It was possible that TWA was refueling right now, that they were passing over them at this very moment... Mitch narrowed his eyes as though that would help him see more clearly, and Alma picked up the binoculars she kept in the pocket beside her seat.

"Anything?" Mitch asked.

She was silent for a long moment, balancing the binoculars lightly in her hand to minimize the vibrations, but then she shook her head. "I don't see anything. Which doesn't mean—"

"I know," Mitch said.

The port engine coughed once, and caught, then coughed again.

"Time to switch over," Alma said.

"Yeah." Mitch reached for the controls, cutting off the lines that led to the rear tank, waiting a heartbeat, and opening the lines to the main tanks. They probably could have waited a little longer, but there was no point in losing performance to drain the dregs. There was plenty of fuel on board to get them into Little Rock.

Beneath them, the land changed again, the houses thinning, then becoming farmsteads set in fields not yet green with spring. Some of them wouldn't be, Mitch thought, banking to catch the next road that was his target. This was ranching country, not the kind of farmland he'd known as a boy. It looked brown and barren; if there were cattle there, he didn't see them.

The sun was behind them now, and Alma lifted the glasses to scan the sky ahead without result. Off the port wing, a line of darker green marked a river, and Mitch banked to run parallel with it for a while. Beneath them, the land slowly changed again, brown giving way to green, the familiar patchwork of fields.

"Texarkana," Alma said, and pointed.

There were buildings beneath the wing, and, on the roof of someone's barn, the arrow and compass pointing toward the airport. Mitch glanced at the clipboard instead, and turned gently onto the heading that would bring them into Little Rock. About a hundred and forty miles, give or take. An hour and a bit before they knew if anyone had found a way to beat them. TWA couldn't, not in a Ford, not with the narrow lead they had. Refueling would eat up every minute of their advantage. Even so, it took all Mitch's willpower not to advance the throttle, pour on the power to get them in any minutes sooner. Haste made waste, literally in this case. Alma had worked out the optimum speed, and he would hold to it.

Below them, the ground was wooded, hilly. The race route suggested following a state highway, but there was no sign of it, no obvious break in the woods. Mitch looked at the compass again, making sure he was on the right line, then back at the ground. Still nothing.

"I don't see the highway," he said.

"I don't either," Alma answered.

The choice was obvious: cast around for the landmark or follow the compass bearings and hope for the best. "We'll pick it up later," Mitch said, and hoped it was true.

The trees crawled past beneath the wing. Now and then a field appeared, pale between the groves, a mule straining against the traces of an old plow.

"There," Alma said, and pointed.

Dust rose between two stands of trees, trailing behind a battered Model A.

"You think that's our road?" Mitch asked. The bearing looked all right, but…

"Yes," Alma said, with a firmness that Mitch suspected hid an uncertainty that matched his own. Still, it was the best bet they had, and he banked the Terrier to line up on the narrow strip of gravel.

An hour passed, the road snaking beneath them, still on the right bearing for Little Rock. Another ten minutes, and Alma pointed ahead, where a clump of buildings rose out of the trees.

"Arkadelphia."

Mitch glanced at the fuel gauges again, turning the numbers over in his head. They were making better time than he'd expected, had more fuel left than he'd thought, and he advanced the throttle another notch. For a second, he thought Alma was going to scold, but instead she nodded.

"Now's the time," she said, and he let it out another notch. The sound of the engines changed, deepened, and he watched their air-speed creep up again.

And then at last they saw it, the first buildings on the city's western edge. The field was on the eastern side; Mitch put them into a slow descent, and Alma squirmed in her seat, scanning the sky with the binoculars.

"I don't see anything," she said. "But there's the tower."

"Yeah." Mitch banked the Terrier, bringing her in low and steady to circle the field, wagging his wings to request the landing. A flagman broke from the tower, ran toward the longest of the grass-covered strips. Behind him, Mitch caught of glimpse of stands, not quite full, but certainly occupied, and then the flagman was waving them down. The windsock hung limp on the tower, barely twitching; he lined up in that general direction, centered on the landing strip, and let the Terrier find her own way down.

The flagman steered them off the landing strip—not toward the hangars, Mitch realized, but toward the terminal and the waiting grandstand. Behind him, the cockpit door opened, and Lewis leaned in, bracing himself on the door frame.

"There's nobody on the leader board."

Alma grinned, crossing her fingers, and the flagman waved them to a stop. Mitch set the brakes, and cut the engines, and in the sudden silence there was a noise he identified after a moment as cheering from the crowd. Lewis disappeared again, and there was the rattle of the stairs going down. Alma hauled herself out of her seat, and Mitch followed, blinking in the relative dark of the cabin. Lewis stepped back, letting Alma out first, and there was another cheer from the crowd. Mitch worked his shoulders, suddenly aware of the work he'd put in, the stiffness in his back and belly, and climbed after her, Lewis and Jerry trailing behind. A man in a race referee's blazer beamed at them from the edge of the paved area beside the terminal.

"Congratulations, Mrs. Segura, gentlemen! You're first in!"

Mitch glanced over his shoulder, automatically checking the sky, but there was no sign of another plane. They'd done it, then, thanks to Alma.

The referee was rattling on, "And you're likely to be the only ones in for a while. TWA left Dallas at noon, and Texarkana just phoned to say someone buzzed the tower. They couldn't quite make out the markings, I'm afraid—" He broke off as a boy came running with a slip of paper, took it and scanned the penciled scribble. "But they do say they have Harvard in sight and coming in to land."

Mitch closed his eyes. They were going to come out in first, that was the main thing; even if it was TWA who were passing Texarkana, they were still more than an hour out, more like an hour and a half. Gilchrist had started the day only forty minutes behind the leader. Alma's grin was blinding.

"If you don't mind, Mrs. Segura," the referee said, "I know the folks in the stands—and the boys from the papers—would like a few words from you."

Alma's smile was fierce. "We'd be delighted."

Mitch dredged up a smile of his own, and followed.

Chapter Eleven

It was roulette again, another giant wheel turned by girls in pretty dresses, though this time they wore demure white ball gowns and diamanté clips in their determinedly waved hair. The ballroom was hung with swags of red and white, pinned with bright blue rosettes, and the women passengers had been given matching blue corsages. Jerry and Jed Pelletier had been given scarlet boutonnieres, and Pelletier fingered his warily when he thought no one was looking. Probably he hadn't worn flowers since his wedding, Jerry thought. If then.

He was feeling a bit light-headed himself. They'd won the stage by just over two hours, for a net lead of fifty-two minutes, and that had meant two hours for the reporters to swarm them, bombarding them all with questions about the supplemental tank and how in the world Alma had thought of it. Some of it had been genuinely admiring, and some had been barbed, none-too-subtle hints that this was close to cheating. Alma had handled it all admirably, Lewis glowering at her side but smart enough not to say anything in complaint, but this was one time Henry's jovial presence would actually have done some good. Except Henry had gone on to New Orleans along with most of the other sponsors, and the teams were left to fend for themselves. He was just glad that this stop didn't involve another trivia contest.

On the other hand, the organizers in Little Rock had been determined to make it more than a contest of mere luck. Each space on the wheel held a prize donated by a local business—a cabinet radio from O.K. Houck, a fur coat, a jewelry set, a fancy wristwatch, plus cash amounts ranging from ten dollars up to a hundred dollars—as well as a hidden time bonus; if you didn't like what you'd gotten, you could swap your prize with someone else's. The catch was that the time wouldn't be revealed until everyone had had their turn, and all the trades were made.

At least there were two fewer teams to worry about now. Both Consolidated and Bestways had had engine problems that dropped them back with American; Alma thought Bestways had an outside chance to make up the time, but Consolidated was more than three hours back, and had proved to have the shortest range of any of the competitors. Everyone else was still in the running, but Comanche was out of its regular territory, and had managed to stray off course. They were back in sixth place now, and Lewis was looking palpably relieved.

Jerry frowned at the wheel. The prizes weren't the real issue, the main thing was to keep Miss Ruby Lee of TWA from getting the one big fifteen minute bonus that was hidden somewhere on the wheel— beneath the radio, he thought. If the reporters wanted cheating, well, this probably was it, but he was determined to do his part to keep Gilchrist solidly in the lead. He'd always had a knack for games of chance, and Gil had taught him how to manipulate them on the fly—it was just a matter of concentration and focus. He could do this.

It was May Saltonstall's turn—Harvard had managed to vault to fourth, on the strength of McIsaac's piloting—and she stepped up to the wheel with a determined look.

"Give it a good spin, Miss Saltonstall," the master of ceremonies urged. He was the president of the local Chamber of Commerce, a handsome, well-spoken man named Jewell, who was sweating under the twin obligations of keeping the competition moving and getting the prize donors' names on the radio as often as possible.

May obliged, and the wheel spun, clicking loudly, to settle at last on a picture of a lady's wristwatch. She smiled with what looked like genuine enthusiasm, and the two ball-gowned girls clapped politely.

"Congratulations," Jewell said, leaning close to the nearest microphone. "That's a beautiful lady's watch, platinum set with real diamonds, from the Elgin Company, courtesy of Pfeiffer's Department Store, Sixth and Main, right here in Little Rock!"

Ten minutes, Jerry thought. He was pretty sure the watch carried a ten minute bonus, and that was all right.

"Miss Laura Bainbridge of United!" Jewell announced. "Step right up, please, Miss Bainbridge. There are still some nice prizes left—that fine mink coat, courtesy of Gus Blass Company, or how 'bout that radio, from O.K. Houck?"

The mink was five minutes, and so was the ladies' dresser set, Jerry thought; the money all carried ten minutes. It was the radio they had to worry about. He focused his will as the blonde reached for the wheel, and Pelletier nudged him in the ribs.

"Not bad, huh?"

Jerry winced, concentration broken, and forced a smile. "Not bad, no."

The wheel clicked to a stop on the radio.

"And that's the cabinet radio from O.K. Houck—don't worry, Miss Bainbridge, Houck ships nationwide!" Jewell waved for a helper to trundle the radio forward, three feet of polished maple inlay on elegant clawed feet. "But, if you'd like, there's always the chance to trade. Look around, see if there's something out there that you like better."

Miss Bainbridge made a production of looking up and down then line, then shook her head. "Thank you, Mr. Jewell, but I quite like what I have. It's a lovely piece."

"Huh," Pelletier said, with a sideways grin. "If I didn't know better, I'd think you were stuck on the Harvard girl."

"Miss Saltonstall is very nice," Jerry said, his voice prim. Inwardly, he was seething. All right, it wasn't so bad that United had the time, but there was still room to trade…

"From Transcontinental and Western Air, Miss Ruby Lee!" Jewell waved her forward, and she posed for a moment beside the wheel before reaching for the lever. The wheel spun, and it seemed to take forever before it began to slow. It clicked toward a stop, past ten dollars, twenty, and settled at last on the mink coat.

"A beautiful mahogany mink coat cut to the latest fashion," Jewell announced, as another assistant brought out the gleaming fur and laid it gently in Miss Lee's arms. "From Gus Blass, in the 300 block, Main Street. It's a gorgeous coat, Miss Lee, but—you always have the chance to trade it for something better. Will you keep it, or will you trade?"

Miss Lee stroked it, looking up and down the line, and then leaned close to the microphone. "It is beautiful, Mr. Jewell, but—I'm a California girl."

Not the radio, Jerry thought. Not the radio.

Miss Lee stopped in front of May Salstonstall. "Sorry, honey," she said, "but I sure like that watch a lot."

"A trade!" Jewell announced, as the women exchanged items to a smattering of applause. "Miss Lee takes the watch, and Miss Salton-stall gets the mink. I don't think anyone loses there."

"And last but not least—last because he's first—Dr. Jerry Ballard. Let's have a hand for Gilchrist Aviation!"

Jewell beckoned, and Jerry managed a smile, leaning on his cane as he stopped beside the wheel.

"Go right ahead, Dr. Ballard, give it a whirl."

Jerry took a last look at the wheel. The hundred dollar prize was still there, and it carried a ten minute bonus. He focused his will, and pulled the lever hard. The wheel spun noisily, slowed, and settled onto the hundred-dollar space.

"One hundred dollars!" Jewell said. "One hundred dollars and a time bonus! But before we find out just how much time our contestants receive, we have one last round of trades. Ladies—and gentlemen—are you satisfied with what you have?"

There was a moment of silence, everyone looking to see what the others would do, and then Miss Saltonstall stepped forward.

"I want to trade, Mr. Jewell."

"Miss Saltsonstall wants to trade." Jewell looked up and down the line. "Anyone else?"

Mrs. Jezek was biting her lip, teetering on the edge of a decision, and Jerry couldn't resist. Just a little push, he thought. Just a nudge toward the extra time, which would help Corsair and not hurt them. Pick the radio. Choose the radio.

"Yes," Mrs. Jezek said. "Yes, I would like to trade."

"And Mrs. Jezek wants to trade," Jewell repeated. "Anyone else? No one? All right, then. By the rules of this contest, the lowest ranking team chooses first, so that's you, Mrs. Jezek."

"Thank you." She took a deep breath. "I would like the cabinet radio, Mr. Jewell."

She held out the money she'd won to Laura Bainbridge, who took it cheerfully enough, and one of the assistants pushed the radio over to her. The audience applauded happily.

"And you, Miss Salstonstall?" Jewell asked. "What would you like instead of that gorgeous mink?"

Miss Saltonstall's grin was utterly mischievous. "One hundred dollars, Mr. Jewell."

Before Jerry could react, she was holding out the coat. He took it, helplessly, the audience laughing and clapping. Miss Saltonstall took the hundred dollars and the envelope with the time bonus and returned to her place, her heels snapping on the wooden stage.

"And that's today's modern woman, folks," Jewell said, to more laughter. "Entirely practical! And now, ladies and gentlemen, it's time for the time. You'll each find an envelope attached to your prize. Have you all got it? Everyone? Then it's time. Open your envelopes, please!"

Jerry wrestled the heavy fur into the crook of his arm—God, it was an awkward bundle—and used both hands to tear open his envelope. As he had expected, the slip read "five minutes" and he held it up to the audience. The others did the same, Mrs. Jezek with a little bounce of pleasure as she showed fifteen minutes, and Jerry couldn't help smiling. It didn't hurt him, and Corsair could use all the help it could get.

After that, the contest wrapped up quickly, Jewell urging everyone to come out to the field to watch the take-off in the morning. Jerry hoisted the unwieldy coat onto his shoulder and levered himself down the stairs to the tiled lobby. It was crowded, even this late at night, and he recognized several of the reporters who had been following the race. Beyond them, Alma and Lewis stood by the doorway of the hotel's restaurant, obviously waiting for a table, and Jerry started toward them.

"Dr. Ballard!"

Jerry turned to see Winchell's stringer Carmichael grinning up at him, notebook open in his hand.

"So, your wife is going to love that baby."

"I'm not married," Jerry said. There was no good place this conversation could go, and it took all his willpower to hold a pleasant smile.

"That's probably good enough to get you engaged," Carmichael said. "That's one expensive fur. Got a lady-friend you're going to share it with?"

No good place, Jerry thought. He took a breath, looking for his best out, and saw Alma wave to him from the restaurant door. "This is all about the team, Mr. Carmichael," he said. "If you'll excuse me?"

He stepped around the smaller man, shifting the coat in his hands. The conversation had attracted attention from some of the other reporters, but he ignored them, smiling at Alma.

"I think this is yours," he said, and set the coat on her shoulders. She blinked, surprised and then pleased, her hands going to the fur to stroke the collar. Lewis lifted an eyebrow, and Jerry shrugged. "What was I going to do with it?"

Flashbulbs popped, and Alma swore. Lewis glared at the photographers, his expression enough to discourage even the most persistent reporter's questions, and Mitch came up beside him, looking from one to the other.

"What the hell?"

"Your table is ready, Mr. Segura," the maitre d' said from the door, and Jerry followed them into the restaurant. Somewhere, he thought, Gil was laughing.

Lewis followed the others down the alley, Alma's sleek new fur catching the light from the alley's mouth. It was really too warm to need it, but it looked as though she wasn't going to let it out of her hands until they got back to their room. Mitch had slipped the waiter a five-spot, and the man had let them out through the kitchen, directing them toward a "private club" two blocks from the hotel, and so far they seemed to have avoided the reporters. Not that Lewis cared if they were seen visiting a speak—who didn't, really?—but he was thoroughly tired of the flashbulbs and the innuendos. The least they could do was take Alma seriously. She was the smartest pilot in the race, that much ought to be obvious to everyone.

They turned right onto Second Street, then left onto Louisiana, a streetcar rattling past in the distance. Lewis heard music, and then it was cut off as though a door had closed.

"There," Mitch said.

Lewis looked where he was pointing, automatically offering Alma his arm as they crossed the street. It was an ordinary-looking store-front—no, not the storefront, but the steps that led down to a basement entrance, where imperfectly curtained windows let slivers of light onto the iron stairs.

Mitch led the way, and rapped briskly on the door. Lewis could hear music again, not quite stifled by the door and the heavy curtains, and after a moment, a peephole opened.

"Yeah?"

Mitch held up the card he had gotten from the hotel doorman, but the man shook his head.

"This is a private club, buddy."

Mitch reached into his pocket and pulled out a dollar bill, wrapped it around the card. "We'd like to become members."

The doorkeeper snatched the card out of his hand. "Why didn't you say so? Come on in, folks."

Mitch signed the guestbook as "Smith" with an indeterminate squiggle for a first name; Lewis identified himself and Alma as Mr. and Mrs. John Jones, and drew a sardonic grin from the doorkeeper.

"Don't get many Joneses around here, mister."

"It's an unusual name," Lewis said, solemnly, and followed Alma into the main room.

It was hot and crowded, the air hazed with smoke. In one corner, a jazz trio tried to keep the music going without actually elbowing any of the dancers; the dancers, a good half-dozen couples, tried to keep from stumbling into the musicians or the tables that surrounded the postage stamp of a dance floor. Mitch checked at the edge of the crowd, looking for a table, and Lewis put his hand on Alma's waist, less to steady her than to keep close to her.

"Are there tables?" he asked.

Before Mitch could answer, someone shouted, "Segura! Over here!"

Lewis peered through the smoke to see Comanche's Rayburn halfstanding, waving them over. His team had commandeered several tables, and they and the Harvard team were crowded around them, along with the pretty girl from Consolidated and one of the pilots from the Corsair. He didn't see any other tables, so he shrugged and made his way toward them, still keeping his hand on Alma's waist. Mitch followed more slowly, and they reached the tables just as the band finished its song.

"Nice job, Mrs. Segura," Rayburn said, with what sounded like genuine admiration, and Lewis let himself relax a little.

One of the Harvard boys shot to his feet, offering her a chair next to Miss Saltsonstall, and Mitch managed to find chairs for the rest of them. The Harvard boy winked at Lewis, and offered his hand to the girl from Consolidated.

"I don't suppose you'd do me the honor, Miss Gray? I've never had the chance to dance with a movie star before."

She laughed, and let him lead her away, and Alma looked at Rayburn. "Thanks. But it was Mitch who did the actual flying,"

Rayburn nodded to him as well. "And a damn nice job. But that was a hell of an idea, putting in that tank. I won't pretend I wasn't mad when the judges said it was ok, but—hell, you beat us fair and square. And smart."

"Thank you," Alma said, and held out her hand. They shook on it, and Rayburn grinned.

"But don't think we're giving up. It's a straight speed run tomorrow."

"That's going to be interesting, all right." Rob Roy McIsaac leaned across the table, raising his voice to be heard. Lewis hadn't had the chance to speak to him before, and looked him over curiously. Rumor said he'd been a rumrunner in the Gulf before Mobile and New Orleans got too hot for him, then headed north to take up the same business in New York and New England. "Any of you folks flown into New Orleans before?"

"Paulie's been there a couple of times," Rayburn said, nodding to his teammate, who grinned and lifted a drink. "Anything we ought to know about it?"

"Nothing that wasn't in the race papers," McIsaac answered. "Grass field, no tower, runway's just a hair short for my taste. But no one's going to be flying heavy this time."

He grinned at Mitch as he spoke, and Mitch smiled back. "Thanks for the warning."

A waiter appeared, and Lewis leaned back to order a round of cocktails for the three of them, on the theory that a mixed drink was somewhat safer than pure moonshine. By the time the man returned and Lewis had paid, the Consolidated girl had returned, perching on the Harvard boy's lap because there was no chair to be found.

"I've heard terrible stories about New Orleans," she said. "Gangsters and voodoo—all kinds of awful things."

"It's not so bad, Miss Gray," McIsaac said. "Why, I lived there almost twenty years, and nobody shot at me—well, no more than twice. Maybe three times…"

Miss Gray laughed along with the others, and reached for her glass. She was a little tight, Lewis thought. The Harvard boy—Newhouse, his name was—was having a bit of a time keeping her balanced, though he didn't seem to begrudge the effort..

"I heard there were some terrible murders there in the teens," she said. "Somebody hacked women to death with an axe."

"And here I thought that was a New England thing," Paulie said. "Lizzie Borden took an ax—"

"Oh, can it," Mitch said.

Lewis glanced at him, startled, and McIsaac raised an eyebrow.

"You know about our Axeman, Mr. Sorley?"

Mitch shook his head. "I've never been to New Orleans." He tossed back the last of his drink, reached out to grab a passing waiter.

"So it's true?" Miss Gray said.

McIsaac shrugged. "It's true that there was a murderer with an axe who scared the daylights out of people back in '19. And, no, they never caught him."

"I remember that," Rayburn said, slowly. "A bunch of Italian women, wasn't it? And he wrote to the papers and said that he was the Devil himself but because he was a jazz man that one night he wouldn't enter any home where his own music was playing. The Devil's own jazz."

"The Axeman's Jazz," McIsaac said. "Some damn fool even wrote the song for him."

"Did it work?" Miss Gray asked. "Did he keep his promise?"

"I was living in the Quarter then," McIsaac said. "He wrote to the Times-Picayune and said he'd pass over the city on St. Joseph's Night, but he'd spare any home where jazz was playing. I remember his exact words: 'some of those people who don't jazz it on Tuesday night will get the axe.'" He shook his head, his accent suddenly stronger. "You never saw so many parties, and there wasn't a musician in town, good, bad, or indifferent, who didn't have a gig that night. My boss had a party that night himself, and come midnight, every girl in the house was in the middle of the dance floor, jazzing it as though her life depended on it. And maybe it did. But nobody died that night. Not then."

"But he came back," Miss Saltonstall said.

McIsaac nodded. "Four times more. Four more people dead. Eleven of them in all."

"That's horrible," Miss Gray said.

"It's like Jack the Ripper," Charlie Saltonstall said. "He wrote to the papers, too. And they never caught him."

"It's a load of crap," Mitch said. He drained his fresh drink. "The Devil writing letters to the newspaper? Come on, McIsaac."

Alma was frowning, visibly worried, and McIsaac spread his hands.

"Nobody knows if the letters were real," he said. "But the bodies sure were."

Mitch started to say something more, and Alma kicked him under the table, catching Lewis a glancing blow. Mitch closed his mouth, scowling, and pushed back his chair. "Sorry, I'm not good company," he said. "I'm heading back to the hotel."

Lewis looked up at him, wondering if he should go with him. Except that meant leaving Alma, which wouldn't do, and Mitch— surely he wasn't drunk, even on two quick drinks.

"You want us to go with you?" Alma asked, and pinned him with a glare.

Her tone seemed to get through to Mitch, and he visibly relaxed. "No. No, I'm just beat, I think. A good night's sleep, and I'll be fine."

Alma hesitated, obviously on the verge of going with him anyway, and Mitch managed an almost normal smile.

"Really, Al. I'm fine."

"All right," she said, and Mitch turned away, threading his way through the tables to the door.

"We don't have to stay too long," Lewis offered, as the conversation began to pick up again around them.

"We probably shouldn't," Alma said. Her eyes were still on the door, and Lewis leaned close. To a casual observer, he might just be whispering endearments.

"Do you have any idea what's going on?"

"None at all," Alma said. "None at all."

The dream, Lewis thought suddenly. Jazz and nightmare and a killer in the dark, staying his hand just as long as the music wailed, intoxicated by his own power. "The Axeman. That's what my dream was about."

"What?" Alma leaned back to look at him.

"McIsaac's story." Lewis shook his head. "But why I'd dream that…"

"You're sure it's not a prediction?"

"I don't know." Lewis closed his eyes for an instant, trying to recover the feelings that had come with the image, but there was too much noise, too many people, and he shook his head again. "I didn't think so at the time. I don't really think so now, not directly. But…"

"We need to take it seriously," Alma said, and he nodded.

Jerry made his way back to his room, leaning heavily on his cane. His stump was hurting, the dull pain that came from standing too long, and he dropped onto the bed with a sigh. It would have been nice to go with the others, have a drink in the discreet speakeasy around the corner, but the walk would have left him aching, and he wanted to be fresh in the morning. He'd never really thought that being a passenger would be quite so much work.

He slipped off his glasses, throwing his arm up to cover his eyes. In just a minute, he'd start the tedious business of getting himself ready for bed, but for now—no. No, he'd get up and do it now, and then he could really relax.

Jerry hauled himself upright again, wincing as his weight came down on to the wooden leg. If he wasn't careful, he was going to get a raw spot on the stump, and that would be almost impossible to heal while they were in the race. He went into the bathroom, shedding jacket and tie on the way, and busied himself at the sink and toilet. As always, the frustration clawed at him: if he were whole, he could lie down any time he wanted to, could do things without worrying about the consequences, but instead he had to plan every step so that he wasn't caught without his leg, forced to drag himself on crutches or, worse, hop or crawl. And even with the best planning, the most careful choreography, there was no real dignity left.

He scowled at himself in the mirror as he splashed warm water on his face, the stubble rough beneath his hands. Tonight he looked every day of his years, every sharp edge blunted, and he wished that Gil were here to tease him out of this mood. For a moment, he could almost see Gil's face behind him, the wry smile curving his mouth, tightening the wrinkles at the corners of his eyes. Gil had been skin and bone at the end, but still himself, though that had been a mixed blessing.

He swore under his breath and swung away from the sink, pausing only to pick up the Dopp kit he'd left on the sinkboard. It was time to patch up his leg and go to sleep and hope for better in the morning. He tossed the kit onto the bed and wrestled himself out of his clothes, then sat down to unfasten the harness that held the wooden leg in place. The straps had bitten into his skin, leaving familiar marks, but there were no particular sore sport, and he eased the leg off the stump with a sigh of relief.

After he'd been hit, the damaged foot had festered, healed, and festered again, the infection simmering in the bones, until a year after he'd come back to Chicago. The fevers had come back, and the swelling, and in the end the surgeons had amputated his leg just below the knee. He'd been lucky, they told him, lucky to still have the joint and enough leg left below it to allow for a prosthesis, but he wasn't in the mood to count his blessings. He cocked the stump over his good knee, wincing as he probed the new red patches. More ointment on the raw bits, and extra moleskin in the socket, and it if wasn't enough, well, he'd just live with it.

He reached for the tube of ointment, and instead his fingers found silk: Henry's necklace. He froze, remembering the look on Alma's face when she'd handed it to him. Better to leave it where it was—except that he was curious. He pulled it out, unexpectedly weighty in his hand, unfolded the pale blue silk. Iron flowers, a hard, unlikely beauty, each dull black blossom perfect, each paired with two leaves and a delicate bud. It would lie heavy on a woman's neck.

He knew the story of Berlin iron, for all that it wasn't his period. The ladies of Prussia gave up their jewels to finance the war against Napoleon, pledged themselves to wear only worthless iron until the monster was defeated, wore it in defiance after Napoleon crushed them, and in celebration when he was finally exiled. Henry had said this piece was cursed, that a dying woman had cursed the soldier who took it, thief and murderer, and that every woman who had worn it since had died a violent death. French women, most of them, Bonapartist women—plenty of them had sought refuge in the Americas.

He spread the handkerchief on his thigh, laid the necklace across it, the metal cool even through the silk. It was easy to imagine those women—he could almost see them, an aging exile with gray in her short black curls, the pale eldest, the proper middle sister, the last-born girl as wild as her mother. Two died at their husbands' hands, the proper one in a robbery, the youngest in her box at the theater, the iron necklace she flaunted bright with blood. All of them sacrificed to the curse, blood on pastel satin, smearing silken skin. Another stranger shot by moonlight, the necklace black against her skin; later still, a night of rain, the gas flames shivering in their lamps, a thread of blood in the gutter, trailing past a kid-leather shoe and a crumpled shape in a dress that had once been palest ivory.

And why not? Why should they live? Theirs was a crime of blood, let it be paid in blood. Why should anyone live? Too many good men were dead in the War, too many worthless souls alive in their stead. The War had taught him that there was a certain pleasure in the kill. There was a razor in his kit, honed to a perfect edge, the ivory handle easy in his hand. It wouldn't be hard. And it would serve them right, all of them who were alive when Gil was dead…

And not a single death, not a single drop of blood, would make Gil live again. He caught his breath like a drowning man, and carefully folded the silk back over the necklace, tucking the ends tight around the iron flowers. Gil was dead, and nothing would change that, true; but nothing could change what they had had. He put the necklace back into the kit, nestling it as far from the razor as he could manage, and reached for the cream to tend his raw leg.

The maid had left the window open, and a breeze curled in from the street, smelling of rain and the dusty street. For an instant, the scent was almost the same as memory, spring rain on cobblestones, and Jerry closed his eyes.

They had managed leave together, in the spring of 1918 before the Army got properly organized, and he and Gil had holed up in the back room of the penzione, huddling into the featherbed against the draft, the window cracked open to let out the smoke of the fire and the cigarettes and the smell of sex. The lamp flickered, drawn perilously close to the bed, and he sat up over the book Gil had brought him, printed in 1805 with engravings from much earlier, feeling the ritual take shape in his mind, correspondence leaping to join correspondence, all the things he had believed dead suddenly alive and waiting.

"It's all real," he said, still needing to hear the words, unable to keep the wonder from his voice, and beside him Gil rolled to face him, draping an arm across his thighs.

"I told you so," he mumbled, his face still in the pillow.

"No, it all makes sense," Jerry said, and pushed his glasses up on his nose. He only needed them for reading, especially in this light, and to decipher the marginal notations someone had left in blue ink and a sprawling hand, and there hadn't been time to get them fitted before he shipped out. "I can see—I want—do you have an ephemeris?"

"Yes." Gil didn't open his eyes.

"Well, where is it?"

"In my pack."

Jerry pushed back the covers, but Gil's arm tightened, and he stopped. "What?"

Gil levered himself up onto one elbow. "It'll be here in the morning, Jer."

"But—" Jerry stopped, and Gil sat up, holding out his hand.

"Give."

Reluctantly, Jerry handed over the book. Gil found the ribbon marker, tucked in into the pages, and set the book firmly aside.

"The stars will be better in the morning anyway," he said.

Jerry frowned. "Not necessarily—you have no idea what the astrological conditions are, do you?"

Gil grinned, not the slightest bit abashed at being caught out. "Nope."

"So in fact this could be the correct hour for—" Jerry stopped abruptly as Gil's hand slid beneath the edge of the heavy sweater he was wearing, began plucking at his undershirt.

"It's a better hour for this."

Jerry grinned in spite of himself, leaned in to the exploring hands. "God, Gil, there's so much to learn, so much—I thought it was all dead."

Gil reached up to cup his cheek, his expression for once serious and tender. "The Gods aren't dead, you know."

"No," Jerry said, and couldn't repress his own smile. He shrugged out of his sweater, and slid down into Gil's embrace.

The hotel room smelled more insistently of rain and gasoline, the exhaust from a truck passing beneath the windows. Jerry took a deep breath, his eyes stinging. That was the Mystery, the thing Gil had given him that could never be taken away. *The greatest of these is love.*

Chapter Twelve

"A jealous Latin husband. How boring!" Stasi folded the tabloid newspaper next to her morning coffee cup with the picture on top. There, in lovely black and white, Alma Segura walked across the tarmac of some landing field or another, her arm around Mitchell Sorley's waist. Behind, Lewis Segura brooded jealously. Actually, Stasi thought, he looked more uncertain and perhaps annoyed that there were photographers there, but it was close enough to make the caption work. "Enchantress of the air Alma Gilchrist Segura and decorated ace Mitchell Sorley have been business partners for ten years as well as sharing a house. Mr. Segura is a recent addition to the ménage."

"New Orleans! End of the line! New Orleans!" The conductor came through the café car. "Ten minutes, ladies and gentlemen. New Orleans!" Out the window Stasi could see the waters of Lake Ponchartrain, the train and trestle reflected in shadow. The sun had risen and to the east waterbirds were rising toward the sun.

With a smile, Stasi picked up her handbag and the paper. Thanks to the paper, she knew exactly where the crews for the Great Passenger Derby were staying, and so upon alighting from the train it was the work of a moment to find a taxi.

"Hotel Denechaud," she said as the driver held the door and she swung her feet in primly, not showing an inch of the hem of her slip, her backseam stockings absolutely straight.

They'd better be. The Hotel Denechaud was everything the name promised, one of the finest hotels in the United States. It wasn't enough to say that it was a model of Edwardian grace. No, it was working hard at being a palace. The enormous columns of Italian marble holding up frescoed ceilings trimmed in gilt and hung with enormous chandeliers dangling with Czech crystals were just the beginning. That didn't even begin to encompass the Louis XV statuary, the gilt cherubs, or the marble balustrade trimmed with onyx and bronze ormolu. It was really, Stasi thought, a bit much. Well, perhaps not for a casino in Monte Carlo, but since she'd never actually been in the casinos in Monte, maybe even there?

The desk clerk looked her up and down as she approached, his back stiffening. Of course. Her dress and hat were quite ordinary, not at all appropriate for the Hotel Denechaud. "Can I help you, madam?" he asked, his lower lip all but dripping with disdain.

"I do hope so!" Stasi gushed, letting a bit more of her accent out. "I'm the wife of one of the pilots in the Great Passenger Derby, and I just arrived by train to meet him. I'd like to go ahead and check in, if I may."

"Ah." That syllable encompassed a world of comprehension. It enclosed fully the understanding of why a woman of such markedly modest means would set foot in the Denechaud.

"It's a lovely hotel," Stasi said sweetly, looking wide-eyed at the chandeliers. "I'm sure we'll enjoy staying here so much."

"Of course," he said, consulting his books. "And what name is it, madam?"

"Mrs. Mitchell Sorley," Stasi said. She laid the paper on the counter, picture uppermost and gave the desk clerk a flat smile. "He doesn't know I came to join him. I hope you won't tell him when he checks in. I'd like it to be..." her eyes flicked to the picture, Alma's arm around Mitch's waist, "a surprise."

"I quite understand, Mrs. Sorley," the desk clerk said. She could almost see the dollar signs floating over his head. A nice little brouhaha of the wife showing up would be worth something to the reporters. He handed her the key. "I hope you enjoy your visit."

"Thank you," Stasi said. "I'm sure I will." She tucked the key into her handbag. "Oh, and is there a telephone I might use?"

"To the left, madam," he said, far too well trained to point.

"Thank you." It was an elaborate Edwardian phone booth, dark walnut panels and a door with glass panes that closed. She shut it carefully and asked for the exchange, waited until it picked up. "Mr. Lanier?"

"Yes?" His voice was genial.

"This is Miss Ivanova," Stasi said. "I wanted to let you know that I plan to deliver your necklace to you tonight."

Lewis made his way to the lobby, leaving Alma still in the bath. It was cloudy out, and when he stopped at the desk, the clerk reported that the Weather Bureau was predicting rain. Not storms, Lewis thought, glancing at what he could see of the sky through the open doors, but low clouds and probably rain: not a fun day for flying.

Jerry was ahead of him in the dining room, sitting at a table set for four, coffee in one hand and the morning paper folded in the other. He put it down at Lewis's approach, turning it over as though to hide something, and Lewis frowned. There was something odd about Jerry—he looked washed out, like a man whose fever has broken, but the waiter arrived, bearing coffee in a silver pot, and the vision vanished. Lewis accepted the coffee gratefully, and looked at the paper.

"What's up?"

"Where's Alma?" Jerry asked.

"Getting dressed," Lewis answered. He reached across the table for the paper. Jerry made a face, but didn't stop him. Lewis turned it over, to see a photograph of Jerry draping the fur coat around Alma's shoulders, himself and Mitch in the background looking startled. Well, Mitch looked startled, Lewis thought. He himself was frowning again, and looked almost annoyed. The caption read, "Mrs. Lewis Segura claims another trophy in the Great Passenger Derby."

"Oh, boy," he said.

Jerry lit a cigarette, shaking the match out with vigor. "Yeah. Al is not going to like that."

"No." Lewis refolded the pages and handed it back across the table. "Did you have to give her the coat right then?"

"What else was I going to do with it?" Jerry asked. "I'd look damned silly in a mink."

Lewis felt himself blushing—no, Jerry wasn't that sort of man at all—and looked up gratefully as the waiter arrived with their orders. He reached for his fork, and another shadow fell across the table.

"Mr. Segura and Doctor Ballard."

It was Carmichael again, and in spite of knowing better Lewis scowled. The reporter grinned back at him. His eyes were bloodshot and his suit was crumpled, but he was clearly still going strong.

"That's a heck of a nice coat, Doc. I'm sure Mrs. Segura appreciates it." His eyes were on Lewis as he spoke, and Lewis bit back a curse.

"As I said before, this is a team effort," Jerry said. If you didn't know him, Lewis thought, you'd think he was completely calm. "Mrs. Segura is the only one of us who could get any use out of that prize."

"How do you feel about that, Mr. Segura?" Carmichael rested both hands on the back of the empty chair, and Lewis repressed the urge to kick it. "Your wife getting presents—well, not exactly from strangers—"

"Ok, that's enough." Lewis shoved back his chair, came to his feet with his fists clenched. "You've got no business insinuating things like that, and if you do it again, I'll knock your block off."

He was bigger than Carmichael, but not by much, wasn't at all sure what he was going to do if the reporter didn't back off. To his relief, Carmichael straightened.

"What's to insinuate? I just report the facts."

"For Winchell to repeat," Jerry said, and for a second Carmichael's face darkened.

"I've got a byline of my own, Doc, don't forget it." He swung away, and nearly collided with Mitch and Alma. That brought a new grin to the reporter's face, and he tipped his hat without sincerity. "Mrs. Segura, Mr. Sorley. Good to see you joining the party."

"What the hell does that mean?" Mitch demanded, but Carmichael was already gone.

"Problems?" Alma asked, and Lewis held her chair for her.

"Nothing we haven't already heard," he said.

Jerry started to slide the paper out of sight, but Alma caught it.

"Let me see."

"Al," Lewis began, and Jerry shrugged.

"Go right ahead."

Alma turned it over, her frown deepening.

"Maybe I'll just head back to my room," Jerry began, and Alma gave him a look.

"You will not. You'll stay right here, and we'll all have breakfast together. Like the friendly team we are."

"Do I want to know?" Mitch asked.

"No," Lewis said, and Alma handed the paper across the table.

"Oh," Mitch said. He passed the paper to Jerry, who folded it

again and tucked it in his lap. "Al, I'm sorry—"

"There's nothing to apologize for," Alma said. Her voice was grim. "And as long as we act like there isn't, the papers won't have a leg to stand on."

"There's something else," Jerry said, lowering his voice. "Henry's necklace—we need to do something about it. The damned thing is dangerous."

"We know that, Jerry," Alma said.

Lewis winced. They should probably try to tie it up in some more complicated working, some sort of protective spell of their own—

"There's no time for that," Mitch said, echoing his thought, and Alma nodded.

"We'll give it to Henry in New Orleans and let him deal with it. There's nothing else we can do right now."

She forced a smile as the waiter approached, gave her order in a voice as brittle as it was bright. Mitch glanced at his menu, frowning over the decision, and Lewis looked at Jerry, who gave a tiny shrug. It wasn't true, the papers would continue to have a field day with the gossip no matter what they did: a woman in charge had to be mannish or a vamp, and nobody could call Alma mannish. Everything any of them did, no matter how innocent, was going to be seen through that lens.

"Gilchrist Aviation! Smile for the *Democrat*, folks!"

Lewis looked up, annoyed, and the flashbulb went off almost in his face. Alma gave a smile that didn't hide her anger.

"I'm sure you'd get much better pictures if you'd give us a little warning."

"That's ok, Mrs. Segura," the photographer said, backing away. "I got the picture I need."

"I just bet you did," Jerry muttered, and ground out his cigarette with extra force.

"Fine," Alma said. She picked up her knife again, looking as though she wanted to stab someone with it. Mitch cleared his throat, gave her a meaningful look, and she shifted her grip to something less threatening. "All right. From now on, everyone smiles."

Mitch slumped in the back of the bus, wishing he could shake whatever was bothering him. Outside the window, crepe paper bunting waved damply in the breeze, courtesy of the girls of Little Rock High, and he was vaguely sorry for them. Their efforts deserved a better day than this, low cloud and a chill, intermittent drizzle. Maybe it was just the weather, he told himself. Maybe he was just reasonably anxious about flying into a strange airfield—a strange, short airfield with a sod runway—on a wet day. Not to mention that navigation was going to be a treat… No, he couldn't convince himself that this was any ordinary worry.

The problem was, he wasn't worried—didn't feel a whole lot of anything, really. It was as though he was caught in fog, as though there was a veil between him and the world. He almost wished for a headache or chills or the sniffles, anything to make it possible to believe this was just something physical, an illness coming on.

Coming down with a cold didn't make you behave like a jerk, though, and he'd been a jerk last night. He'd been unpleasant to Miss Gray, and he'd been rude to McIsaac, though for the life of him, he couldn't remember why. He braced himself against the edge of the seat as the bus rounded a corner, concentrating on the way the metal resisted his strength, the tightness in his muscles as he pushed back. He hadn't been that drunk, hadn't been drunk at all, not on two cocktails, not even knocking them back the way he had. What the hell had they been talking about?

It came back to him then—New Orleans, the New Orleans Axe-man—and he relaxed with a sigh. Ok, not a nice thing, but at least he'd remembered. And he supposed that explained why he'd been in a bad mood. Girls could be the worst ghouls sometimes. Maybe that was what had bothered him.

Alma elbowed him, and he jumped, turned to see her forehead creased with concern.

"Are you ok?" She kept her voice low, barely audible above the rumble of the bus's engine. "Lewis or I can take this leg if you need."

Mitch hesitated. Maybe it made sense, feeling as weird as he did. The weather was—well, not precisely bad, but the ceiling was low, and there was a good chance they'd be flying by dead reckoning at least part of the way. Maybe he should let Lewis take over. Except this was his job. "No," he said, before he'd realized he'd made up his mind. "I'm fine, Al. Just a little tired."

"I'd rather have you rested for the last leg," Alma said. "There's no need to push yourself right now."

Mitch forced a smile. It felt stiff, but Alma seemed to relax. "You or Lewis can take Pensacola," he said. "That'll give me plenty of rest."

"I want you for the mail drop," Alma said. "That's your baby. You've done it a hundred times."

Mitch forced himself to pay attention. The New Orleans-to-Pensacola section of the race was a pure stunt run, a short timed leg between the two cities in the morning, and then a pylon race in the afternoon. If that wasn't bad enough, each plane had to make a mail drop at some point in their ten laps, fastest time to win. Bonus points for accuracy. It was the sort of thing he could do in the Terrier pretty much in his sleep—which might be a good thing, if he couldn't pull himself together. He shook his head. If he didn't feel better, Lewis could do it. Or Alma. Either one of them was more than capable of it. But in the meantime, he wanted to fly today.

"So you take half this leg," he said. "That'll be a couple hours for each of us, and I'll be fine."

"All right," Alma said. She leaned forward to see past him, scanning the still-damp street. "I think maybe it's clearing?"

The bus pulled up in back of the terminal, on the runway side where the stands had been erected. They were close to full in spite of the damp, and as they climbed out he saw more people on the roof of the terminal. The race was certainly living up to its publicity. Ahead of him, Alma stopped to listen to a reporter's question, Lewis at her side. Mitch ducked past them, following the porters with their suitcases, and escaped into the safety of the hangar. It was quieter there, the smell of gas and machinery steadying, and he opened up the Terrier, unlocking the baggage compartment for the porters and folding down the cabin steps. He double-checked the baggage compartment once the porters were gone and carefully re-locked it, then climbed into the cockpit and settled himself at the controls.

He ought to begin the preflight, but he couldn't seem to make himself move. Instead, he stared blindly through the windscreen, not really seeing the TWA team busy across the hangar. He felt as though he was caught in a downdraft, as thought the bottom had dropped out of the sky and taken his stomach with it. He wanted—well, he couldn't say exactly what he did want, but he didn't want to go to New Orleans.

The realization shocked him back to himself, and he reached for the clipboard, shaking his head. That was ridiculous. He'd never even been to the city, there was no reason for the wave of reluctance that washed over him. Maybe it was something he'd eaten, or maybe he was coming down with something—maybe he should let Alma fly today.

He considered that for a moment, then shook his head. The Terrier was his baby, and this was a straight speed run, no need to worry about fuel consumption. Better he take the controls and let Alma do the dead reckoning—she was better at it than he was. And then he could rest up in New Orleans. He could always skip the party that had been laid on for the competitors and get a good night's sleep— they were staying at the fanciest hotel in the city, the rooms ought to be something else. He'd be good for the pylons then, and for his share of the last leg into Coconut Grove.

He glanced over his shoulder as the cockpit door opened, and Alma slipped into the seat beside him, one hand full of flimsies from the Weather Bureau.

"Any good news?" he asked, and Alma grinned.

"Well, no bad news, anyway. Clouds and drizzle all the way, but it's not a front, so we shouldn't have thunderstorms to worry about. The ceiling's only 800 feet here, but it's supposed to lift by the time we get to New Orleans."

"Could be worse," Mitch agreed, and began the start-up procedure.

They were first out, trundling out onto the soggy runway to the approval of the crowd. Mitch could see them waving and clapping as he turned the Terrier into the wind, lining her up on the runway.

"Flag," Alma said, and he opened the throttle, feeling the engines roar up to speed. The Terrier lifted easily, and he banked wide over the field, settling onto the heading that would take them to New Orleans.

To Alma's relief, the ceiling stayed high enough that they never had to resort to dead reckoning. She took over the controls after the first hour, settling just below the cloud deck; the air was rough, but not unbearably so. They hit harder rain near Greenville, flying in and out of sudden downpours that rattled on the cabin and momentarily obscured the windscreen, but by then they were following the Mississippi, and even the rain couldn't hide that landmark. The weather cleared as they approached Vicksburg, but she stayed on the line of the river for a little longer, until she was sure the clearing was going to last, before striking off cross country. Mitch had the list of landmarks ready, calling them off as they approached, and by then the ceiling was almost 1300 feet. She lifted the Terrier again, gaining the better view, and at last she saw the wooden beacon tower that marked New Orleans Airport.

Of course, it started to rain again, not hard, but a thin sprinkling that would make the sod runway thoroughly slick under the tires. She swore under her breath, hoping the rain wouldn't actually reach the ground, but it still streaked the windshield as she put the Terrier into a gentle descent.

"Want me to take it?" Mitch asked, and she risked a glance at him. He was looking better, his color and expression more normal than it had been, and she suppressed a grimace. It wasn't that she couldn't, she was perfectly capable—but this was his baby. He was the one with the most hours in the Terrier, and there was no point risking a stupid accident. It was one thing to lose a race through bad luck; she'd be damned before she'd lose it to a mistake.

"Yes," she said, and circled the field, gaining a little height while they made the switch.

Once Mitch had the controls, she leaned against the window. The field's flagman was out, signaling that they were good to land. She pointed, and Mitch banked the heavy plane, lining it up on the longest of the two runways. It was still spitting rain as they came down, trails of liquid crawling along the window, and the Terrier rocked in the unstable air. Mitch controlled it easily, shedding speed until they were almost stalling, set the Terrier down with a thump and a bounce before it finally settled. Alma felt the brakes catch and the tires slide and grip and slide again before they finally caught. Mitch let them run the full length of the runway, bleeding speed to nothing, before he turned and began the slow progress back to the terminal.

Alma took a deep breath. She could have done that, yes. She knew her limits, and that landing was within them, but—Mitch was so damn good. She tapped his shoulder lightly, won a quick glance and a fleeting smile.

"Nice work," she said.

The reporters clustered around Alma, Jerry stuck in the press, while Lewis went with Mitch to the desk of the Hotel Denechaud to check in. It was quite a place. Everything was marble and velvet and gold mirrors, just like pictures of palaces from newsreels, though none of them were in living, vibrant color like this. It made Henry's house look normal.

"Sure is something," Lewis said to Mitch under his breath.

"Yeah." Mitch always managed to look more confident than Lewis felt, probably because he was a university man, but even Mitch looked wary and uncomfortable today.

Lewis signed the register carefully, "Mr. and Mrs. Lewis Segura, Colorado Springs, Colorado." This time it was 100% true.

The desk clerk handed Mitch two keys. "You and Dr. Ballard have adjoining rooms with a shared bath," he said. He leaned forward confidentially, dropping his voice. "Mrs. Sorley has already checked in."

"She has?" Mitch blinked.

"Yes, sir. Several hours ago." The desk clerk twitched an eyebrow. "She said she wished it to be a surprise."

"Oh," Mitch said.

"What?" Lewis said.

"Mrs. Sorley?" Mitch said.

"Yes, sir." The desk clerk seemed to be expecting a tip, probably for giving them the keys, so Lewis gave him two bits.

"Thank you," Lewis said, taking his own key. "Let's give Jerry his."

"Right," Mitch said. He looked confused.

"What the heck?" Lewis asked. "Mrs. Sorley?"

"Probably some racing fan," Mitch said. His brow furrowed. "Or somebody working for another team who wanted to get in our rooms."

"We don't keep anything important in our rooms," Lewis said. "Anybody who wanted to sabotage the plane would be at the field."

"What else could it be?" Mitch said. "It can't be the countess, anyway."

Lewis lowered his voice. That was an unwelcome thought, all right. "We do still have the necklace—"

"Yeah, but she's on her way back to LA." Mitch actually sounded faintly sorry about that, but Lewis was careful not to look surprised.

"A reporter, maybe," he said. He paused. " You don't actually have a wife, right?"

"No, of course not." Mitch scanned the massive lobby again. "I don't think."

Lewis stopped short of Alma and the crowd of reporters. "You don't think?"

"I don't. I'm not married." Mitch squared his shoulders and plunged in among the reporters. "Jerry, here's your key. Lewis and I are going to check the rooms."

He turned away before Jerry could ask, and Lewis frowned. Something was not ok—well, something was wrong with Mitch as well as with the rooms, but he knew better than to push. Trying to push Mitch was like pushing a brick wall.

They rode up to the fifth floor in silence, the elevator operator deferentially silent. Lewis took a deep breath before he flung his door back fast, but there was nothing in the room except two beds piled high with pillows and expensive-looking linens. Feeling increasingly foolish, he checked the bathroom and the closets, and then under the bed. There was nothing, not even a scrap of paper, and he opened the door again to see Mitch peering out of the room opposite.

"Anything?"

Mitch shook his head. "Not even a mash note. Must've been a reporter."

"Jerry's room?"

"Nothing there either."

"I don't like the idea that someone's got a key to your room," Lewis said.

"Me, neither. Maybe we can change rooms," Mitch said. He pulled the door closed behind him, and tested the door. "Damn reporters."

"Yeah." Even as he spoke, Lewis felt the hairs prickling at the base of his neck. Something was definitely wrong—but at least they'd be getting rid of the necklace tonight, handing it over to Henry. That would be one less thing to worry about.

Chapter Thirteen

There were no rooms to spare at the Hotel Denechaud. The entire hotel was booked because of the race, and after a long conversation with the front desk clerk, Mitch had decided it was too much trouble to try to find people willing to switch with him and Jerry. It was only for one night, and if it did have something to do with Henry's necklace, well, they were giving it back to Henry tonight anyway. It wasn't like anyone was going to try to attack them, not in a place like this. And besides, he didn't really want to have to explain about the key and the person who claimed she was his wife, especially not when Jerry was listening. Because if it was Miss Rostov—though of course it couldn't be. She was on her way back to LA, and even she wouldn't have tried a lie like that. Even Gil wouldn't have tried something that outrageous, though it would have been kind of fun to see how Miss Rostov would have tried to pull it off. He put that thought aside with unexpected reluctance. It was five thirty, and he just had time for a shower before the evening got started. It felt good to stand under the hot water, to let the steam ease all the kinks in his back out, to ease the aching muscles in his belly from so many long flights back-to-back.

And it felt even better to be in first place. Into New Orleans at 3 pm, six hours and eight minutes out of Little Rock. When they'd left the airport the second place team hadn't even gotten in yet, more than an hour behind. Yep, Mitch thought. Alma's plan was solid and they were going to roll this race up. Two more legs to go—a short stunt run to Pensacola, and then the long leg from Pensacola to Miami—but with the kind of lead they had somebody was going to have to sprout rockets to catch up.

It would be a beautiful evening in New Orleans, carefree and fun with that $25,000 prize almost in reach. There was a party in the main ballroom of the Hotel Denechaud, which looked like it would live up to its reputation as one of the finest hotels in America, and they were the guests of honor. This was pretty much what it was like to be on top of the world. He ought to try to relax and enjoy it.

Mitch turned off the water and got out, reaching for the towel. He rummaged around in his shaving kit for his toothbrusth and tooth-paste. The tube wasn't there. And now that he thought about it, he could visualize just where he'd seen it last—sitting on the edge of the sink at the hotel in Little Rock that morning. "Aw, damn," Mitch said. Well, Jerry wouldn't mind if he borrowed his. Tying the towel around his waist, he went out into the other room. Jerry's suitcase was on the stand, the shaving kit on top. He unzipped it. Where did Jerry…? There was the familiar Colgate tube.

A silk handkerchief twisted, dislodged by his hand, and fell to the floor with a heavy sound, the molten thud of something in it. Mitch leaned over and picked it up. It was the necklace, smooth links of wrought iron like flowers, cool and dark, like the scent of jasmines on a rainy night. It was beautiful.

And familiar. He'd seen it before. He'd seen it before so many times.

Mitch picked it up, weighed it in his hands. The scent of jasmine, the sound of the rain…

Rain like a drum. Rain coming down and down and down, wash-ing blood into rivulets on the street, sliding down the storm drain toward the river. The river just rolled on, oblivious to blood or night or anything. Rain crushed the jasmines, leaving them bloodless and pale against the cobblestones…

And then there was nothing but rain.

"Al, have you seen Mitch?"

Alma was putting her shoes on to go to dinner when Jerry barged into their room without knocking. "No. Should I have?"

Lewis looked over from the dresser where he was dealing with an uncooperative Windsor knot. "I thought he went to take a shower."

"That was hours ago," Jerry said.

"Maybe he went down to the lobby or something," Lewis said.

"He's gone," Jerry said. "Suit, shoes, hat, and Henry's necklace."

Alma jumped up, one shoe on and one off. "What?"

"The necklace is gone," Jerry said. He pushed his glasses up on his nose. "It was in my shaving kit wrapped up in a silk handkerchief. The handkerchief was on the floor next to my suitcase. The necklace is gone. And so is Mitch."

Lewis frowned. "Maybe someone stole it and he went after them."

"Without calling us?" Alma stood on one foot to fasten the straps on the other shoe. "Mitch wouldn't do that." She looked at Jerry. "That thing exerts a powerful pull."

"That's what I'm worried about," Jerry said, meeting her eyes.

"Oh crap," Lewis said.

"He's not a woman," Alma said sensibly. "Putting it on won't kill him."

"But who knows what it wants him to do?" Lewis said.

Alma felt the dread expanding in her stomach. "I don't know, but it can't be anything good. We need to find him right now." She looked at Jerry. "Before something awful happens."

There was a streetcar and then another. Dusk crept in, and lights shone down from windows above, shadows barred from the louvers of each shade. He walked through the city just as he had so many times, alone in the dusk, listening to the devil's music. The sound of jazz followed him, dip and turn, wail and recall, and the sweet soft notes of a woman's voice.

No one turned to watch him. Why should they? He was an ordinary-looking man in a gray suit, a plain fedora, clean shoes. No one noticed Mitchell Sorley.

The clear blue notes of a tenor sax drifted out into the street and he paused. The devil's music for certain, it crawled under your skin, wiggled into your brain with promises that even New Orleans could not fulfill. The world is full of promises that can't come true. The world is full of things that begin only to die, flat and faded and utterly pointless. There are hungers wine can't quench, that friendship can't quiet. Jazz celebrates them all.

He used to love to dance. He remembered that. He loved to move with someone's arms around him, loved the sweet scent and the pressure of a woman's hands, loved grace and fire and dawning need—whoever she was. They were all beautiful, whether they were pretty or plain. Dancing made them beautiful. And in jazz anything was possible.

Almost anything.

Mitch leaned against a wrought iron railing, listening to each note washing over him. Cold iron, cold as disappointment, cold as forgetting. In New Orleans you could forget anything. He crushed out a cigarette on the pavement and went on.

Lewis, Alma and Jerry rushed along the hotel hall.

"Where the hell could he have gone?" Alma demanded. "Did he say anything to you, Jerry?"

"Not a word," Jerry said, leaning heavily on his cane and hitting the button for the elevator. "The last thing he said was that he wanted to clean up. That's all."

"Where would he go? Does he know New Orleans?"

"I have no idea," Jerry said. "He never talked about it if he does."

"Wait," Lewis said, catching Alma's arm. He put his finger to his lips and pulled her away.

Jerry's eyebrows rose, but he followed after as quietly as possible.

Lewis held up one finger. Wait. He quietly backtracked a few steps to a door marked "Linen". Alma stood to one side as Lewis reached for the handle and whipped it open.

A woman fell out. She'd been leaning against the door, and now she stumbled out onto the carpet. She was wearing a smart gray silk dress and strappy heels, but the finger waves were unmistakable, even before she picked herself up from the floor.

"You," Alma said, advancing on her. "What have you done with Mitch?"

"I thought we left her in Flagstaff," Jerry said. "The countess, or whoever she is."

"So did I," Lewis said grimly.

Alma dragged her to her feet, shoving her back against the wall roughly. "Where is Mitch?"

"Darling, how should I know?" the countess gasped.

"Don't darling me, and don't play stupid," Alma said. "You know perfectly well that necklace is a cursed article of malevolent power, and you've done something with both it and Mitch. Now you'd better start talking before I lose my temper. These gentlemen may be too well bred to sock you, but I'm not."

"I know what it is," she said. "But I don't have it!"

"Where is it?" Alma gave her another shove. "Where is Mitch and what have you done with him?"

"I haven't any idea where he is," the countess said. "I haven't laid eyes on your Mr. Sorley since the speakeasy in Flagstaff!"

"What speakeasy in Flagstaff?" Lewis demanded.

Jerry let out a long breath. "The one Mitch went to after we all went to bed."

Alma shot him a sharp look. "You let Mitch go to a speakeasy by himself?"

"He's a grown man!" Jerry snapped. "I'm not his chaperone! He wanted to go get a drink. He went. He came back forty-five minutes later and went to bed. Why would I do anything about that?"

Alma tightened her grip on the countess' arm. "What happened in the speakeasy?"

"Nothing. We had a drink. We talked for a few minutes. I swear I didn't do a thing to him," the countess squeaked, her voice going up with injured innocence that Alma didn't believe for a second. "He loaned me a few dollars for the train back to LA."

"And yet here you are in New Orleans," Jerry observed. "In a very pretty new dress that you didn't seem to have on the plane in Flagstaff. And here Mitch isn't. And oh, coincidentally the necklace is missing again, which it seems to be whenever you're around."

"And I mean to search her," Alma said. "To the skin." She dragged the countess down the hall to her room, Lewis at her shoulder. "You can let me search you. Or you can let Lewis do it. Your pick."

The countess tossed her head. "As if that were a choice."

Alma gave Lewis a nod and closed the door, hearing the comforting familiarity of him leaning against it. "Strip," she said.

The countess started unfastening her dress. "Why are you so worked up about it? It's not your necklace."

"Because that thing kills people," Alma said. "Innocent people. And one of my men is missing."

"Your men." The countess pulled her dress over her head and stood in her slip. "They're all yours?"

"They're my responsibility," Alma said.

"As if you were a general?"

"Something like."

The countess' brow wrinkled. "Just what do you think you are?"

"The Magister of their lodge," Alma said sharply. Yes, it was probably unwise to say, but the worry for Mitch crawling inside her loosed her tongue. "Now raise your arms and turn around."

"Okey-dokey," the countess said, and jabbed out with her elbow, catching Alma in the stomach.

It hurt. A lot. For a moment she couldn't catch her breath. I've had worse, Alma thought. A lot worse. It's not that bad, not that much. She looked up at the countess, eyes watering, her left arm coming up in a vicious sideways blow that caught the countess in the side of the head and knocked her over, crashing against the dressing table.

"Ok in there?" Lewis called through the door.

Alma kicked the back of her knees, dropping her onto her butt. "Fine," she called back. She looked down at the countess. "Now. Cooperation?"

Lewis winced at every thump. "Think we should go in?" he asked Jerry.

"Give her five more minutes," Jerry said, glancing at his watch. "Unless someone screams."

Lewis nodded. "Sounds good."

In two minutes the door opened. The countess had a bleeding cut at the corner of her mouth and Alma looked like she was getting a black eye. Both of them seemed decently dressed and reasonably sedate. "Come in," Alma said. "Stasi was just about to tell us about the necklace."

Lewis looked at Jerry and Jerry shrugged. "Let's hear it, then." They came in and sat down side by side on the bed. The countess had the chair, and Alma prowled around the room barefooted. One of her new shoes seemed to be missing its heel.

"Can I have a cigarette at least?" the countess asked.

"Sure," Lewis said, and lit one for her.

Jerry looked at her cynically. "So, is the necklace your family heirloom from the Old Country that you had to get back to comfort your dying grandmother?"

"No," she said shortly. "I was hired to steal it."

"By whom?" Alma asked.

"By a client here in New Orleans, a man named Lanier."

"You really are a professional thief," Lewis said, with interest. He'd never met one outside of the pages of a magazine.

"I do odd jobs." The countess took a draw from her cigarette. "A girl has to make a living."

"Lanier," Alma said. "Who is he and why does he want it?"

She shrugged. "I don't know," she said. "He's got money. He said it was valuable to him, an antique. It's not worth that much on the open market, and he paid me $500 to get it for him. That's good money. There's a Depression, you know."

"We know," Lewis said.

"It was supposed to be a very simple job," she said. "Go to LA, break into Kershaw's safe, and walk out with it. Kershaw wouldn't even notice for a couple of days, and by then I'd be in New Orleans delivering it to Lanier. Only I didn't want to be walking around with it all night, so I stashed it. And then somebody called the police and I had to leave it there, because if I'd tried to walk out with it I would have been caught."

It couldn't have been that simple, Lewis thought. The office was warded. Which meant the countess knew a few occult tricks of her own, beyond the business with the cards, enough to baffle Henry's wards.

"You hid it on the plane," Jerry said. The color was high in his face. "And then sneaked on the plane the next morning to get it back. We know that part. What about the part with Mitch and the speakeasy?"

"I was trying to get one of the other teams to give me a ride to San Angelo," she said. "Your Mr. Sorley came in and we had a chat. He loaned me money to get back to LA. Instead I wired for more cash and took the train to New Orleans." She shrugged. "I knew that you had to fly a longer route. A direct train would beat you here. It's easy to find out where the contestants are supposed to stay, so I checked in as Mrs. Sorley and I was hiding in the linen closet waiting for you to go to dinner. As soon as you did I'd just use the key to let myself in." She took another long draw. "Then I'd nip in, grab the necklace, and be gone before you knew it."

Alma looked at Lewis. "What do you think?"

There was no cloud around her, no sense of deception, though whether he was good enough to tell was the real question. Still, Alma was asking and he shouldn't second guess his abilities. He should rely on them as she did. Lewis shook his head. "I don't think she's lying," he said.

The countess snorted. "And what are you? A lie detector?"

"A medium," Alma said.

"What a coincidence! I'm a medium too!" She gave Lewis a brilliant smile.

"Can we stay on the subject?" Jerry asked.

"I have no idea where the necklace is, or where your errant knight has gone," the countess said. "What's the big deal anyhow?"

Alma leaned back against the dressing table. "I meant it when I said the necklace is cursed," she said. "Every woman who puts it on dies soon, and by violence." She met the countess' eyes. "So if Lanier didn't warn you about that, he certainly put you in a nice spot. Did you put it on?"

"No," she said slowly. "I never had a chance."

"But you wanted to," Lewis said. He knew that suddenly, as clearly as if she'd said it. He leaned forward. "You felt it too, didn't you? The way it draws you."

She nodded. "I wanted to on the plane. But I didn't. I didn't for some reason."

"The plane's protected," Lewis said. The sigil. His own protection, painted on the tail, protecting everyone aboard, even the stowaway.

The countess looked at him sharply. "Yours?"

Lewis nodded.

"That's a nice piece of work."

He felt his face heat. "Thanks."

Alma crossed her bare feet. "The necklace exerts a powerful and malevolent draw," she said. "As I'm sure you noticed. It wants to be worn... It wants women to wear it and die."

"And it wants men to kill," Jerry said. "That's what it wanted from me."

Lewis looked up. "And—from Mitch?"

"Oh, yes," Alma said, her voice grim.

"The dream," Lewis said. That had to be what it was about, murder in New Orleans, warning him of what might happen.

"Oh yes," Alma said, not taking her eyes off the countess. "It's a very dangerous thing. And now it's on the loose with Mitch, who, given the draw it exerted on the rest of us, is probably snared. We have no idea where he is or what he's doing, but we have to find it before it carries out the things it's cursed to do. Before it kills again."

The countess' face was white, and Lewis thought her expression of shock was genuine. "I had no idea."

"Well now you do," Alma said. "So I suggest you get out of here and keep your head down and avoid your friend Lanier. I don't expect he'll be pleased with you."

The countess stubbed her cigarette out in the glass ashtray. "What are you going to do?"

Alma stood up. "We're going to find Mitch." She glanced at Jerry. "And then we're going to get the necklace back before anyone gets hurt."

"Why is it your problem?"

Lewis knew that expression. He must have worn it himself, not long ago, when Alma told him what the Lodge did. He knew how unbelievable it sounded. It still did. But it was true, and he knew the rightness of it in his bones. "Because it's our job," Lewis said.

"I thought your job was to win an air race."

"Our job is to preserve the world," Lewis said gently. "If we don't, who will?"

Something moved in her eyes, something that half wanted to believe, something real and tender as new grass. "And Mitchell Sorley is part of your Lodge?"

"Yes," Alma said. "And we're going to find him before anyone gets hurt. Thank you for telling us the truth. You're free to go." She got up and rummaged in her suitcase for her old, comfortable shoes.

"I can help," the countess said.

Jerry snorted.

"No, really. I can," she insisted.

"You just want to tag along while we find the necklace for you," Jerry said. "Thanks but no thanks."

"I'm a medium," she said. "I can hear the dead."

Lewis looked at Alma, who shook her head. "I think we're fine with just our own wings. And you understand why we can't trust you."

"Of course, darling." The countess got to her feet. "Well, it's been lovely. I suppose I'll see you around." She gave Lewis a brittle smile. "Ta and all that."

"Bye," Lewis said, feeling that it was rather inadequate.

The countess swanned out the door. After a second Jerry went and opened it. "She's gone," he said.

Alma was already changing into slacks and a blouse. "Ok," she said. "We need to find Mitch."

A woman was singing the blues. She was tall, with tawny skin and a rhinestone clip in her hair, leaning against the piano while the notes floated out into the night. He looked in through the window of the bar, watching her, watching the way her hand rested on the piano, so graceful and so light.

He'd heard this song before. Or maybe he'd heard her sing before, twelve years ago. He couldn't remember which. He couldn't remember the name of the bar either, but his feet had found it. He'd found it. It was still here, packed and busy.

The blues were songs about death or about lost things that could never be found—youth or love or pride. The blues were true songs. She had red, red lips and her voice purred on the low notes, a jazz diva holding court for a room full of jesters, true as if they'd worn Mardi Gras costumes, harlequins all. A harlequin, a devil, a prince... Who could tell who anyone truly was? Sometimes the prince is a devil in disguise. And sometimes he's nobody at all.

Mitch stood under the awning, listening to the blues. He might as well listen one more time before the end.

Chapter Fourteen

Stasi hurried out through the front of the hotel, holding her handkerchief to her eye as if she'd been crying. The bell captain looked concerned. "Are you all right, ma'am?"

"Oh yes," Stasi said with a sob in her voice. "I need a taxi. Please, will you call one?"

"Of course, ma'am," he said, his face creasing in a concerned frown. "Are you sure...?"

"Just the taxi," Stasi said, dabbing at her eye. She was certain he could see she'd been punched, and if she were running away from a man... "As quickly as possible."

He snapped his fingers, calling one from down the block. "Here you go," he said, opening the door. "I won't tell anyone where you've gone."

"Thank you," Stasi said, sliding in quickly. "Corner of Chartres and Esplanade, please." She hoped she was lucky tonight. She hoped he was still there.

"Ok," Alma said. "Lewis, go down to the desk and see if you can get a street map. Surely they have some. Jerry, we need something of Mitch's, preferably with a material correspondence. A comb or a brush with hair in it would be perfect."

Jerry nodded. "There's one in his shaving kit. I'll get it."

"We're going to dowse for Mitch?" Lewis asked.

Alma nodded. "We don't have anything on the necklace, but we should be able to find Mitch. That's the best idea I've got, unless somebody knows where he might go in New Orleans?"

Jerry shook his head. "Not me. I've never heard him say a word about it."

"Then let's do this," Lewis said. "I'll go get a tourist map."

***

The cab pulled up on Chartres Street, hugging the curb in the narrow way, and Stasi hopped out, paying the driver and craning her neck at the same time. It was nine o'clock, and the restaurants along the street were busy. Was he there? Oh yes. There he was, a familiar pudgy figure in a Panama hat pacing up and down the street in front of a restaurant while living people walked straight through him.

Stasi stood up, shaking her gray silk dress out in folds around her, waiting for the taxi to move before she stalked across the street. "You!" she shouted silently, mental voice ringing like her heels on the cobbles. "I need to talk to you!"

The dead man spun around as if he'd seen a Fury. "Ma'am?"

"I need to talk to you," Stasi said, gaining the curb on his side of the street. She glanced in through the lighted windows of the restaurant. "And why are you still here anyway? Didn't your brother get the message I left for him?"

"He did." The dead man took his hat off and twisted it around nervously in his hands. "But he didn't believe it, you see. He thought somebody was playing a joke. So I'm trying to get somebody else to do it. It's not that I don't appreciate you writing it out, Miss." He looked at her curiously. "But why are you looking for me? I'm just a dead man."

"I need your help," Stasi said. "I need the help of the dead of New Orleans. And I'm willing to pay for your trouble."

"Pay?"

"I'm looking for a man who's under a terrible curse. The sooner I find him the more likely I can keep something awful from happening. The Dead who helps me and finds him will be fairly paid. I'll be their medium, any message they want to any person they want, delivered in person with full voice possession." Stasi lifted her chin. "Find this man for me, and I'll let you talk to your brother Milward yourself. And you can use my body to do it."

The dead man's eyes lit. "Truly?"

"I give you my sacred word on it," Stasi said. "And if more than one person helps find him, I'll give each their fair turn. The Dead can find anything faster than a living person and can go anywhere."

He put out a hand. "It's a deal." She looked at it and he stuffed his hand in his pocket embarrassedly. "Sorry. I forgot I can't."

"That's all right," Stasi said. "This is the man."

She made the mental picture as vivid as she could. A big man, 6'1" or 6'2", broad shouldered but not heavy. Brown hair, blue eyes, a face that must have been truly handsome before middle age started creeping up on it. Wrinkles at the corners of his eyes, a sag to his jawline... Still handsome, really. He had a mischievous expression, at least he did when he looked at her, like they were sharing some joke rather than that the joke was on him. And she liked his voice, a slow drawl associated with nitwits and hillbillies, but there were no fleas on Mitch. He was sharp as a tack under that lazy expression. He'd have to be, wouldn't he? You didn't get to be an ace in the air by being slow.

The dead man's voice was sympathetic. "Your sweetheart?"

Stasi opened and shut her mouth again like a fish. "I hardly know him," she said.

"Oh." The dead man frowned. "Lots of trouble for someone you hardly know."

"It's about a curse," Stasi said. "That's the important thing. I need to find him before something bad happens."

"We'll do our best," the dead man said. "Lots of the Dead'll want to take you up on your offer."

"Just find him," Stasi said.

Midnight, and another bar, this one at the corner of Iberville and Burgundy, on the edges of Storyville. Twelve years ago this had still been the red light district, regardless of all efforts of social reformers to stamp out the brothels that had made this the most famous den of iniquity in the western hemisphere. Despite official closures, there had still been plenty of places to play for a guy who was so inclined.

Mitch took a long drink from the glass in his hands, Cuban rum straight up. You can buy anything in Storyville, the saying went, even after they'd stopped publishing the notorious Blue Books, guides to the brothels and the specialties of the house. Almost anything. There are things no money can buy.

He'd have one more drink. Why not?

Henry hovered in the lobby of the Hotel Denechaud. The sponsors' party had started almost an hour ago, and everyone was there except the Gilchrist team. The delegation from TexAv was starting to ask questions, and he could hardly blame them for being annoyed. This was supposed to be the chance for the people who'd put up the money for the race—for the fuel, for the hangar space, for the fancy hotel rooms and the restaurant meals, none of it exactly cheap—to hobnob with the flyers, to bask in a little reflected glory and get their names and businesses in the papers. And Alma wasn't here.

It wasn't as though she didn't understand what was at stake— she'd proved that she was almost as good at the publicity as she was at flying. Which meant something was wrong.

He shook his head. There couldn't be anything wrong. They couldn't have gotten into anything like serious trouble in the six hours between landing and the party. Not even in New Orleans. Maybe Alma was sick? Mabel said she always got her monthly visitor at the most inconvenient time imaginable…

There was movement in the doorway of the ballroom, one of the TexAv bigwigs checking the lobby, and instinctively Henry stepped into the shelter of a pillar. There was a house phone in one corner, and he crossed to it, lifting the receiver to summon the hotel operator.

"Mrs. Segura's room, please."

"One moment."

The phone rang, and rang again. Henry waited. He probably should have asked for the room under Lewis's name, it wasn't fair to fuel the gossip—and all the gossip in the world wasn't going to matter if they didn't show up soon. Ten rings, twelve…

"I'm sorry, sir," the operator said. "There's no answer."

"Try Dr. Ballard's room," Henry said. "Please." He should have started there, he thought. Jerry at least was unlikely to be out running around the city at this time of night.

"One moment."

The telephone rang ten times. Henry hung up before the operator could interrupt again. Not in their rooms, and not at the party. Maybe something had gone wrong with the Terrier? That jarred him into motion, sending him toward the telephone cubicles in the alcove farthest from the front desk.

"Number, please."

"New Orleans Airport, the office there. I don't have the number."

"Fifteen cents, please."

Henry fished in his pocket, came up with three nickels and fed them into the telephone.

"Thank you. One moment."

There was a long silence, and then a telephone began to ring. He counted five rings, six, and finally a breathless voice said, "New Orleans Airport."

Thank God there was still someone in the hangar. Henry said, "I'm trying to reach the Gilchrist Aviation team. I heard they were there—"

The man interrupted him before he could finish. "Mister, there ain't nobody from any of the teams here. There's just me and Hank and the dogs and the shotgun. That good enough for you?"

"Yeah," Henry said, and hung up. What the hell had gone wrong?

Alma pushed her hair back from her eyes, swinging her wedding ring over the tourist map that Lewis and Jerry tried to hold steady in the alley behind a closed shop. Fortunately, a little light came from the streetlight on the corner so that it was at least possible to read the map. Concentrate. Concentrate.

"He's moved west now," Jerry said, squinting at the map. "Jesus Christ, Mitch! Can't you stay in the same place for twenty minutes?"

"Basin Street?" Lewis shook the map, and Alma lost the trace.

She folded the ring into her hand and slipped it back on her finger, the piece of string balled in her palm. "How far is it?"

"Thirty blocks," Jerry said grimly.

"Oh, Jerry." There was no way to keep this up. Jerry couldn't hike around like this, and cabs were getting few and far between after midnight. Alma thought this through. "Ok, you go back to the hotel and get hold of Henry. He's probably having a fit by now. Tell him what's up. Lewis and I will go to Storyville."

She thought for a second that Jerry would protest, but instead he broke out laughing. "There's a story for the newspapers! Aviatrix photographed in house of prostitution!"

"Is that what it is?" Lewis boggled.

"Storyville is the red light district," Jerry said.

"It used to be," Alma said. "Supposedly they cleaned it up after the war."

"Not so much," Jerry said.

"Why would Mitch…?" Lewis stopped, his ears flaming.

"Ours is not to wonder why. Ours is but to do or die," Jerry intoned.

Alma swatted him with the map. "Is this silly season? Can we keep our minds on what we're doing?"

"At least you're only taking one man to Storyville," Jerry said with a bitter laugh. "Instead of your usual harem."

"I don't think…" Lewis began.

"Jerry, go find Henry. Lewis, let's get moving." Alma folded the map and shoved it in her pocket. Thirty blocks was a long way.

"You didn't tell me it was about this." The woman put her hands on her hips, a pretty Italian woman just past thirty in a white negligee. For the moment her negligee was clean, though Stasi imagined that it often appeared soaked with blood.

"About what?" she asked. She was sitting in a wrought iron chair in front of a café long closed, no doubt a pleasant place to watch people in Jackson Square at a time other than one in the morning.

"About the Axeman." The dead woman put her hands on her hips. "You told Morton it was about finding some man. You never said anything about the Axeman."

"I don't…"

"Come on. New Orleans' own Jack the Ripper. It was only twelve years ago. It was in all the papers."

"I wasn't in the United States twelve years ago," Stasi said. "I'm sorry. I've never heard a word about it."

"He killed eleven people and then disappeared," the dead woman said. "Just vanished. Nothing supernatural, of course. He left town."

Stasi felt a cold chill run up her back which had nothing to do with talking to the Dead. "What does that have to do with the man I asked you to find?"

"Nothing. And everything." The woman shrugged. "You didn't say anything about the Lanier necklace either."

"I said there was a curse."

"The Lanier necklace is cursed, all right," the dead woman said. "We all know that." She looked at Stasi keenly. "You didn't put it on, did you?"

"No," Stasi said.

"Good, because if you did you'd be joining us soon. Just like the rest of them." She gave Stasi a hungry smile. "It's always nice to make new friends."

"Where is he?" Stasi asked. "Tell me or don't, but if you want the reward you'll tell me where the man is with no more crosstalk about it."

"On Canal Street walking down toward the levee," she said. "Just about Decatur."

"The levee." Stasi jumped up. "That big thing that keeps the river back. You can't get up it, can you?"

"You can at the Canal Street ferry terminal," the dead woman said cheerfully. "There's the Algiers Ferry. No ferry running at this time of night, of course."

"How far is it?" The river was right in front of her, on the other side of the square and the street and the levee, of course. If she just turned right and followed the levees…

"Far enough."

"Thank you for your help. How far is it?" Stasi snapped.

"Six blocks." The dead woman flowed along behind her. "But you won't make it in time. He'll be fished out tomorrow with the Lanier necklace in his pocket." She smiled happily. "I imagine it will be in all the papers."

"Do me a favor and go see where he is now," Stasi said.

The woman shrugged. "Aren't you paying up?"

"Tomorrow," Stasi said.

"You didn't say tomorrow."

Stasi stopped, hands on hips. "I didn't say now either. I didn't specify, and Morton didn't ask. So I suggest you wait patiently until tomorrow. I know how bargains with the Dead work, and I didn't promise a time."

"I've done my bit. I'm not doing any extra," the dead woman said. "And I'll see you tomorrow, Miss Medium."

"Fine," Stasi said as she vanished into not so thin air. Six blocks. And damn these shoes!

The lights of Algiers shone over the water, reflecting in the dark surface of the Mississippi. Was Algiers a separate town or just a faubourg, as they called it here? Mitch couldn't remember. There were a lot of things he couldn't remember. Like most everything the last time he'd been in New Orleans.

Mitch leaned on the rail that normally kept people from boarding the ferry until they were allowed. Now, in the middle of the night with the ferry not in, muddy water swirled around just beyond and six feet down. Nothing stopped the river, not now, not ever. Mother of Waters, someone had said once. It sounded like something the Indians would have called the river, but he couldn't remember where he'd heard it. It didn't matter. One more thing he didn't remember, like how long he'd been here, or why he'd left.

Mitch pitched his bottle in the water. It was empty. It had been full, once. Of something. Not sure what. It made a loud splash, bobbed and righted itself on the current.

It wouldn't take much to go after it. And why not? There wasn't anybody in the world who would mind for long. His mother, maybe. She'd be sad. But he hadn't seen her in four years, and she had sons aplenty, sons who were right there with wives and children and who sang Christmas carols around the tree and ate poundcake and smoked on the porch and talked about how the country was going to hell. Alma and Jerry would be sad, but they'd get over it. Jerry would understand. Jerry of all people would understand and not be surprised at all. There was only so long you could keep smiling.

Besides, Jerry was better now. No, he'd never have exactly the life he'd wanted, but scholarship was coming back. He was writing articles, doing peer reviews. If he'd ever get out of Colorado Springs he'd meet somebody, and yeah, the guy wouldn't be Gil, but there was probably somebody out there in the big world, somebody who would really go for Jerry. He had options.

Just a step or two. It wouldn't even hurt. They said drowning was the easiest way to go. The hard part would be not to swim. That would be hard.

"Yoo hoo!" a cheerful voice squeaked behind him. "Yoo-hoo! Darling! What an amazing coincidence to run into you here!"

Mitch turned around. It was a little difficult to get his eyes to focus right.

The countess whose name was really Stasi was teetering up the ferry dock on high heels at a brisk jog, silk flapper dress blowing around her in the river breeze, waving for all the world as though it were perfectly normal to run into someone on a ferry dock in the middle of the night. He gaped.

"Darling!" she said, gaining his side and twirling him around like an ingénue, putting herself between him and the river. "It's so lovely to see you!"

"It's nice to see you too," Mitch said politely. The world seemed very tippy when she twirled him around. "I thought I left you in Flagstaff."

"You did, but I'm here now." She tucked her hand through his arm and steered him back down toward Canal Street. "My goodness how busy you've been!"

Mitch tried to focus on her face. "You're after the necklace," he said.

"Well, it would be better if you handed it to me just now."

"I don't think so," Mitch said. His voice was very slow and he enunciated carefully. "I'm pretty sure you stole it and hid it on the plane."

"I did, but that's all in the past," she said. She looked at him more critically in the light of the first street light. "Mitchell Sorley, you're drunk!"

"Absolutely blotto," he said.

"Honestly," Stasi said. She shook her head. "All this time you've been on a bender."

"All what time?"

"All the time that you've been missing."

Mitch frowned. "For seven months?"

"For seven hours," Stasi said.

Which didn't make sense, because he was sure it was much longer than that. He grasped for something he could be sure of, further off in the dark. "Gil wired me," he said.

"Who's Gil?"

"He wired me. Last week."

"Fine," Stasi said, steering him down the street. "I'm so happy for you. Where have you been?"

"Bourbon Street. Storyville. There were some other places too." It all blurred together, like the scent of jasmines after rain. "They're going to worry about me," he said.

"Yes," Stasi said.

"They're all going to worry. In Eden."

"What?"

Mitch shook off her arm. "I've got to get back to Eden. They're going to worry."

Stasi blinked, looking around like she was wishing for a payphone. There wasn't one in sight. "What's Eden? How do you get there?"

"On the St. Charles streetcar," Mitch said.

Lewis and Alma stopped outside a bar on Basin Street in the block between Iberville and Canal. "We've got to check again," Alma said.

Lewis shook his head, moving to block what she was doing from the windows of the bar. The lights of a theater marquee provided some light as she swung the ring over the map on its thread, her eyes half closing. He hated doing this in full sight of any passer by. And there were still plenty at nearly two in the morning in New Orleans. It took Alma longer than he expected, and he watched her face tense, strained with not only the long night but the continued effort. The ring swung wildly, refusing to settle, tracing a long tangent to the southwest.

"How is he moving so fast?" Lewis asked. Not another taxi. His wallet was nearly empty from the amount they'd spent on taxis tonight, not to mention the problem of telling a taxi driver to go thataway with no idea where they were going or how far.

"I don't know," Alma said, opening her eyes and folding the ring back into her hand. "A car, maybe."

"Where would Mitch get a car?"

"I don't know. But it's that way." Alma pointed. "And here we go again."

"Surely he's got to get tired sometime," Lewis said.

Jerry ducked into the men's room to try to freshen up. He was horribly late, and hardly dressed for the sponsors' party, the biggest social event of the entire race. All the teams were supposed to be there—he'd bet money the Harvard boys had packed black tie for the occasion—and it looked like hell for the leaders to be missing. He could probably plead some kind of problem with the Terrier, Henry would back him on that, he thought. But it didn't look good at all.

He wet his pocket comb and ran it through his hair, sleeking it back into good order, and carefully redid his tie. The suit was respectable, old-fashioned enough in cut to look faintly formal, and well enough made that a few hours dashing around the French Quarter hadn't rumpled it too badly. His stump was burning, but there was nothing to be done about that right now. Well, maybe a quick drink, he couldn't believe the party would be dry, but he needed to keep his wits about him. He glanced at his reflection a final time, adjusted his cuffs, and walked back into the lobby.

There was a bellman in uniform at the door, checking tickets, and a hatcheck girl beyond, who flashed him a smile as she handed him the metal disk. The ballroom itself was packed, about two-thirds of the couples in black tie and evening dress, the rest—mostly the teams and their connections—in their nicest suits and dresses. The crystal chandeliers glittered overhead, each in its own segment of the coffered ceiling, brilliant against the honey-colored marble walls and the darker gold pillars that made parallel rows down the length of the room. They were marble, too, but set in square bases covered with fleurs-de-lys and crowned with acanthus-leaf capitals; the floor was marble inlay, patterned like an oriental carpet, and the portraits on the wall were of men and women from the beginning of the eighteenth century—and utterly genuine, if he was any judge.

He rested his weight on his good leg, easing his stump, and looked around for Henry. No sign of him, but at least there weren't as many reporters. It looked as though the organizers were only admitting the more respectable ones, the ones with bylines for the national papers. And Carmichael, of course, but for the moment he seemed busy with one of the boys from Harvard's team—yes, in a tuxedo, and seemingly unworried by Carmichael's jabs. Good luck to him, Jerry thought, and turned toward the bar. He really needed something for his leg, and it was as likely a place to find Henry as any.

"Dr. Ballard!"

He didn't know the voice, but turned anyway to face a stout man in a tuxedo that had been tailored for a younger self. There was a woman on his arm, her lilac dress far more flattering to her round figure and matronly rolled hair, and Jerry recognized her as Mrs. Paul Altner, a feature of the western society pages. That meant the man was probably Paul Altner, majority owner of Texas Aviation Fuels and one of the major sponsors of the race—yes, that was a TexAv pin on his lapel. Jerry forced a smile. "Mr. Altner?"

"We've been waiting for Gilchrist all evening," Altner said. He was smiling, but there was a definite edge to the words. "Glad to see you've made it."

"Ah." Jerry kept smiling, though his hand tightened on the cane. "I'm afraid I'm the only one here yet. Mrs. Gilchrist found a problem with the plane…"

"Oh?" Altner's attention sharpened, and Jerry could almost see the calculations flickering through his mind. Gilchrist was popular, yes, but if they were having mechanical issues, that would give the other teams a chance to catch up, open the chance of a fight to the finish. "I'm sorry to hear that. What's the problem?"

"I really don't know," Jerry said. He turned up his free hand. "I'm afraid I'm not a mechanic." He glanced past Altner's shoulder, saw Henry moving toward the bar. "Would you excuse me? I've got a message for Mr. Kershaw."

"Of course," Altner said, and his wife echoed, "Good luck, Dr. Ballard!"

Jerry made his way across the marble floor as quickly as he dared, the knob of his leg skittish on the polished surface. The last thing he needed was to go sprawling and draw any more attention to who was here and who wasn't.

"Henry," he said, and caught the other man's sleeve.

"Christ!" Henry visibly bit back whatever else he was going to say, his expression murderous. "We need to talk."

"Yes," Jerry said. "But I want a drink first." He pushed past Henry to the bar, nodding to the nearest bartender. "Is the scotch drinkable?"

"The bourbon's better, sir. Less you prefer a cocktail."

"Bourbon on the rocks," Jerry said. "Make it a double."

The bartender grinned and poured. Jerry laid a dollar on the counter, and turned away with the drink in hand. Henry caught him by the elbow before he had a chance to take even a sip, steering him firmly toward the wall and away from the milling crowd.

"What the hell is going on? Where's Alma? For God's sake, everyone's waiting to talk to them."

"We've got a problem," Jerry said. He took a quick swallow of the bourbon, letting it burn its way down to his stomach. "Mitch has done a bunk, and Al and Lewis are looking for him, but we haven't the foggiest where he's gone."

"Christ," Henry said again. "Well, if worst comes to worst, you can fly with two pilots—"

"Al's not going to leave him," Jerry said. "No more will I."

"I'll stay and search," Henry said. "I'm not saying abandon him. What do you think I am? But there's a race to win."

"Al's not going to go for that," Jerry said. "And anyway, I don't know where they are. They were heading for Storyville when I left them."

"Of course they were," Henry said. "What the hell is Sorley's problem?"

"Your damn necklace," Jerry said. "That's the problem."

"My necklace?"

"The one that got stolen the night before the race," Jerry said. "The one with the curse."

"That thing's dangerous," Henry said, and looked genuinely alarmed. "And if it's here—it'll only be stronger here."

"Tell me about it."

"Wait—if you had the necklace—how did you get the necklace?"

"It's a really long story," Jerry said. "We don't have time."

Henry looked as though he wanted to pursue the matter, then shook his head. "All right. Have you talked to anybody?"

"Mr. Altner buttonholed me when I came in," Jerry said. "I told him Alma was dealing with a mechanical problem."

"Goddamnit," Henry said. "They'll know she wasn't at the field."

"You got a better idea?" Jerry glared at him.

Henry took a breath, visibly tamping down his anger. "No."

"We'll think of something else to tell the reporters in the morning," Jerry said. He took another gulp of the bourbon. "And Al's the most level-headed woman I've ever met. She'll call the hotel as soon as she knows anything."

"She'd better," Henry muttered.

"She will," Jerry said, and hoped it was true.

Chapter Fifteen

Well, Stasi thought, I'm on a streetcar in the middle of the night with a lunatic.

At least it wasn't possible to throw oneself in the river while riding a streetcar going somewhere random but apparently away from downtown. He certainly wasn't the only guy on the streetcar who'd had way too much to drink, nor was she the only woman trying to get some sizzled guy home without a disaster. Would that they were going home, or at least back to his hotel! Instead they were going somewhere named Eden where Mitch insisted he was missed. And he still had the necklace, though it was too much to hope he'd just hand it over to her.

He leaned on her a little and said in a quiet, conspiratorial voice, "You're pretty. What's your name?"

"Stasi," Stasi said.

He appeared to think about it hard. "Milly will be jealous."

"Is Milly your wife?" It was a guess in the dark, but worthwhile.

He laughed, a brittle kind of sound without any drunken joy in it. "No. Never had a wife. Always thought there was time, before. And then there wasn't any. That's how it goes." He picked up her hand and examined it as if looking for the traces of a wedding ring under the glove. "You married?"

"No," Stasi said.

Mitch looked abashed. "Oh right. He was killed in the war. I'm sorry."

"Well," Stasi said. "These things happen." Easy enough to imagine that boy instead, some quiet upper crust boy who'd been in the Russian army. He wasn't like anyone real.

"I'm still sorry," Mitch said. "Bad things oughtn't happen to someone like you."

"Darling, I'm the very definition of someone to whom bad things happen," Stasi said airily. "I'm a bad thing waiting to happen."

His blue eyes focused very seriously on her face. "Doesn't that get tiring?" he asked quietly.

Stasi leaned back against the window, between him and the side of the streetcar, glancing out at houses darkened against the night. "You have no idea, darling." Bone tired, all the way to the core. "You run and you run and you run and you stay one step ahead, knowing one day you'll stay too long. One day you'll miss a step and then there's nothing under you but air."

He squeezed her hand. "Air's ok if you've got enough lift."

She laughed and rested her head against the glass. "I expect you'd say that, being a pilot. I bet you love the air."

"It's the only thing worth living for," he said.

"Then why wasn't it tonight?" Stasi asked. His hand was cold in hers. "Do you think that might have something to do with the necklace in your pocket?"

"What necklace?"

"Never mind." Stasi shook her head. Some kind of lunatic fugue. There wasn't going to be any sense out of him. She'd call his team's hotel and see if she could get Mrs. Segura, but that would require a telephone, and if she left him alone long enough to make the call she'd probably lose him again. And the necklace. Was the necklace this bad, or was it just that he was on the edge to start with?

There was a long silence. "Do I know you from somewhere?" Mitch asked curiously.

"My name is Stasi," she said.

"Garden District?" Lewis said, squinting at the map. "He's way down there now. That's quite a ways."

Alma blew out a deep breath. "Ok, time for a cab."

"Going where?"

Alma pointed somewhere in the general vicinity. "Pick a street," she said. "Or how about Kindred Hospital? There are reasons why people might take a taxi to a hospital in the middle of the night."

"That does it for me," Lewis said. "It's that or Lafayette Cemetery."

"Please not a cemetery," Alma said. "Do we have to be that gothic?"

"You tell me," Lewis said. "Would Mitch go hang out in a cemetery in the middle of the night?"

Alma looked sober. "He might," she said. "I have no idea where he might go. He probably…" Alma glanced away, shaking her head. "After he got back from Europe he wandered around for a while. Gil would get telegrams from him from random places, New York, New Orleans, Fort Worth… I asked him about it later and he said he didn't remember where he'd been. That he'd genuinely forgotten." She took a deep breath. "That worried me, of course. But as far as I know it never happened again."

"It takes you that way sometimes," Lewis said, and he did know. "You see things you just can't think about anymore, so you forget. You've got to. If you remembered you'd just keep on remembering. So you don't. You shut it off and put it in a box."

Al nodded. "I get that. I just don't know what's happened now."

"The necklace opened the box," Lewis said grimly.

There was a house. It was three blocks from the streetcar line, down a tree lined side street. No lights shone in the windows. Why would they? It was three o'clock in the morning. It was a very nice house, Stasi thought. It had double porches and a wrought iron fence, the finials of the posts decorated like the Berlin Iron of the necklace. The paint was faded in places, and there was a crack in one of the bricks of the walk. Time didn't stand still, and here like everywhere there were the marks of the Depression, paint jobs deferred, minor repairs left for another, more prosperous day.

"Is this your house?" Stasi asked quietly as Mitch opened the iron gate. A little faded sign by the gate proclaimed its name: Eden.

"No," he said. His voice was also low. "I'm just staying here."

"Oh." Friends of his. That would be good. Perhaps they'd have a telephone and know what to do. Stasi followed him up the walk and up the five brick steps onto the porch. Bougainvillea bushes grew up around it and jasmine twined around the columns, small white blossoms lending fragrance to the night.

Mitch knocked on the door. "Milly?"

There was no answer. The house was quiet. The neighborhood was quiet. Not a dog barked. There were no sounds of cars, no sound but the wind through the branches of the big old trees.

"Milly?" Mitch knocked again.

"She's probably asleep," Stasi whispered. "It's three in the morning."

"Milly!" He raised his voice, banging on the door with his fist. "Let me in! Milly!"

"Maybe we should come back later," Stasi said. "Mitch…"

"Milly! Milly! Open the door!"

At this rate someone in the neighborhood would be calling the cops. "I think we should…" Stasi began.

"Milly! Open up! Milly!"

The door opened and for a moment Stasi stood there speechless. There was a man in a bathrobe, a flashlight in his hand, which he shone in their faces. "Milly doesn't live here anymore," he said genially. "She moved to Bienville Parish when she got married ten years ago."

Mitch flinched at the light. "Married? Ten years ago?"

The light played over his face. "Mitchell Sorley," the man said evenly. "Well, this is a surprise."

"Jeff," Mitch said.

The light hit her in the eyes. "And Miss Ivanova. An even better surprise. Should I trust you've brought my necklace?"

"Mr. Lanier," Stasi said, and was proud that she could toss her head.

"You know each other?" Mitch asked.

"He's the man who hired me to find Kershaw's necklace," Stasi said.

"My necklace," Lanier said sharply. "It was in my family for a hundred years before Milly sold it. She had no right. She sold it and kept the money for herself, used it to help that husband of hers open a car dealership! She had no right at all." He smiled at Stasi. "So I hired you to get it back, fair and square. Have you got it?"

Stasi nodded.

Mitch looked at her. "You have Milly's necklace?"

"It's not Milly's," Lanier snapped. "It belongs to the family. She had no right to sell it."

"Mr. Lanier," Stasi began. "There's a curse on it, you see…"

"I know all about the curse," he said, holding out his hand. "We all do. Believe me, no one will be more careful with the necklace than I."

Mitch shook his head. "I thought you'd gone into a sanitarium. That's what Milly said."

Lanier's face changed, hardened. "She put me in one after the war. That wasn't right either. It wasn't right, locking her own brother up like that! She blamed me, you see, for what you did."

"Milly was a good person," Mitch said. His voice slurred a little, much the worse for drink.

"Milly was a spoiled little brat," Lanier snapped. "I never told on you. I never ratted you out. You were my brother in arms, and I never said a word."

"Jeff," Mitch said. "No."

Lanier looked at Stasi. "Has he told you? Has he told you what he is? Leading Milly on, getting his jollies on the sickness of it all?"

"No," Mitch said quietly. "That wasn't what happened."

"Has he told you?" Lanier shouted. "Has he told you he's a god-damned eunuch? He had his balls shot off in the war. I let him stay with me, brother in arms, and he went after my sister and then when he couldn't get it done, he moved on to carving up whores in Storyville with an axe!"

Mitch opened his mouth but nothing came out, and Stasi flinched.

"Give me the necklace!" Lanier shouted. "Give it to me now!"

Mitch rushed him.

Lanier hadn't seen it coming and Mitch was bigger, a tackle that sent the flashlight flying and both of them crashing into the door.

"Oh hell," Stasi said, and got out of the way. The necklace spilled out of Mitch's pocket, glittering cold and evil on the boards of the porch. She scooped it up.

Lanier scrambled up, grasping for something inside the door, a small trickle of blood coming from the corner of his mouth. "I'll kill you," he said. "I will." Something equally dark and deadly glimmered in his hand as he rummaged on the hall table.

"Come on!" Stasi grabbed Mitch by the hand, dragging him to his feet and down the steps. The shot went over their heads, slicing through the leaves of the tree above as they ran for their lives.

Lewis tensed, his head going up like a hunting dog's. "That was a shot," he said.

"North of here," Alma said. They stood on the sidewalk a block from Kindred Hospital, watching the tail lights of the cab disappear.

"You want to bet?" Lewis asked.

"I wouldn't bet against it," Alma sighed. They must have covered sixty blocks tonight, all told. Running was out of the question, but they could probably manage a brisk walk. "Let's go."

Well, Stasi thought, I'm in a cemetery in the middle of the night with an axe murderer. Life does have its little quirks.

They'd run down first one street and then another, dodging one more shot and trying to stay in the shadow of the trees, but short of barging into a house there really wasn't much cover. Of course there were bushes and plants, fences and flowers, but they were as much hindrance as help. Blossoms fell, leaving a trail. Roots were something to trip over. And towering live oaks didn't provide much of a place to hide unless you were Tarzan, which she decidedly wasn't. Ducking behind a tree truck might work for a pursued ingénue in the movies, but it didn't work in real life, not for two people with one of them drunk and both of them winded. The gates of Lafayette Cemetery offered the perfect refuge.

Unlike most cemeteries Stasi had seen in the United States, Lafayette Cemetery seemed mostly above ground rather than a graveyard. Mausoleums large and small glimmered white in the dark, marble reflecting palely. It was like a city of the dead, streets green with grass between crumbling monuments, walls of vaults stacked four high, each body behind a neat plaque. It was like cemeteries in Europe meant for feasting the dead on tombstones with walks where children could run shouting between the bones of their ancestors. There were plenty of places to hide. Unfortunately it was a little hard to hide when you had an axe murderer noisily being sick on a wrought iron fence beside you.

Stasi looked anxiously up and down the "street." Not a shadow moved. The mausoleums were silent, their white edges marked sharp against the dark of a few towering magnolia trees. Perhaps they'd lost him. It was possible.

Mitch straightened up. "I feel better," he said. Whether that was the result of being sick or getting rid of the necklace was a moot point.

"Good," Stasi said.

There was a step, a sudden movement, and a bullet came singing along the row, plunking into a mausoleum, sending shards of the facing marble flying. Mitch knocked her flat between two platform tombs.

"Ow," Stasi said.

"Keep your head down!"

"I'm keeping it down!"

"And be quiet!"

"You were the one who started talking!"

"He has a gun and we don't," Mitch said. He was rather heavy to have on top of one. Also, he didn't smell particularly good.

"Oh well observed! I hadn't noticed he had a gun," Stasi whispered furiously.

Footsteps coming closer.

"How about we get out of here?"

"What an idea!"

Mitch clambered to his feet and she dragged herself after him, dodging around the corner of a mausoleum just as Lanier reached the end.

"I know you're here," he called. "Miss Ivanova, I've got no quarrel with you. You can leave if you want. This is between me and Mitchell Sorley."

Stasi slipped around the back corner of another tomb, drawing Mitch after her. That put two between them and Lanier.

"You should go," Mitch whispered in her ear.

"You think I believe him?" Stasi whispered incredulously. "He'll let me go when hell freezes over. I'm the one who knows that he hired me to steal the necklace."

Another series of steps. He was coming closer.

"I could get the jump on him."

"And get shot."

She could see Lanier's shadow thrown against the opposite wall, gun extended. No, anybody going for it might take the shot at point blank range.

Instead she backed away, trying to make no sound, pulling Mitch along. At least he seemed soberer. He'd lost his hat, and the shadows through the magnolia branches shifted across his face as she drew him along, tiptoeing among the tombs.

Around another set of tombs, across a path and between the next set. These were newer tombs, only a few decades old. 1890 gleamed out at her from incised marble letters. Larger ones too, providing more shelter. There was no sound. Who knew where Lanier was?

There was a sudden movement ahead and Stasi shrank back.

Not Lanier.

The woman stood in the shadow of a monstrous live oak, beside a marble urn that graced a mausoleum, dark hair falling in ringlets around her face, a fan in her other hand. Her white dress glimmered like moonlight in the dark, and her eyes found Stasi's unerringly as she raised one hand to her neck.

"Who are you?" Stasi whispered.

"My name is Emilie." She tipped her head, the gesture of a coquette in days gone by, as antique as her century-old dress.

"Who are you talking to?" Mitch whispered, looking around.

"The Dead," Stasi said.

The woman took a step closer, stronger and more solid. "I can help you," she said.

"Why would you do that?" Stasi asked, and then she knew. "You're one of the necklace's victims."

"Emilie Rose Angelique Marie Daigle Lanier," she said. "I am the third woman it killed." She took another step closer, her eyes not leaving Stasi's. "I was killed in my theater box by my husband because he thought I had a lover. He lost his temper and stabbed me." She stopped, swaying in her long pale skirts.

"Lanier," Stasi said.

"What?" Mitch said, glancing around wildly.

"My son was twenty months old," Emilie said. "He was raised by my sister when my husband was hanged. Until the necklace killed her too." She opened her fan like a gesture of long habit, a secret smile crossing her face. "She's named for me, you know. Milly. Emilie. That's her real name but they call her Milly. She escaped. She got rid of the necklace. Maybe it will never touch her or her girls either. She has two daughters now, away in St. Bienville. And I thought the curse was finally done."

"It's not," Stasi said grimly.

"Who are you talking to?" Mitch whispered again.

"A ghost," Stasi said. "And maybe she can help us. Now hush."

"I can help you," she said. "And I will help you if you'll promise to take that necklace far away from here and lock it away."

"We can promise that," Stasi said. "But not if we don't get away from your descendant. He's trying to shoot us."

"I know." Emilie lifted her head, looking down the long row of tombs. "He hasn't been right since the war. It takes some men that way." She glanced back at Stasi. "But isn't it so pretty? Nothing like the shadow of old blood to make a man attractive. It does lend an air of virility."

"Yes, well, right now he's going to shoot us," Stasi said. "We need a place to hide until morning, or we need to get out of here without him seeing us."

"Hiding is better," Emilie said. "There's only one entrance and you'd have to go past him to get to it. And frankly you're not that quiet." She glanced at Mitch appraisingly. "Or that sober."

"Yes, I've noticed," Stasi said.

"Noticed what?" Mitch demanded in a whisper.

"That you're blotto. Now be quiet and let me talk." She squeezed his hand tightly.

"I suppose I am," Mitch said thoughtfully.

Emilie shook her head. "Men! They're all the same," she said in her lilting accent. "I've seen this one before. He's a big boy, isn't he?"

"Are we going to gossip or are you going to help us hide?" Stasi asked. "Because frankly we don't have all night."

"Come this way." Emilie turned, slipping between two mausoleums. "Quietly."

"This way," Stasi said, dragging Mitch behind her. He didn't resist, just followed after like Theseus on the thread.

Between tombs, around corners, down a long avenue where a wall was filled with tombs four high, like a catacomb only above ground, each one marked with names and dates, into the older part of the cemetery. The tombs were closer together here, a neoclassical façade almost wall to wall with the ones beside it. Over the door was a Latin inscription, and before it an empty urn.

"Here," Emilie said. "The door will open if you give it a little push. They didn't get it quite to catch the last time they came."

"Are you sure about this?" Mitch asked, swaying a little in the moonlight, bareheaded and rough looking. "In a tomb?"

"It's all right," Stasi said, glancing at Emilie. "The owner doesn't mind." She pushed on the bronze door and it gave on well-oiled hinges. She went in and closed the door behind them. It was pitch black.

"There," Emilie said. "Now you stay here until morning, and I'll go lead him off."

"You can do that?" Stasi whispered.

Emilie laughed. "Of course I can," she said. "He's my own bone and blood. I'll keep you safe until dawn, and you make sure that necklace leaves New Orleans."

"Deal," Stasi said. There was a warm breeze, or rather the absence of Emilie's cold.

"What's the deal?" Mitch asked. He was breathing hard.

"It's a long story," Stasi said. "But we should be safe now. Do you still have your lighter?"

There was the sound of fumbling, and then the Ronson lit, Mitch looking around in the narrow space.

It was quite nice, actually, and not ghoulish at all. There were six spaces, three to each side, each covered in a marble slab with names and dates. Stasi traced the first one, not at all surprised. "Emilie Rose Angelique Marie Daigle Lanier, August 4, 1797—January 8, 1826."

Mitch put his hand out to steady himself. "That's the ghost you were talking to?"

"Your Milly's great grandmother ," Stasi said. Her fingers slid down the marble to the one beneath it. "Charles Felix Daigle, 1769—1834. He followed the eagles." The marble was smooth and hardly worn at all. "Her father, I suppose."

"Another sister?" Mitch said, looking at the other side. "Victoire Louise Justine Daigle? They're all Daigles here."

"Of course they are, darling," Stasi said, sinking down to sit with her back to the tombs. "Every last one of them following the eagles." She looked up at him. "Why don't you sit down before you fall down?"

"That might be a good idea," Mitch said. "Ouch!" The light went out abruptly as the Ronson got too hot. She felt rather than heard him slid down beside her.

"Oh, my feet," Stasi said, folding her legs and massaging her instep. "Give me the lighter, darling. I think I saw a votive candle over here." She felt around in the dark until she found the glass, leaning across

Mitch's lap. There was a little puddle of wax in the bottom as she'd hoped. "There."

His hand bumped her breast. "Sorry," he said. "Trying to give you the lighter. I can't see."

"Because it's dark," Stasi said, taking the lighter and flicking it, coaxing the little bit of candle left to light. It caught at last, a faint gold and blue flame at the bottom of the glass. "Isn't that better?"

Mitch leaned his head back against the mausoleum and closed his eyes, his face gray.

"We'll just wait him out," Stasi said. "It can't be more than three hours until dawn."

"Sure."

She looked at him closely. "Are you all right, darling?"

Mitch didn't open his eyes. "For a drunk lunatic in a fugue state, I'm doing pretty well."

"What's my name?"

He almost smiled. "I have no idea," he said. "You said your name was Rostov but Jeff called you Ivanova, and I wouldn't take any bets on either one being true. What's your real name?"

"Darling, that's like asking a woman her real age," Stasi said. Oh her feet hurt. But any one you could walk away from was a good one. "Let's try this. What's Lanier's real name and how to you know him?"

He still didn't open his eyes. "Jefferson Murat Lanier," Mitch said. "I was in the army with him. He was transferred out of the Veneto to the Western Front. I ran into him again after the war. He and his sister had inherited that house in the Garden District, Eden. I stayed with them for a while." He moved his head a little, like a man in a dream. "I don't know how long, so don't ask me. And I don't know why I left or when. Gil had been wiring me, asking me to come to Colorado Springs. At some point I did. Couldn't tell you why. I don't remember most of 1919 and part of 1920. Jeff's right that I'm a certifiable lunatic."

"Oh," Stasi said. She moved her toes back and forth. Yes, they still moved. "And he thinks you…seduced his sister?" she asked delicately.

Mitch's mouth thinned, closed eyes twitching. "I'm pretty sure I didn't do that."

"Ah," Stasi said. She took a deep breath, leaning back against the stone beside him. "And that's where you saw the cursed necklace before."

"Yeah. That's where I saw it. I guess Jeff's got it back now. I dropped it in the fight."

"I've got the necklace, darling," Stasi said.

At that he opened his eyes and blinked at her. "You do?"

She nodded. "The question is what to do with it."

He frowned. "I thought he paid you to bring it to him. Why don't you just hand it over and collect the money?"

"Because now I've seen what it does," Stasi said. "And I'm sorry but I don't think he's able to prevent it from wreaking havoc. It wants to kill and it's terribly strong. It belongs somewhere it can't harm anyone, or it needs to be destroyed."

His frown deepened. "And that matters to you?"

Stasi stretched out her leg and smoothed her tattered silk dress. "Darling, it may come as a complete shock to you, but I have a problem with killing innocent people. Unlike some present company."

He didn't look away from her. "You think I'm the Axeman."

"Are you?"

Mitch took a deep breath. "I don't know."

"Well," Stasi said.

"I don't remember killing those people, but I don't remember much of anything from that year. The killings stopped about the time I left town." Mitch shook his head, leaned it back against the wall again. "I don't know."

Stasi looked around at the pale tombs. "I could find out," she said.

"How?"

"The Dead probably know." Stasi smoothed her dress again. "I'm sure at least one of the Axeman's victims is still lurking around. Given a few days I could probably find one. Mind you, it's terribly difficult getting a witness description, you know how that is, darling, and it's worse when it's someone who was very upset, which the victim usually is. Ma'am, would you mind giving me a description of the man who killed you? Terribly awkward. But I could certainly ask them if they recognized you. Though it would probably be better to do something more like a police lineup. More scientific."

He closed his eyes. "I'm not sure I want to know."

"Ah," Stasi said.

"What's that?" Lewis pulled up sharply and Alma stopped on his heels. Ahead of them were the gates of Lafayette Cemetery, a wrought iron arch overhead proclaiming its name.

"What's what?" Alma asked quietly.

"That." Something dark lay in the gutter like a dead animal. Lewis jogged across the street and investigated, then picked it up as Alma came over.

"Mitch's hat," she said. She took it from him and turned it around in her hands. No blood, thank goodness. It smelled like smoke and booze but nothing worse.

Lewis looked toward the cemetery gates. "If he was running and dropped it…"

Alma let out a long breath. "I can't think of any good reason to run into a cemetery in the middle of the night." She looked at her watch, tilting her wrist to catch the light from the nearest streetlight, and suppressed the urge to swear a blue streak.

"What time is it?" Lewis asked.

"Quarter till five," Alma said. "We're supposed to be at the airport ready to take off in two hours and fifteen minutes."

"Crap," Lewis said. He looked at the gates again. "We should…"

Alma closed her eyes. "We have to find Mitch," she said. They were in first place. They were winning. Forty five minutes drive out to the airport, and nobody had slept a wink. Henry would be chewing the wallpaper. And if they missed their start time they'd lose their lead and everything they had invested in this. If they didn't win a purse they'd have to sell the Jenny when they got back to Colorado. She took a deep breath. "We don't leave our people behind."

Lewis nodded. "Let's find him. At least in daylight we can get a cab to the airport more easily."

"And let's hope Jerry has packed for us," Alma said. "And that he assumes we'll meet him there."

Chapter Sixteen

Jerry let the curtain fall, turning away from the street and the cars still parked below, no longer gray in the rising light. He'd managed to snatch a few hours' sleep, despite waiting for a telephone call that hadn't come; now he was busy throwing things into suitcases, ready for the moment Alma walked in the door. He reached into his pocket and checked his watch: quarter past five. Their start time was seven o'clock, first out, and they had to reach Pensacola by noon if they wanted to take part in the pylon race. Forty-five minutes to the airfield… He went back to the window again, peering out into the light. Oh, Alma, where the hell are you?

There was a soft knock at the door, and he lurched to open it, almost falling in his haste. His shoulders sagged when he saw Henry in the hallway.

"Anything?"

Jerry shook his head, stepped back to let the other man in.

"Damn it to hell," Henry said. He was keeping his voice down with an effort that made the veins on his forehead stand out. "Where are they?"

"I wish I knew," Jerry snapped. "If I knew, don't you think I'd tell you?" He controlled himself with an effort. They wouldn't get anywhere shouting at each other. "I've got everything packed up. We can leave any time."

"But will they go to the field?" Henry asked. He went to the window in turn, looking down on Poydras Street as though he could make them appear by sheer force of will. "if they come back here, waste time looking for you –"

Jerry took a breath, made himself focus, shoving aside the worry and the sleeplessness and the night's confusion the way he'd learned in the War. "She'd call," he said. "Alma knows how close it's getting, she'd find a pay phone and call the hotel. We can leave a message with the switchboard, have the operator tell her we've gone on to the field."

Henry nodded slowly. "All right. That makes sense." He crossed to the telephone, dialed the operator and left his message, then ordered a bellboy and cab with the absent ease of a man who did this regularly. Jerry latched Alma's suitcase, gave the room a quick search to be sure he wasn't leaving anything important.

What the hell had Mitch been thinking, to let that thing get hold of him? But it wasn't about thinking, he knew that from his own encounter with it. The curse was worked deep into the iron, growing in strength with each death, with every drop of blood and every tear. It tugged and it probed until it found a weakness – he'd felt it himself, and seen the look on Alma's face when she handed it to him. And somehow, somewhere, it had found something in Mitch that it could use.

Henry was finished with the phone, had gone back to the window, and Jerry looked at him.

"What else do you know about the necklace?"

"What?"

"The necklace," Jerry said. "Anything more you can tell me about it. Maybe we can figure out some way to find it, or something."

"I told you what I know," Henry said. "It came with a questionable history, like I said, and when I hired a guy to look into it, he came up with the story about the curse. Which he thought was pretty much someone trying to drive up the price, but I'd gotten my hands on the thing by then, and – I knew. My safe's warded as well as locked – and they're damn good Chubb locks, by the way – and I figured it would be safe there." He shook his head. "I guess I was wrong."

"Yes," Jerry said, but closed his mouth over any further complaint. There was nothing more he could do here.

"What in the merry hell?" Alma's scathing voice cut across his sleep, and Mitch woke with sunshine in his eyes.

"Um?" he said, squinting. It was way, way too bright for his pounding head and he felt vaguely nauseated. He was leaning back against the wall inside a mausoleum in Lafayette Cemetery with the sun streaming through the open door, his arm around a disheveled looking brunette in a torn silk dress, with pretty much zero recollection of how he got there. Except that from the smell it must have involved rum. "It's not what it looks like?"

"I am going to kill you and suck the marrow from your bones," Alma said.

"Oh please don't," the woman said, untwining from where she'd been using his shoulder as a pillow. "It's not every day one has a lunatic fugue."

"You?" Lewis said disbelievingly, to the brunette, and Mitch looked down at her as well.

"Hey," he said slowly. "I know you."

Alma snorted. "I should hope so! What in the hell happened here? No, wait. Don't tell me. Tell me this instead. Do you have any idea what time it is?"

Mitch blinked again. He had the feeling this was a trick question. "Um, no?"

"Twenty minutes after seven," Alma said sharply. "Seven. AM. Our takeoff time."

And then it all came flooding back. "Crap."

"Lewis and I have been hunting for you for the last eleven hours," Alma snapped. "We've been hunting through the cemetery for two hours, wondering if we'd find you or your dead body. And instead we find you canoodling in a mausoleum with our little stowaway!"

Mitch got to his feet, which was a bad idea both because it made him dizzy and because it involved dropping Stasi on her behind. "We have to get to the airport," he said.

"No kidding!" Alma shouted. "Right this very minute we are losing our first place lead! And where the hell have you been?"

"I can explain," Stasi said, getting to her feet. "I'm not sure he remembers where we've been."

"I wish I didn't," Mitch said. Which he did. A lot.

Alma pulled herself up to her full height, dirty man's shirt, black eye and all. "You can explain on the way to the airport. And I'll decide if I'm going to kill you myself."

They took a cab out to the airfield in the dawn light. The sun wasn't fully clear of the horizon, spreading molten between the distant trees, throwing elongated shadows. The light was brassy, tilting everything to yellow, even the still water in the ditches that ran beside the elevated road.

The same light caught the white-washed hangars and the beacon tower, darkened the sod as though it were soaked with rain. Henry directed the cabbie to the main hangar, and they climbed out. Henry left Jerry to supervise getting the suitcases to the plane, and disappeared into the shadows.

"Say," the cabbie said, as Jerry fumbled for a tip. "I didn't realize y'all was Gilchrist."

Jerry paused, forced a smile even as he found a third quarter in his pocket. "That's right."

The cabbie grinned. "Hell of a lady, Mrs. Segura. We been listening on the radio. I'm sorry I didn't get to drive her."

"Thanks," Jerry said. He couldn't think of anything helpful to say, so he handed over the tip.

"Thank you, sir." The cabbie touched his cap. "Good luck."

We'll need it, Jerry thought. The other teams were starting to arrive, loading their planes, turning over engines. He craned his neck every time another cab pulled up, but it was only more of the contestants, or reporters.

Where the hell were they? And what the hell was wrong with Mitch? He shook his head. He'd been in pretty bad shape himself when he'd come to Colorado Springs the first time, still recovering from the infection that cost him his lower leg. Gil had told him once that Mitch had had a bad time since the War, but at the time, Jerry had still been too weak to think much about it, to ask questions. By the time he'd been well enough to notice much more than people's general presence, Mitch had seemed ok and the chance had passed. Had there been something he should have seen? Something he should remember? Gil had said—Gil had said that Mitch spent some time traveling before he'd come to Colorado, that it was a touchy subject, something Mitch didn't want to talk about. No, didn't want to remember—couldn't remember? Surely not that. That would be… potentially very bad.

Henry came striding back across the hangar, waving off a reporter, his coat flying open unbuttoned. "Anything?"

Jerry bit back a profane response—did Henry think he'd smuggled the team into the Terrier? "No sign yet."

"Call the hotel," Henry said. "I'm going to try to get the referees to let me start fueling without them."

Jerry pivoted on his artificial leg, stalked across to the pay phone by the door. Luckily, he still had a handful of change, and fed it into the machine at the operator's instructions, then waited while she raised the hotel switchboard. The operator was polite, but unhelpful. No, Mrs. Segura hadn't left a message for him, nor had Mr. Segura or Mr. Sorley. She rang their rooms, and Jerry listened to the bell jangle on and on without an answer until the operator came on again.

"I'm sorry, sir. There's no answer."

"Thank you," Jerry said, and hung up. He hadn't felt a knot of fear like this since Italy, waiting for the balloon to go up, not knowing for sure if they'd get support, or even if their spotters had found the right targets... He shook the thought away, and turned back toward the plane.

"Dr. Ballard."

At least it wasn't Carmichael, Jerry thought, and forced a smile. He kept walking, the reporter falling into step at his side.

"Mrs. Segura and the rest of the team—it's less than an hour till they're due to take off. Any idea when they'll be here?"

Jerry shook his head.

"Any idea where they've gone?"

"Into the city," Jerry said.

"Any word on why?"

"I can't answer that," Jerry said—it was literally true—and waved to Henry. "Any luck?"

Henry nodded, his face grim. "I've got them to agree to fuel her up, and I can move her to the start line if I have to, but anything more—like flying her myself—disqualifies us." He stopped, shoving his fists into his pockets. "No word?"

Jerry shook his head again. "They haven't been back to the hotel."

"Goddamnit!" Henry glared at the hovering reporter. "Look, buddy, you'd better clear out. There's nothing for you here."

"Missing aviatrix? In a city where all kinds of weird things happen?" The reporter was careful to stay out of reach, Jerry noticed. "That's a story, Mr. Kershaw,"

Henry controlled himself with an effort. "I'll grant you that," he said, and his voice was almost his usual good-tempered baritone.

"But that's happening there, not here. We're as much in the dark as you are, Thompson."

"The team owner doesn't know?" Thompson asked. "Come on, Doc, you must know something."

Jerry shook his head, not trusting himself, his hand tight on the crook of his cane.

"Nope," Henry said. "We don't know anything." He paused. "You want the real story of the morning? The referees are over there right now trying to decide if they're going to disqualify Gilchrist altogether if they miss their start time. There's a story for you."

"Yeah?" Thompson cocked his head in disbelief.

Henry nodded. "Check it out for yourself."

Thompson backed away, and Jerry looked at the other man. "Is that true?"

"Oh, yes." Henry's fists were clenched again, and he looked more than ever like a baited bull. "Some of the sponsors feel this is showing disrespect for the event, and Alma traipsing around with her harem in tow—her husband and her boyfriend and God knows what they think you are—that doesn't exactly make this easier."

"You know damn well that's not true," Jerry said.

"I know." Henry had the grace to look abashed. "I do know that. But Winchell's been making hay with it, and some of the sponsors are a little skittish. A sexy vamp is all well and good, but they don't want to be associated with actual immorality. Luckily Altner just thinks it makes everything more exciting, and he's putting up most of the money."

"Will they be disqualified?" Jerry asked. They'd staked everything on the race, just as much as Jezek had. If they didn't win—if they got kicked out because of Henry's damned necklace—If they'd just managed to get rid of the thing in San Angelo the way they'd planned— He swallowed his anger, knowing it was useless here.

"I think I've talked them out of it," Henry said. "I hope I have. But, remember, whatever happens, they still have to get to Pensacola by noon."

None of it made much sense to Lewis, and by the time the cab tore up to the airport terminal at 8:33 Lewis didn't feel he was much the wiser. He had a few points—the guy who hired Stasi to steal the necklace had tried to shoot Mitch, who was apparently in a lunatic fugue and thought it was 1919, but Stasi had gotten him away and dragged him into the cemetery. Mitch might or might not be the New Orleans Axeman. Mitch mostly sat with his head back against the seat and his eyes closed, looking grim and gray and ill, interjecting little into the narrative.

Meanwhile the clock was ticking, their lead evaporating.

The sound of a trimotor taking off split the air as the cab pulled up, Lewis paying the driver without waiting for change. "Who is it?" he asked, not looking up from what he was doing.

"Comanche," Alma said. "They were in seventh."

Mitch muttered something under his breath and staggered out of the car.

"Darling, can you walk?" Stasi asked, running around to get under his shoulder.

"The hangar. Now," Alma said, taking off at a run through the doors.

"This is not going to be pretty," Lewis muttered, leaving the countess to drag Mitch along. Even if Jerry had gotten the plane fueled, the preflight was going to take a few minutes. He hurried along in Alma's wake.

She broke into a sprint across the flight line, running for the Terrier pulled up on the apron outside the hangar. At least someone had gotten it fueled and ready to go. Jerry was standing on the tarmac. With Henry. Henry must have pulled the plane out. He'd been a pilot himself, and while he couldn't fly the race without disqualifying them he could do that much. But thunderclouds were friendlier than the look on his face.

"Lewis, take the seat," Alma shouted back to him. "I'll get clearance."

"What in the name of heaven?" Henry demanded, grabbing Alma by the arm. "You people! What the hell?"

"I can talk or I can fly," Alma snapped back. "Jerry, get Mitch onboard."

"Where have you…?" Jerry started, and Alma cut him off with a look.

Two of the reporters who had been photographing the Comanche plane taking off hurried over, getting between Lewis and the door with cameras. "Mr. Segura, why does your wife have a black eye?"

Lewis punched him.

It was quite a roundhouse. The reporter went down, limbs flailing.

Henry threw his hat on the ground and stomped on it.

Lewis dove through the hatch and into the cockpit, flipping the ignition as he went. Preflight and warm up. He could do that while Alma spoke to the referees, got them to phone the tower.

She was right behind him, sliding into the co-pilot's seat. "Get us out of here as quick as you can," she said.

"You don't have to tell me twice."

Lewis was dimly aware of voices in the compartment behind, but he tuned them out. Nothing mattered but the plane. Nothing mattered but the flight, cold and adrenaline-fueled in the bright morning just like he'd been on many a flight line during the war. Just get it right, Segura. Just get it perfect.

And it was. At 9:08 the Terrier soared into the air, an hour and thirty three minutes behind the leader, in dead last place.

"We are completely screwed," Mitch said, leaning his head back against the seat.

"Would you like to tell me what happened?" Jerry's voice was completely even.

Mitch closed his eyes. "I was going to borrow some toothpaste," he said. "Out of your shaving kit. The necklace fell out and…" He shook his head, a bad idea as it brought the nausea back. "I don't know what happened next." It was all foggy, bits and pieces of memory. "I went to a bar. I walked around town for a while. I ran into Stasi." Mitch stopped. And then he'd been convinced it was 1919, that twelve years had completely disappeared. Gil was alive and was wiring him from Colorado, asking when he was going to come out and go into business with him. He was living with Jeff and Milly. It had all made sense, all seemed logical at the time.

"And then?" Jerry asked gently.

"I don't know."

Jerry leaned over and patted his shoulder. "Why don't you try to get some sleep? There isn't anything we can do until we get to Pensacola." He heard Jerry get up heavily and go to the cockpit door, leaning in with it half ajar, heard the sound of his voice but no words were distinguishable over the sound of the engines. No doubt he was talking to the others, talking about him.

The seat beside him gave again and Mitch looked up. "You're still here?"

"I seem to be," Stasi said brightly. Her hair had fallen down and her silk dress was ripped and she looked decidedly the worse for wear. "I love fleeing town with the clothes on my back, darling! It's what I live for."

"You didn't have to."

"Lanier was trying to shoot me, and between you and me, he didn't look all that sane himself, if you understand what I mean. And I've heard Florida's lovely this time of year. Pensacola, is it?"

"It is," Mitch said. His mouth tasted like ashes. "We were in first place. Now we'll be lucky if we can stay in the race at all."

Stasi glanced out the window. "I suppose it's a big prize."

"We have to win a purse," Mitch said. "We're flat broke. The company is going under if we don't place. We're going to have to sell off the planes and my car." He took a deep breath. "We could have won."

"Don't you think you might still?"

Mitch snorted. "Dead last? With only two legs to go? We had our one good trick, and we've used it. It put us number one. That was what we had. That was the game plan."

"Then you'll have to find another one, won't you?" Her eyes had dark circles under them but she sat there in her ruined dress, thin and beautiful and indomitable.

"It was the White Terror, wasn't it? In Hungary," Mitch said before he could stop himself. "On the Austrian side of the war, not the Russian."

She looked away, glancing out the window as though some of the scenery was of passing interest. "Darling, one revolution is very like another."

"I'm just saying," Mitch said, groping for the words through his throbbing head. "If it was the Austrian army, I don't hold a grudge that way." An Austrian shell over Austrian lines, but that was how it went. Not her fault, no more than anyone else's in the world gone mad.

She looked at him sideways. "You're a lunatic."

"Pretty much," Mitch said, and closed his eyes.

Chapter Seventeen

Jerry glanced over his shoulder. Mitch was leaning back in his chair, eyes closed, while the soi-disant countess calmly fished a battered pack of cigarettes out of her purse and fitted one into a slim black holder. Mitch's cigarettes, Jerry was willing to bet, and turned his back before she could expect him to offer a light.

Alma and Lewis had left the cockpit door open, clipped back against the forward bulkhead, and Jerry braced himself in the frame, leaning awkwardly in. The position made his leg ache, but he doubted they could be heard over the engine noise.

"What the hell?" he said.

Alma didn't take her eyes off the horizon, but the set of her shoulders and her white-knuckled grip on the wheel betrayed her fury. Lewis glanced warily over his shoulder.

"We found Mitch," he said, with the air of a man struggling to find a silver lining, and Jerry stared back at him.

"So I see. Stinking of rum and with extra baggage."

"Baggage." Alma's voice was a snarl. "I'd like to murder them both."

"Did Mitch say what happened?" Lewis asked. "He told us he couldn't remember."

"It was the necklace," Jerry said. "He wanted to borrow my toothpaste, and it fell out, and—Al, you know what that thing's like." He winced then, unsure of how much Alma had told Lewis, but Lewis nodded.

"It's strong," he said. "Really powerful."

"After that..." Jerry shrugged. "He got drunk. He ran into whatever-her-name-is."

"She said she found him on the Algiers Ferry Landing," Lewis said.

Jerry whistled.

"Yeah," Lewis said. "She said she tried to get him to stop, but he was bound and determined he was going to get to a house called Eden. Which turned out to belong to somebody who he'd known in the war—"

"And who, incidentally, was the man who hired Miss Rostov to steal the necklace," Alma interjected.

"It was some sort of family heirloom," Lewis said. "And somebody sold it? I'm not very clear on that part. But she says the guy pulled a gun on them, and that's how she and Mitch ended up hiding in the cemetery."

"Of course they did," Jerry said.

"That's assuming we can believe a word that woman says," Alma said.

"I think that part's probably true," Lewis said, frowning. There was something in his expression that made Jerry frown in turn.

"What else did she say?"

"She said this guy—Lanier, his name is—"

"Jeff Lanier?" Jerry interrupted. "He was in the Lodge in Italy—before you joined, Al, he got transferred right after Mitch was shot up. He should—he must have known what the necklace was."

"Maybe?" Lewis shook his head. "That's not the important thing. Miss Rostov said he told her that Mitch was the Axeman."

Jerry took a deep breath, bracing himself against the frame of the door as though he was warding off a body blow. The New Orleans Axeman, the South's bloody answer to Lizzie Borden, eleven people hacked to death in their beds and the shadow of the devil and his music over it all… Not Mitch. It couldn't be. Except he'd been in New Orleans at the right time…

"I don't believe it." Alma's voice was flat, her eyes fixed on the horizon. "You can't seriously believe that."

"I don't want to," Jerry said, and it was the truth. The trouble was, it made a kind of dreadful sense. Mitch had been missing for a year and a half, Gil had said, eighteen months of occasional telegrams and scribbled postcards, and when he'd finally fetched up in Colorado Springs, he'd had thirty dollars in his pocket and no real memory of where he'd been. Mitch wasn't a killer; if he had murdered those people, he would have to have been under such a terrible compulsion that his only possible defense lay in a failure to remember.

"Mitch wouldn't," Alma said. "He doesn't like killing. He never did."

That was true, Jerry thought. Mitch didn't take any particular pleasure in the kill. But he was more than capable of it, the ace with seven dead men. "You might as well say I couldn't kill," he said, and this time Alma did turn, one quick glance in his direction.

"I said he wasn't a killer," she said. "No more than you are. That's different and you know it."

"I do," Jerry admitted. "But, Al—"

"Yes, he was missing," she said. "Yes, he—he wasn't well when he came home. And yes, he told me, told Gil, that he couldn't remember where he'd been. But that doesn't make him a murderer. And it certainly doesn't make him the Axeman."

"It also doesn't prove he isn't," Jerry said. "I'm sorry, Al."

"I don't believe it," Alma said again. "Not Mitch."

Jerry looked at Lewis. "What do you think?"

Lewis shrugged. "I don't know him like you do, so—I just don't know. I had a dream," he said slowly. "Months ago, when we first talked about entering the race. It was about jazz and New Orleans—I see that now. I didn't recognize the city when I dreamed it because I'd never been there. I think—I think it was a memory of the New Orleans Axeman."

Alma took a deep breath. "Did you see a killing?"

"No." Lewis shook his head. "I didn't. I just saw the streets and the rain and heard the music. I didn't see anyone actually die. I don't even know for certain it was Mitch."

"But you don't know it wasn't."

"I don't know either way," Lewis said. He glanced at Alma, his face lined with exhaustion from the sleepless night. "And—I'm sorry, Al, but I think we've got other things to worry about right now. There's got to be a way to get us back in the race."

"I'm damned if I see one," Alma said.

"We'll think of something," Lewis answered, but his voice wasn't as certain as the words.

Jerry tightened his hold on the frame as the Terrier lurched under him. "First we get to Pensacola before noon," he said. "Then we see."

Mitch leaned back in the seat, his eyes closed. He wouldn't bet two bits on their chances now. Two bits. That's what a girl was worth in Budapest in 1919. Twenty five cents, the price of a dozen eggs today. He'd seen the bread lines. He'd seen the cost of food skyrocketing a hundred times, every loaf of bread going through the ceiling, the currency becoming worthless. And when it did, so did people.

Mitch had been transferred right after the Armistice between Austria and Italy. For the last few weeks he'd had command of the squadron, taken over after Gil was wounded, taken his best shot. He did ok. He must have, because they made him a brevet major and sent him to Budapest, military attaché to the diplomats who were supposed to turn a cease-fire into a peace treaty. Just who they were supposed to make a treaty with was a good question. The Austro-Hungarian Empire was over—just last week—the end of four hundred years of near absolute monarchy. The new government, the Hungarian Democratic Republic, lasted not quite five months. He'd been there all of them, except the last week, when the diplomatic personnel had been pulled out when it got too dangerous. Another day, another revolution, this time Communist, and a Red Terror that lasted five months. Then the counterrevolution, a White Terror that in turn sent more waves of refugees fleeing, had more neighbors killing neighbors.

Mitch was long gone by then. He didn't remember quite where he was, but it wasn't Budapest. That had been the winter before.

Mitch kept his eyes closed, listening to the sound of the Terrier's engines. It wove in and out of his dreams, half dozing. Sometimes Stasi said something to someone else and it took him back, the sound of her voice, that particular accent.

"Two bits, soldier? Anything you want for two bits?" She was fair, not dark. She didn't look a thing like Stasi, that girl on a rainy night in Budapest thirteen Februaries ago. Not a thing like her, bundled in a scarf against the cold, drops standing like icicles on her hair where it escaped in the front.

Two bits was almost nothing. It would be warm inside. Everything would be warm, and maybe...

Her room was tiny but big enough, her pressed up against the door, arms passionless but her face so pretty, the soft touch of her hair, the color flaming in her thin cheeks. She ought to have been intoxicating, rather than a mistake, like everything that happened after.

The Terrier shifted, beginning a long, slow banking descent. He knew her, his Terrier, felt the change in movement in his gut, and Mitch opened his eyes.

"We're arriving in Pensacola," Stasi said, glancing over from the other seat, her legs folded in front of her in their tattered silk stockings.

"I know," Mitch said. "I can feel it."

Alma brought the Terrier down onto the long runway, pointing the Terrier's nose into the wind, all her attention on the feel of the plane as she slowed toward stalling. Station Field was part of the Navy base; the runways were paved, impeccably maintained, and she let the Terrier drop onto the tarmac with hardly a bounce.

"Just gone eleven," Lewis said.

Alma allowed herself a sigh of relief. She'd been certain she could get them into Pensacola before noon—it was only about a two hour flight, after all—but the way things had been going, she'd been tensed for further trouble, engines or weather or almost anything. She turned the Terrier toward the hangars, following the flagman, and winced as she saw the crowd still waiting, filling the temporary bleachers and crowding the roof of what had to be the administrative building.

"Looks like we might have made up a few minutes," Lewis went on. "Maybe ten?"

"That's good," Alma said, but the words felt hollow. The press would be waiting, and the race authorities—what the hell was she going to say to them? More important still, could she be sure Miss Rostov would go along with them, and not go running to the papers with what would be the biggest scoop of the race? No, she thought. That wasn't going to happen, because Miss Rostov knew perfectly well that they'd accuse her of stealing Henry's necklace in the first place.

There was no time to do more than be sure the Mitch was awake and capable of walking on his own before Lewis opened the cabin door and they were besieged by reporters. Lewis let the stairs fall into place, nearly hitting several of them, but they pressed in close, while a referee worked his way though the mob. Alma braced herself—she knew she looked like hell, the same clothes she'd worn the day before, the black eye in full bloom—and fixed her attention on the referee.

"Mrs. Segura," he said, and stopped. "Sorry, I'm Theo May."

"Mr. May," Alma said, warily, but held out her hand. The organizers could still throw Gilchrist out of the race; they'd still been arguing about additional penalties when the Terrier took off for Pensacola.

"I have a wire from New Orleans," he said. "The sponsors have agreed that you will not be disqualified for the late start."

Alma reached out to grab the stairs' narrow rail. "That's good news." Her lips felt stiff. Lewis pressed closer to her, steadying her.

"And they've also agreed that no further penalty will be assessed," May said. "Given that you'd already lost a significant amount of time."

"Also good news," Alma said. It felt as though a weight had lifted from her shoulders. The situation was bad enough, but at least it wasn't going to be any worse. And somehow they'd figure out how to make up time… After the mail drop, she reminded herself. Lewis was going to have to fly that, not Mitch, but Lewis was just as experienced on the mail runs. He could handle it, even if the Terrier wasn't exactly the ideal plane for it.

"Mrs Segura!" That was one of the reporters. "Mrs. Segura, exactly what did happen? Why the late start?"

"Just a minute," Alma said, and looked back at May. "Thank you, Mr. May. Was there anything else?"

"The mail drop begins at noon," he answered. "You'll be starting sixth, so you can expect to start at two-thirty."

Dead last, Alma thought. The only people behind them had already dropped out of the race. She forced a smile anyway. "We'll be ready," she said.

"Good luck," May said, tipping his hat, and turned away.

"Mrs. Segura!" That was another reporter, hat pushed back on thinning hair. "Can you tell us what happened last night?"

Alma took a deep breath. She could almost hear Gil's voice in her ear: *if you're going to tell a lie, Al, make it a whopper.* "Gentlemen." She raised her voice to carry over the buzzing voices. "Gentlemen! I know everyone wants to know what happened to us—"

"Why the shiner?" somebody yelled, and she ignored him.

"—And I'm very willing to tell you, as I hope it may help the police turn up the malefactors." *A whopper, Al, but not necessarily the big words.* She lifted her hands again, begging for silence, and the reporters quieted reluctantly. "Last night, my co-pilot, Mr. Sorley, left the hotel to run an errand, and someone slipped him a Mickey Finn. Fortunately, Miss Rostov, here, recognized him and realized he was in trouble, and called me and my husband at the hotel. With Miss Rostov's help, we were able to find Mr. Sorley, but as we were trying to get him back to the hotel, we were jumped by a gang. Or at least I assume they were a gang. In any case, we were attacked, and—well, you see what happened." She spread her hands in what she hoped was a disarming gesture. "We're going to have to work hard to get back into the race, and I suspect that's exactly what was intended."

"Are you saying someone wanted to make you lose the race?" someone shouted.

"I can't think of any other reason for this to happen," she answered.

"You're sure there's nothing more personal going on?" That sounded like Carmichael, but Alma couldn't spot him in the milling crowd.

"I can't imagine what you mean."

For a second, she thought he might call her bluff, spell it out in lurid detail, but someone interrupted.

"What about Miss Rostov? Who is she, and why did you bring her with you?"

"For her protection," Alma said promptly. "We couldn't leave her in New Orleans, not with these people still on the loose."

"Yeah, but who is she?"

Stasi lifted her hand like a schoolgirl. "I'm a friend of Dr. Ballard's. An old friend."

For a second, Alma thought Jerry was going to explode, but he controlled himself, and even managed a tight smile.

"How good a friend, Doc?" Carmichael called, and Jerry pretended not to hear.

"Looks like you were in a heck of a fight, Mrs. Segura," a new voice said. She thought it was the man from the New York Post, but all the faces blurred together at this point. "Are you going to be physically able to continue the race?"

He was on their side, she realized abruptly. Whatever he thought they'd actually been up to—and maybe he even believed her—he wanted them to continue, and was offering them a chance to make their case.

"I hope so," she said, with what she hoped was a game smile.

"We're a bit bruised and battered, as you can see—"

"But you should see the other guy?" The Post reporter grinned back.

"I certainly hope we left our mark," Alma answered. "But—to be honest, gentlemen, we grabbed Mr. Sorley and beat it out of there. With Miss Rostov's help, to be sure."

"Did the gang say why they attacked you?"

"What do the police say?"

The two reporters spoke almost at once, and Alma raised her hands again. "Mr. Kershaw is dealing with the police for us," she said. She'd have to remember to tell Henry that. "Our main concern was making it back to the airfield in time for our takeoff. As for why—as I said, I believe someone was trying to spoil our chances of winning the race."

Lewis cleared his throat. "I've heard there's a fair amount of money being wagered on this race," he offered. That was indisputably true, Alma thought, but she suspected the silence that followed was more shock that Lewis had spoken.

"And now—gentlemen, we have a lot of work to do if we're going to get ready for the next part of the race," she said. "I'll be happy to give interviews later, but right now, we need to get to it."

For a moment, it hung in the balance, but then a couple of referees came forward, pointing them toward their place in the hangar, and the reporters moved grudgingly away.

"All right," she said, willing herself to concentrate. "Lewis, you're flying. Do you want a nap first?"

He considered for a moment, then shook his head. "I'm all right. If I sleep now, it'll just make things worse."

Alma nodded, recognizing that state of exhaustion. "Mitch, are you fit to help with the engines?"

"I'll try."

He looked like death, but she needed him. "Ok. Jerry, keep an eye on Miss Rostov."

"We can play gin," Jerry said. "Right after she hands over the necklace."

Alma swore. Of course in all the confusion at the airport they hadn't managed to get rid of the damned thing. "We're going to have to do something about it," she said, and Jerry nodded, holding out his hand to Stasi.

She made a moue of distaste, but produced the necklace from somewhere within the rags of her dress. Jerry nodded, and gestured for Stasi to precede him up the steps. "Please, Miss, after you."

Lewis touched Alma's arm, and she took a deep breath. "Right. Let's get to work."

Lewis braced his thigh against the top of the ladder, putting his full weight on the wrench to tighten the last bolt on the engine cowling. He and Alma had been over the engines and all the control lines, making sure that everything was in perfect shape after the morning's flight, and now—he pocketed the wrench and slid back down the ladder, hearing another plane's engines revving outside the hangar. Now it was just waiting for the start, though from the sound of things it wouldn't be long.

He folded the ladder, carrying it out of the way, and as he came back to the Terrier, Alma emerged from the passenger compartment.

"Ok," she said. "I found some clothes for Miss Rostov, and she's volunteered to do the suitcase run in Jerry's place."

"That's good," Lewis said. She definitely couldn't go on in that ripped cocktail dress, not showing that much thigh. He could feel the color rising in his face just at the thought, and hastily turned his mind to the suitcase race. Jerry had never been going to do well in that—pack a suitcase and then carry it over an obstacle course; they'd intended to get a waiver from the race officials to have him do it, on the grounds that Jerry couldn't very well be expected to run on his wooden leg. Miss Rostov was a better solution, even if it would make Jerry furious.

"Jerry's not happy," Alma said, as if she'd read his mind, "but he sees the necessity."

Lewis nodded. They moved together toward the hangar door as another plane revved its engines, got there in time to see the Corsair flash past, barely a hundred feet above the runway. The course was set up using the shorter of the landing strips; the pylons rose at each end of the shorter east-west strip, lightweight fifty-foot towers topped with short, bright flags that rippled in the steady breeze. The Corsair tipped sideways, turning tight and steep, easily a sixty-degree bank as it swung through the turn, and straightened, engines howling, to flash back down the course to the west.

"Tight," Alma said, and sounded for a moment dismayed.

Lewis nodded. You wouldn't have to take it that close, of course; make the turns a little wider, and you'd only have a thirty-degree bank, and much less chance that one failed engine would drop you out of the sky. But tight was also fast, and Jezek was taking full advantage of their plane's smaller size. The Fords could never make that turn, not with their wingspan, and the Fokker would be cutting it dangerously close. The Terrier... He squinted into the sun, watching the Corsair's wings flash as it tilted into another tight turn. Maybe. Mitch could do it, probably, on his best day, but—Lewis shoved the thought aside. He was flying, not Mitch, and that was all there was to it.

The Corsair flashed past a final time, the announcer proclaiming the end of the final lap, heading out to sea to make a more reasonable turn back toward the main runway.

"The best time of the day!" The announcer's voice crackled over the loudspeaker. "Jezek Air is now in first place for this leg of the competition. And don't forget, folks, every second won in this race turns into two minutes in the main race!"

Lewis tuned him out, watching the Corsair drop daintily onto the runway, while the Harvards' Fokker gunned its engines at the edge of the field.

"Twenty seconds." Alma caught her breath sharply. "Forty minutes. If we could do that—"

If. Lewis shaded his eyes, gauging his approach to the pylons. The Terrier was bigger than the Corsair, less maneuverable, but it was still more maneuverable than the Fords. The Fords would definitely have to take the turns at a shallower angle, a wider radius, which meant they'd definitely be slower. The Fokker—that was harder to tell.

The Harvards turned into the wind, lifting easily off the tarmac. From the look of it, the way they caught the air, they were flying light, cutting back on fuel to make them as maneuverable as possible. And they'd left their passenger on the ground: May Saltonstall stood near the hangar entrance, her arms folded tight across her chest. Lewis looked back at the Fokker, circling lazily back toward the field, lining up for the entrance to the course.

"And the flag is up!"

Lewis's muscles tensed as though he was flying himself as the

Fokker dropped lower, two hundred feet, a hundred, seventy-five, flashing over the start line painted on the ground and into the first turn. They were on the Corsair's line, or very close to it, left wing pointed almost at the ground as they made the turn. McIsaac must be on the ragged edge of control, Lewis thought. They'd have to make the mail drop, of course, but it looked as though they were going to hold that for an ending lap.

The Fokker swung around the far pylon, wing down as though they were pivoting on the tip of the pylon itself.

"That's cutting it awfully close," Alma said, over the noise of the engines.

"Yeah." Lewis nodded, shading his eyes again as the Fokker headed back toward the ocean. It banked again, wing tilting toward the pylon, and the plane staggered. Clipped the top of the pylon, he knew instantly, as the flag fell like a streamer and the Fokker tipped further, pitching sideways. He heard Alma gasp, and someone screamed. Miss Saltonstall had both hands over her mouth, her eyes wide with fear. Somehow McIsaac wrestled it back, not to level, that was too much to expect, but into the opposite bank, pointing it down the long runway away from the crowd. The tip of the left wing was damaged, and the Fokker was going down, wobbling toward the end of the runway. Too fast, Lewis thought, and it hit, the wheels collapsing under its weight. It skidded down the runway on its belly, the left engine smoking now, rudder hard right to spin it, slow it against the ground.

Bells clanged in the hangar, and a fire truck was already moving, rolling out even before the Fokker ground to a stop, half a dozen men clinging to the side of the tank. The left engine was still trailing smoke, but the smoke was fading, maybe not going to burst into flames. Alma grabbed his arm, her fingers digging into his biceps, her face like chalk. Come on, Lewis thought, willing them to be alive.

"Come on, get out of there—"

He hadn't realized he was speaking aloud until he heard Alma's breath catch again. And then at last the hatch opened, a black gap in the fuselage, and a figure climbed awkwardly down, turned back to help another. Two, that was two of them—and there was the third, holding one arm close to his body, the others supporting him away from the plane.

The truck was there, water playing on the engine, on the Fokker's wooden body, and Lewis heaved a sigh of relief. No one dead, not even too badly hurt, just the plane cracked up, when he'd expected, they'd all expected, to see the Fokker cartwheel across the runway shedding fire like a lit Catherine-wheel. Out of the corner of his eye, he could see Mrs. Jezek and the girl from Consolidated hovering over Miss Saltonstall, who was weeping in Mrs. Jezek's embrace.

Lewis took a deep breath and then another, letting the adrenaline drain out of him. They were all more or less ok, and that was the main thing. And, God forgive him, he could see just where they'd gone wrong. He could do this—all right, he couldn't make up all the time they'd lost, but he could get them twenty minutes, maybe half an hour, maybe a hair more, if the wind stayed just where it was, and steady. And then it would be up to Al.

Chapter Eighteen

It took the better part of an hour to get the field cleared, and even then the wreck of the Fokker was merely dragged to the side of the airstrip. It didn't look as though the Harvards were going to be able to get it back into the race—the undercarriage was shattered, and the tip of the left wing looked as thought something had been chewing on it—but at least they were all alive. McIsaac had broken his wrist, and been carted off to the nearby Navy hospital to have it splinted, but that was nothing. Not compared to what could have happened.

Lewis allowed himself a last drink of water, warm and flat and odd-tasting, and turned back to the Terrier. It was almost time, and he couldn't afford to worry about the Harvards right now. The main thing—the only thing—was the pylon race. The mail drop first, he thought. They weren't allowed to do it on the first lap, but if they made the drop on the second, they could build speed the rest of the way. They still probably couldn't beat the Corsair, it was just a better plane for the job, but they should be able to make up time on everybody else. And the Corsair was going to struggle on the last leg anyway.

He ducked under the Terrier's tail, came up the fuselage to find Alma standing at the top of the steps, looking down at Mitch. Mitch looked better than he had, some of the color returned to his face, but for once the stubble stood out sharply against his skin.

"I can do it, Al," he was saying.

Alma shook her head. "No. I'm sorry, but—"

"You don't trust me."

"You're in no shape right now," Alma said. "And even if you were—I'm going to need you tomorrow."

Mitch's breath caught, a sound something like laughter. "Al, we're out of it. And, yeah, it's my fault. Let me at least go for the prize this leg."

Lewis hesitated. He'd never heard Mitch like that before, and if Mitch thought the race was over—well, maybe it was. He knew the Terrier better than anyone, and if he didn't think they could make it…

"Mitch." Alma's voice was compassionate but firm. "You're not flying this leg because I need you to take the second leg tomorrow. That's final."

Mitch shook his head. "Al—"

"I need you more tomorrow," Alma said. "Lewis is going to get as much time back as possible and then—then I've got ideas."

Oh, Al, Lewis thought. He knew her well enough by now to know when she was stretching the truth, and that was definitely a stretch. She saw him then, and met his gaze without apology. Mitch's shoulders moved as he took a heavy breath.

"Ok," he said, "but—"

Lewis took a step forward. "I'd like Mitch in the co-pilot's seat," he said, looking from Alma to Mitch. "If you don't mind."

"I'll do it," Mitch said.

Alma opened her mouth as though to protest, then nodded. "Ok. I'll handle the mail drop."

"On the second lap," Lewis said. "And then—"

Alma gave a tired grin. "Strap in and hang on."

They were last onto the field, a bit past three in the afternoon, the sun seeming to hang just above the western pylon. That would make things a bit more difficult, Lewis thought, but at least the breeze had died to almost nothing. Weather tomorrow, he was willing to bet, but he shoved that thought out of his mind. The only thing that mattered now was the mail drop and the pylons.

The engine sang as he lined the Terrier up on the main runway and opened the throttles, the big plane lifting easily with its light load of fuel. There would be ample for the race, but they'd left the tanks half empty to spare the weight. Mitch swore the Terrier would dance Swan Lake with this load, and Lewis hoped it was true.

He leveled off at two hundred feet, circled back toward the hangars, getting the feel of the air. The sun was awkward, but not as bad as he'd feared, and he swung back over the course, mapping the long oval.

"Yellow flag's up!" Alma yelled from the cabin.

Lewis nodded, easing the Terrier into a gentle descent, heading for one-fifty, and Mitch shouted back, "Ok."

They had one practice lap after the yellow flag, and then the green went up and the timer started. Lewis shoved the throttle forward, searching for the line. This was the easy way, a wider loop around the pylon, thirty degrees of bank and then steady down the course, the sun turning the sky white with glare. There was the flag, the second pylon, and this was the turning point, the Terrier hard over. Maybe she wouldn't dance Swan Lake for him, but she was quick and light under his hands as he straightened for home.

"Green flag!" Alma shouted.

"Ok," Mitch answered.

Lewis pushed the throttle forward just a little more. There was no point in trying to get up to speed just yet, not with the mail drop to come on the next lap. Instead, he focused on the most efficient path, the exact moment to begin the turn. The Terrier heeled, swung to face the sun, and he leveled out again.

"Next lap," he said, and Mitch repeated it.

This time as he rounded the pylon and flattened out, he dropped lower still. He kept his eyes on the eastern pylon, but he couldn't help picturing Alma crouched in the cabin's open door, the mail bag ready at her feet. She wore a harness, of course, but even so it was dangerous… He shoved that thought aside, throttling back just a little as they approached the drop zone.

"Bag's away!" Alma yelled, and Lewis shoved the throttle forward.

"Hang on," Mitch shouted.

Lewis ignored them both, the geometry suddenly clear. No need to gain altitude, they'd waste time and upset the Terrier's balance. Instead, he picked the point of his turn, closer than before, letting the Terrier tip up to sixty degrees, turning on her downward-pointing wing. And then they were past the pylon, flashing into the sun. He leveled her, engines howling. No more power, she wouldn't take it, just the steady rhythm of the course, the turn made just here, just that deep, standing her on her wingtip to rotate past the pylon and then out again. The sea in his eyes, and then the sun, and the sea again, and then at last Alma was yelling from the cabin.

"Yellow flag! We're done! Yellow flag!"

Lewis aborted the last turn, let the Terrier bore on out over the

water, gaining height and shedding speed for a decorous run back
to the field.

"Nice flying," Mitch said, and when Lewis glanced warily at him,
the smile was genuine. "Hell of a nice job."

Alma leaned in the cockpit door, her hands braced on the frame.
"My God, Lewis. Beautiful."

"Let's see what our time is," Lewis said, and would have crossed
his fingers if he could.

He brought the Terrier down neatly onto the main runway, taxied
back to the hangars at standard speed in spite of the desire to rush,
to see where they'd finished. The reporters were waiting, of course,
flashbulbs popping as Alma lowered the steps and they climbed out
of the plane. The air was hot and still, the last of the breeze vanished,
and Lewis felt the sweat standing out on his skin. Alma kissed his
cheek for the reporters, and he managed a game smile, but his eyes
were fixed on the board where one of the referees was chalking up
the new results.

Second place. Second place behind the Corsair, and fourteen seconds ahead of the next competitor. Twenty-eight minutes off their
time. It was better than nothing. It was a lot better than nothing,
twenty-eight minutes off meant that they were only an hour and five
minutes behind. But—Mitch might have been right, that might just be
too much to make up on the last long leg into Coconut Grove.

Alma would think of something. Surely. He glanced at her, tired
and dirty, her hair held back by a faded kerchief, no sign of the sexy
world traveler haircut she'd worn from Hollywood. But she was still
Al. She'd find a way.

The reporters claimed Alma for her promised interviews, and Mitch
and Lewis followed her, but the hangar was still buzzing with reaction to the Harvards' crash and the results of the pylon race when the
referees began collecting the passengers for the suitcase race. Jerry
couldn't help flinching—one more reminder that he was a cripple—
but he schooled himself to impassivity and offered Miss Rostov his
arm. She had managed to find a dress of Alma's that would fit her,
and though it hung loose on her skinny body she moved like the
countess she claimed to be.

Not that Jerry believed that for a second. A cheap grifter, getting

too old to get by on looks alone, so why not try a different con? Spiritualism was a good game, especially when you could tie it to exotic Russia. Except that her talent was real. That was one of his gifts, to recognize talent in others, and he could feel it in her, humming in her fingertips where she rested them lightly on his crooked elbow. Real, and she knew it, used it knowingly and with care: there was none of the tangling, the static, he felt when someone tried to use their gift without understanding what they had. She wasn't trained in his traditions, but she knew what she was doing. The stream of her gift ran straight and clear.

She looked up at him, not smiling, the circles dark under her eyes. "Well, darling, do you like what you see?"

You could take that half a dozen ways, Jerry thought. "How'd you find Mitch?"

She blinked once, and then a penciled eyebrow rose. "I asked the Dead. They know everything, darling, especially in New Orleans."

She expected him to scoff, he realized, but in fact he did believe her. It was probably the first thing she'd said to him that he did believe. "You must have made some pretty promises for that."

She looked away, one corner of her painted mouth quirking up in a wry smile. "Not that it really matters, but, yes, I did."

"I'm curious," Jerry said. And he was: what had she thought it worth, and why?

"I told them I would be their medium," she said. She must have seen his expression change, because she shrugged, tossing her head without disturbing her jet-black hair. "So, yes, darling, I'm in for a few days of tedium when this is all over."

"I reckon so," Jerry said, startled out of his careful vowels and proper grammar. That was more than tedious, it was hard work, hard as digging ditches except that there was always the chance that some discorporate soul might try to take up permanent residence. And it was also a bargain easily broken, at least in the beginning. All right, Miss Rostov was probably planning to keep her end of the deal primarily out of self-protection, but there were plenty of mediums who'd try to weasel out of it.

They had reached the area in front of the tower where bleachers had been set up, and he swallowed any further questions as a referee bustled up to them.

"Dr. Ballard," he said, consulting his clipboard. "And—Miss Rostov, is it?"

"That's right." Stasi favored him with a wide smile.

"Oh, Dr. Ballard." That was Miss Saltonstall, hurrying toward them, her sensible heels clicking on the pavement. "I wondered—oh."

She flushed to the roots of her hair, and Jerry tipped his hat, giving her a careful smile. "If it's what I think," he began, and she shook herself.

"I thought—since we had to withdraw I thought I might be able to run in your place. If that would be helpful."

"It's very kind of you to offer," Jerry said, and suppressed a curse as Carmichael came to a stop beside him.

"An embarrassment of riches, Doc," he said. "You're quite the ladykiller."

Jerry flinched at that, and Miss Saltonstall lifted an eyebrow. "I beg your pardon?" Her voice was cut crystal, Brahmin to the core.

Even Carmichael seemed momentarily taken aback. "I just—"

Miss Saltsonstall swept on without waiting for him to finish. "Dr. Ballard is a friend—a former colleague—of my Uncle Philip, the current Senator. I'm sure you'll excuse us if we have a private conversation." She hooked her hand through Jerry's free arm and drew him away, Miss Rostov following gracefully like a kite on a string.

"Neatly done," she said, nothing put out, and Jerry nodded.

"Is he a senator? Your uncle, I mean."

Miss Saltsonstall grinned. "A state senator. But he did used to teach classics before he went into politics, so you're sort of colleagues."

"Thank you," Jerry said.

"I should have guessed you'd have made arrangements," she said, and smiled at Miss Ivanova, all embarrassment overcome. "I'm glad."

"Miss Rostov was kind enough to volunteer," Jerry said, feeling clumsy again. Harvard had taught him to move in good society, but nothing had ever taken away the sneaking sense of fraud every time he tried it.

He made the introductions, and when Stasi offered her case, lit cigarettes for both of them. He lit one for himself as well, inhaled the smoke as though it might help somehow. "How's McIsaac doing?"

"Better." Miss Saltsonstall sounded grateful to be on more solid ground. "His wrist's broken in a couple of places, but the doctor thinks it will heal cleanly. If he doesn't put stress on it too soon."

"And your brother? And Mr. Newhouse?" Behind her, Jerry could see the organizers laying out the suitcases and the contents.

"Bruised and shaken up," Miss Saltonstall answered, "but not seriously hurt, thank goodness." She held out her hand. "Good luck, Miss Rostov."

"Thank you, darling." The two women clasped hands, and Miss Saltonstall moved determinedly away.

"Are you ready?" Jerry asked, and glanced down at her feet. She was still wearing her black pumps with the high heels that she'd been wearing at the Hotel Denechaud. "I mean—can you run in those?"

Miss Rostov extended one foot, considering it critically. "Darling, all I've been doing in these shoes is running."

Jerry grinned in spite of himself.

"Besides," she said. "The point isn't to go fast. It's to show lots of leg and make the photographers happy. And be faster than the others."

"We need the time," Jerry said. If they hadn't, he would never have let her do the job. For an instant, he wished he could call Miss Saltsonstall back. He trusted her, which was more than he could say for the so-called countess.

"Darling, don't worry," she said. "They don't want to see my legs."

Jerry couldn't help laughing at that. She waggled her fingers at him and went to join the others.

The race itself didn't take long. Jerry leaned heavily on his cane, easing his stump, while the announcer ran through the rules. When the starter's gun went off, each passenger had to pack her suitcase— the table was stacked with clothes and shoes and what looked like an alarm clock for each of them. Once packed and secure, they were to take off for the opposite end of the course, where they had to hand over the suitcase to a referee to confirm that everything was there, and run back to the starting point. And if any of the alarm clocks went off—the announcer sounded almost indecently gleeful at the idea—that person had to stop and turn it off before she could continue. Silly season, Jerry thought, and remembered Pelletier's comment at the beginning of the race. Games for dames. He was shamefully glad he didn't have to play.

The passengers took their places, four women and one man, all that was left of the teams who had started the Great Passenger Derby. The trouble was, they'd lost enough time that they were still behind some of the teams who'd dropped out. They'd pass them tomorrow, but—that only put them into fifth, out of the money. Jerry shook the thought away, and the starter lifted his gun and fired.

The passengers leaped into action, tossing clothes into the cases, jamming the lids down and fumbling with the old-fashioned straps that held them closed. Pelletier got his fastened first, swung away, only to have the alarm clock go off with a muffled clamor. Jerry saw him swear, but he dutifully stopped and silenced the clock before moving on. Miss Rostov was third away from the table, but she made up time as she ran, the suitcase banging at her knees. Mrs. Jezek took three steps with her suitcase, stopped, and kicked off her pumps, to start again at a better pace. The girl from Consolidated was ahead of her and gaining, holding her skirt out of the way with one hand.

Jerry swore under his breath. All they needed was for Consolidated to get more bonus time—but then her alarm clock went off, and Miss Rostov surged past. She was first at the referee's table, smiling and vamping as he went down the list, then snatched up the suitcase, empty now except for the alarm clock, and darted for the finish line.

"Come on," Jerry said, through clenched teeth. He felt like he was betting on a long shot at Santa Anita. "Come on…"

The alarm clock went off. Miss Rostov stopped, glanced over her shoulder to see Pelletier and Consolidated coming fast, and banged the suitcase on the ground. The alarm clock went dead, and she sprinted for the finish.

"It counts," Jerry said. "Oh, God, let it count…"

Miss Rostov swung the suitcase onto the table with a triumphant cry. The nearest referee opened it, looked at the alarm clock, and nodded.

"First place to Gilchrist Aviation!" The announcer's voice crackled from the loudspeaker. "First place, and the fifteen minute bonus, for Gilchrist Aviation!"

It would work out to about seven minutes off their deficit, Jerry thought, as he shouldered his way through the crowd to collect Miss Rostov. Consolidated and Comanche had both gotten small bonuses, but overall they'd made up more time. If he had the numbers right, they were less than an hour behind.

And he never could have done that, not in a million years. He wasn't even sure he could have made it to the end of the course without falling. Miss Rostov turned away from the judges, her winner's bouquet tucked in one arm—very like the winner at Santa Anita, Jerry thought. She gave the photographers a final wave, and Jerry tipped his hat.

"Thank you," he said, and she gave him a startled glance.

"You're welcome, darling." She tucked her hand into his arm, and they started back toward the hangar.

Their hotel room in Pensacola was a suite—two bedrooms with a small sitting room in between, beautifully appointed with white French Country furniture and pale blue walls, a glorious view of the Gulf of Mexico through the windows. Alma twitched the curtains aside and looked out. It was a gorgeous evening, seventy nine degrees, wind out of the south southwest at five miles per hour, perfect flying weather. Tomorrow was supposed to be warmer with a chance of thundershowers. If they weren't starting tomorrow in dead last place…

Alma leaned her forehead against the window. They'd come so close. But not even the best flying in the world was going to make up an hour of time. They might finish fifth or even fourth rather than dead last. Third place would get them $5,000, a ten-fold return on the entrance fee, not leave them flat broke, but that would require some kind of minor miracle. Maybe a complete breakdown from one of the leaders. That was possible. But three or four breakdowns? No, they had lost. She couldn't see any way out. Not this time. The late start from New Orleans had doomed them.

At least Mitch was making sense now. He hadn't been, and that disturbed her more than she could say. She was protective of him, she admitted to herself, as if he were the younger brother she sometimes felt he was. Maybe that was guilt. Gil had said so, once. "Al, nobody could have done anything. You did your best." She had, first aid on the field, but there were things that were beyond her. No reason to feel guilty for not making a miracle.

Which brought it back to that again. She couldn't make miracles. Magic didn't let her pull rabbits out of her hat to repair everything.

Lewis came and leaned against the window beside her, arm companionably about her waist. He looked out at the sea, steady and solid as always. "I wish we hadn't taken out the auxiliary tank in Little Rock," he said.

Alma nodded. "If we could skip the refueling stop in Lake City we'd still have a chance." She blew out a long breath. But wishes weren't horses. They'd left the tank, and Henry didn't even have a shop in Pensacola, nor anywhere near enough to get it by morning. His nearest shop was in Miami, and if they were in Miami they would have already won. She looked out over the sunlit sea.

And then it came to her in a moment, something so risky... It might work. It might just work. It would depend on the tiniest of margins, just a hair.

"Lewis," she said, turning away from the window, "Do you have that almanac of airfields handy?"

"It's in my bag," Lewis said and went to get it. He knew better than to ask.

Sheets of hotel stationary, a pencil... It might work. It just might work. It would depend on the fields. The map was right in front of her in memory. "What kind of field is there in St. Petersburg? Or Sarasota?"

Lewis paged through wildly. "Um, Alfred Whitted in St. Petersburg is under construction. That doesn't help. Fuller Airport in Jungle? Doesn't have full field service. How about Sky Harbor Airport on Weedon Island? It says there's regular passenger service from Eastern Air Transport and National, so it should be a full service field."

"Weedon Island," Alma said. "Where's that?"

Lewis frowned. "In Tampa Bay," he said. "It's a little further." He looked up at her. "Are you thinking what I think you're thinking?"

"Yes," Alma said. Her eyes met his, daring and willing to try whatever the plan was. "You know I am."

"Will it work?"

"I need the exact mileage," Alma said. "You've got to get me an almanac. I need the exact mileage to Lake City and to Weedon Island."

Lewis jumped up. "I'm sure there's a Florida map downstairs at the desk."

"That will do," Alma said. The exact miles. She thought it was about the same, though Weedon Island was much further south. Their fueling stop was supposed to be Lake City, a long flight across the Florida panhandle, and then turn south for Miami. But if they could refuel in Tampa instead…

Straight across the Gulf of Mexico, a flight on the edge of their fuel over open ocean, with no margin for error… It would make up time. It might save an hour, maybe a little more. But if they miscalculated, even by a tiny amount, there would be no second chances. They'd have to ditch in the Gulf of Mexico miles from land, and nobody would even know where to look for them. For a moment, she wished she could grab the long distance operator, call Henry and tell him the new plan, but he would be on the train to Miami already, unreachable. A cable, maybe, sent to the hotel to wait for him, just as insurance. But if they told anyone what they were going to try to do, even the Western Union operator, a reporter would get hold of it. Then one of the lead planes would try it too and they'd still be behind. Their only chance was if nobody else was desperate and crazy enough to try it. It was crazy. But it just might work. It might work if the numbers added up.

Jerry listened to the sound of water running in the adjoining bathroom—Mitch taking a bath and getting cleaned up after last night's romp through a graveyard and drinking binge—which was all to the good. Mitch would be busy for a few minutes while Jerry figured out what to do with the necklace. Like it or not, they were stuck with it for another 24 hours. Short of just leaving it in the hotel, which would be incredibly irresponsible as it would mean the necklace would fall into the hands of some random innocent person, they needed to hang onto it until they could give it back to Henry.

Of course if the bogus Countess hadn't stolen it in the first place it would still be secure in Henry's nice, warded safe! This was absolutely all her fault. If she hadn't stolen the damn thing none of this would have happened, including whatever had broken Mitch up so much in New Orleans. They'd still be in first place, and Mitch wouldn't have that haunted look on his face. He'd been kind of a mess when he'd first come to Colorado at Gil's invitation. Of course Jerry'd had problems of his own at that point, still learning to walk on the wooden leg, still trying to figure out what his life might look like. But once he'd wrestled his own life into something like order, and seen what Mitch was going through, he'd figured he was better off than Mitch.

He'd said as much to Gil, curled up in the four poster downstairs in the drawing room they'd turned into Jerry's room so he wouldn't have to climb stairs, the rain beating down on the tin roof of the porch outside. Gil had grinned, his hand straying over Jerry's chest. "You'd rather lose your leg than this?"

"Any day," Jerry had said fervently, and he meant it. His leg wasn't essential to who he was. It wasn't the thing he'd feared, a head wound that would take his mind away, leave him grasping for simple sums, all stories erased, all knowledge forgotten. It wasn't the end of intimacy, the end of this. Gil loved him as he always had. He could see the day—not today, not soon, but someday not infinitely far away—when this might feel normal.

Jerry shook his head. Not normal, not quite. Not ever. But not terrible either, even without Gil. And losing Gil had been worse than losing his leg.

Mitch had been on thin ice then, but Jerry'd thought it was better. It had been years since Mitch seemed out of it, years that he'd seemed cheerful and laid back, but Jerry supposed it had all been lurking just under the surface, kept at bay with friendship and flying. Mitch had a lot of friends. He had the kind of easy comraderie in the American Legion that Jerry had never been able to manage—too much of an egghead to talk football and motors. Mitch moved back and forth between worlds seemingly without effort, following Jerry's excitement about some new inscriptions deciphered from an ancient temple and talking sports at the Legion. It was easy to miss that nothing seemed very deep, nothing cut to the heart of it. You could talk to Mitch all day and not realize you were the one doing all the talking, come away from it thinking he was a great guy and not adding it up that you didn't know one single thought of his deeper than an eggshell. Whatever was going on in his own private world, it stayed private.

This thing had just been waiting to happen, Jerry thought. Yes, the necklace started it, but it just built on the pain that was there. That's what it did. That's what it was designed to do. It could only plow a fertile field.

Well then, Jerry said to himself grimly. Time to get busy. Time to figure out how to contain this thing for another 24 hours.

Ideally he'd have some kind of prepared container to keep it in, a silver or lead box properly warded to neutralize its power. However, as usual, things weren't ideal. Hotels in Pensacola didn't generally have lead boxes lying around. His best bet was wood, and that at least he could get.

Jerry rang for the bellboy, meeting him at the suite door and pressing a dollar bill into his hand. At least he still had some cash. "Can you get me a box of Havana cigars? And keep the change."

The boy grinned, gap teeth showing. "No problem, mister. You want Hermosillos? Or I can send out for something different."

"Hermosillos will be fine," Jerry said. They came in a nice wooden box. "You have them at the desk?"

"Sure thing," the bellboy said. "And twelve kinds of cigarettes. I'll be back before you count to ten!"

"That's fine," Jerry said, and he waited by the door, wondering if anybody had a supper plan or if that was one of those things that had slipped everyone's mind. Alma and Lewis were in their room, and the countess was nowhere to be seen. Maybe she'd taken herself off to greener pastures. It could happen.

Once the boy returned, Jerry took the box into the room he shared with Mitch. The sounds of splashing from the bath told him Mitch was still busy for a few more minutes. He tipped the cigars out into his suitcase and methodically stripped the labels off the box. This would do for now. Instead of a lead lining he'd have to use his silk handkerchief, but silk was a perfectly reasonable material for this.

Jerry stood, turning off the lamp so that only the evening light came in through the window, thin undercurtains drawn though they stirred a little in the sea breeze. He closed his eyes, composing himself and reaching for the center of calm, for that cool certainty that stood in the stillness, the point where the universe stood poised. "Ateh malkuth ve-gevurah ve-gedulah le-olahm." The motions were second nature, the Kabbalistic Cross painted across his body with his movements, calling upon the powers of the Archangels and of the Most High to protect him, to clear the space of all malevolent energies. In a way, for all its trappings of high ritual, what he did was quite simple. Instead of casting a circle and asking its mighty guardians to temporarily ward the space of a room, he called them instead to a circle much smaller, collapsed to the size of the cigar box. Instead of knife in hand to delineate the wide spaces of the circle, he had a fountain pen instead. The pen is mightier than the sword, Jerry thought with an inward smile. This was one instance where that was quite literally true.

Instead of setting each quarter at a cardinal point around the room, east and west, south and north, he marked each in ink on a face of the box. "On my right hand, Raphael," Jerry said, drawing the symbol on the right end of the box. "On my left, Gabriel." Michael went to the south, as though the box itself were a map or a compass face, Uriel to the north side with its box flap. Ink was not much to seal such a binding, not even consecrated ink, but just indigo from the hotel bottle on the writing desk, but it would hold for 24 hours. Quick and dirty.

Do we ever do it any other way? Jerry thought. For all that he sometimes disagreed with Henry, he missed the beauty of the large rituals, of the meticulous planning and grace that comes from having all the right things, not just making do.

And that was distraction, which he should avoid. Perhaps it was the necklace, pushing in the only way it could, trying to find a seed of dissatisfaction to grow.

No, Jerry said silently, and put the necklace still knotted in the silk handkerchief inside the box. He closed the lid, hand flat against the smooth surface. "Amen," he said, and bent his head a moment, eyes closed in service. "Amen." When he opened them the room seemed lighter, though it had actually grown darker, sunset over and night falling. The sounds in the bathroom had stopped. Presumably Mitch had gone out into the sitting room. Yes, he heard his voice and the voices of the two women. Which meant the countess was still here.

Jerry put the box in the bottom of his suitcase and closed it up tight. That was the best he could do for now, and it was enough. It would hold long enough for them to get to Miami, and that was all it needed to do.

He opened the door to the sitting room, and Alma looked up, warmth in her face. "Room service is on its way up. I thought that might be the best thing tonight since we're all tired." And tired of dealing with the press, Jerry thought, though of course Al didn't add that.

"Absolutely," Jerry said. "I'm ravenous."

Stasi turned over on the rather narrow couch in the main room of the hotel suite, pulling the spare blanket around her. The windows were open to catch the breeze off the sea, drawing in voices of the last diners finishing their drinks on the terrace below. One bedroom was for the Seguras and the other for Mitch and Jerry. It had been a fairly wordless agreement that if anyone was taking the couch, and the room with the outside door with no one else in the room, it wasn't going to be Mitch. Which meant either Jerry shared the other room with Mitch or she did, and it would hardly be decent for her to. So she got the couch.

Not that this didn't make it easy for her to simply trot off. All she would have to do would be open the door and go down the hall. Very easy to disappear. No trouble at all. Maybe they hoped she would. Or figured she would. That would be like Mrs. Segura. She'd let her go, or at least give her the opportunity to, with hours of head start and nobody bothering to follow in the morning. Nobody would have time, and probably nobody would care what had happened to her. She was simply a picaresque adventure that had crossed their lives, an entertaining story for after dinner drinks one day.

Stasi squeezed her eyes shut. And that's what she ought to do. Get up, put on her one pair of shoes, fish the money she had left out of where it was pinned in her combinations, and figure out what to do next. A cab to the train station and go…somewhere. Another town where nobody knew her, another new beginning, another dead end. Not enough money left for the train all the way back to LA, but there were other towns.

She'd work it out. She always did.

Only she was so tired. It had been a long night spent chasing and running and hiding in a graveyard, and then a long day after. So tired, bone tired. The couch was thin and uncomfortable, but it was flat and it was warm, the whisper of the sea breeze over the blanket, the voices of people below. She could just close her eyes for a few minutes. She could rest a few minutes before she left, before it was time to start over again. It wouldn't hurt to just stay a few minutes longer.

Henry made his way to the dining car for the night's final seating, the evening paper from their last stop tucked under his arm. According to it, the Harvard team was out after an impressive crash, and Gilchrist Aviation, having gone from first to last by missing their takeoff time, had made back thirty-five minutes of their deficit. He nodded to the steward, slipped him fifty cents with a murmured "private, if you can," and was led a moment later to a table at the rear of the car. The waiters came hurrying with water and iced tea and the menu, and he tried to focus on his choices.

Why the hell had he ever agreed to sponsor Gilchrist anyway? Ok, yes, the publicity had been good, but this latest stunt was only going to undo everything. His planes were going to be associated with a scandalous aviatrix who'd disappeared, failed to show up at the biggest event of the race, and reappeared with a black eye and a strange woman to add to her male harem—no, that didn't bear thinking about, and he hoped none of the papers decided to make anything of that aspect of the story. You couldn't get away with that even in Hollywood.

What in God's name was wrong with Sorley, anyway? Henry had always picked him for the reliable one. If Ballard was right, and it was the necklace—well, that was one more thing to worry about later, after he'd dealt with the disaster that was the Great Passenger Derby. The last thing he needed was for Republic to be associated with unreliability.

"Take your order, sir?"

Henry glanced up at the hovering waiter, ordered the steak dinner as the most predictable choice, and accepted another glass of iced tea. What he really wanted was a stiff scotch, but that would have to wait until he was back in his sleeper. He should have known better than to sponsor Gilchrist. Yes, they'd saved his life on Independence, and probably the business, too, but right now they were on the verge of costing him far more than the eight hundred dollars in entrance fees, or even the lost prize money.

"Henry? Major Kershaw? It is you, isn't it?"

Henry looked up again, frowning for a moment before he recognized the man. Older, yes, and a bit heavier, shadows dark as bruises under his eyes, but it was still Jefferson Lanier. He and Gil had both been sorry when Lanier was posted away from the Veneto; he'd been a good comrade on the lines and in the Lodge. "Jeff," he said, with genuine warmth. "What are you doing here?"

"I'm on my way to Miami," Lanier answered. "Family business. I suppose you're heading for the finish line?"

"Yes," Henry said, and motioned to the seat across from him. "Have you eaten? Why don't you join me?"

"I ate already," Lanier said, "but if you don't mind, I'd be glad of the company." He slid onto the bench across from Henry, and the waiter bustled over. Lanier accepted a cup of coffee, and leaned back against the burgundy leather. "It sounds as though you've been having quite an adventure."

For an instant, there was an odd note in his voice, almost gloating, and Henry gave him a sharp glance. Lanier's expression was open, relaxed, and Henry decided he'd imagined it.

"A bit more of one than I'd hoped for, I'm afraid."

"What in the world happened to your team?"

Definitely an off note, Henry thought, and couldn't hide a frown. Lanier spread his hands.

"Sorry. You know Mitch Sorley was a friend of mine. I was real sorry when he dropped out of sight after the war."

They had been close, Henry remembered, and he knew how the loss of those wartime friendships could smart. "I wish I knew. Al— you remember Alma Sullivan, she married Gil Gilchrist right after the Armistice. She was in the Lodge, too, but after you were transferred."

"She was one of the ambulance drivers," Lanier said. "Tall blonde. Yeah, I remember her. Nice girl."

That was one adjective Henry would never have chosen, but he didn't disagree.

"I've been following them on the radio," Lanier said. "It's been quite an event. That stunt you pulled, with the extra fuel tank—damn smart."

"Al is damn smart," Henry said. "That was all her idea."

The waiter returned with his dinner, a decent-sized steak with mashed potatoes and mushrooms and a wedge of lettuce on the side. The meat was tough but tasty, and Henry wrestled with it, paying more attention to it than the conversation. He hadn't realized until the food appeared just how hungry he was. And Lanier was good company, happy to hash over the old days and genuinely glad to hear about Henry's business. He was less willing to talk about himself, and

Henry guessed that the family was hurting. He tried a couple of care-ful questions, but Lanier deflected them deftly. There was nothing to be ashamed of, Henry thought. Plenty of people were in trouble these days, out of work and out of luck. But Lanier had always been painfully proud.

The waiter brought pie and more coffee for Lanier, and at last Henry settled back, replete. Lanier gave him an almost wistful smile.

"I envy you," he said. "Even if you don't win—it sounds like it was a hell of a ride."

"It has been," Henry said. "It certainly has been. Look, I'm giv-ing a party the night of the finish." And a useful investment that was turning out to be, his last chance to make sure Republic got good press and would be remembered as something separate from Gilchrist Aviation. "I have a house in Coconut Grove. If you'd like to come, you'd be more than welcome."

"That's really nice of you," Lanier said. "I believe I will. I'd like to see Mitch again."

Stasi woke to bright sunlight in her eyes and the sounds of tentative footsteps. The sun was rising somewhere behind the hotel, and the sea was smooth as glass under the dawn, pink clouds streaking the sky with impossible tropical colors. Mitch Sorley stood beside the windows in shirt and pants, barefooted since his shoes must have been set out to be polished. He had big feet, and his white shirt was rolled up halfway to the elbows, baggy and not freshly pressed at all. "Red sky at morning," he said, one hand on the window screen.

"Sorry. What does that mean?" She sat up, pushing her hair back out of her face.

"Bad weather later." There were creases at the corners of his eyes from squinting into the sun. He must be forty if he was a day, or nearly so, and the years hadn't been good to him. Well, she could talk. Looks lasted longer if they were tended, but it was a bit hard to keep up a routine with cold cream while on the lam.

"Lovely," Stasi said. "I expect we won't enjoy that."

"We?" He looked around with a quizzical expression on his face.

"Of course, darling," she said, the decision made in that moment. "I'm coming on to Miami with you."

"You are? Why?"

Stasi shrugged. "Look at this place. There's nothing here. Miami has far more potential for mayhem."

"I'll believe that," he said. "South Beach and Coconut Grove, play-grounds of the rich and dissolute."

"My kind of town," Stasi said. She shoved the blanket back and stretched. Alma's dress was much too big on her, designed for curves, not angles. "I like rich and dissolute. Or rich without dissolute. And dissolute without rich has some potential."

The corner of his mouth twitched. "You make a good living as a jewel thief?"

Stasi got to her feet and padded across the carpet to look out the window beside him. "It comes and goes." She reached around him and rummaged in his front pocket to pull out his pack of Camels. "Frankly it's not all glamour, darling. But it's often better than the alternatives. How's aviation cracking up as a career?" She tapped one out of the box quickly.

He reached in his other pocket and got out his lighter. "I live over my friend's garage and fly planes." He didn't look at her as he lit her cigarette. "As you say, it's not all glamour but it's better than the alternatives."

"Well," she said, bending her head to take the first draw, the ciga-rette still between his fingers. "I suppose saving the world never pays very well." She took it out of his hand. "Oh, that's perfect! I'm simply useless before my first ciggy."

His eyebrows rose. "Alma told you that?"

She shrugged.

"I guess it sounds crazy, doesn't it?"

Stasi lifted her head, blowing the smoke out through the screen. "Darling, revolutions always do. And most of the time the world just goes right on doing what it was, only maybe worse. Rich people play and poor people starve and so on to the end of everything. And all the guns and cannon can't do anything except change who the mas-ters are, not a hair's breadth of difference between them. Ideals kill, darling."

Mitch shook his head, his eyes meeting hers. "No. People kill."

She stopped, the cigarette halfway to her lips, feeling stark and naked in the morning light, though she was completely dressed. "You really do think you're saving the world. You—the Lodge—you people.

You really believe that."

"We're trying," he said simply.

She put her hand on his arm, sleeve and flesh beneath it, warm and alive. "The world can't be saved."

He shrugged. "Maybe not. But what else am I doing with my life?"

No speeches. No oaths. No promises that no one could keep.

"Well," Stasi said. "If you put it that way."

The door to the Seguras' room opened and Alma emerged, Lewis behind her. "Good, I'm glad you're up, Mitch. I've got an idea I need to talk to you about."

Chapter Nineteen

The weather report was better than Alma had expected after the shocking pink clouds at dawn: there was weather behind them, yes, and the usual chance of scattered thunderstorms across the panhandle, but nothing they shouldn't be able to avoid. There was a bit of a headwind, though, not much, but predicted to last the entire trip, and she scowled over her calculations, running them twice and then three times, before she was sure of her result.

"Well?" That was Lewis, leaning into the cabin. The others had left her the privacy in which to work: they all knew, even the countess, that this was their only chance of winning. If they couldn't make the jump to Weedon Island, there was no real point in continuing.

Alma looked at the numbers straggling across the page, line after line of figures, each result worked and reworked half a dozen times. "We can do it," she said, and saw the smile break across Lewis's face. If she said it, he believed her, and for a moment the responsibility terrified her. But she knew what she was doing, knew her job, and the numbers didn't lie. "As long as the headwind doesn't pick up more than another 15 knots—and that's highly unlikely, given the weather pattern, we're more likely to see the wind change to a cross wind once we leave the coast—we'll make it. We'll even have a little margin for error."

"I'm not planning on making errors," Lewis said solemnly, but amusement was lurking in his eyes. "Mitch says they've packed the fuel cells as full as they'll get."

"Good," Alma said. For a moment, she wished again that they hadn't removed the supplemental tank in Little Rock, but there was no point dwelling on things that couldn't be helped. Outside the hangar, she heard the familiar roar of a Ford getting ready for takeoff. "Let's get started, then."

They were last off, still, a total of fifty-eight minutes behind the leader: not a margin that could be made up by any normal means, not sharing the refueling stops with other competitors. Alma let the Terrier trundle down the runway, weighed down by the full fuel load, hauled it reluctantly into the air and let it climb north for a bit before turning to follow the other competitors. Comanche was just visible in the distance, dark against the hazy sky; the rest were strung out ahead of them, boring on down the panhandle toward the recommended refueling stop at Lake City. As long as nobody else had the same idea they did—but nobody else was that desperate.

She settled onto the compass heading, checking it against the landmarks and the map. She'd worked out the magnetic variation the night before, was sure she could navigate across the Gulf and into sight of Weedon Island, but it was good to confirm that everything was working as she'd expected. There was only the possible head wind to worry about, but she'd taken that into account, too. Her planned heading would bring them in a little north of the island, she could fly down the coast a bit and be sure of her landfall. Though they'd be on the ragged edge of their fuel if she missed it by too much.

She adjusted the fuel mixture, setting it to an economical mix, and tried not to watch the fuel gauge. She'd given herself half an hour to be sure fuel consumption was where she expected, half an hour to be sure this was going to work before she committed them to the open ocean. And she had to be sure. If they tried it and failed, they'd be going down in the Gulf, and no one would know to look for them there.

She put that thought aside, concentrating on maintaining her heading and her speed. Beneath her wing, the land rolled past, deep green giving way to creamy beaches. There was a bit of haze, but not enough to hide the landmarks; a few early thunderheads rose in the distance, but the towers were widely separated, easily avoided. To her right, the Gulf beckoned, clear aqua flecked with foam.

"Time," Lewis said.

Alma took a deep breath. The fuel was right where she'd known it would be, consumption just where she needed it. The compass was accurate, the weather good. It was their only chance.

"Right," she said. "We're going."

She tipped the Terrier into a wide bank, turning away from the land, pointing her nose toward the open Gulf. She steadied onto their new heading, resisting the urge to open the throttle just a hair. This was the best speed, the safe speed that would get them into Weedon with even a bit of fuel to spare. She had the discipline to maintain it.

She glanced out the side window, seeing the land retreat. The other planes were out of sight, boring on up the panhandle toward Lake City. In just under an hour, they should see Apalachicola off the port wing, the first and last landmark of the trip. And then it was open water all the way across.

Everything was fine. Lewis looked over the instruments one more time, not that Alma wouldn't have said something immediately if something were off. Everything was fine. A few distant thunderheads to the west marred the sky, but they must be fifty miles away or more at the base, far off their course to the southeast. Ahead, the waters of the Gulf of Mexico looked still from this altitude, variations in wave height erased at five thousand feet. Which meant there wasn't much variation, another good thing. Strong storms, strong winds would kick up waves. If these swells weren't running more than three or four feet, then there wasn't anything to trouble the waters.

And yet. Lewis shifted in his seat. Something bothered him. It wasn't anything in the sound of the Terrier's engines. They sang along at their usual pitch. And besides, Alma would notice any variation of handling, Mitch any difference in sound even though he was in the back right now with Jerry and Stasi. No, it wasn't a sound. It just felt like a sound, like something just below hearing. Something off.

Lewis closed his eyes. It was easier to concentrate without distraction. He could feel the plane around him, feel his friends nearby, Alma beside him a bright fire of concentration, focused completely on their course. And still something was wrong. The sigil on the tail glowed in his mind like a lamp, like the lantern at the stern of a sailing ship, pushed here and there by the winds.

"Hey Lewis?"

His eyes popped open.

Alma glanced at him sideways. "Don't go to sleep on me now. If you're that tired, go on back and have Mitch spell you."

"I'm ok," Lewis said. He glanced out the side window. There off the wing was the golden streak of barrier islands off Apalachicola. St. Vincent Island and St. George Island, the last landfall before a hundred and twenty miles of open sea, blue Caribbean almost teal in the morning light. Below the sun caught on the white sails of a ship, a following wind belling out a huge spinnaker, skimming over the sea back toward Port St. Joe and Panama City.

Hang in there, Segura, he thought. Just hang in there and make it count.

Apalachicola had disappeared into the haze astern almost twenty minutes ago when Alma felt the first niggling hint that something wasn't right. It was hard to tell, but it felt as though the fuel gauge was dropping just a little faster than she had calculated—just a hair under where she'd projected it would be at the end of the first hour. But that could just be the gauge itself, an artifact of the instrument. She'd need to let it ride a little longer before she worried.

Everything else was good. The compass was steady, magnetic deviation exactly as she'd set it, judging by the position of the sun— they could find the Florida coast by the sun any time she needed, just put the sun in her eyes and they'd hit it eventually. If they had the fuel. She looked at the gauge again. Had it dropped? It was hard to tell.

She glanced at Lewis. He was looking out the side window, frowning slightly, and she felt the first touch of fear.

"Lewis?"

He turned back to her, more perplexed than worried, but the knot of fear didn't diminish.

"Are you all right?"

He hesitated, then shrugged slightly. "Something feels—off. I can't put my finger on it, though."

Alma's eyes went to the fuel gauge again. Nothing had moved, but she couldn't shake the crawling sense of unease. If Lewis was worried—she'd learned to trust that feeling. She took a breath, resisting the urge to meddle with the settings.

"See if you can pin it down," she said, and made herself look ahead, toward the horizon and the invisible coast. Out of the corner of her eye, she could see him take a deep breath and then another, hunting his center as his eyes closed gently.

Ten minutes, twenty... The fuel gauge was definitely dropping, a full notch below where it should be. She glanced at Lewis again, but his eyes were still closed, and she looked away. Ok, what could up the fuel consumption? She'd worked out the optimum mixture before they left Pensacola, done the numbers so many times she knew she was right on the knife-edge of perfect efficiency. That wasn't the problem. They were steady at the perfect cruising speed, altitude just right, high enough to ride above the buffeting surface winds...

And that was it, that had to be it. The headwind that she'd been warned about had to be stronger than she'd anticipated, making the Terrier's engines work harder to cover the same amount of ground. But she'd done the math, worked it all out—the wind had to have increased by more than fifteen knots, and that made no sense at all.

But it had happened. She stared at the horizon, juggling the variables again. She'd cut it close, yes, but there was still a little room. A leaner mixture? No, any leaner and the engines would lose efficiency, they wouldn't gain anything there. Certainly not less throttle, that would just leave them more vulnerable to the wind. More throttle, to fight it better? Maybe, but that would cost all the fuel reserve. Better to see if they could find better air. If the headwind was stronger at altitude, maybe they could get below it.

She put the Terrier into a shallow dive, watching the numbers tick off on the altimeter. Four thousand fee, thirty-five hundred... She leveled out at three thousand, feeling the first kick of the surface winds, let the Terrier drone on to the east, steady on the heading for Tampa and Weedon Island. Out the window, she could see a boat crossing their course, heading north and west, sails full-bellied with wind. Not a good sign, she thought, but she waited, watching the fuel, until she was sure. The wind was the same or even a little worse, and she pulled the nose up again, rising back toward her planned altitude.

"Al?" Mitch leaned in the cockpit door. Of course he'd felt the unexpected maneuver, and come to see what was up. "Everything all right?"

"Fuel consumption is off," she said, and heard her voice tight and wrong. "It looks as though we've got more of a headwind than we expected."

She couldn't turn to look, but she could feel his reaction, the way his whole body stiffened as though he'd been struck. Or maybe that was just her, imagining how he had to feel.

"What's our margin?" Mitch asked. He paused. "What's with Lewis?"

"Sorry." Lewis opened his eyes, shaking himself like a dog emerging from water. "I just—I had a feeling, and I was trying to pin it down."

"Oh?"

If anything, Mitch sounded more worried at that, and Alma couldn't really blame him. Lewis's feelings were rarely a sign of anything good.

"We've got some margin," she said, to Mitch, and looked at Lewis. "Anything?"

"The headwind," Lewis said, slowly. "It's not—right? Something's not right about it? But—that's pretty big stuff, changing the wind. You can't do that with, you know, magic. Can you?"

Mitch let out his breath in an explosive sigh. "Goddamn."

"You can," Alma said. "If there's something to start with, and if you know what you're doing "

"Jeff was part of the Lodge." Mitch's voice was steady, no sign of the pain he must be feeling. "He knows that much."

"Crap," Lewis said. "What do we do about it?"

That was the thousand dollar question, Alma thought. And she was Magister, and it all came down to her. She looked at the fuel gauge again, seemingly stuck just under where it should be, and repressed the urge to tap the covering glass.

"How far south have we come?" Mitch asked.

"About sixty miles."

He knew the map as well as she did. Once they were past Apalachicola, the Florida coast bowed away to the north and east, fifty, seventy miles at the very least just to land, and God knew how far to the nearest airfield. It was about twice that far to Weedon Island, but at least there was a field, and fuel. If they turned inland now, they'd definitely lose the race. If there was an airfield to serve them.

"Lewis," she said. "Check the almanac. Is there anything at all on the coast west of Gainesville?"

He reached for the little book, paged quickly through it. "That's all swamp," he said, after a moment. "I'm not seeing anything." He turned pages again, shaking his head. "The nearest field along there is Lake City."

"Well," Alma said. That made the decision easier. It was just as far to Lake City as it was to Weedon Island, might as well carry on. Except that crashing in a swamp might be marginally preferable to going down in the open ocean… The point was not to crash. "Mitch, talk to Jerry. Lewis, go back and help them. See if there's anything we can do to counter whatever Lanier's doing."

"Right," Mitch said, and backed away.

Lewis scrambled out of harness and seat, careful even in his haste. He paused just long enough to touch her shoulder, and disappeared.

"Keep me informed," she called after him, but there was no answer. And that was part of being Magister, she knew. She had her job, and they had theirs, and she would have to trust them. Just as they would have to trust her.

Mitch went back into the Terrier's cabin and took a deep breath. Jerry and Stasi were ignoring each other completely while reading different parts of the same newspaper. "Jerry," Mitch said. "We've got a problem."

Jerry straightened up, a familiar expression of keen intensity on his face. An occult problem obviously. If it had been something mechanical, Mitch would have gotten Alma or Lewis. "What's wrong?"

"Jeff Lanier's called an eldritch wind." There wasn't any good way to put it, no way that wouldn't hurt. Maybe Jeff had tried to kill him in New Orleans and maybe not. That shot could have been meant to warn, way wide of the mark. But this… This wouldn't just kill him, but Jerry and Al and Lewis who Jeff had never even met. If they went down at sea there would be no survivors.

"Ok." Jerry put the paper down as Lewis followed Mitch back into the cabin. "What's it doing?"

"Slowing us down," Mitch said grimly. "It's a headwind. We're still on course, but we're burning fuel a lot faster than Alma figured. At this rate we won't make the coast."

Stasi looked alarmed. "Crashing at sea?"

"Yes," Mitch said shortly. They shouldn't conduct Lodge business in front of her, but given that there wasn't any other room to put her in, short of locking her in the baggage compartment again, it had to be. Besides, she'd proved her worth, and that was good enough for him.

"I don't like crashing at sea," she said.

"Can we skip the hysteria?" Jerry said. "Do you have any idea what protocol Jeff is using?"

"None," Mitch said.

"I don't even know what a protocol is," Lewis said, frowning.

"The method he's using, the symbols," Jerry said. "But if we don't know, we don't. Alma..."

"Is flying the plane," Lewis said. "And she needs to, because she's the one who handles the fuel consumption best. It's up to us."

No, Mitch thought. It's up to me. This isn't Jerry's kind of thing, quick and dirty and literally on the fly, with no proper procedures or equipment.

Jerry put his head to the side, considering. "A simple negation? The negation of air is earth."

"I don't think we can do that in an airplane," Mitch said. "We're depending on the flow of air over the control surfaces. On lift. I don't think we can negate that safely."

"Can we use the tail sigil?" Lewis asked. "That helped before."

"That's to protect the plane," Jerry said. "A headwind doesn't harm the plane or its occupants. The sigil's not going to work counter to something that isn't in itself harmful."

"It will be harmful if we crash," Lewis said.

"Yes, but wind isn't harmful. It's not malevolent." Jerry glanced over at Stasi. "Not like the necklace is. There's nothing innately bad about wind out of the southeast. And the wind isn't trying to harm us. It's just that the results of the wind are dangerous."

"We need to attack him," Mitch said.

Lewis's eyebrows rose.

"Break his concentration, break his hold on the wind," Mitch said. "Hurt him if we can." He looked at Jerry. "Sometimes the way to get a guy to quit is to punch him in the nose." The amount he'd like to do that beggared description. If he could get his hands on him right now...

"I'm not arguing," Jerry said. "If a guy is trying to kill me, I have no compunction about punching him in the nose, physically or otherwise."

Lewis looked troubled. "How do we do that? I have no idea how you would even start doing something like that."

"Not that you're pissed off, darling." Stasi crossed her legs negligently.

Mitch ignored her, answering Lewis instead. "Magic is energy, right? Energy is creating airflow—the wind—just like it does when a prop turns. You can trace the crankshaft that turns the prop back to the engine, right?"

"Well, sure," Lewis said.

"And then you can see what makes the engine work—the internal combustion—provided by the spark plug and the magneto. That's where the energy is coming from. The prop turns, creating airflow, because of the application of energy upstream. So what we can do is trace the energy back from the airflow to the magneto. From the wind to the magician." He couldn't quite bring himself to say 'to Jeff.' He couldn't believe it, not deep inside, even if it were true. Not that killing the Axeman wouldn't be justice. But there were the others.

Lewis nodded solemnly. "And then?"

"And then you use a counterspark," Jerry said. He leaned forward in his chair. "If I'm following your engine metaphor."

"Like an engine with one spark plug," Mitch said. "There's the possibility of uneven burning if the fuel isn't high enough octane, like if you're burning regular gas instead of aviation fuel. A second spark creates an unsynchronized flame front."

Stasi put down her section of the paper with an incredulous look on her face. "A what?"

"A knock in your engine," Lewis said. "It tears up your engine."

"You are out of your mind with your spark plugs and things! What are you talking about? Magic or mechanics?" Stasi demanded.

"There isn't any difference," Mitch said.

"There certainly is."

"Look, are you going to help or not?" Mitch asked, putting his fists into his pockets. "If not, that's fine. But we need to talk about it."

"Oh, I'll help," Stasi said grimly. "Crashing in the ocean isn't my idea of fun, darling."

"What do we do?" Lewis said.

Mitch looked at Jerry and Jerry gave him a nod. "Your operation."

"Ok. Let's set up a basic circle. Then Jerry will help me establish the connection. I'll trace it back and drop a match in his engine. Lewis and Stasi, you'll lend energy and stabilize the circle."

"With no ground," Jerry said.

"Our ground is flying the plane," Mitch said. He looked at Stasi.

"Unless you happen to be a strong earth sign?"

"You must be kidding," she said. "I'm all air and fire, darling."

"That makes me the ground," Jerry said. He shifted in his chair. "Do we have to get on the floor?"

"You stay in the chair," Mitch said. "I'll sit on the floor."

"I'm already on the right side," Jerry said. "Starboard is west, more or less."

"Since we're going southeast, that will do," Mitch said. He sat down on the deck with his back to the cockpit door. "Lewis, you sit to my right. Stasi, scoot your chair closer to Jerry's so that you're opposite me."

"North is a perfectly good position for a medium," Stasi said. She moved her wicker chair, making room for Lewis to sit on the floor beside her feet.

"Hands around then," Mitch said, and closed his eyes, reaching. Lewis to his right, a firm grip like a handshake, the solid grip of a new friend. His energy was bright, constant, clear as a stream of pure current. Jerry to the left, precise, Jerry's hand on top ready to pass counterclockwise, all of the conventions observed without thinking, professional as they come. And Stasi across, hard to feel at first, through the other connections or because she wasn't putting much into the web, but strong. There was more energy than he'd expected there, not as deep as Alma but as practiced as Jerry, just in an entirely different tradition.

Mitch took a deep breath, opening his hands flat against the Terrier's body beneath him, cool metal under his fingers, smooth as soft skin. His lady. His plane. His Terrier. She struggled against the wind, holding her own, nose into the eye of the wind, only a faint shudder down her body telling her strain. The wind moved over every surface. He could almost feel the eddies, feel the lift beneath her wings, the turbulence in the wake of her props, the silvery path of her slipstream. She could take more than this, his gallant lady, but she was burning fuel to do it. Using energy. She was using energy to fight the wind, certain as a woman struggling to walk in a gale, certain as the figurehead of a sailing ship pointing the way home. She couldn't go on forever this way. Fuel would fail.

I won't fail you, he whispered to her, fingers against her metal flesh. I'll get you respite.

Wind. There was energy behind it. Something moved it. Somewhere, out in front along their course, air particles moved in response to energy, a stream of energy unmeasurable by modern standards but nonetheless there, atoms responding to changes. The air moved. Wind was created.

And the energy, the untraceable track of protons and electrons… it could be followed. It could be followed if you knew how, if something in your own mind was similar enough, if you had energy of your own. He did. He had fuel, and more poured in from Lewis in a steady, solid stream, Jerry regulating it carefully, Stasi on the edge of his consciousness, an auxiliary fuel tank barely tapped.

Back along the course of the energy over green seas, a diagonal path over deep waters, the Gulf of Mexico warm in the sun. He could follow it. Not a place, not a thing, but a person. Jeff. He'd worked with Jeff this way, his touch as familiar as Lewis'. He knew him. He'd trusted him.

Mitch gathered the energy up, pooling it, like making a snowball of energy, his and Lewis' and Jerry's and Stasi's, compacting it like ice, harder and tighter and brighter. A snowball. An energy ball. A flame to the engine, a second spark, an unsynchronized flame front that would burn entirely wrong, that would send the stream flying off in unpredictable directions, disrupted entirely from its purpose.

Jeff. The sense of him, suddenly, surprisingly, open and real as though he had come upon him startlingly quick, walked up behind him wherever he was sitting and grabbed his collar and yanked him to his feet. A punch in the nose, the snowball of energy thrown into the operation, falling straight down the line of energy to its source, exploding into fire, the unsynchronized front that tears up your engine. There was nothing subtle about it. It was a sock to the jaw, all the energy he could muster, fueled by a rage he didn't realize he had. Rage. Pain. Shame. All of it fed a roundhouse of energy, a hit with all his strength.

He had half a moment to feel the shock, and then the contact broke, the energy trail dissipating, and he rocked back, fingers against the cool metal skin of the Terrier.

The last of the power wrapped around him, and he felt Jerry grounding it, pulling it down, spreading it between them to absorb evenly. Mitch opened his eyes.

"Ok?" Jerry said. His glasses reflected the light and there was a thin smile on his face.

"Ok," Mitch said. He lifted his hands from the deck, flexing his fingers. They were cold. It was probably from the metal, but it felt instead like all the anger had burned out of him like tobacco out of a cigarette, leaving ash in the shape of the paper behind.

"That was interesting," Stasi said. She looked worried, or maybe that was what respect looked like from her.

"Did it work?" Lewis asked.

"Ask Al."

Lewis opened the cockpit door. "Hey Al? How's it looking?"

"I think the wind's dropped," she called back. "She's handling differently. Come up and see."

Lewis scrambled over Mitch and went back into the front, while he leaned back against the door, suddenly tired. The Terrier's engines droned on, but he thought she was laboring less. He thought. So tired. He closed his eyes and let the sound of the engines lull him. Paper. Ash on the wind, the thing that the fire leaves behind.

"Let him be," Jerry said in some distant place, kind and warm. "We've done all we can for now."

Chapter Twenty

The Terrier was moving easier, and Alma eased back on the throttle again, returning it to the setting she had calculated would be the most efficient. They'd burned off ninety, maybe a hundred gallons of fuel in the time since she'd first spotted the problem, and that was thirty or forty gallons more than she'd planned for, cut at least half an hour off the time they could stay in the air. They'd burned more before that, too, maybe another twenty gallons extra, maybe even a bit more, as Lanier built the headwind against them. At least Mitch had stopped that.

She glanced sideways at Lewis, who was flipping through the almanac again as though he might find a field he hadn't seen before. "How's Mitch?"

"Ok, I think." Lewis didn't look up from the flimsy sheets. "Sleeping."

"Good." Actually, it wasn't all that good, not if she wanted him sharp for the last leg into Coconut Grove, but a working like this, spoiling something as big as Lanier's wind—that took energy, took it out of everyone. Mitch's pockets weren't as deep as hers, but even she would be exhausted by the amount required. "How about you?"

"Fine." Lewis did look up then, a quick, rueful glance as he put the almanac back into the flap beside his seat. "A little tired, but nothing serious."

"Good," Alma said again. The sun was almost at the zenith, easing the glare; there was a streaky haze of cloud a thousand feet above them, and thunderheads to the northwest, marching slowly down the coast. At least they were less likely to run into them on this route, though that wasn't much of a silver lining, not when the cost of failure was crashing in open ocean…

"How did he find us?" Lewis asked. "He couldn't have known

what we were trying—could he?"

"A headwind would have slowed us down, made sure we couldn't win," Alma said. "Which I expect he wants. If I were doing it, I'd have dowsed for us, and then I'd have seen what we were trying. He was a flyer, too, you know. He was in the Lodge with Gil and Henry and Mitch and Jerry."

"I should have seen it," Lewis said.

Alma looked at him quickly, but he looked more thoughtful than guilty.

He gave a quick smile, as though he'd guessed her thought. "I'm not beating myself up, I just—I was thinking about sailing ships, that the sigil on the tail was like a stern lantern, and—well, that was the answer, wasn't it? We had a wrong wind. Only I couldn't read my own mental handwriting."

"It takes a while to learn your own symbols, I think," Alma said. She was grateful for the distraction, something to keep her mind off the pointless calculations, her hands steady on the wheel, not fiddling with throttle and fuel mixture. "We've got to find someone who can teach you."

"I'd like to learn," Lewis said. "But it's not like you can afford for me to take a couple of months off."

"No," Alma said. Nor could they afford to hire someone to come to them, though she could probably find a tutor if she really tried. Not that she wanted to ask Henry particularly: she wasn't as much of a purist as Jerry, but Henry's lodge worked in an entirely different tradition. Bullfinch belonged to a more congenial group, and would certainly know someone; Jerry had an even wider range of connections they could tap, but all of those people would need to be paid. At the moment, they were barely making ends meet. Which was why they'd gotten into this whole air race thing in the first place... She shoved that thought aside. They were going to survive, and they were going to win enough money to keep the business going. Somehow. The Terrier bored on to the southeast, the haze thickening to cloud ahead of them.

Twenty minutes more, and she was worrying again, eyeing the fuel gauge warily. Fifteen minutes more, and she was sure: even at the most economical speed and fuel mixture that she could manage, she wasn't going to be able to stretch it out to make the coast. She scowled at the instruments, everything perfect except the one crucial gauge, the numbers flickering through her mind. They were coming up about fifty gallons short, half an hour's flying time or a bit more. If she thinned out the mixture any more, they'd lose airspeed, and going slower wasn't actually going to help the problem. The slower speeds still burned fuel, and took longer to cover the ground; 80 knots was their most efficient speed, and she'd been holding to that all the way across the Gulf, except when the headwind forced her to increase power. .

Eighty knots was a given. Any faster, any slower, they'd just run out of fuel sooner—She stopped abruptly, frowning. Eighty knots was the most efficient speed on three engines. On two… She closed her eyes for a moment, juggling the numbers. On two engines, the best speed was around seventy knots; that would get them into Weedon Island in about an hour and a half, and they had just about that much fuel remaining. It would be close, so very close, but it should work. It had to work.

"All right," she said. "Lewis, I want you to shut down the center engine."

He gave her a sharp look, but reached for the controls, closing the fuel line and readying the engine for shutdown. "Ok."

And that was Lewis for you, she thought. He's not going to flail or ask pointless questions, he's just going to do what needs doing. The engine sputtered, the last of the fuel feeding in, and Lewis switched off the spark.

"Done," he said. "Fuel still a problem?"

Alma nodded. "We'll be ok now," she said, and willed it to be true.

Mitch woke to a change in the engines, a shift in the steady drone. He sat upright, his body reacting before his mind had caught up: they were down an engine. He looked at Jerry, who shrugged.

"Alma shut it down."

Ok, that was better than a mechanical failure, but still not good. He jammed both hands into his hair, tugging at it as though the pull would help wake him up. Across the cabin, Stasi sat bolt upright, legs crossed, one foot swinging in its pretty shoe. She was scared, he thought, but determined not to show it. He couldn't quite manage a reassuring smile, and hauled himself to his feet to lean in the cockpit door.

"Al?"

"We burned up too much fuel fighting the wind." Alma spoke without turning. "But we can make it on two."

"Ok." He'd learned years ago to trust Alma's calculations. If she said they'd have enough fuel this way, then they would. They'd be losing time, but Alma would have factored it in, and, anyway, they had to make it to Tampa Bay without crashing if they were going to have any chance of winning. He braced his hands on the sides of the doorframe. "How far out are we?"

"I make it about fifty miles from Weedon Island," Alma said. She nodded to the windscreen. "Closer to the coast."

Sure enough, there it was, a line on the horizon, sand rising out of the sea. The question was where they were, exactly, whether they were north or south of the field. A light flashed then, a single point a few degrees north of their heading; a moment later, a double flash appeared in the same spot.

"That's the Anclote Key light," Lewis said. He passed the map over his shoulder, and Mitch took it. "About thirty-five miles north of Weedon Island."

"Ok," Mitch said again. He turned the map in his hands, matching the light's flash to the markings. Alma was keeping the Terrier on a heading that ought to cross the coast just about Clearwater, and from there it was a straight run across the little peninsula to Weedon Island. "Do you want me to take the landing?"

"Yes." Alma's eyes were on the instruments, her hands steady on the control yoke. "You can swap with Lewis whenever you're ready."

Fifty miles, at their most economical cruising speed… Before he could say anything, Lewis said, "Why don't you take it now?"

"Thanks," Mitch said. If it was him, he'd hate to give up the co-pilot's seat—but Lewis was a good guy, entirely sensible. Too sensible to take it as a slight on his flying, or as anything but acknowledgement that he, Mitch, had the most hours in the Terrier. Lewis struggled free of his harness, slipped past Mitch into the cabin, and Mitch took his place in the second seat. Alma gave him a quick nod, but all her attention was focused on the Terrier, nursing it toward the coast.

They crossed the coast over Clearwater at a thousand feet, crossed the peninsula's narrow waist, and turned further south to follow the coast of old Tampa Bay, Alma beginning the shallow efficient descent as they crept southeast toward the field. Mitch glanced at the fuel gauges. They were low, but not yet on the reserve: good enough, close as they were to the Weedon Island field. Yes, there was the bridge that was their first landmark, the coast swelling to the east, swamp running dark green to the water. And there at last was the flash of flag streaming from the Sky Harbor tower, rising fifty feet above the tin-roofed hangar. The field was empty except for a pair of stub-winged biplanes tied down on the verge.

"Time to fire her back up," Mitch said, and Alma nodded.

"Go ahead."

Mitch reached for the controls, began the starting sequence. He pumped the primer, then checked to be sure the throttle was closed. The starter was on, the starter dog engaged; he switched on the ignition and the booster magneto. The engine coughed, caught, and died again.

"Damn." Mitch reset the controls, ran through the sequence again. The engine coughed again, but refused to turn over. "Come on…"

"We're on the reserve," Alma said, quietly.

"Come on," Mitch said again. More primer, more fuel, the mix boosted to "Full Rich"; the starter and the booster fired. The engine coughed, caught, and failed again with a shudder that shook the entire airplane.

"Mitch," Alma said.

They couldn't run rich like that, not if they wanted to have enough fuel to land. His hands were already moving on the controls, adjusting the mixture. Alma brought the Terrier around again, lining them up for another pass. Mitch could see people on the ground outside the hangar, staring up at the strange plane.

"One more time," Mitch said.

"Go," Alma answered, and he reached for the controls, began the sequence once again.

The engine shook and sputtered without result. Maybe a clogged line somewhere, Mitch thought; but then, it was always tricky restarting in midflight, the slipstream playing merry hell with the spark and the gasoline. Alma looked sideways at him, and for the first time,

Mitch thought he saw fear in her eyes.

"Can we land on two?"

No. That was the simple answer: the manual strongly recommended only doing landings and takeoffs with all three engines, and disclaimed any responsibility for the crash that it implied was inevitable if you were stupid enough to try it. There was enough power, even on two engines there was enough to bring the Terrier safely down. It was just that there was no margin for error, no chance of changing your mind once you'd picked your line, and God forbid there be a gust of wind, a glitch in the other engines, or any other minor problem. "We're going to have to," he said, and knew he sounded grim.

"You'll have to take it," Alma said. Her voice was tight. "Get ready to switch over."

Mitch was already busy with the controls. "Ready."

"She's yours," Alma said.

Mitch felt the controls come alive in his hands, the Terrier swinging east over the swamp. The reserve tank was ticking down, but he took his time getting the feel of the air, the way the Terrier handled on two engines. One chance, that was all he was going to get.

He brought the Terrier around in a gentle turn, heading back toward the field. No steep angles, no sudden moves, nothing to shake her out of true. The runway was dirt, empty of traffic, but there were even more people outside the terminal and the main hangar, all staring up at the Terrier. A flagman waved from beside the tower, and Mitch wagged his wings in answer, acknowledging the signal, but kept on past the terminal, making another long, gentle turn to bring them into the wind. Into the wind and in line with the runway, bare dirt with sod to either side. He cut his speed, not quite to stalling, letting the Terrier drop from three hundred feet to two to one hundred. He could feel the air under the wings, right on the edge of a stall, the two working engines straining to keep power. Fifty feet, and the dirt rushing to meet them, a glimpse of the flag on the tower, above him now as he brought the Terrier down. Twenty feet, ten, and he dumped the last of the lift, the Terrier dropping the last few feet. She landed hard, bounced, wings wobbling, then settled, rumbling across the uneven ground. Mitch allowed himself a sigh of sheer relief, and Alma reached across to grab his shoulder.

"Beautiful flying," she said.

It had to be, he thought. He owed them for screwing up so badly in New Orleans. Necklace or no necklace, he knew better—"We shouldn't have had to do this," Mitch began, and she shook her head.

"Stop it. This is not the time."

She was right, and he nodded. He brought the Terrier around in a sharp turn, no longer worried about losing an engine, heading back toward the terminal and the people who'd gathered there to see the unexpected arrival.

"Are you fit for the last leg?" Alma asked.

"Yeah." Mitch took a breath, letting the tension drain out of his muscles. He could feel it, all right, but the reserves were there, the old familiar strength, steady and waiting. In spite of everything, that, at least, was still there. "I can handle it."

Alma smiled and touched his arm again, then hauled herself out of her seat. "Good."

Alma climbed out of the Terrier, working her shoulders to relieve some of the tension of the long flight. They'd made it, that was the main thing, and now it was just a matter of refueling as quickly as possible and getting in the air for Coconut Grove. Just under two hundred miles to the finish line, a couple of hours' flying at their fastest cruising speed—

She broke off as a man in khaki pants and a blue shirt with "Sky Harbor" embroidered above the breast pocket came to meet her, taking his hands out of his pockets.

"Boy, we were worried there for a minute," he said. "Engine trouble?"

Out of the corner of her eye, Alma could see Lewis negotiating for the use of a ladder, ready to check out the center engine. Mitch was standing ready under the nose, squinting up at the magnetos.

"I hope not," she said. "Mostly we were out of fuel."

"That we can fix," the man said. "We've got fuel. No mechanic service, though." He held out his hand. "Joe Christie."

"Alma Segura." Alma returned the handshake. She was so tired, she'd almost said Gilchrist, and she stretched her shoulders again. "I think we're all right. It's just the fuel. We'll need a full load, though."

That was the other piece of the gamble, that this small field would be able to supply them. Eastern flew out of here regularly, she knew, but there was no knowing how much other traffic there was.

"We can do that," Christie said again. "How much do you need?"

"Four hundred gallons, give or take." Alma crossed her fingers, and was relieved to see him nod.

"Ok. That'll run you twenty-eight dollars. Cash."

Alma blinked. She'd gotten so used to having the gas supplied by the race organizers that she hadn't exactly considered how she was going to pay for this. She had three dollars and forty cents in her purse; after all the taxis in New Orleans, she doubted Lewis had much more. Mitch—well, you didn't get that drunk cheaply. Jerry might have money, but she hated to have to borrow from him. But of course she had the business checkbook with her. "Will you take a check?"

Christie shook his head. "Sorry."

"Hold on just a minute," Alma said, and turned toward the men working on the engine. "Lewis "

He looked down at her from the top of the ladder. "Good news. Everything's fine here."

"Good," Alma said. "How much cash do you have left?"

"Um." Lewis blinked, then braced himself against the top of the ladder to reach into his pocket. "Four bucks and change."

"Damn." Alma looked at Mitch. "How about you?"

Mitch flushed. "Two bits, if we're lucky. Sorry, Al."

Not quite eight dollars. "Never mind," she said, and climbed back into the plane. Stasi was still sitting in the rear seat, swinging one foot in her pretty shoe, and Jerry looked up from his newspaper.

"Everything ok?"

"No," Alma said. "How much cash do you have on you, Jerry?"

He reached into his pocket without question, hauled out his wallet. "Nine dollars. Plus some change. What's wrong?"

"We have to pay for the fuel here," Alma said. "We're off the race route, nobody's made any arrangements."

"Hell." Jerry handed over the bills, and reached into his other pocket for the change. "That's a buck twenty."

Alma took that as well. "Thanks." She looked at Stasi. "I don't suppose—?"

"Darling, I'm nearly flat broke," the countess answered. "Two dollars until I can wire for money."

Nineteen dollars. More than half. Maybe she could talk Christie into taking a check for the rest. "Thanks," she said again, and climbed back out of the plane.

Christie was still waiting at the edge of the airstrip, talking now to Mitch, his arms folded across his chest. A woman was with him now, a heavy-set woman in a blue print dress, her corset losing its battle with her figure.

"Great Passenger Derby?" Christie said, and Alma could hear the disbelief in his voice. "You're a bit off-course."

"We cut the corner," Alma said briskly. "We're Gilchrist Aviation. We have a lot of time to make up, so we took the direct route."

"Across the Gulf?" Christie's eyebrows rose.

"That's right," Alma said. "Look, I've got nineteen in cash. Will you take a company check for the rest?"

Christie shook his head again. "We're a cash business—"

"Yes, we will," the woman said.

Christie looked at her. "But, Mother—"

"Don't you listen to the radio?" She looked at Alma with a smile that showed a missing tooth at the side of her mouth. "TexAv will pay us, anyway, you know that. If you give us a check, Mrs. Segura, we'll hold it for security."

Alma let out a breath she hadn't realized she was holding. "Of course—Mrs. Christie, is it?"

"That's right, dear."

"I'll write that out right now," Alma said.

"And I'll get Billy to bring the truck around," Christie said.

"Thank you," Alma said, and ducked back into the Terrier.

Mitch watched the fuel truck pull away and heaved a sigh of relief. The tanks were full, and it had only taken thirty minutes, less time than it would have taken to refuel in Lake City with everyone else ahead of them. He had no idea how Alma had pulled it off, but that was the sort of thing she always did. It was why she was Magister after Gil. And somehow Jerry had found sandwiches. They weren't fancy, or even particularly good, just cheap white bread and mayonnaise and lettuce with a few slivers of ham tucked into them, but they were something. He stuffed the last bite into his mouth and washed it down with the rest of the rather better coffee.

He shook the last drops of coffee out of the cup and set it on the bench where the passengers waited, then turned to look at the Terrier.

Lewis ducked under the nose of the plane, just forward of the wheel struts, and checked, seeing him. "Oh," he said. "Al wanted me to tell you that the main engine checks out fine."

"That's good." Another man might have resented his wife coming behind him, looking over his work, but not Lewis. He knew his skills and his limits, and Alma was the best mechanic of any of them. And Alma would never question his flying or the things he was learning to see.

"Yeah," Lewis said. He paused. "Who do you want for co-pilot?"

Mitch hesitated in turn. It was probably Al's right, but she had to be beat from the flight across the Gulf, and Lewis was the better navigator. "Why don't you take it?" he said, and heard Alma's light step behind him.

"Lewis should co-pilot," she said, and stopped, seeing Lewis's expression.

"Already settled," Mitch said. "Are we ready?"

Alma nodded. "She took my check for the whole thing."

"Well, that's a break," Lewis said. "We still got the countess?"

"Jerry hasn't let her out of his sight since we landed," Alma answered. "Let's go."

Mitch settled himself into the pilot's seat, adjusting the controls as Lewis arranged himself beside him. The engines started on the first try, even the center, roaring to life as though there'd never been a problem, and Mitch shook his head, smiling. "Atta girl."

Lewis grinned, and reached for the map. "You've got a choice. Do we go straight across the swamps, or follow the roads?"

"What's the difference?" Mitch had to raise his voice over the sound of the engines, sweet and strong at full throttle. He cut them back reluctantly and turned the Terrier toward the runway.

"I make it about forty miles," Lewis said. "That's why I asked."

Mitch nodded. Forty miles wasn't much of a saving, a little less than half an hour's flying time. He could see all the reasons it might make more sense to take the safe route, follow the roads along the edge of the swamp so that there was no chance they'd miss the landmarks that would bring them in to Coconut Grove. But if they were going to win, they needed every minute they could scrape up, and he trusted Lewis's navigation.

"Straight through," he said, and turned the Terrier into the wind, opening the throttle for takeoff.

She rose easily under his hands, catching the wind as they turned south and east. Lewis gave him the heading, and Mitch opened the throttle further still. Two hundred miles, and full tanks: they could afford to waste a little fuel now, to gain speed. To gain time. He only hoped it would be enough.

Chapter Twenty-one

Henry paced the tarmac, stopping to light another cigarette and glancing at his watch. Ten or fifteen minutes, tops, until the first plane was sighted. His fellow in Lake City had phoned as each plane landed and left, refueled and ready for the flight down the length of Florida. United had fifteen minutes on the nearest competitor, with Comanche in second. Consolidated was half an hour behind, with TWA limping in at the back on two engines. They'd finish the race, but for a plane that had started the day in second it was a big comedown. Henry shook his head. Mechanical trouble, his man said. One engine down.

And no sign of either the Corsair or his plane. Henry paced back in the other direction, shaking ash into the breeze. Easy come, easy go. It was always something with that lot. Probably they'd limp into some field anytime now. Surely. They wouldn't have gone down. Not them.

There was a shout and a cluster of reporters pointing, all hands raised to the north, cameramen vying for the first decent shot. RKO's newsreel photographers turned their big camera on its tripod. "Who is it?" Henry asked the nearest man with binoculars. "United?"

"I don't see the red wings," he said. He squinted into the binoculars. "White and blue. Consolidated? How'd they get up this far?"

Henry yanked the binoculars away from him, not even saying *excuse me* to his "Hey, mac!" White and blue. He focused on the distant speck, ignoring the roar of the crowd as they saw the first plane and behind it at the horizon another, no more than two or three miles behind, a photo finish, right down to the wire just the way the newsies liked it. The cant of the wings, the shape of the fuselage against the sky, larger than a Ford trimotor... It was all Henry could do not to shout. It was all he could do not to leap in the air.

"That's my plane," he said, and his voice didn't even shake. "That's a Kershaw Terrier." Eight miles out, and United just behind, a third plane behind that, the small, light shape of the Corsair.

"Man, what a finish!" the RKO guy said, his eyes to his lens, the movie camera cranking.

"Think they'll make it, Mr. Kershaw?" the first reporter asked. "United's going to finish strong."

"Sure thing," Henry said, and clenched his fists in his pockets.

They made good time across the swamps, the headwind shifting as the day went on, becoming more south than east. Mitch did his best to compensate, keeping the Terrier steady on the direct line to Miami, but he wasn't entirely surprised to see Lewis scanning the ground ahead with increasing concern.

"Trouble?"

"We ought to be seeing Miami by now," Lewis answered. "At least the area around Hialeah."

"We're probably west of our line," Mitch said.

"Yeah, but how far?" Lewis consulted the map again, then looked out the windows. "Wait. There."

The line of a road cut through the swamp, concrete showing pale between the overhanging trees. It ran east-west, and Mitch looked back at Lewis.

"That's the Tamiami Trail," Lewis said. "Ok. Yeah, we're west of where we should be, but if we follow that to the first town, that's Tamiami "

"We can cut southeast again from there," Mitch finished. "Got it."

He put the Terrier into a turn as he spoke, lining her up on the flash of the road. This was easy flying, high and fast, the ground reeling past under them. Four and a half hours in the air from Pensacola, plus the forty minutes on the ground: the race route notes said they should expect the Pensacola to Coconut Grove leg to take about six and a half hours including stops, though he and Alma had guessed they could do it in a bit over six. Another half hour or so to the field, if Lewis was right and they hadn't come too far west, which still put them in just ahead of the best time they thought anyone could make. It might all just work. In spite of him.

He concentrated on the feel of the controls, air on the wings and flaps translating to pressure against his hands, the engines strong and steady. All that mattered now was crossing the finish line. Get to Coconut Grove and cross the finish line, the literal white line painted across the end of the runway. And then they'd see.

"Tamiami," Lewis said, pointing, and sure enough the ground was changing, swamp giving way to solid ground. He consulted the map again, gave a new heading. "That should bring us into the field from the west."

"Ok," Mitch said, and banked the Terrier, watching the compass swing. He opened the throttle, feeling the revs increase.

Ten minutes, then fifteen, houses and yards and streets reeling past beneath their wings. Lewis made a small course correction, and for an instant Mitch thought he caught the flash of a tower light on the horizon. It came again, more definite this time, and he gave a whoop of joy.

"There. That's got to be Coconut Grove."

"Yeah," Lewis said, looking from map to horizon. "That's it." He looked as though he didn't quite believe it.

"How far?"

"About five miles."

We can do it, Mitch thought. They'd be first in at the field, and that might just be enough to make up the difference. The houses flashed past beneath them, the streets broader, busier now that they were over Miami itself. Even if it didn't put them into first place, it should be enough for second, and that was still good money. They'd said from the start that second would still be good enough.

"Mitch." Alma leaned in the cockpit door, her voice tight and controlled. "There's another plane in sight to the north. I think it's United."

"Goddamnit." Mitch craned his neck to see. There were clouds to the north, the tail end of the line of thunderheads that was still building. For a moment, all he saw was cloud, but then he saw it, a fleck of brighter white against the sky, drifting for an instant into the edge of his side window, and out again. "Damn it to hell."

His hands were already moving on the controls, shoving the throttle to full, canting the Terrier into a shallow dive that would bring them in fast and low. No need to worry about the fuel now, no need to think about economy, all that mattered was raw power, power and speed and the rush toward the field. He could see the tower now, windsock lifted by a decent breeze, and he banked a final time, lining up to cross the finish line squarely, broadside to the cameras.

Alma had disappeared again, but a moment later Stasi took her place, clinging to the frame with both hands. "Mrs. Segura says there's a second plane."

"What?" Mitch didn't try to look. They were behind him, almost on his tail, old instincts screaming to peel off, get the drop on them. But this was a race, not a dogfight; he kept the Terrier coming, dropping further still. "How far back?"

Stasi relayed the question, and shook her head. "She says maybe a mile. They're neck and neck."

Let them fight each other, Mitch thought. Let us get away. "Are they overtaking?"

"She says—no, she can't tell."

"Damn it," Mitch said again. There was no more power left to give, all the engines opened full, the Terrier shuddering faintly under the pressure. United was behind him, and the second plane, but he couldn't even look to see what they were doing. All he could do was keep the Terrier straight and level, arrowing toward the finish. He could see it now, the white line splashed a yard wide across the concrete. Come on, darling, he thought, hunching forward as though she were a horse, as though he could urge her to just that little bit more effort. Come on—

"There!" Lewis yelled, and Mitch saw the line flash beneath the nose. He kept the power full on, pulled up and left, coming around in a broad turn, craning to see what was behind him. A smaller plane was just crossing the line, diving like a kestrel—Jezek, he realized, the Corsair, dropping toward the landing strip as though they were low on fuel. United was only a few thousand feet behind them, pulled up and away with a waggle of wings, acknowledging defeat.

"We did it!" Alma leaned in the cockpit again, her grin incandescent. "My God, we did it!"

"A little too close," Lewis said, but he was grinning too.

"We won it fair and square," Alma said, and squeezed Mitch's shoulder. "And damn good piloting."

Mitch couldn't help but respond to that smile, grinning himself as he circled back to the end of the runway. The flagman was out, signaling a clear field, and Mitch brought the Terrier gently down, wheels kissing the tarmac. Safely down, and in first place: it almost seemed too much to believe.

Mitch stood at the bottom of the Terrier's steps, one hand resting lightly on the plane's aluminum body as though that would help ground him. The referees were still working the numbers, Henry and the delegation from United and Connie Jezek all crowding around the office door waiting for the results, but even as he watched Henry pried himself away and came striding back across the tie-down area, scattering reporters as he came.

"We've won," he said, to Alma, and she flung her arms around his neck, kissing him soundly. He clasped Lewis's hand, and Jerry's, and touched the brim of his hat in Mitch's direction before looking back at Alma. "They're just trying to figure out where Jezek will finish. It's going to be very close for second."

"I hope they get it," Alma said.

And that was Al for you, Mitch thought. Generous to a fault. He felt weirdly distant, as though he was looking at everything through a pane of glass, as though he could see but not touch. The office door opened, and the referees emerged, their leader holding up his hands to silence the waiting crowd. His words came disjointed through the continued noise from the stands and drone of distant engines.

"Gilchrist Aviation first, Jezek Air second—United third."

There were cheers in answer, the sound spreading to the crowd still waiting in the stands as the announcer repeated the finish, his words crackling over the loudspeaker. A handful of reporters darted for the nearest telephone; the rest surged across the concrete toward the Terrier.

"Mrs. Segura! How do you feel about your finish? First to last and first again!"

And if I hadn't screwed up, Mitch thought, we wouldn't have had to do that. No dangerous flight across the Gulf, no on-the-fly ritual that barely pulled us out, no crazy landing, just a straight flight down the Panhandle and on into Miami. No drama, and no danger, none of them at risk. Lewis was grinning at Alma's side, the worried frown he'd worn for most of the race finally erased: the newspaper would have better pictures of him at last. Jerry leaned on his cane, relaxed for the first time in days, and the black-haired countess was talking to one of the reporters, her head cocked to one side like a bird. He hoped she wasn't going to get them tangled in some improbable story—or, worse, tell the reporters exactly how they'd made it across the Gulf—but then, no one would believe her anyway.

"Mitch!"

Alma waved to him, and he came forward to pose for the first round of photos, Al with one arm around his waist and the other around Lewis on the opposite side, her body warm against them both. That probably wouldn't quell any rumors, Mitch thought, but she'd earned it. "Mrs. Segura!" One of the referees was pushing through the mob of reporters, waving. "Mrs. Segura, you and your team need to come with me. We have a truck ready for your victory lap."

"Our what?" Lewis asked.

"Please, gentlemen," the referee went on, offering the reporters a placating smile. "The whole team will be happy to answer your questions, but we've promised the crowd a chance to cheer our first three finishers. Ladies, gentlemen, this way, please."

Mitch followed the others into the hangar, where three open-bed trucks had been drawn up, their sides draped with red-white-and-blue bunting. Signs hung from the rails as well, the teams' names with their marque painted beside it. Made up at the start of the race, Mitch was willing to bet, to be ready for any eventuality. No one could have expected Jezek to do so well.

Jerry balked at the truck, shaking his head unhappily at the referee. Alma linked her arm in his and smiled, and a few moments later someone hurriedly pushed a set of steps up against the truck's tail. Alma climbed up, and turned at the top, holding out her hand to steady Stasi. Jerry hauled himself grimly onto the bed, his hands white-knuckled on the rail, Lewis following close enough to catch him if his leg failed. And I should have done that, too, Mitch thought, climbing up after them. Stupid and careless…

The truck lurched forward, gears grinding, and he caught Stasi as she stumbled against him.

"Thank you, darling," she said, straightening with a brilliant smile, and braced herself more carefully against the rail.

The truck pulled out onto the wide turn-around in front of the hangar. The stands were set up a little further down, between the hangar and the terminal, and a roar went up as the trucks appeared. The sound was deafening, almost palpable, like the noise of the barrage, and Mitch flinched in spite of himself. From the look on his face, Jerry had the same thought, but was bracing himself to endure it. Only Lewis didn't look spooked, waving with one hand and steadying Alma with the other.

The truck reached the end of the turn-around, and swung left to retrace its path, idling to let the other trucks finish their first pass. In the relative quiet, Alma said, "I'm sorry."

"What?" Mitch frowned, not at all sure what she meant.

"I'm sorry I yelled at you," she said. "In the cemetery. I shouldn't have said that."

"I screwed up," Mitch said. "I should be the one apologizing."

"No," Alma said. She glanced sidelong at him, her mouth twisting in a wry smile. "That necklace—do you think you were the only person it tried to influence? I know how powerful it was."

"It did influence me," Mitch said. He fixed his eyes on the stands, the restless mass of people still cheering for them: anything to block out the memory of Eden and Jeff Lanier in the hall…

"Somebody gets the short straw," Alma said. "I'm sorry it was you. And I'm sorry I yelled."

In spite of everything, Mitch smiled. "Did you really mean you'd suck the marrow from my bones?"

"At the time?" Alma's answering grin was unrepentant. "Absolutely. But I am sorry. About everything."

The truck lurched into motion again, and the noise of the crowd drowned any further conversation.

The Biltmore might actually be the fanciest hotel they'd stayed in over the course of the race, Alma thought, or maybe it was just that she had a moment to enjoy it. She let herself slide down a little further in the enormous bathtub, a cool breeze belling the gauze curtains. In three hours, they would have to be at the victory party, dressed in their best and ready to make more speeches to the reporters and polite conversation with the sponsors, but for now… She splashed more water on her face and let her head rest gently against the edge of the tub. For now, she was going to enjoy every bit of this, from the soap that smelled of exotic flowers to the soft cotton dressing gown that hung on the wall. Henry had already arranged for a hotel maid to do her hair for the evening.

Lewis knocked at the door, came in without waiting for her answer, a tall glass in each hand filled with pale green liquid.

"Limeade," he said, and Alma thrashed herself to a safer position to take it from him. She took a sip: gloriously sweet and tart and with a definite kick of gin.

"Thank you."

"Compliments of the hotel," Lewis said.

"Including the gin?"

"I'm getting the very strong impression that Prohibition isn't popular here."

That was the sort of thing that made people think Lewis was naive, but Alma saw the amusement in his eyes.

"They also sent up some sandwiches and fruit," he went on. "I thought you might want some before you had to start getting ready."

"I probably should." Alma handed him back the glass and hauled herself out of the tub, shivering a little at the breeze on her skin. Lewis watched with frank appreciation as she dried herself with a towel twice as soft as anything she'd ever had before, and handed her the robe from the door.

The bedroom was enormous, almost the size of a studio apartment in some of the places Alma had lived as a child, the bed set between two arched windows, a sofa and table and chairs set closer to the door. The carpet was plush under her bare feet, the inlaid marble chill, and she wiggled her toes a little at the contrast. The tray, sandwiches and fruit and a dish of celery olives, sat on the table next to the sweating pitcher of limeade, and she realized she was hungry after all. She grabbed the first sandwich that came to hand—crustless bread with cucumber—and then a slice of orange, all trace of pith peeled away to show only the jewel-colored fruit.

Lewis settled himself on the sofa. "When we get home, I need to find a way to learn more about what I'm doing. I know we need the money, but maybe now—if I'd known how to read my own mind, understood what I was showing myself—you know what I mean— we might not have had to cut it so close."

Alma topped up her glass just to use the crystal pitcher. "You need more than any of us can teach you," she said. "And with the prize money—I know we can find someone. Jerry or Henry will know someone."

"I'd rather go with someone Jerry picked."

"Henry's a good guy," Alma said.

"I know," Lewis said. "I do know. I just think Jerry's friends are more likely to be—congenial."

Alma nodded. "Maybe. But I promise, we won't put it off any longer."

"Thanks," Lewis said, and Alma settled into the curve of his arm. For a moment, she wished they could stay like that all night, together in a room that didn't move and didn't smell of metal and gasoline—but the party was part of the price of victory, and one she would gladly pay.

Chapter Twenty-two

"What the hell is that?" Lewis said, then blinked self consciously at Mabel Kershaw. "Beg your pardon." In the trees above their heads roosted a flock of…something. Bigger than big geese. Big as swans. In the dusk they looked something like ostriches.

"Peacocks," she said.

"Peacocks?"

"One of our neighbors thought they'd be lovely," Mabel said wearily. "Ornamental. They'd walk around the lawn and look pretty. Only they got away, and when their wings aren't clipped they fly rather nicely."

"They shit on my cars," Henry said loudly. "Useless damn birds. They roost on anything and they shit on my cars and anything else that goes under them. So watch out."

Lewis cast a worried glance treeward. He was wearing his brand new white dinner jacket, and the last thing he wanted was for a bird to mistake him for a bathroom. And Alma would kill him if anything looked wrong for the reporters.

She looked stunning. Her dress was white, absolutely simple with a plunging neck that showed off her tanned skin and made her blue eyes bright as stars. They were the same age, Lewis and Alma, but while not quite forty-two years had marked him with streaks of early gray at the temples, her hair was untouched yet. Or maybe you just couldn't see it as well against blond hair as you could against Lewis' black. Stopping beside Henry and Mabel for the photographers to get a shot, they looked like they belonged together. And they ought to. On top of the world, the big winners.

"How does it feel to have proved you're the best pilots in America?" one of the reporters asked.

"You know, I don't think that's a fair question," Alma said. "I think the finest pilots in America are the search and rescue pilots who fly every day to protect lives, not people who compete in an air race. We're lucky and we're good, but the only thing we risked was losing. The unsung reservists who fly the skies of this country to help those in trouble risk their lives all the time and we never know their names."

One of the other reporters, one who'd done his homework, piped up. "Aren't you a reserve pilot, Mr. Sorley? Mr. Segura?"

"Um," Mitch said. Stasi stood between him and Jerry, her black dress set off nicely by their black tuxedos.

"Mr. Sorley is a major in the reserves of the US Army Air Corps," Alma said. "Mr. Segura is a captain."

The reporter turned to Lewis. "And you fly search and rescue missions?"

"When I'm called to," Lewis said, glancing sideways at Alma. "People lost in the mountains, accidents, avalanches, that kind of thing. Situations where some eyes in the sky can see what people on the ground might miss."

"Are there special planes for that?" the reporter asked. "What planes do you fly for the Air Corps?"

"We fly our own planes," Mitch said. "There aren't any special ones. We just fly our own. The Air Corps doesn't have a lot of money."

The reporter's eyebrows rose. "You fly Gilchrist Aviation planes? The same plane you flew in the air race?"

"Not usually the Terrier," Mitch said. "It's a bigger plane and it needs a real runway. We usually take the Jenny." He looked at Lewis. "Usually, right?"

"Pretty much," Lewis said.

Henry was smiling beatifically. "See boys? Not just winners, but real American heroes. Now come on in and grab a bite of grub. Maybe something stronger, if it's not against your principles."

"We won't tell on you, Mr. Kershaw," one of the reporters grinned. "We never see any bathtub gin."

"Well, I hope you won't see good Scotch whiskey either," Henry said, clapping the reporter on the shoulder. "Or there's champagne." He gave Alma a wink as he led them inside.

One of the reporters hung back waiting for Stasi. "So what do you do on the plane, Miss?"

"I'm ornamental," Stasi said, twining her arm with Jerry's. Jerry looked like he wanted to deck her. Mitch looked like he was trying not to laugh.

The reporter laughed. "You sure are. But you came on halfway through. What's the story?"

Stasi tossed her head. "You see the other team's passengers. Mrs. Segura thought she needed a babe too, and I'm an old family friend, so why not?"

The reporter had his notebook out. "You're an old family friend of Mrs. Segura's? What's your name, honey?"

"Anastasia Natalia Elisabeth Maria Ivanova Rostov," Stasi said. "Countess Pancetta."

Mitch made a strangled noise, but he didn't say a word, standing quietly behind Jerry and Stasi, who had twined her arm with his lovingly.

"Italian?"

"My husband was Italian," she said, a little quaver in her voice. "My dear Count Pancetta served with Dr. Ballard in the war. In the Veneto. He was killed. It was terribly sad. Dear Dr. Ballard was a lifeline for me. Simply a lifeline!"

The reporter looked up. "Isn't pancetta a kind of ham?"

"It's named for the village where it was first produced, darling," Stasi said. "Like Weinerschnitzel. My dear husband's family had been there since the fourteenth century when the first Count Pancetta fought against the Moors!"

The reporter glanced up at Jerry. "And after her husband's death you...comforted the widow?"

"He did, darling." Stasi beamed at Jerry. "I probably would have killed myself if it weren't for him. Dr. Ballard gave me a new reason for living!"

"I..." Jerry began.

"Shhh," Stasi said. She looked coyly at the reporter. "Don't give away our secret! Let's wait and announce it properly."

Jerry looked like he was on the verge of a stroke, so Lewis dove in. "I think Alma and Henry want us inside," he said, tugging on Stasi's arm. "Sorry, but we need to go." He all but dragged Stasi along, Jerry helpless in her wake since she had his arm in a vise-like grip.

Behind him, Lewis heard the reporter ask Mitch, "Have you known Countess Pancetta long?"

"Just met her this week," Mitch said cheerfully.

The house was a cozy bungalow bloated to outrageous proportions. The living room could have comfortably housed a game of field hockey. At the other end of it double doors led to a screened porch arranged elegantly with potted palm trees and white wicker furniture and several long white wicker plant stands filled with some kind of lily. Alma had drawn Henry onto the porch and she glanced back meaningfully at the others. It was as far from the bar as possible, so there was no one else there.

"Once more into the breach," Jerry said grimly. "Let's go explain this latest fiasco to Henry."

Mitch shrugged. "He won't be too upset," he said. "We just won his air race."

"We did," Lewis said. It still seemed kind of incredible. He had just won a coast to coast air race. He was just what they said, one of the top pilots in the country. And it felt good. Alma might hate having their pictures on the front page, but Lewis couldn't help but be proud. He'd worked hard, he'd risked his life on Alma's gamble, and every gamble had paid off. They belonged. If he never did anything else in his life again he was still the guy who had won the Great Passenger Derby. He'd flown Alma's plane, risked everything on her word, and now he laid the trophy at her feet. This must be how a knight felt, Lewis thought, the tournament over and to the victor the spoils, for friends and company and his unconquerable lady fair!

Alma looked at him, her expression growing quizzical. "What?" she asked, turning so that he could say something quietly.

"I was thinking that I love you," Lewis said. A slow blush rose in her cheeks, speechless as she sometimes was. "Just saying so," he said quietly. "Because I do." Her smile could have lit an aerodrome.

"What did you want to talk to me about?" Henry asked. "If it's to give me a song and dance about missing the refueling stop, I've got to say I don't care. I don't care how you did it. You did it."

"No," Alma said. "I wanted to give about this." She gestured to Jerry, who reached in his pocket and produced a silk handkerchief wrapped bundle. He handed it to Henry, who took it gingerly. He untied it, and the links of iron slid out into his hand, steel flowers delicate and dark.

"This is Miss Rostov," Alma said, not quite pushing Stasi forward. "She stole your necklace and now she's returning it."

Henry looked baffled. "What?"

Stasi cleared her throat. "I was hired to steal it. But I'm terribly sorry and I'm bringing it back. So we're completely clear and friends, yes?"

Jerry made a sound like he wanted to disagree, but Alma gave him a quelling look. "Miss Rostov is contrite," she said. "And she did help us win the race. So it would be nice if you didn't call the police, Henry."

"I'm terribly sorry," Stasi said in a tone that Lewis didn't think was entirely convincing. "I've absolutely reformed. I will never steal your necklace again. Or anything else," she said brightly. "I'm sure my darling Dr. Ballard will keep me straight."

"I don't think straight is the word here," Henry snapped. "I'll believe Jerry's reformed you with his love shortly after hell freezes over! What kind of BS is this? You expect me to just drop the charges because you apologize?"

"There's no harm done," Alma said. "Come on, Henry. Be big."

"Mr. Kershaw! We'd like a picture of you with your winning team for the Miami Herald!" A reporter and a cameraman crowded in. "Can you all stand next to each other and smile?"

Henry slipped the necklace into his pocket. "Of course, boys. Happy to! Alma, you stand here next to me. Lewis, on the other side, that's right." He looked at Stasi. "And we'll talk about your problem later, Miss."

Lewis shook his head and got into line, Mitch on his other side. Henry would come around. Probably.

"Let's have a shot of the big winners," the cameraman said. "Smile." *Flash.*

The mellow sounds of Mood Indigo floated across the terrace from the bandstand under the trees. Strings of electric lights hung from the branches of the live oaks, a glittering fairyland that half-illuminated the elegant crowd enjoying hors d'oeuvres and dancing on the terrace. It was a pretty good band. Mood Indigo sounded about right. To the left one of the canals was overhung with picturesque palm trees bending toward the water under the light of the enormous golden moon. The moonbeams made a path across the water, just like they always did in movies.

Mitch leaned against the rail at the top of the steps down to the little boat house on the canal—just a couple of steps down, really. There wasn't any actual high ground around here, not two blocks from where the canal let into a little lagoon and a sandbar. Beyond was nothing but the Atlantic Ocean, just rolling water from here to the coast of Africa. Maybe someday there would be planes that could do that flight in one hop. No refueling in Newfoundland, no flying south to Rio and then across. Just spread your wings and take the whole Atlantic in one swoop, like the airship Independence had.

Of course the Independence had crashed. Which was always the problem with high flying fantasies. There was no sense in wanting things you couldn't have.

Was that what had started the whole thing in New Orleans? What had happened in New Orleans, anyway? It's a hell of a thing not to be sure if you're an axe murderer or not.

Mitch supposed the best move was to go turn himself in. Maybe the police in New Orleans would be able to figure it out. Maybe they could check his fingerprints against something. Or maybe there wouldn't be any evidence one way or another, not after eleven years. Maybe they'd put him on trial and he'd go to the electric chair. If he had done it, he owed the victims that much. Or maybe they'd find him not guilty by reason of insanity. He was certainly insane. Normal guys don't forget a year of their lives.

It was just cowardice that he hadn't done it, gone and taken responsibility and confessed. That and not being sure. But Jeff sounded sure. What had Jeff seen? Not the murders, surely. But maybe Mitch sneaking home, bloody and guilty. He hadn't gone to the police or Mitch would have been arrested. Had he thrown him out? Was that what had happened?

Mitch leaned against the rail and closed his eyes. If only he could remember.

…Eden, and a hazy summer night, the darkened hall, the stairs to the second floor in shadow. He stood by the door looking out at the night. Jasmine blossoms had fallen on the porch, on the porch steps, crushed by someone coming up, giving off their scent. Jasmine and blood. There were drops of blood on every step, dark against the white petals.

He went to wash the steps, bringing a bucket from the kitchen and cleaning each one. The help would come in the morning. But the blood would be gone. He'd wash it all off and none of it would have ever happened, swept off the steps like the crushed flowers…

"Don't tell me you're going to jump in the canal."

Mitch opened his eyes. Stasi was standing against the rail beside him.

"It can't be more than four feet deep, darling. It would simply be ridiculous."

"I think I killed those women," Mitch said. His throat was dry. "All those people."

"We could find out," Stasi said. She lifted her chin thoughtfully. "I have to go back to New Orleans anyway because I made a promise to the Dead. We could find a victim and ask if you're the killer." She glanced down toward the waterway. "No sense in doing anything silly until you know for certain."

"I suppose." Mitch nodded shortly. "It doesn't bother you that I might be a killer?"

"Darling, I already know that," Stasi said. "Real live ace, remember? That means you get a prize for killing at least five men. Only you did that with a license. If it's official they give you a medal and if it's not…" Stasi shrugged. "Lots of things happen in war, don't they? Men get decorated and women just have to do what they have to do. And lots and lots and lots of things happen that nobody brags about when they get home."

Mitch just stood there. Words deserted him.

"Besides," she said contemplatively, "I don't think you're that type of lunatic. Not the psycho-sexual axe murderer type at all. I did a little asking around with some of the reporter boys. Did you know the Axeman killed men too? And the whole story about how he just killed Storyville prostitutes? Not true, darling. That charming man, Billy Beaufort, used to work for the Picayune. He said that was just popular twaddle, New Orleans' own Jack the Ripper. He thought it was about the Mob, that most of the people killed were connected to the Mob or were related. That the whole story about an insane copy-cat killer was made up to cover Mob hits." Stasi leaned on the rail. "I don't think there was actually an insane killer at all. Often the truth is a lot more prosaic than the story."

Mitch shook his head regretfully. "I wish I could believe that," he said. "But there was something. There was something that happened that was so bad that I forgot the whole thing. And I have no idea what it could have been if it wasn't..." He swallowed hard. "I can even think of a motive, kind of."

"For killing Italian grocers? You once had a horrible experience with an eggplant?" Stasi crossed her ankles. "No, darling. No insane killer. Just an enterprising mobster who sent a letter to the paper to throw the police off the scent."

"As charming as Miss Ivanova's theory is, unfortunately it's wrong," said a friendly voice. At the bottom of the steps beside the boat house stood Jeff Lanier. He gave Stasi a gentlemanly nod. "I'm sorry to say, Miss Ivanova, that there really was a New Orleans Axeman, and Mitchell Sorley knows perfectly well who he is." He glanced up, smiling. "Don't you, Mitch?"

Mitch didn't move. He stood stock still while Jeff pulled the revolver out of his pocket and pointed it at Stasi.

"I suggest you come on down here so we can talk," he said cheerfully. "I'm sure you could run or do something else foolhardy, but I have this gun aimed at Miss Ivanova. I don't think there's anything you can do that will prevent the first bullet from hitting her. I suppose you could throw yourself in front of it or something, but then you'd be shot and the second one would be for her, so..." He shrugged.

"I thought you had nothing against me," Stasi said.

"I don't," Jeff said. "But you make a good hostage." He gestured with the gun again. "Come on down here, Mitch."

He didn't see an alternative. He could yell and someone at the party would hear, but not faster than Jeff could shoot Stasi. So instead he started down the steps, Stasi ahead of him.

"There's a flaw in your logic," Jeff said to Stasi. "The Mob doesn't hit women and children. It's against the code. Women and children are off limits. And that's where this story starts—with a mobster who wanted to kill his wife."

"So he hired a hit man to make it look like an insane serial killer?" Stasi asked, walking out on the boat dock. She looked as calm as if she did this every day, no hysterics, no sobbing. She was as glacial as a dame in Black Mask, the gun moll who's been around the block more times than you can count.

"Another fascinating story!" Jeff said. "You do spin them, don't you? I bet you'd like to be on the other end of this gun. How many men have you killed?"

Her face was deadly calm. "Probably more than you."

Jeff laughed. "Oh, I doubt that," he said. "Mitch and I are natural born killers, aren't we, Mitch? That's what they said about us. Natural born killers. They never did find out what happened to that girl in Venice, did they? Who did it? I don't expect the Italian police ever made an arrest."

Mitch swallowed. "Are you saying...?" He couldn't finish, not with the taste of bile in his mouth.

"That it was the Axeman? Oh yes. That was the Axeman's first murder, in Italy in 1918. They never linked it. But you were there, weren't you? Just like you were in New Orleans—a freak with an axe to grind, no pun intended."

Stasi lifted her chin. "What does that have to do with the mobster using the necklace to kill his wife?"

Mitch blinked. "What?"

Jeff laughed. "She's a smart cookie, Mitch. A lot faster on the uptake than you." He gestured for them to precede him down the dock. "There was a mobster who wanted to kill his wife. Only it had to look like an accident. They don't kill women and children, remember? He could kill fifty men, but if he'd killed his wife he would have been out of the club, a pariah. That's how it works, Mitch. Kill five men and they give you a medal. Kill five women and they lock you up. And keep your hands where I can see them."

Jeff was behind them, probably not with a clear shot at Stasi. But the barrel of the gun poked firmly at the middle of his back. Not good odds, Mitch thought.

"He had one of his guys offer Milly a thousand dollars for the necklace! He'd heard about it, you see. Any woman who wore it died by violence. Just buy the necklace, give it to his wife, and let the curse work. And Milly... She was a spoiled little brat, Mitch. That necklace had been in our family for a hundred years and she knew perfectly well what it did, but offer her a grand and she just passed it over! She sold it without even telling me. But I knew. I knew." He edged them toward a motor launch moored at the end of the dock. "The wife died, all right. There was a hit. A bunch of rival mobsters with Tommy guns shot up the car. She was killed alongside her husband who'd given her the necklace. And I knew what had happened. I got it out of Milly then. She was upset because it had killed and I asked what she'd thought it would do? Do you remember that, Mitch? Do you remember?"

"No," Mitch said. There was something, something vague, an argument between Milly and Jeff, something he said wasn't hers to sell… And that was it. It all washed away like bloodstains in water.

"I had to get it back. It was mine. It should never have gone anywhere. And so…"

"And so you killed everyone connected with it," Stasi said, turning around just short of the launch. "Starting with Joseph Maggio, who had been the mobster's bodyguard. Maggio and his wife were the first victims. Louis Besumer was the next, who presumably was also connected."

Jeff grinned. "Oh you have done your homework, Miss Ivanova! You've got all the victims in order! I wonder which press boy gave you that."

Stasi didn't answer. Instead her eyes were on Mitch, trying to communicate something, though he was damned if he knew what.

And then it sunk in. "What?" Mitch turned around. "You killed all those people?"

Jeff gave Stasi a little bow. "Well played, Miss! He didn't suspect until the night Sarah Laumann was killed. And then I'm afraid it became all too clear. She spattered too much."

Mitch closed his eyes.

…blood on the steps, crushed jasmine flowers. Jeff had just come in and gone upstairs. Mitch could hear him in the bathroom, hear the sound of the water running. The blood drops led right to the door, blood and a few scraps of flesh, a mat of long blond hairs. They glittered like gold when he washed the blood off them, roots and all. It took him with cold horror and he sat there looking at them, smoothing them on his knee, until Milly came out…

"She sent you to a sanitarium," Mitch said quietly. "And the killings stopped."

"Damn her!" Jeff shouted, and Mitch opened his eyes. Jeff was waving the gun wildly. "She called the doctor, called the judge who'd been our father's friend, told them what happened. There was a court order that I was criminally insane, all hushed up nicely. A good boy, the judge said. A good boy who went to war and went off his rocker. Not a bad boy. Just insane. He needs to be locked up for his own good and that of other people. The police would never get a conviction. Best to just handle this ourselves, a court order and a quiet sanitarium."

"You killed all those people," Mitch said. "It had to be." A strange peace was settling over him.

"It did not! I'm no worse than you! No worse than anyone else!" Jeff gestured with the gun again. "No worse than those mob hit men I killed."

"Sarah Laumann was no mobster," Mitch said. "She didn't do anything except go with a boy who worked for them. You liked it. You liked killing and you didn't want to stop, even when it was women who had nothing to do with your necklace."

"She put it on!" Jeff shouted. "She had it coming! I'm nothing but an instrument of the curse." He waved the gun again, and Mitch didn't even see it coming, didn't expect it until it connected with the corner of his mouth, pistol whipping him across the face.

Pain and clarity. They had to end this or someone was going to die. He thought that as he reeled back tasting blood in his mouth.

The same instant that Stasi hit Jeff's forearm square on, her other arm hitting his wrist from the opposite direction and sending the gun flying. There was a very satisfying splash as it landed in the canal.

"Help! Help! Help!" Stasi screamed. "Help! He's trying to kill us!" They probably heard her on the other side of the Atlantic.

There was nothing to do except stagger up and tackle Jeff. Unfortunately, Jeff wasn't such a bad fighter, and he rolled to the right just as Mitch grappled. Mitch hung on, his head still spinning. Crap, he thought, as they rolled together off the dock into the canal.

Chapter Twenty-three

Stasi looked around for a weapon. Unfortunately the gun was in the dark water, and even if she could find it, it wouldn't fire. There was the sound of shouts above, but they would probably be too late. Lanier would have drowned Mitch by then. They were pitching around in the water, but it looked like Lanier was generally on top.

An oar. There was a pair of oars on the wall of the boathouse. Stasi grabbed one and hauled back and gave Lanier a whack. At least she thought it was Lanier. It was a bit hard to tell who was who, given two identically clad men in black suits who both had brown hair and the same build struggling in the dark in four feet of water.

"Let God sort them out," Stasi muttered as she brought the oar down good and hard a few more times. It ought to buy some time at least. Whack, whack, whack. Good solid body hits probably wouldn't kill anyone.

Running feet, and Lewis Segura all but jumped down the steps, white dinner jacket open and tie flying. He didn't hesitate, just jumped straight off the dock and made a grab for the first flailing body he found. Stasi held off whacking him.

Others were right behind him, three or four men Stasi didn't know, and Alma Segura and Henry Kershaw. "What happened?" Kershaw yelled.

Alma ran down the steps looking as if she intended to jump in too, but the men in the water had surfaced, Lewis and Mitch holding onto Lanier between them, blood beading at the corner of Mitch's mouth.

"That man tried to kill us," Stasi said clearly. "He threatened to shoot me if Mr. Sorley didn't do what he said. He was talking crazy! He said that he was going to kill me!"

"Come here, you," Lewis said, dragging Lanier toward the dock. Another man and Kershaw leaned down to help pull him up.

There was a bright flash, a reporter's camera flash going off. Stasi held the oar.

"Don't let him get away," Alma said, stepping in. Kershaw jostled past Stasi, brushing against her as he went, and the idea came to her fully formed.

"No chance of that," Lewis said, manhandling Lanier onto the dock.

"Call the police," Kershaw said grimly.

Stasi blinked right into the camera, into the reporter's faces. "I think he dropped this," she said innocently, holding up the Berlin Iron necklace.

"Oh my God," Alma said.

For once Kershaw looked utterly dumbfounded. "That's my stolen necklace!" he said.

Flash bulbs went off wildly. Stasi laid it in his hands. "I don't know why that man was screaming about it," she said.

Lanier saw it and twisted around in Lewis' grip. "It's mine!" he screamed. "It's mine! It kills! You know that! I'm just its instrument! I'm just the instrument of the curse! Give it to me, you little whore!"

Stasi widened her eyes. "I've never seen it before five minutes ago. Is it yours?"

"Yes," Kershaw said. His face was beet red.

"How clever of you to have found it," Alma said, her hand on Kershaw's arm.

"I'm going to kill you!" Lanier shouted. "I'm going to kill you and Sorley both! I'll see you in hell, both of you! That necklace is mine! I'll kill you, Mitchell Sorley! You're marked! Let that be known!"

"Not going to happen," Lewis said grimly, never letting go. "The police should be here soon."

"He's raving," one of the gathering crowd said.

Mitch climbed up on the dock heavily, soaked tuxedo dripping.

"I'll kill you!" Lanier shouted at Stasi. "Bitch! Whore!"

"That's no way to talk to a lady," Lewis said, hustling him toward the stairs.

"I think you need to calm down, buddy," one of the other men said.

"My necklace," Kershaw said, blinking at it.

One of the reporters was keen. "The one that you reported stolen in Los Angeles just before the race?"

"Yes," Kershaw said.

"It's mine!" Lanier shouted as the men bundled him up the steps, still struggling. "Mine! I hope it kills you and your wife too! The Devil's in it! May you burn in hell!" He twisted around. "May you burn in hell, Mitchell Sorley!"

Mitch shook his head, shaking water out of his hair, a rueful expression on his face. "This is hell," he said. "Nor am I out of it."

Lanier screamed. "I'll kill you! You wait!"

Reporters' flashbulbs went off again, and Stasi blinked and smiled, holding the oar. "Tell me, Miss," one of them said. "Why did he use you as a hostage?"

"I suppose because I was talking to Mr. Sorley," Stasi said. "I imagine he thought that Mr. Sorley would do what he wanted rather than risk him injuring me."

"Do you know each other well?" another reporter asked, elbowing in.

Stasi shook her head, all big innocent eyes. "I only met him a few days ago. I came to the party with Dr. Ballard. Where is he, anyway?"

"Here," Jerry said, coming carefully down the steps. "You all right, Mitch?"

"Yeah."

Jerry handed him his handkerchief. "Your lip is bleeding. And the Marlowe is a bit much."

Mitch looked sheepish.

Stasi twined her arm around Jerry's. "I might have been killed if not for Mr. Sorley, darling."

Jerry didn't actually flinch this time. "I'm glad everyone is ok," he said.

"Sweetheart," Stasi said, and smiled for the camera flash.

Alma stood by Jerry, watching Henry, Mitch, Lewis and Stasi talking to the police, Mitch still dabbing at the corner of his mouth with a napkin. For once the police had nothing to say to Alma or Jerry. Stasi was obviously the center of attention, gesturing wildly and animatedly. From the bemused expression on Henry's face, Alma could bet that anything unusual in the story was being washed away by a torrent. The police wouldn't even remember to ask by the time she got done.

"Doesn't seem fair, does it?" Alma said, taking Jerry's arm.

"What doesn't?"

"She helped us win the race and now she's high and dry again," Alma said.

Jerry sighed. "You want to give her money. Al, she broke into Henry's safe and burgled him! Yes, she was helpful in Pensacola, and yes, she's been helpful tonight, but Al..." He shook his head. "You know the nicest thing you can say about her is that she's a crook."

"I can think of a few nicer things to say," Alma said, watching Lewis talking to the police under Stasi's attentive eye, keeping all the stories straight. "We're not so different."

"The colonel's lady and Rosie O'Grady are sisters under the skin?" Jerry quoted, raising an eyebrow.

"Something like that." Alma leaned on his arm. "Jerry, where do you think I'd be if I'd never met Gil?"

Jerry blinked. "What?"

"Where do you think I'd be?" Al shook her head, looking across the crowd. "You know what I was when you met me, an ambulance driver, a girl who knew what was what and didn't take any guff, but what do you think I'd have been when the war ended? I've never had any graces or accomplishments, nor a single class over junior year when my Pa died. He left me forty dollars and a saddle. What kind of work do you think there is for a girl cowpoke? Maybe I'd be a wildcatter? Work an oil rig? Cut stock?" She gave Jerry's arm a squeeze. "You think anybody would hire me for those kinds of jobs if I weren't a man, and tell me what respectable job I could do? Be a school teacher without a diploma myself? A nurse?"

"You're a fine nurse," Jerry said. "And I ought to know."

"Nursing school costs money, Jerry. Not so many scholarships for girls who can't recite and stand up straight." She shook her head again. "I loved Gil, no doubt about that, but there's also no doubt he was a fine thing for me."

"That's not why you married him," Jerry said.

"No, it's not." She tightened her fingers on his arm. "But it's true what people said, a good catch for a girl like that, a man with education and a pension coming, the kind of man who buys a house for cash and sets up his own business. If she's got to nurse him a bit, well, that's what she pays for what she gets."

Jerry looked vaguely appalled. "That's not what happened."

"It's not. And it is. Don't you think Gil was aware what a good thing he was doing for me?" She didn't let her voice shake. "He left me my freedom, Jerry. He left me wings and a business and a home and he made sure I'd never have to scrape around from town to town like she does. The only difference between the colonel's lady and Rosie O'Grady over there is that she never had Gil like we did."

"Everything he touched, he transformed," Jerry said in a low tone.

"Especially us." Al blinked hard. "All the terrible ways our stories could have ended, if Gil hadn't been bound and determined to save the world…"

"I'd have died alone in that boarding house," Jerry said. He laced his fingers with hers tightly. "I couldn't have done it alone, Al." He looked away. "Waifs and strays, all of us. Mitch too. A pack of pound puppies Gil took in and turned into a family."

"Sometimes pound puppies make the best dogs," Alma said. "Don't you think we owe it to Gil to give her a chance?"

"You know if you put it that way I can't say no," Jerry said.

Alma nodded cheerfully. "I do."

Jerry let out a breath. "What are you going to do?"

"I'm going to offer her a job," Alma said. "A legitimate job, working for Gilchrist Aviation as our new office clerk."

"Do you actually need an office clerk?" Jerry asked. "I've never heard you say you wanted one before."

"We could probably use one," Alma said. "Handling the office drives me crazy, and we can pay her out of the winnings that go into the business. And it's better than giving her a lump sum. If she takes off she doesn't get paid anymore, but if she stays and works she keeps on getting a check. And jobs aren't easy to come by these days, especially with no references."

Jerry shook his head. "Only you would hire a jewel thief to work the front office."

"Besides, she can teach Lewis," Alma said practically. "You know perfectly well that none of us have the right mix of skills to go any further with him. He needs a medium, and that's what she is."

"I do see the value of that," Jerry said. "But Mitch won't like it. And he is the co-owner."

"Oh, Mitch will be ok," Alma said. "I expect he'll get used to her."

Stasi looked around the room in the Biltmore Hotel with satisfaction. This looked exceedingly comfortable, even though it was one of the smaller rooms, with a big fluffy bed with a headboard of white quilted leather and a window that looked out toward the water. Not that you could see the ocean from this angle, but it was there even if you couldn't. Three floors below there was a terrace that opened onto the ballroom, palm trees in pots nodding in the breeze, a few little tables here and there to catch the view, little lanterns hung among them to make a fairyland. The music drifted up from the orchestra playing in the ballroom below. And there waited an actual bed, nice and flat, with perfectly enormous pillows and soft, soft sheets. It was big enough for a small army, much less for just her.

Mitch opened the door and came in, taking off his wet tie, and stopped short when he saw her. "I'm pretty sure this is my room," he said.

"Really? I'm practically certain that Mrs. Segura said it was mine," Stasi said airily.

The ghost of a smile crept over his face. "I'm pretty sure she didn't, but it's ok. I'll share with Jerry."

"It would be gallant," Stasi said. "Unless you'd like to share with me. With a sword down the middle of the bed, naturally. Though we probably wouldn't need it, as that bed's so big I doubt we could find each other in it if we tried."

"I think I'll take my chances with Jerry. Let me get my suitcase."

"Of course," Stasi said. The orchestra was still going, an upbeat number that was cheerful and bright. "You can probably trust me not to take terrible advantage of you, though I imagine I could ruin your reputation for being an upright all-American hero."

"More likely the reporters would turn it into a terrible rivalry between me and Jerry." He sounded amused. "Here I am, going after Jerry's fiancée, after all we've been through together."

"Are you cheating on Alma with me?" Stasi asked. "How positively caddish of you, given that she's cheating on you with Jerry."

"And on Lewis with me." Mitch shook his head. "You know that's not true, right?"

"Yes, darling. I'd figured that out."

He picked up his suitcase from the bench along the wall and sat it by the door. He still squelched a little when he walked. "What were you and Alma talking about for so long?"

Stasi wandered over to the window, smoothing her hair back from her forehead. "She offered me a job. At Gilchrist Aviation. Working in the front office. I'd be your typewriter girl."

"Can you type?"

"No." The moon was postcard perfect across the tops of the palm trees, swaying hauntingly in the wind. "But how hard can it be, darling?" Stasi shrugged. "LA has gotten awfully hot for me. It might be a good idea to get out of town for a couple of months and lie low until things settle down."

"I can see that." Mitch came around the bed and stood beside her at the window, looking out at the night, just as he had at the terrace rail.

She looked sideways at him, wondering how to ask. Perhaps flat out was just best. "And the necklace scrambled your memories?"

He shook his head, not looking at her. "No, that's just me. I told you I was a lunatic."

Stasi shrugged. "Well, as insanity goes, I suppose it's not so bad. Lots of people have things they'd like to forget, darling. It's just that your brain has managed it."

"A little inconvenient, don't you think?"

Her voice was light, she supposed. "Only if you go wandering off again. But I expect I could keep an eye on you and drag you back if you do. After all, if the worst you're going to do is go on a bender every few years, that's practically normal, darling."

Mitch looked at her sideways, eyebrow rising. "Compared to what?"

"Aren't you relieved to find out you're not an axe murderer?"

His mouth tightened. "And that one of my best friends is?" He took a deep breath. "Jeff was real good to me, a good guy, a good man. The war did this to him. He was the kind of guy you could always count on. He had your back. No, I'm not relieved to find out he's an insane murderer. This isn't a win, Stasi. Not for me."

She glanced away, back out at the trees, so she wouldn't see anything she shouldn't in his face. "What's going to happen to him now?"

"There isn't any evidence to link him to the Axeman's murders. Just a guy who's off his head raving and confessing to stuff that was in the papers years ago. And Henry's not going to press charges about the necklace, especially given that he knows Jeff didn't actually steal it and it would be kind of hard to come up with evidence that he did when he was in New Orleans at the time it was stolen in LA. So I expect he'll go back to a sanitarium." Mitch's voice sounded choked. "That's probably the best thing that can happen. Milly will be his guardian and he'll be locked up somewhere for the rest of his life."

"Well," Stasi said. "Maybe he'll get out. Maybe he'll get better and he'll be well again."

Mitch looked at her evenly. "You know there some kinds of wounds that never heal."

"I know that," Stasi said.

The melancholy strains of "Goodnight, Sweetheart" floated up from beneath the trees, the band starting their last number, sweet and sharp as knives.

"Dance with me," she said, and turned toward him. "Dance with me, darling. I haven't had a dance all night."

"If you like." He looked bemused, but he did it anyway, damp tuxedo and all, one hand at her waist and the other clasping her hand, and she rested her head on his shoulder. He moved well, slow steps that were easy to follow.

"You're a good dancer," she said.

"I used to like to dance," Mitch said.

Stasi smiled. "Then dance with me until the music stops."

About the Authors

Melissa Scott is from Little Rock, Arkansas, and studied history at Harvard College and Brandeis University, where she earned her PhD in the Comparative History program. She is the author of more than twenty-five science fiction and fantasy novels, and has won Lambda Literary Awards for *Trouble and Her Friends*, *Shadow Man*, and *Point of Dreams*, the last written with her late partner, Lisa A. Barnett. She has also won Spectrum Awards for *Shadow Man* and again in 2010 for the short story "The Rocky Side of the Sky" (*Periphery*, Lethe Press) as well as the John W. Campbell Award for Best New Writer. She can be found on LiveJournal at mescott.livejournal.com.

Jo Graham worked in politics for fifteen years before leaving to write full time. She is the author of the Locus Award nominated *Black Ships* and the Spectrum Award nominated *Stealing Fire*, as well as several other novels, including the *Stargate Atlantis* Legacy series and *The General's Mistress*. She lives in North Carolina with her partner and their daughter. She can be found online at jo_graham.livejournal.com.

About the O. C. L. T. Series

There are incidents and emergencies in the world that defy logical explanation, events that could be defined as supernatural, extra-terrestrial, or simply otherworldly. Standard laws do not allow for such instances, nor are most officials or authorities trained to handle them. In recognition of these facts, one organization has been created that can. Assembled by a loose international coalition, their mission is to deal with these situations using diplomacy, guile, force, and strategy as necessary. They shield the rest of the world from their own actions, and clean up the messes left in their wake. They are our protection, our guide, our sword, and our voice, all rolled into one.

They are O.C.L.T.

TALES OF THE O. C. L. T.

AVAILABLE NOW:

Brought to Light: An O.C.L.T. Novella by Aaron Rosenberg
The Temple of Camazotz: An O.C.L.T. Novella by David Niall Wilson
The Parting: An O.C.L.T. Novel by David Niall Wilson
Incursion: An O.C.L.T. Novel by Aaron Rosenberg

UPCOMING:

The Highjump: An O.C.L.T. Novel by David McIntee
Schrodinger's Tomb: An O.C.L.T. Novel by David Niall Wilson
Digging Deep: An O.C.L.T. Novel by Aaron Rosenberg

NOTE: The Order of the Air series connects to the O.C.L.T. series but is not part of it.

Want more O.C.L.T.?
Turn the page for a sneak peek at

Prologue

"Damn it!"

He ran, brushing limbs and branches from his face as he moved, the needles and leaves stabbing at his hands and wrists above his leather jacket and tugging at his long hair in its braid. In the dark they were mere shapes, fluttering shadows that blurred by as he moved, feet churning, his heavy boots stomping flat leaves and cones and bristles alike as he charged headlong through the night.

And behind him, the wind howled in the trees, and it sounded like screams of rage.

He'd tried to warn them, he reminded himself as he ran. He'd warned them not to do it, shown them the right way and urged them to follow it—but of course they wouldn't listen. They never did. Why had he thought this time would be any different?

But this time *was* different.

This time their arrogance might prove fatal.

And now he was caught in the middle.

"I'm sorry!" he shouted over his shoulder, the wind taking his words and whipping them away into the dark. "I tried to stop them!" That was a lie, though. He had warned them, yes, but had he really done anything to stand in their way? Had he really put forth his best effort to prevent them from moving forward with this insanity?

Or had he let them sway him from his own better judgment, and cow him into keeping silent?

Deep in his heart, he knew the answer to those questions, and the shame of it made him weak.

But was that enough reason for him to be facing this himself?

He didn't think so.

So he ran on, stumbling over sticks and roots, reeling as branches struck out at him, and crying as the wind continued to howl behind him and alongside him.

And then the tenor of the wind changed.

Its howls shifted, shortened, rose in pitch, became thin, reedy whistles.

And the whistles surged forward, circling him, ringing him in.

Surrounding him.

"I'm sorry!" he called out again, the words little more than a sob. "I'm so sorry! Please!"

He raised his hands high even as he dropped to his knees.

One of the flickering shadows detached itself from the darkness and raced forward, trailing his descent. Long and slender and lightning-swift, it took him just under the chin, and he felt his life leave him all in a rush, not gently tugged free but roughly shoved aside, slammed from his body by the same lethal impact that took his last breath and made his vision go dark.

He toppled to the ground, blood bubbling up in his throat and choking him, the rich scent of the earth filling his nostrils as his head hit the thin grass and the loose soil beneath, and he spasmed, unable to control his body's last urges—

—and all around him, the whistles continued through the trees, and they sounded like laughter.

1

"**R**emind me again what we're doing all the way up here?" R.C. muttered as he turned off Interstate 90 and onto the narrow two-lane. The sign by the road read "Flathead Indian Reservation" but there wasn't a gate or even a fence, and the land they were now driving through looked much like what they'd seen for the past hour since landing at Missoula International. Western Montana wasn't known for its variety. Or its densely populated areas.

"Just taking in the scenery," his partner Nick answered, waving one hand at the sights in question. "Which includes mountains, rivers, a lake or two, possibly some valleys—oh yeah, and a few dead bodies."

"Ah, now you make it sound interesting." R.C. grinned at her, one big hand wrapped loosely around the steering wheel and the other resting casually on the lip of the door just below the window, and she laughed and grinned back.

"You're a terrible vacation buddy, you know," she pointed out, still laughing as their rental barreled down the road, raising dust all around them in a thick cloud.

"Maybe, but I'm a good partner," he countered. That quieted them both for a second, and he cursed himself in his head for not thinking before he spoke. Would he ever learn?

Probably not.

"Where're we heading, exactly?" he asked instead, and Nick looked just as grateful as she pulled the map from her purse and checked where it had been marked.

"Pablo," she answered finally. "That's the home of the tribal headquarters, as well as the BIA local office, the Flathead Tribal Police Department, and the Salish Kootenai College. And it's only seven miles south of Polson, which is the largest community out here, at a whopping eighty-five hundred residents. Polson's also the county seat for Lake County, and home to the Kwataqnuk resort and casino."

"Thank you, Miss Tour Guide," he told her. "But no gambling while on duty, remember?" For a second he worried that he'd strayed too close to dangerous topics again, but she smiled and he relaxed a little.

"Look at that!" she said a few minutes later, as the road crested a small rise and they spotted a wave of dark shapes moving through a valley below. "Aren't they amazing?"

R.C. glanced over briefly, and had to agree. Even from this distance the massive, woolly-coated bison were impressive creatures, and the surge of their herd running full out across the plain shook the road beneath their wheels and filled the air with the pounding of their hooves. He'd never seen anything so majestic, or so powerful, at least not in person. It was truly awe-inspiring.

He wondered if the rest of this trip would prove to be as pleasant, or as easily spotted.

It took them another three hours to pull into Pablo. They'd passed five or six other communities along the way, none of them more than a few dozen homes and buildings clustered around the main road and perhaps one cross street, and the few people they'd seen had barely bothered to glance their way. But then R.C. supposed they were used to visitors. The reservation made a lot of its money off the casino, so there were always people heading too and from Polson, plus students going to the small community college in Pablo. And then there were the tourists here to see the Kerr Dam, or the Flathead Lake State Park, or seeking the St. Ignatius Mission, or looking to walk through the National Bison Range.

And then there were people like them.

"Special Agent Reed Hayes, FBI," R.C. announced after he'd parked in front of the two-story adobe council building and he had Nick had climbed the front steps and stepped into the dark, cool inner lobby. "This is my partner, Danika Frome." He showed the woman behind the front desk his badge and ID, and beside him Nick did the same. "We'd like to speak to the tribal council."

"Just a minute," she told them, and then turned away, whispering into the mic at her throat. She was short, dark, and heavy-set, though not nearly as dark as R.C. himself—he was way beyond Native American in coloring, just as Nick was nowhere near. He knew they made a striking pair, him tall and broad-shouldered and still fit even with the gray starting to show in his short dark hair, and her average height and slender but still curvy, with her blonde-brown hair cropped close and her pale skin and big blue eyes. Even in the fitted suit, Nick didn't look like any FBI agent he'd ever imagined before joining the Bureau.

But the times, they'd certainly changed.

"Special Agent Hayes? Special Agent Frome?" The man who approached them was young, maybe thirty, with the typically glossy black hair pulled back in a ponytail, and his face was round and very friendly. He wore jeans and a denim shirt, though his leather belt had a hand-tooled silver buckle, a braided rope-tie with a carved turquoise eagle hung around his neck, and moccasins adorned his feet. Tribal casual, R.C. guessed. "I'm Detective Jonathan Couture, with the Flathead Tribal Police Department. I was assigned to the murders. Right this way."

R.C. shook hands with him, as did Nick, and then they followed him through the doors at the far end of the lobby, and up the broad staircase to the second floor. Along the way R.C. set his phone to "voice recorder" mode, and spotted Nick doing the same. It was the quickest and easiest way to take notes on the situation—they'd download those to their laptops later, run them through the dictation software to translate the audio files into text, and then clean them up to use as the basis for their status reports. He did carry a small notepad and a pen in his jacket, of course, but that was more for doodling or jotting down reminders to himself than for any real note-taking.

He was glad to see that the local cops were already on the case. The FBI took charge of any situation it was in, and some local authorities didn't appreciate being ordered around. He tried to keep things on as friendly a basis as possible—he'd always believed it was better to have willing partners than grudging assistants—and the detective's friendly attitude suggested that wouldn't be a problem here, plus obviously he would be the man to ask for details about the situation.

Detective Couture led them down the hall to a wide room that took up the entire middle of the floor, the sides of which were filled with tiered wooden seats facing a long table. It was like a courtroom—or a council room.

Ten men sat that table, most of them older if their gray-streaked hair was an indication, and all of then Native American. The reservation actually had many non-Native residents—in fact, only eight towns here were predominantly Flathead Indian, or Bitterroot Salish as the largest tribe was called—but the tribe still controlled the reservation as a whole, and non-Natives couldn't be members of the tribal council.

"Welcome, agents Hayes and Frome," one of the men announced. He didn't look like the oldest member present—that honor was reserved for the elderly gentleman to the far right, whose braids were almost snow-white and hung down his chest probably to his waist—but his face was deeply lined and his braids were adorned with feathers and beads. He was wearing jeans and a denim shirt as well, though his shirt had embroidery woven into it at the collars and cuffs and down the front panels, and his bolo tie had a silver and lapis image of a leaping trout. "I am Willy Silverstream, chairman of the tribal council. Your superiors notified us that you were coming. We appreciate the FBI's help in this matter." That was a good sign, as well—the federal government didn't have the best track record of treating Native Americans fairly, especially with regards to the reservations, and many Native Americans still resented them, but it sounded as if the council leader really was happy to have them here.

"Glad to be of service," R.C. answered, giving the old man a polite nod. He wasn't sure he could refer to him as "Willy" and still keep a straight face, and hoped it wouldn't come to that. "Why don't you tell us exactly what's been going on here, and we'll see what we can do to help?"

"Of course." Willy frowned and placed both hands flat on the table— they were lined and wrinkled, but still looked strong, the fingers thick and blunt and marked with tiny scars here and there that showed white against his weathered skin. "Men have been dying, out in the woods."

"What men?" Nick asked. "How long ago, and how often? And where in the woods?"

The old man's gaze flicked to her for half a second, and R.C. wondered if they were going to have a problem, but if the tribal elder didn't like speaking to a woman he didn't let it show in his face or his tone. "Three men so far," he answered instead, "starting a week ago. The first one, Elk in the Trees, was hunting. The second, Peter Colman, was a student at the community college, studying animal husbandry, and had been given an assignment to study the local wildlife—easy enough to do around here. The third, Roger Tanner, was a fisherman."

"All of them had lived here on the reservation their whole lives," another of the council members offered. "None of them had any enemies beyond the usual rivalries and minor arguments. Elk in the Trees was a widower with grown children, Peter Colman was engaged, and Roger Tanner was married with one small child and another on the way."

"Any connection between them, beyond being here on the reservation?" R.C. directed that question to Detective Couture, and wasn't surprised when the local cop shook his head. Of course they would have investigated that.

"How did they die?" R.C. didn't miss the pause after his question, or the way neither Willy nor this other council member would look him in the eye. He knew Nick hadn't missed it either.

It was the detective who finally answered. "They were each shot through the throat. With an arrow."

R.C. studied him, but the younger man wasn't smiling or laughing. "An arrow? Each of them? Through the throat?" He scratched at his jaw. "So we're looking for William Tell here?"

"That was a crossbow," the oldest elder corrected, though there was a trace of humor in his raspy voice that R.C. saw was mirrored in his sharp blue eyes. "Better to say you are looking for Robin Hood. But a Salish version."

"Fair enough." R.C. considered the matter seriously. "Do you have anybody who could make a shot like that, repeatedly? I'm assuming it wasn't at close range or these guys would have run, or fought back, or something?" He knew from his time on the firing range that hitting a target as small as the human throat wasn't easy, especially if you needed that first bullet—or arrow—to be a kill shot. That took real skill.

"That would make sense, yes," Willy agreed, finding his voice again. "But we don't know for certain. There were no witnesses with any of the deaths. Each time the man in question was alone in the woods, and his body was found the next day."

"So each of these attacks occurred at night?" Good of Nick to pick up on that.

"We think so, yes."

"Where did they happen?" was R.C.'s next question. He could tell from the muffled growl behind him that he'd beaten his partner to the punch on that one, and he hid the smirk that threatened to cross his lips. He could rub it in later.

"Along the edge of the Hog Heaven range," Detective Couture replied. There was a large map of the reservation tacked to the far wall above the massive stone fireplace that took up the space between two wide windows, and he stepped over to it and gestured toward an area near the northwest corner. Polson and Pablo itself were a bit south of the northeast corner, which was dominated by the lake.

"All three of them?" R.C. moved closer to study the map, Nick half a step behind him. "How big is the reservation, in all?"

"Almost two thousand square miles," Willy answered proudly. "We are one of the largest reservations in North America."

"And yet all three deaths occurred in one area," Nick pointed out. She caught R.C.'s eye. "I think we'd better take a closer look at this mountain range."

He nodded. "Can we get a guide to show us the way, and the original locations of the bodies?" He made a mental note to ask about autopsy reports as well. Assuming any had been performed.

Willy nodded, but before he could speak Detective Couture stepped forward. "I can show you," he offered, with a glance at the council members, who silently nodded permission after a second. "I know the area well, and I know where each of them were found."

"Perfect." Something else had been caught his attention, and R.C. figured he'd better mention it now before they really got into anything. "Where's the BIA in all this?" The FBI was tasked with investigating major crimes on Indian land, but the BIA, or Bureau of Indian Affairs, was responsible with maintaining law and order on the reservations otherwise, including police matters. He'd expected to find a BIA officer here waiting for them, and didn't want to step on any toes, especially if that could foul the investigation later.

A few of the elders made harrumphing noises, but they seemed as much amused as annoyed. "That would be Martin Proudfoot and Isaiah Fisher," Willy explained after a moment. "They're the only two manning the local BIA office—the rest are up at the regional office in Portland. But Martin broke his leg a few days back, bike accident, and he's stuck in traction for a bit. And Isaiah's wife's expecting—their first, and there's some complications, so he's sticking to her side over at St. Luke's." He removed a folded-up paper from a pocket in his vest, smoothed it out, and slid it across the table. "Isaiah dropped this off, though, says they were duly notified of your presence and cooperate fully, so you're in the clear." He was definitely holding back a grin, and though his lips only twitched his eyes crinkled and the lines around his mouth deepened so much they looked like furrows.

Nonetheless, the news was good. As long as the BIA knew they were here and didn't have a problem with it, R.C. wasn't too worried. He'd copy any reports to their regional office, of course, just to keep them in the loop, but honestly this way was probably better. Now he didn't have to worry about some paper-pusher dogging his steps along the way.

He turned back to Willy and the others. "We'll let you know what we find, of course. Hopefully we can resolve this quickly, and before anyone else gets hurt."

Willy nodded. "That is our hope as well. Thank you."

There were nods all around, and then Detective Couture led them back out into the hall. "The council's booked you into the Hawthorne House, a really nice bed-and-breakfast over in Polson," he explained as they headed down the stairs and outside. "Did you want to rest for a bit, or head straight out?"

"We should probably check in and drop off our bags," R.C. decided. "But I'd like to get going right after that. How long will it take to get over there?"

"A few hours," the detective answered. "I'll get my Jeep and meet you over at the hotel in a few minutes."

"Sounds great." R.C. shook hands with him and watched the young Native walk off, then turned to his partner. "What do you think?"

"He seems like a straight-up guy," she answered as they unlocked their car and got in. "And this could be as simple as one crazy guy staking out an area and shooting any 'trespassers.'" Her tone said she wasn't convinced, however, as did the sigh she released right after that.

"But?" he urged as he backed out and drove to the bed-and-breakfast.

She gave him a tired smile in reply. "But when is it ever that easy?"

2

"**I still don't see why they couldn't have booked us there instead**," Nick groused for the tenth time as they walked. She'd been complaining about the accommodations off and on since they'd checked in, and R.C. knew she was only half-kidding. The Hawthorne House where they were staying at seemed decent enough—big airy rooms, clean whitewashed walls, hardwood floors, high ceiling beams, nice big beds.

But Nick was stuck on the fact that there was a resort only a few blocks away. And that they weren't staying there.

"We're just government grunts," he reminded her yet again. "We're lucky the council is putting us up at all." Most of the time they had to arrange their own accommodations, and pay for them, too. The Bureau would reimburse them, of course. Eventually. After a mountain of paperwork and what seemed like an eternity. This time, they didn't have to deal with any of that. The council was covering their room and board, which was a lot more generous than most local agencies that had asked for their help.

But that still wasn't swaying Nick any.

"In for a penny, in for a pound," she grumbled. "It's not like we're asking to gamble. But a massage sure would be nice."

R.C. almost offered to give her one, then stopped and cursed himself for that impulse. Then cursed again for stopping what would have been a completely reasonable and harmless remark, but now would seem either forced or salacious. Damn it! Would this ever get any easier?

"It's just up ahead," Detective Couture called back. He was obviously at home in the woods and had quickly moved in front of them, though perhaps that was just to get out of range of Nick's complaints. "Where we found Elk in the Trees."

"Did you find him?" R.C. asked, pushing away questions of his partner's comfort level and focusing on the investigation again.

"No, it was a young family, the Singing Doves," their guide replied. He slowed to let them catch up a little so he didn't have to shout. R.C. had already learned that Detective Couture was very helpful but also very soft-spoken—nice when sharing a car ride but not good when trying to be heard while climbing a mountain.

Not that they were really climbing a mountain, of course. The Hog Heaven Range might contain some genuine mountains, but they were only in the foothills here. There were some decent peaks and valleys, to be sure, but R.C. had gotten used to Denver these past two years. Compared to the heights around that city, these were barely speed bumps.

The land did have a rugged beauty, however. They were well beyond any towns or villages out here, and as far as the eye could see there was nothing but thick grass and tall trees, broken here and there by a jumble of rocks or a narrow, swiftly flowing stream or a small, dark lake.

There were birds aplenty, their calls and cries and wingbeats echoing all around. R.C. had spotted a few deer as well, and Nick swore she'd seen wolves peering at her from behind a fallen tree. Detective Couture had assured her that wolves would never attack three armed men—he'd brought a hunting rifle along, grabbing it from the Jeep's back window probably out of reflex, and R.C. had decided not to raise a fuss about it. They were the guests here, after all.

"They were out on a nature walk," the detective was explaining, and it took R.C. a second to rein in his thoughts and return to the subject. "Their little girl, Sophie, ran ahead to pick some wildflowers, and then screamed. Her parents came running, and that's when they found him." The three of them topped a low crest, and Couture surveyed the area from beneath one hand, then pointed. "Right over there."

R.C. followed him across the small valley, scanning the area for signs of trouble or ambush. Old habits died hard. He'd been in the Army a long time, mostly Military Intelligence but you still had to serve a stint of active duty and he'd never forgotten those skills, or lost those reflexes. Which was a good thing—he was fairly sure he would have died on the job several times otherwise.

But the area seemed clear, aside from a lone falcon and a few small deer, plus the ubiquitous birds. The spot in question was right at the edge of a small clearing, the first trees of the renewed forest springing up just beyond, and R.C. crouched down to study the area better.

Much of the ground had been trampled here, unfortunately. Probably one of the local officers and whoever had collected the body, plus anyone out to help and whoever took the Singing Dove family home, and then anyone who'd heard about the incident and wanted to see for themselves.

Christ.

"Yo, check this out." Nick hadn't stopped with them, and now she was calling from just inside the treeline, some fifty feet beyond. R.C. joined her, and found her kneeling in the loose underbrush.

"What've you got?" he asked.

"This." She indicated a spot just to her side. "I figured the space right around the body would get too much foot traffic but if we were lucky the killer might have struck from back in the trees, where nobody thought to look and thus destroy the evidence." Her smug expression finally gave way to a grin. "Guess I was right."

R.C. studied the spot she'd gestured down at, and stiffened when he realized he was looking at a shape depressed into the leaves and moss and pine needles that coated the forest floor.

A shape that looked an awful lot like a footprint.

Fishing out his phone, R.C. snapped a photo of the print. Then he ran the image through a special FBI app, one that stripped out everything but the outline and a few pertinent physical characteristics.

A few second later his "Message Waiting" icon blinked on. He checked the phone's logs and found the image there, waiting.

But when he'd called it up, all he could do was stare.

"That can't be right," he muttered. He glanced down at the actual print, then back at the display, which did appear to match.

But it didn't make any sense.

"What's up? Let me see!" Nick demanded, practically ripping the phone from his hand.

"Here." R.C. showed her the image. After a second she shook her head as well.

"What the hell did that?" she wondered aloud. R.C. didn't answer. He was still trying to process what he'd seen. Even if it didn't make sense.

Just like a certain incident many years ago.

But he tried very hard not think of that anymore.

Especially at times like this.

The print was a footprint, all right. The program had rendered it out, clear as day. It was a left foot, and bare, with long, thin toes spread wide—

—and a total width of no more than two inches, but a total length of close to eighteen. Which made it half again as long as one of his own feet—and only half as wide. No way a man had a foot like that. A monkey, maybe, or some kind of lizard, though whatever had cast that print had five toes and a heel, and the general shape was a lot more like a man's than it was any sort of animal R.C. had ever seen. Still, he freely admitted he wasn't exactly a wilderness expert.

Fortunately, they were with someone who was.

"Detective!" Their guide had been studying the body's final resting spot, still, and glanced up at the call. A minute later he was crouching beside them.

"What's up?" R.C. pointed to the print, and held up the phone as well, but the young local shook his head. "I don't know—I haven't ever seen anything like that. I'd say it was a man's, but horribly stretched."

"Is it a prank?" Nick asked. "There is a college near here—could this have been some kind of game or hazing ritual gone horribly wrong?"

"Maybe, but only one of the victims was a college student," R.C. pointed out. "And it was the middle one. Besides, the college is in Pablo, near the tribal headquarters, right? Long way to go for a prank." He spread his hand over the footprint for a second, then rose and took a single long stride past it and into the woods. He didn't spot any marks on the ground there but the print had been far longer than his own feet so he took half another stride—and saw a second print beside a tree's roots. It matched the first one except that this was clearly a right foot.

Another step and a half brought him to a third print, this one a left again.

"We've got a trail," he called back over his shoulder. But each print had been a little shallower, and though he did find a fourth it was barely visible as an impression in the leaves. There wasn't a fifth.

So much for the trail.

Still, they had proof that someone had been here. Someone with a stride significantly longer than R.C.'s own.

Which would suggest the stranger was significantly taller as well. Almost half again as tall. And R.C. was a few inches over six feet.

That would make their quarry one of the tallest men alive.

Curious about other Crossroad Press books?
Stop by our site:
http://store.crossroadpress.com
We offer quality writing
in digital, audio, and print formats.

Enter the code FIRSTBOOK
to get 20% off your first order from our store!
Stop by today!